D1255114

THE WILL

BY RICHARD MARTIN STERN

The Bright Road to Fear 1958
Suspense 1959
The Search for Tabatha Carr 1960
These Unlucky Deeds 1961
High Hazard 1962
Cry Havoc 1963
Right Hand Opposite 1964
I Hide, We Seek 1964
The Kessler Legacy 1967
Merry Go Round 1969
Brood of Eagles 1969
Manuscript for Murder 1970
Murder in the Walls 1971
You Don't Need an Enemy 1972
Stanfield Harvest 1972
Death in the Snow 1973
The Tower 1973
Power 1975
The Will 1976

THE WILL

Richard Martin Stern

Doubleday & Company, Inc.
Garden City, New York
1976

PRINTED IN THE UNITED STATES OF AMERICA
FIRST EDITION

Library of Congress Cataloging in Publication Data

Stern, Richard Martin, 1915–
The will.

I. Title.
PZ4.S83945Wi [PS3569.T394] 813'.5'4
ISBN 0-385-11084-7
LIBRARY OF CONGRESS CATALOG CARD NUMBER 75-30460

To D.A.S. as always,
with love

THE WILL

PROLOGUE

There were stirrings and whisperings in the courtroom, and Judge Steven Geary was not pleased. "If need be," he told the spectators, "I will have this courtroom cleared. This is a trial, not a circus, and I will have order."

We could damn well sell tickets, the judge thought bitterly, just because of the magic of that name in California: McCurdy. And also because everybody knows that in a family-will contest, nobody wins—and family secrets that shouldn't be revealed usually are.

On one side of the courtroom was Paul McCurdy; Marty McCurdy was on the other. *McCurdy versus McCurdy*, Judge Geary thought; damn fools both.

And counsel, he told himself; they too are bound to make this into a fight.

Billy Gibbs was representing Marty McCurdy. Gibbs was tall, tanned, and fit, bringing into this San Francisco courtroom a hint of Southern California beaches, of booming surf at San Onofre and a dozen boards catching the swell, seizing the downhill momentum, cutting across the face of the curling wave. The word flamboyance came to mind. In the judge's view, Southern California, or at least its beaches, seemed peopled by a race of tanned and overly healthy barbarians.

As Paul McCurdy's lawyer, John McKenzie seemed the exact opposite of Gibbs. McKenzie was a proper San Francisco lawyer—lean and grizzled, sober in dress and manner—and far more to the judge's taste than Gibbs. But taste doesn't count, the judge told himself.

"Mr. Gibbs," he said, "you may proceed." And he leaned back in his leather chair and half closed his eyes to listen—although he already knew what he was going to hear, even if the jury did not.

Mental incapacity, coercion and undue influence—the classic lines of attack in any attempt to break a will. . . .

"We will show," Billy Gibbs told the jury, "that after the stroke which incapacitated him, and most particularly during the time when he was making his will, Joseph McCurdy, ill and almost bedridden, was helpless to resist . . ."

Joe McCurdy helpless? The judge wondered. Old Joe McCurdy, Paul's father, Marty's grandfather. He had built the McCurdy National Bank from a neighborhood institution to what it was now, one of the stalwarts of the West Coast's financial structure, and part of the backbone of the nation's economy. It was hard to think of his being helpless. But of course strengths did dwindle, and old men's minds did lose their keen edge. It was always possible that the evidence would be persuasive. I hope it isn't, the judge thought, and strove to put bias from his mind. He looked at the jury.

Eight men, four women; one black, two of Oriental descent, one Chicano. The rest what the judge believed in some sections would be called Anglos. They were merely names and unfamiliar faces now, but as the trial went on, as always happened, they would take on personalities and the judge would learn, as opposing counsel would too, at whom to look for reaction. It would be like trying to read tea leaves as far as predicting a verdict was concerned, but the temptation to try would be irresistible.

He glanced at Paul McCurdy.

With his father and now his brother dead, Paul was head of the bank and of the family; to all appearances a man fit for his position and responsibilities. San Francisco born and bred; Stanford and Stanford Business School; from the beginning groomed to take over. "It's all yours, boy"—the judge could almost hear old Joe McCurdy saying it. "Take hold, and goddamn it, see to it that when you leave, you pass along at least as good as you got." Well, as far as the judge knew, Paul had been equal to the task.

And young Marty McCurdy, sitting quiet and confident at his table. He was cut from the same cloth as his counsel, Gibbs: tall, tanned, solid and healthy, a young barbarian up from the south to challenge his uncle, just as he would step right up and challenge anything or anybody that got in his flamboyant way. He was now about thirty, some twenty years younger than Paul. But age meant nothing to youth; they already knew it all, and then some.

"Further, ladies and gentlemen," Gibbs was saying, "we contend that the trust established by the will, because of its terms, is not a valid trust at all. It has been held that when the trustees of a trust are also its beneficiaries . . ."

Well, yes, the judge thought. And then again, no—but, as Calvin Coolidge once said: don't quote me. That is a point of law upon which I shall instruct the jury after I have listened to arguments and studied pertinent references with what I hope will be an open mind. But the fact of the matter is that no matter what is decided here in this court, there will be cries of "foul!" and accusations of bias. In judgments concerning great wealth and power, it is always so. And most especially when the contest concerns a will. Because a will contest, almost any will contest, is a family gnawing at its own vitals.

There will be no winner, the judge told himself, there will only be losers. Because when judgment is rendered, whatever it may be, there will remain a legacy of pain and hurt and estrangement, civilized counterparts of a hill-country feud which will savagely endure. The judge was a compassionate man, and these were dismal, even painful predictions.

Is there a possibility of compromise? the judge asked himself. Can I find grounds that have not yet been explored, some way to achieve peace and save face at the same time? Some out-of-court settlement which might terminate the battle without bloodshed?

The judge was conscious that Paul McCurdy watched him without expression. He tried to ignore it. They were friends, from similar backgrounds, with almost identical views; but now, and until the end of the trial and perhaps beyond, they were at arm's length, nodding acquaintances only. So be it.

But why, the judge wondered, why had matters been allowed to reach this point of public confrontation? What led up to it? What were the seeds that had germinated and produced this unhealthy result? In these futile questions was there the possibility of settlement?

He was conscious that the courtroom had fallen silent and he roused himself. The jury was watching him. "Have you finished, Mr. Gibbs?"

"For the present, your honor." Smiling, polite barbarian, exuding confidence. And maybe the confidence was real at that, the judge thought. He watched Gibbs walk back to his table and sit down. He moves, the judge told himself, the way Joe DiMaggio used to move, and maybe still does—like the superbly conditioned athlete that he was.

Looking at the two together, Marty McCurdy and Billy Gibbs, client and counsel, the judge thought: There is neither fear nor awe in them, nor even respect for what is and what has been. Rightly or wrongly they will challenge, they are challenging, the established system. This is going to be worse than I thought, worse even than I feared.

"Mr. McKenzie," he said tonelessly, "you may proceed."

I
THE ROOTS

1

On a mild autumn day with only moderate smog in the Los Angeles Basin, the Coast Aircraft twin-engine Executive flying at three thousand feet was in clear view of the tower. It was from the tower operator, a man named Peterson, that the eyewitness account came:

"It could have been a backfire. I don't know. But all of a sudden his port engine was on fire, and I mean *fire*, you know? Flames, not just smoke. He came over the hills and he flipped up on his starboard wing and started to turn, coming around to head for the flat. The fire must have gotten to the main tank, I guess; anyway she blew. Just like that—whooom! Whoever he was, he didn't have a chance."

The man in the plane had been Joseph McCurdy, Jr., age fifty-five, the oldest son and therefore, in effect, head of the California McCurdys, a powerful banking and manufacturing family. And Peterson was right: he did not have a chance.

Burning wreckage from the Executive started half a dozen small brush fires in the hills above Hollywood, but the fires were quickly brought under control. What was left of Joe McCurdy, encased in a rubber bag, was carried down the hillside.

From the almost obliterated registration number, ownership of the aircraft was established. A Los Angeles County deputy sheriff called the McCurdy Aircraft plant, and finally reached Walter Jordan, general manager, who listened in his expressionless way, and then said, "Oh, no!"

"We'll need positive identification," the deputy said. "Next of kin?"

"His son, Marty—Joseph Martin McCurdy III. I'll locate him and tell him." Walter Jordan paused. "Where should he come for the—identification?"

The deputy told him. "I'll see to it," Walter Jordan said, and hung up.

Automatically he took the clean handkerchief from his breast pocket and began to polish his rimless glasses. Without the glasses the far wall of his office was nothing but a blur, but he studied it for a long time anyway, thinking his own thoughts.

He put the glasses back on at last, and summoned his secretary. "I want to talk to young Marty McCurdy," he said. "You'll probably find him down at Newport. Try his apartment and the Bay Club. It's urgent. I want to talk to him before he hears on the radio that his father has been killed."

Marty was sitting with Liz Palmer in the cockpit of his sailboat, *Westerly*, when one of the club waiters came down the ramp and onto the slip to tell him that he was wanted on the phone. "The message is urgent," the waiter said. "At least that's what they told me." He grinned suddenly. "You been up to something, Marty?"

"I've been behaving myself, I think," Marty said, and stepped over the gunwale. To Liz, "Back in a minute. Don't go away." He walked up to the clubhouse in that quick springy way of his, and Liz watched him go.

The waiter said, "Quite a guy. You've seen him body surfing? Or riding a board?"

"No. But I've heard about him."

"You should see him sailing this thing," the waiter said. His gesture included the full length of the sleek forty-three-foot ocean racing yawl. "I crewed for him in one Honolulu race." He shook his head. "He worked our ass off. Him and Billy Gibbs between them. They stood watch and watch, and what I mean, they were sailing to *win*."

The question was expected of her, Liz thought. "And did you?" she asked.

"First to finish, and first overall." The waiter glanced toward the clubhouse. Marty was coming back across the walk to the head of the ramp. "He told me he figures second best is no good. I've known him a long time down here, and that's the way he's always seen it." He headed for the clubhouse himself. On the ramp he passed Marty but it was as if Marty did not see him.

Marty dropped into the cockpit, sat down, and said slowly, "My father just killed himself flying into a hillside."

"What can I do?"

"For the moment, nothing." Marty stood up. "They want me to identify him—"

"Oh, no!"

"Apparently somebody has to. Then—" He shook his head. "I'll have to figure it out as I go along. A call to my uncle in San Francisco—" He shook his head again. "Less than six months ago," he said, "the old boy went, my grandfather; he died in bed. Now this. It—changes things."

"I'm sure you'll be able to cope."

Marty looked at her in silence. "Will I?" he said at last. And then, "We'll just have to see."

Marty McCurdy was almost thirty years old at the time of his father's death. He had his mechanical engineering degree from Cal Tech, and the habit of success at whatever he put his hand or mind to.

The force of the McCurdy name probably had something to do with it. As a McCurdy you were expected to run ahead of the pack; he had learned that early on as a new boy in the school yard.

"You're Marty McCurdy and you think you're real great, don't you?" This in plain hearing of what Marty's teachers would have called his peer group.

Marty didn't know the term peer group, but the situation was clear, and the fact that the other boy was a little bigger than he was didn't change things a bit. "I am," Marty said, "and I do." And he swung as hard as he could for the other boy's nose, landed with a gratifying crunch, tried a left-hand shot for good measure, and that was all there was to it.

Later, in the principal's office, "Yes, sir. I clobbered him." And that too was a McCurdy characteristic: you stood up to be counted. Here in the presence of Authority, his breath came a little faster and there was an uneasy feeling in his stomach, but none of it showed, and he stood firm.

The principal was a kindly man. "Are you a troublemaker, young McCurdy? Because we don't really like troublemakers here."

Marty thought about it. "No, sir," he said. "I don't think so. I never thought about it before."

"Think about it now." The principal took his time. "Are you, for example, thinking of pursuing this—vendetta with young Gibbs?"

Marty looked surprised. The thought had not even occurred to him. He said so.

The principal hid a smile. "Then," he said, "we will consider the incident closed." He raised a hand. "And we will hope that there are no further incidents. Is that understood?"

There were no more incidents; at least none in the school yard. None was necessary. Marty and Billy Gibbs established a satisfactory and in time unshakable one-two relationship; no others stepped up in challenge.

When Marty began to enter sailing dinghy races in Newport Harbor, Billy crewed for him. In later days, first aboard a Rhodes-class knockabout sloop and later aboard *Westerly*, it was the same: Marty was skipper; Billy first kicker. In those two Newport-to-Honolulu races they functioned almost as one.

They body-surfed together, learning the hard way how to handle the big ones at the Wedge, sometimes stunting—hot-dogging, it was called, which meant taking wild liberties with tons of breaking white water and sometimes ending with your nose in the sand and a feeling that you were never going to breathe again, or even long survive.

They rode boards, usually at San Onofre, that curving beach on Camp Pendleton property where the submarine ridge curved the long Pacific swells inward, slowing their centers and on good days piling the surf to unbelievable height and ferocity. There, balanced obliquely on your board, by the tilting of your weight altering course and direction, you could glance over your shoulder, sometimes even up through the fabric of the curl itself, and watch the white water crashing down where, as you cut across the face of the wave, you intended not to be—flying, man!

There were girls, and beach picnics, blankets or sleeping bags and grunting intimacies in the shadows cast by a small flickering fire. There were weekends at Catalina, and wild rides to Tijuana or Rosarita Beach. There was skiing as close as Big Pines; or the longer drive up to the Sierra Nevada ski areas—Badger Pass, Squaw Valley, Alpine Meadows, Sugar Bowl.

Marty went off to Cal Tech, Billy to UCLA and law school. End of what had seemed a lifetime together.

They met occasionally, but not often lately. Billy's world was that of downtown Los Angeles, and a small office in the old prestigious law firm of Gibbs & Carrington; the Jonathan Club or the LAAC for lunch, and squash or swimming for exercise. Marty's world was Newport Harbor, the Bay Club, *Westerly*, occasionally San Onofre, periodic filial visits to his father's new Stone Canyon house, a variety of tanned and bikini-clad chicks—and recently he had met Liz Palmer, who was something else.

Liz was an anomaly. She had her Ph.D. in theoretical physics, a passion for Mozart, Scarlatti, and Louis Armstrong, and a determination to be treated as a pure, empty-headed, unadulterated female whose sole functions were physiological. "The only reason for having a brain," she had told Marty, "is so you don't have to worry about it. The physical side is much more fun." But she could surprise him, too. "There are a couple of things I like about you," she told him once. "For example, you don't seem to wear the McCurdy name around your neck like that sea gull in the poem."

"It was an albatross."

"Yes," Liz said absently, "family Diomedeidae, as we say; more or less the same thing. But," she went on, "the weight of the McCurdy name is still there, and you couldn't walk out from under it if you tried."

"Meaning what?"

"Oh," Liz said, "I suppose catch the torch from the falling hand and all that jazz. You're marking time now, but it won't last forever." They were sitting in *Westerly*'s cockpit, snug in her slip. Liz sipped her drink thoughtfully. "I'll be interested to see how you perform when playtime is over."

"Maybe it won't be." She could reach him and it annoyed him, this strange female. "Maybe I like it just the way it is." The trouble was, you were never certain precisely what Liz was thinking. "Had you thought of that?"

"And rejected it. The word is gung-ho with the McCurdys, isn't it? Whether it's your uncle up in his San Francisco countinghouse, or your father flying airplanes and building pieces of them, or even you, sailing *Westerly* as if every time out were a cup race. I've heard the stories."

"And why isn't that good enough?"

"Is it? Shadowboxing? You've beaten everybody you could find. Now what?"

"That's easy." Marty was grinning. "I'm going to take you ashore, to dinner, and maybe to bed."

Liz's face was thoughtful. "Maybe," she said. "No, probably." Her smile was sudden, brilliant. "But that's only evading the question, just postponing *Der Tag*."

"The day when I what?"

"Stop fooling yourself."

2

Marty sat alone in his own apartment while he placed the call to San Francisco. Beyond the partitioned-off gallery (two chairs, a table, and unlimited privacy) he could watch the always changing face of the ocean, the long Pacific swells rolling in, building their momentum, curling and crashing down on the clean, broad beach, their journey of perhaps six thousand miles ended at last. Their sound reached him clearly. He could stare now at those far-traveling swells and contemplate the emptiness of the unknown.

He heard his call passing through voice after voice in the San Francisco bank, reaching at last his uncle's executive secretary, a Chinese girl, Helen Soong; and to her he said, "It's urgent. My uncle will want to know. There's been an accident."

Paul McCurdy's voice came on immediately. "Yes, Marty?"

"Joe is dead." When had he first started calling his father by his given name? He could not remember. And they had never been close. Why should he think of that at this time? "A plane crash. That's all I know."

There was silence. Then, in that quiet banker's voice, Paul said, "There is no possibility of an error?"

"I'm going up to identify him. Walter Jordan phoned me."

Another short silence. "I see," Paul said. "Keep me posted. I'll come down, of course, whenever you want me. Certainly for the funeral."

"Yes," Marty said.

"And thank you for your call. I—I'm shocked."

"That," Marty said, "makes two of us."

He hung up, and walked out of the apartment down to his car. With his key in the ignition he hesitated, and then got out and went back upstairs. He was just beginning to see some of the things that had to be done, and the Stone Canyon house would be a better base than this. He threw some clothing into a suitcase.

San Diego Freeway to Harbor Freeway to Hollywood Freeway, driving with automatic skill and unconscious attention. So where do we go from here, my friend? And why are you so let down by your uncle's reaction? What did you expect him to do, drop everything and come down to hold your hand?

It was a billion-dollar bank, McCurdy National; Marty had read the figures in a newspaper once. And God knew he had heard enough about the sense of responsibility that went with that much wealth and power.

Old Amos McCurdy had started the bank in the 1890s, nursed it through panic, earthquake, and fire, and passed it along to the first Joseph Martin McCurdy, Marty's grandfather.

The grandfather had expanded it, some said not always gently or even politely; and in his turn passed it along to Paul McCurdy's guidance.

The bank was the family monument and its strength; against it one life snuffed out was a not very important matter. Paul McCurdy would observe the amenities; he had said as much. He and probably Susan would fly down for the funeral; there would be both public and private expressions of sadness and sympathy; some kind of memorial would be thought out; and that would be it. In the meantime, my friend, Marty told himself, it is all up to you.

He found the morgue, identified himself to a not very interested civil servant, and was shown to a room where a sheet-covered body lay on a table. "Not very pretty," the attendant said, and lifted the sheet.

Marty had his one long look, and walked out quickly. The attendant followed, wearing a faint smirk. In the corridor Marty said evenly, "That's my father." And then, studying the attendant's face, he thought: smile just a little more and I'll bust you in the teeth. "Do you want me to sign something?"

He walked out of the building and breathed deeply in the fresh air. Now Stone Canyon, he thought, and the telephoning would begin.

The sycamore trees at the Sunset Boulevard entrance to Stone Canyon were turning gold, and the air itself held an autumn tang. The house his father had built was set well back from the road, hidden; a curving blacktop drive wound between two stone columns.

Marty had always thought the columns were probably the architect's, not his father's, idea.

The house itself was cantilevered out from the hillside with a magnificent view of Westwood and the vast sprawl of Los Angeles, the ocean and the beaches—the Point Firmin headland, even Catalina crouched on the horizon. Built of stone, wood and glass, the clean modern lines of the house blended into the landscape almost as if it had grown there. Despite the stone columns, the architect had known his business.

Molly Moto met him at the door, and it was clear that she had heard the sad news. There were no tears, merely a gentle softening of the usually inscrutable face. "I'm sorry," she said. "I heard on the radio. And there have been telephone calls." She took Marty's suitcase from his hand and held the door wide. "If there is anything you wish," she said.

"Thanks, Molly." He shook his head. "At the moment, nothing." He hesitated. "I'll be in the study."

He sat down for the first time at his father's desk. A silver-framed photograph of his mother looked at him. She was standing beside a gate he did not recognize, probably the gate of the house where they had lived when he was born, long before his father had decided to build this place at Stone Canyon. And as far as that went, Marty knew it was a picture of his mother only because he had been shown other pictures of her. She had died, and he never knew from what cause, when he was only two.

Come to think of it, he really knew very little about his parents, a strange, suddenly uneasy concept—which he would take a longer look at later on. First things, as they said, came first. He began opening desk drawers and closing them until he found the Los Angeles telephone books. Central District it would be, and, yes, here it was. He dialed the number and with the first ring a very pleasant female voice said, "Good afternoon. Gibbs, Carrington, and Gibbs."

So Billy had his name on the door already, did he? Well, well. "This is Martin McCurdy," Marty said. "If he is available I would like to speak to William Gibbs." He waited quietly, thinking: Good for Billy! He is making his way, and only out of law school a few years. And I, what way have I made? The question came out of nowhere, and he found no immediate answer. Maybe the question was without point. Maybe—

"Well, well." Billy's voice. "It's been a while, friend." And then, more quietly, "I've heard the news. I'm sorry."

"Thanks," Marty said, and wondered how to begin. I am in strange waters, he thought, without so much as a single chart. "I have a feeling I need help."

There was a short silence. "What kind of help?"

"I don't know."

Another short silence. "What do you want me to do?"

Marty could smile then and mean it, because this answer was plain. "I want you to come out here to Stone Canyon and sit and listen and tell me what you think."

"Just like that?"

The habit of command was strong. "Just like that."

"Drop whatever I'm doing—"

"Yes." Marty paused. "I saw a plaque once. It read: 'When you are up to your ass in alligators, it is very difficult to remember that your original intention was merely to drain the swamp.' I need somebody to help me get on course and stay there." He paused again. "That means you."

"You're an arrogant son of a bitch. But, then, you always were."

Marty hung up and leaned back in the chair. There was another photograph on the large desk, black and white, leather-framed. It showed his father standing beside the P-47 Thunderbolt he had flown in France and even over the Third Reich itself when he was how old—twenty-one? twenty-two? And there on the study wall in a plain wood frame were the connected, signature-scrawled dollar bills which, Marty vaguely remembered, were called short-snorters, or some such silly name.

"They were the in thing," his father had told him in one of their rare times of ease together. "You carried them with you wherever you went and got as many signatures as you could. Why?" He shrugged. "If there ever was a reason, I've forgotten it. We did a lot of things that seemed right at the time but later seemed pointless." He seemed to understand the question that was forming in Marty's mind, because he smiled in a deprecatory way. "When you get older you keep some of your young things around even if they no longer have much meaning. I'm not sure I know why, except that you wouldn't like everything always brand-new and up to date and functional. It would be like living in a motel room. Can you see that?" The kind of thing older people liked to say.

Marty looked at the P-47 photograph again. Flying was his father's life. Not for him the bank in San Francisco. World War II had taken him and taught him to fly, and that had become his life. And, as Marty understood it, Joe McCurdy had been good with an airplane. Maybe not one of the great ones, a Doolittle, a Tom Dancer, a Pete Lewis, not one of the fabled ones. But of front rank nonetheless. What was it they said, that there were old pilots and bold pilots but no old, bold pilots? He began to flip through the telephone books again.

Coast Aircraft was easy to reach, but within its maze finding one man was a task approaching impossibility. "His name," Marty said, "is Peter Watson, and he's in Engineering."

"This is Engineering. May I help you?"

"I'm trying to reach Peter Watson."

"Yes, sir. Which project?"

"I don't know." All I know, he thought, is that we were at Cal Tech together and he went to Coast. "Isn't there—?"

"I'll connect you with Engineering Personnel."

There was no Peter Watson in Engineering Personnel's current files. "Perhaps he has terminated?"

Perhaps. Marty hung up. Dead end. The hell it was. He called back. To the operator, "Is there somebody in charge of sales and service, a vice-president or somebody like that?"

There was a smile in the operator's voice. "Mr. George Granger is vice-president in charge of sales and service." She spoke the name with deference.

"Let me speak to him, please."

He got a secretary instead, of course. "I am afraid that Mr. Granger—"

"My name is McCurdy," Marty said, "and my father just killed himself in one of your aircraft. If your Mr. Granger isn't interested—" He left the sentence unfinished.

There was a short silence. "Just a moment, please," the secretary said, and almost immediately a new, male voice said, "Mr. McCurdy. Would you be Joe's son?"

"Yes, sir."

"And you said that he—?"

"He's dead. He crashed in flames on a hillside. I've identified him."

"I am very sorry to hear it. Joe was a—friend." The voice paused. "What is it you want us to do?"

"Gather up the pieces and find out what happened."

"I see."

"The insurance people and the FAA will probably take a look," Marty said. "I don't know how these things work, but I assume that's what will be necessary. But you built the aircraft and you have the facilities to find out exactly what happened."

"Tall order, young man."

"Do your aircraft frequently catch fire in the air?"

"You come on strong."

"If that is what it takes."

Granger's voice turned thoughtful. "Do you have some reason to believe that the crash was not an accident? Strike that. We will look into it with an open mind."

They held services for Joe McCurdy in the Wee Kirk of the Heather at Forest Lawn. It was a closed-coffin service. Paul McCurdy, his wife, Susan, and Marty sat in the curtained-off family room to one side and listened to the eulogistic and in Marty's opinion largely meaningless words spoken over the coffin.

When the service was over and they walked out to the waiting family car for the brief journey to the grave site, a wedding party was already gathered and waiting its turn at the chapel. Only in Southern California could it happen, Paul McCurdy thought, but he said nothing.

He was a middle-sized, compact man in his late forties, wearing the habit of quiet importance with ease. He was not without humor, but it was customarily hidden, and the facet of himself which he presented to the world was largely solemn and reserved.

In the rear seat of the car Susan sat, as always tall and straight as she had been taught as a young lady in Brookline. "It was a fine service, Marty," she said in that faint upper-class New England accent. "And all of Joe's friends, so many. He would have been pleased."

"I think," Marty said, "that he'd rather we'd had a cocktail party. And maybe we should have at that." He felt no deep sense of loss, and certainly no overpowering sense of solemnity. His father had

managed to kill himself, although undoubtedly without intention; but sooner or later death happened to everyone, and Marty thought that, given a choice, Joe would have preferred it in this sudden form rather than slowly in a bed. Was he being heartless? He didn't know. He glanced at his uncle. "He had what he wanted," he said.

Paul McCurdy nodded faintly. "You never know."

The banker type, Marty thought, refusing ever to commit himself. That of course wasn't quite right, because banker decisions had to be made, sometimes big ones, and as far as Marty knew Paul McCurdy had never been found wanting in decisiveness in that direction. But the man never seemed to open up. Maybe there wasn't anything inside to come out; maybe the smooth San Francisco exterior covered an unfurnished room, with only a computer bank humming away against one wall.

During the brief graveside service, the three stood together. When the coffin was lowered and the first spadeful of earth thrown in, they turned away, Paul shook hands solemnly with the minister, and that was it.

Marty said, "Are you staying over or flying right back?"

"You might offer us a drink." Paul's voice was expressionless. "Could we go to Stone Canyon? The house is yours now. We have a few things to talk about, I think." He paused. "Although, if you prefer, they can wait."

Marty opened the car door. "Be my guest."

3

From the broad porch of the cantilevered house above Stone Canyon, Susan could see some of the Romanesque buildings of UCLA, and she turned her attention to them, letting the man talk flow past her unnoticed. Only a handful of years ago, she thought, the UCLA campus had been dirt and mud with only a few isolated buildings, Royce Hall, the center, standing almost alone; a poor cousin of the Berkeley campus with its tall Campanile, its mellowed buildings, and its broad green lawns. Now UCLA flexed its own muscles. The word was growth, change; change was the constant here in the West, and some thrived on the impermanence and some did not. I do not, she thought with some bitterness.

"My father and now yours gone within six months," Paul was saying. "What now, Marty?"

Marty thought about it. He had been thinking about it. "I don't know." He looked at his uncle. "You're thinking of the plant?"

"It's yours. The bank, at the moment, has a very small interest in it."

"And the question is how much interest do I have in it?"

Paul was silent. He waited.

"As far as I'm concerned," Marty said, "the plant has always been there. Once upon a time I thought I'd take it over someday and build it up from just a minor aircraft parts and subassemblies vendor into something big." His grin was turned inward, mocking himself. "Very big," he said. "Lockheed, Coast, McDonnell-Douglas, Boeing, and the rest, move over." He shook his head. "Kid dreams. Joe was happy with it the way it is. It runs itself. Walter Jordan copes. He doesn't need me."

"You don't have to do anything, of course," Paul said, his tone carefully uncritical. "You are in a position to do just about whatever you want to do. You will have your father's share of your grandfather's trust."

"Just cash the dividend checks, is that it?"

Paul allowed himself a small smile. "Our trust department does that for you, us."

"So all I have to do is spend the loot." Marty nodded. "The way Joe did."

"He started McCurdy Aircraft."

"And lost interest in it."

Marty stood up and walked to the porch railing, stood for a little time with his back to his aunt and uncle; a big man. Here in Southern California, Paul thought, the children always seemed larger than their parents; and looser, if that was the word, less concerned with traditional appearances, more interested in immediacy than in the eventual results of the long haul. Generalizations, he told himself, and probably only partly accurate. Still. "The question, I think," he said, "is what do you want to do?"

Marty turned slowly. He was without anger or even annoyance, but one or two things had to be set straight. "You're what you might call head of the clan now," he said. "Agreed. You're in the catbird seat as head of the bank, and now that my father is dead, you're the clan head by right of age as well. But don't you think that what I want to do actually comes under the heading of my business?"

"Probably." There was no change in the older man's tone or expression.

"I might want to sail *Westerly* around the world."

"You might. I am sure you could."

"I might want to set this place up as a lush pad and stock it with hot and cold swinging chicks."

Paul nodded. "It would make a splendid private bagnio."

"Or I might want to take *Westerly* down into the South Pacific and go native."

"All distinct possibilities."

Marty sat down again. He was aware that Susan watched him with silent concentration. He ignored her. "But," he said, "you think otherwise, don't you? You think I'll put aside my childish toys. Tell me why."

A fair question, Paul told himself, and wondered how to phrase his answer without waving the family pride like a banner in the wind. He decided that the oblique approach was best. "I always wondered," he said, "why you chose Cal Tech and an engineering course which couldn't have been too easy."

"Because I liked engineering, fooling with things, seeing what made them tick. So did my father."

Paul nodded. "I expect that is the proper answer." His calm was unshaken, seemingly unshakable. "And you accomplished what you set out to do."

Marty shook his head. "Did I have in mind taking over the plant? Was that the reason for engineering? I told you, that was a kid's dream."

"Other people besides kids have dreams. I see people with dreams constantly, or have them brought to my attention at the bank."

Susan, watching, listening now, thought: is that really how he sees them, as dreams rather than as cold-blooded business propositions: dull, dry applications for loans? She had never thought of him in that way before—as a romantic at heart. A lover, yes; there were four children to testify to his performance in that role, and there were times when, thinking about it, she had found his behavior in intimacy with her totally at variance with his everyday banker attitudes. But romantic? Hardly. Still she found herself listening just a little more carefully, as if she were trying desperately to hear the thoughts behind the words.

"The wine industry started with dreams," Paul said. "The movie industry. Those giant aircraft corporations you mentioned. Grown men dreaming, not kids." He smiled faintly in a deprecatory way. "Your great-grandfather starting the bank, barely surviving the 1906 San Francisco fire, rebuilding the bank, and helping to rebuild a ruined city."

"Should I stand up and salute?"

Paul shook his head, expressionless again. "No. You know the story. Either you already appreciate it, or you don't, and nothing I could say would alter your view."

"Then why try?"

"We try a lot of things," Paul said, "even when we know they are futile." He again showed that deprecatory smile. "Pride is a dreadful force. You will learn that one day, perhaps. Perhaps not, too. In the end, it all depends on you." He glanced at his watch, and then at Susan. "There is that three-o'clock flight."

Marty stood up. "I'll drive you to the airport."

"There is no need." Paul was smiling again, the smooth, polite, meaningless banker's smile. "The bank can afford taxi fare, even Los Angeles taxi fare." He held out his hand. "Until the next time, Marty."

In the first-class compartment of the 727, Susan McCurdy in her port-side window seat watched the ocean glisten in the late-afternoon sun. She turned, and through the windows on the starboard side of the cabin she could see snow-capped mountains of the Sierra Nevada. In the foreground, although not visible from her seat, lay the great Central Valley of California called by some the richest agricultural area on the face of the earth.

Long ago, she told herself, she ought to have become accustomed to California in all of its extremes. She had not, and she decided now that she probably never would. Paul could laugh at her in his polite, even gentle way, but he had been born and grew up here, and the vastness that surrounded him he took for granted.

The highest mountain peak in the contiguous United States, Mount Whitney, was right over there in the Sierra Nevada; and not all that far from it was also the lowest point, in Death Valley.

In area the state was far larger than all of New England, New York, and New Jersey lumped together; and if you threw in Pennsylvania as well, you exceeded California's territory by only a little.

Texas and Alaska were larger, as Paul was fond of pointing out, but California with now over twenty million people had passed New York as the most populous state in the Union, and yet there were still vast areas of wilderness.

But more than all this, it was the sense of impermanence that still impressed itself upon Susan's mind, and she knew that it was this quick visit to Los Angeles that had brought out her feelings again.

To Susan's mind, San Francisco was bad enough, but Los Angeles was a disaster, and in a way, she supposed, young Marty typified the place—which was strange, because she liked Marty, even though she could not accept the breezy self-confidence that was his hallmark. "What do you think he will do?" she said to Paul.

She meant Marty, of course; the boy had been in the front of Paul's mind too. "Difficult to tell." Paul leaned forward a little to look out and down through Susan's window. They were over land now. They would be landing shortly. He settled back in his seat again. "He cannot be driven. Joe found that out." He glanced at Susan's smiling face. "I know," he said, smiling in return, "none of us can be driven very well, but Marty is his own man to an even greater extent than most. If he takes it into his head—" He was silent.

"To do what?"

"Anything. Anything at all."

"You'll control him. You are older, more experienced." Susan paused. "And you control the money." She paused again. "Don't you?"

"In a way." Paul smiled again. "In what might be called a left-handed sort of way." My position vis-à-vis Marty is precarious and uncomfortable, he thought, but found no need to spell it out. Susan knew nothing of money and banking affairs, and seemed quite happy in her ignorance.

"What would you have him do?" Susan said.

"I don't know. He has the plant, if he wants to devote himself to it. And I think he might enjoy it once he got his feet wet."

Susan was listening to the harmonics and the overtones as well as to the words. "But," she said, "you are not sure you want him to go in that direction? Why?"

"He plays to win. Always. And he is not above gambling."

Susan smiled again. "Neither was your father. And if the tales are true, your grandfather to an even greater extent."

"That was different."

"In what way?"

Paul had no answer.

A driver and car from the bank were waiting at the airport. Paul and Susan sat silent in the back seat as they rode, gathering traffic, north toward the city. Houses, new houses everywhere, Susan thought; more change, more impermanence. And there were construction scars of the newest proof of change, BART, Bay Area Rapid Transit, the automated transportation wonder that never seemed to work properly. In a way it was comical; in another, tragic.

Is it only change that upsets me? she asked herself. Or is it more? Is it that after all this time I have finally decided that I hate San Francisco, California, the Golden West? And what about Paul? She glanced at him. He was looking out his window, no doubt thinking banker thoughts, Susan told herself, and she felt a sudden impulse to weep, which was ridiculous. But, then, ridiculous impulses were not uncommon these days, and the only thing to do was to stifle them immediately, thereby refusing to give credence to old wives' tales about the difficulties of the change of life. She sat straight and tall and stared disapprovingly at the passing houses.

Joe was dead, Paul was thinking; the fact of death was given finality by the funeral. Marty was on his own now in a way that had not been true before. Should he, Paul, have stayed down in Los Angeles for a few days, maybe a week, to give the boy some kind of counsel or support? Or would he have merely been in the way, an intruder? How did you decide these things with any assurance?

But the question was academic anyway, he told himself. There were too many irons in the fire at the bank for him to sit long in Los Angeles holding a nephew's hand. That sticky business with Wally Trent, for example, which had to be gone into right down to the bottom. As privately as possible. And there was no time like the present to begin. "I'll drop you at home," he told Susan, and failed to see her reaction. "I'm going down to the bank. I don't think I'll be late."

"The twins are coming over from Berkeley for dinner."

"I'll try to be there."

"And Alan is off duty. He's coming too."

"I'll try."

"Is it really that important?" Despite herself, there was annoyance in her voice.

Paul seemed not even to notice. "It is." He smiled his polite banker's smile. "Sorry."

And there it was again, Susan thought: the attitude that "there are affairs women cannot possibly understand." She sat silent and angry, stifling the tears.

4

The main office of the McCurdy National Bank was on Montgomery Street in the bank's own twelve-story building now dwarfed by San Francisco's new high-rises. Old Joe McCurdy, Paul's father, had built it just after World War I when under his guidance the bank was beginning to make itself felt as a financial force in the West.

In its day the building, like the man himself, was looked upon in conservative circles as a thing of flamboyance with too much glass, too much glitter and show, typical, in a way, of the methods the first Joe McCurdy sometimes resorted to to gain his ends.

For the opinions of the conservatives, Joe could not have cared less. He was a big man, a football player at the University of California across the Bay, in his senior year selected for Walter Camp's All-American team as a running guard. "I learned to knock people down," he liked to say. "It works in business just as well. Stir yourselves, goddamn it. Find new ways to put money to work."

Prohibition stifled the California wine industry, and Joe fumed and raged and sent blistering letters off to California's freshman senator Hiram Johnson. "I don't expect results," he told Martha, his wife, "not right away anyway. But you keep hammering and sooner or later something starts to give, and one day the country will come to its senses and repeal that stupid amendment, and we'll be ready to help the wine industry get back on its feet and, by God, start making the French sit up and take notice too."

In the meantime, there was the rich Central Valley with its growing agriculture, and Joe wanted a large piece of that. He opened a branch bank in Modesto, another in Stockton; and through merger, which some considered closer to coercion and blackmail, he opened a McCurdy National branch over in Salinas too, and through it made his financial influence felt as far away as Monterey with its fishing fleet.

San Francisco was *the* port of the Pacific, although Los Angeles by a sniggly bit of business which Joe secretly admired reached out and grabbed a skinny strip of land that ran all the way down to San Pedro. Then, lo and behold, suddenly the inland city of Los Angeles had a seaport and was pushing it for all it was worth. There was, Joe thought, a lot to be said for the attitude of those men who more or less ran Los Angeles, and he craved what would later be called a piece of their action too.

And it was possible because the movement to contain San Francisco financial power north of the Tehachapi failed to stop Giannini and his Bank of Italy, which became the Bank of America; and Joe rode right along behind Giannini into the expanding lushness of Southern California with its citrus groves and its walnuts, its bustling movie industry, its swarming tourists, its building boom, and its new-found oil.

Nor were his eyes always turned inland. There was increasing trade with Japan and the Far East, as well as the expanding population of Hawaii, and, as Joe liked to say, "The oil that lets the wheels of commerce go around is money, and that's where we come in."

His views on banking itself were usually thought of as unorthodox. "I'll lend a million dollars to a man on the strength of his character," he was fond of saying, "but I won't lend a goddamn cent, no matter what the collateral, to a man I can't trust."

He had his twelfth-floor office next to the board room, and he used it about half the time. He also had a desk on the ground floor behind the railing, and he preferred to sit there at his work, able to watch what went on in the bank, to see who came in and how often, who spoke to whom; to be able to pick up small gossip in a casual way, to add to his immense store of local history and current knowledge.

To Pete Mariola, San Francisco's largest produce dealer: "What's your problem, Pete? You've been in the bank three times this week talking with Charlie. Anything I can do?"

"It's transportation, Joe." Pete sat down heavily in the straight visitor's chair. "The Southern Pacific isn't the monster it used to be, thank God, but they run their schedules their own way, and fresh produce won't wait. Now some slowdowns. God knows what next."

Joe took his time thinking about it, and waved at Pete a few days later. "I've got an idea. What about your own trucks, a fleet of them? The highways are free. You can set your own schedules, pick up direct from your growers. And"—Joe grinned maliciously—"screw the Southern Pacific and get some free advertising at the same time."

"Advertising?"

"Paint your trucks red or yellow. Put your name in big letters on the side. Attract attention the way the brewery wagons used to do."

It would be years before trucking became a major industry, and yet the basic equipment was already at hand.

Pete got out a fresh cigar, unwrapped it carefully, and cut off the end with his penknife. "Trucks cost money," he said at last.

"I'll lend you the money."

Pete lit the cigar with care. He studied Joe McCurdy's face. "You think it will work?"

"I'm not in the habit of putting my money on things I don't think will work, am I?"

Pete looked around the bank's main floor. He was still thinking. "This isn't exactly a charitable institution." He had a long puff and blew out a stream of smoke. "Let me think about it."

Joe nodded. "What you do is figure out how many trucks you'd need, what they cost to buy and what they cost to operate—gas, oil, depreciation, repairs, drivers—and what routes you could best use—" He saw the gathering resistance in Pete's face. "Look," Joe said, "I've got a bright young fellow named Potter. He was born with a slide rule in his head. I'll lend him to you to do an analysis. How about that? If you like what he comes up with, you come back here and we'll work it out."

A few called it imaginative banking; most thought it was high-rolling. But throughout the twenties McCurdy National burgeoned as Joe McCurdy went his own way. In a few directions largely unnoticed, he exercised caution.

In his big twelfth-floor office one day in early 1928: "I'm sorry, Frank, I won't lend you the money. Not for stock speculation."

"Joe. It's safe as a church."

Joe leaned back in his chair. "I grew up right here in California.

Let's say I've got a country-boy attitude toward the East. Money slickers dealing in pretty paper. Oh, I don't say there isn't actual worth to stocks, good stocks. In the end they're part ownership of going concerns. But that isn't what you want to buy, Frank. You want to buy a few pieces of paper that you think have a life of their own, and I think you'd be better off in a game of three-card monte. I think a lot of people would, because then at least they would have some part in the play, instead of being totally at the mercy of what happens in downtown Manhattan three thousand miles away." Joe paused. "I don't like the feel of things. No loan, Frank. Sorry."

"You're in the market yourself, aren't you?"

"I am. But I own my stocks. I didn't buy them on margin. I own pieces of big companies I am convinced will be around a long time. I don't expect a quick profit. When I gamble, Frank, it is in something I can at least partly control."

"You're a hard son of a bitch, Joe."

Joe McCurdy nodded quietly. "I have to be. I'm taking care of other people's money."

"And making a pile yourself."

Joe grinned. "Just why in hell do you think I'm in this business anyway, Frank? For the fun of it? Of course I'm making money for myself, and I'll keep right on doing it—just as long as I make the right decisions. Like this one."

Paul McCurdy rode the elevator from the basement garage to the large twelfth-floor offices.

Helen Soong was at her desk guarding Paul's own suite. She got up and followed him into his office. "We weren't sure you would be coming in today, Mr. McCurdy, so I scheduled no appointments." Was there vague reproach in her tone? "Mr. Simpson of Latour Vineyards is anxious to see you. And Mr. Waldo called from Washington." Miss Soong glanced at her wristwatch. "With the three-hour time difference, it will be too late to reach him now."

Paul sat down at his desk. "Just Mr. Trent," he said. "Ask him to come in, please. And no interruptions."

Miss Soong was already at the doorway. "Will you want notes?"

God forbid, Paul thought. He smiled and shook his head.

From the street faint sounds of traffic reached even this high—the blaring of a horn, the heavy sound of a truck engine; distantly a wailing siren quickly faded. Many offices Paul knew were hermetically sealed and filled with cooled or heated, washed and filtered air, but no outside sounds, creating, as far as he was concerned, a mausoleum atmosphere suitable only for walking on tippy-toe and speaking in hushed voices of death and disaster.

Oh, he supposed if, God forbid, he worked in New York or even in Los Angeles, he would find air conditioning welcome, but as it was he would not for the world give up the feeling of being part of the city, a living part. On foggy days he loved to open his windows wide and listen to the foghorns talking back and forth—the Ferry Building, the Bay Bridge, the Golden Gate Bridge, the ships themselves in the Bay. Chauvinism was buried deep in every man, he had often thought, which was probably why Susan had never understood his love for San Francisco. No matter.

He looked up from his desk. "Come in, Wally. Close the door." He stood up and walked from his desk to one of the leather visitor's chairs, indicated another; expression of informality. "Sit down. We'll have a little talk."

Wally Trent was tall, running slightly to fat, with graying hair worn a trifle long. He was the bank's senior vice-president in charge of foreign operations, a bachelor, a gourmet, a near-scratch golfer with an endless list of friends stretching from Pebble Beach to Honolulu, Manila, Tokyo, Hong Kong, and way stops in between. Usually cheerful, he was subdued now. He sat down, lighted a cigarette, and waited.

"What have you been up to, Wally?" Paul said.

Wally blew out smoke, a great deal of smoke. "If it's sugar—"

"Not entirely. There are some yen involved and some sterling and, as I understand it, some gold as well as Swiss francs and a few other currencies which usually don't figure in our foreign operations." Still no overt censure, but the point had been made.

Wally tapped ash into the ashtray. "I've called a few wrong, Paul. I admit it." He smiled suddenly, friendly as a puppy. "You win some and you lose some." He paused and smiled again. "Particularly with things as they are today, uncertain, you know how it is."

There was a short silence. Then: "Which might be a very good reason," Paul said, "for slowing down a little, don't you think?"

Wally shook his head. "We have to keep moving. We can't just sit and stagnate, paying out interest with none coming in. You don't mean that surely? Why, hell, Paul, we talked about this, you and I, before I really went into any foreign-currency deals."

"I don't recall that." He watched Wally shrug. "Do we have any memos on the matter, Wally?"

"Jesus, Paul," Wally said, "has it come to that?" Was his voice overloud? "Does everything we talk about have to be put down on paper? You're making too much of this."

There were times, Paul thought, when the gentle approach simply did not do the job. And lines had to be clearly drawn. "Exactly how much are we in for, Wally?" he said.

"Now, Paul. I don't have the figures right at my fingertips—"

"Why not?"

Wally was frowning now. "It isn't like you to go all hard-nosed, Paul. We've been friends for a long time. You know me, and—" The frown disappeared and he waved one hand expansively. "I know, I know, you're upset about your brother's death, and I don't blame you. But—"

"Wally, Joe's death has nothing to do with this. This is bank business, and all I know so far is rumor. I want facts."

"Charlie Waters has been running to you? Because if he has—"

"If he has," Paul said, "it is precisely because he ought to. You have a great deal of near autonomy. When you're in Manila or in Tokyo obviously you have to make decisions on your own. I understand that, and I wouldn't have it any other way. But after the event, I also want to know what your decisions were and how they affect McCurdy National." He paused. "I want facts now, and I am going to have them."

Wally stubbed out the cigarette and stood up. "I'll have them worked up for you. Anything else?"

"Yes." Paul too was standing. "I think we'll give you an auditor to help you work up the figures. That way we'll both know they are right." His voice was again without expression.

There was shock and incredulity in Wally's face. "This isn't like you, Paul. You've always trusted me. You—"

"My father," Paul said in the same level voice, "used to say that if you skinned a McCurdy you uncovered a bastard. Maybe the bastard in me is showing. Sorry, Wally, but there it is."

Paul went to sit again behind his desk after Wally had gone out, closing the door a little more firmly than necessary. You did what you had to do, Paul thought; how often had that been drilled into him? He could remember sitting in this same office listening to his father: "There are those who say that only the money counts with us, boy. They're both right and wrong, which is true oftener than people think. They're right because money is the *thing* we deal in. They're wrong because the money is only the symbol of what we do; and what makes us handle money and hurt people if they have to be hurt is pride. Your grandfather and I built this bank up to what it is now by doing the job right no matter what it took and no matter what some people thought. If we had turned our backs on what had to be done the bank would have been out of business a long time ago, and a lot of people who trusted us would have wished to hell they hadn't when the money they gave us to handle for them went pissing off down the drain. When circumstances dictate that you have to be a hardhearted son of a bitch, remember that, you hear?"

Paul sighed and punched one of the buttons on his desk. Helen Soong appeared immediately. "Mr. Waters, please," Paul said. Charlie Waters was his personal assistant. And when Helen Soong hesitated. "Yes?"

"Mrs. McCurdy phoned." Helen's face was expressionless. "She asked me to remind you that the children will all be home for dinner tonight."

Paul felt a sense of mild annoyance, quickly gone. Home was Susan's province just as this bank was his, and it was every bit as important, wasn't it? Remember that too, he told himself. "Thank you," he said. "First Mr. Waters. Then I'll go home."

And when Charlie appeared, young and bright and eager: "Have our auditors send over one of their whiz kids," Paul said. "I want him to look into Wally Trent's operation." He saw the surprise and interest in Charlie's face. "And," he added, "I want you to keep it to yourself. Strictly to yourself. Understood?" Word once out turned to rumor. And nothing could be more dangerous than that.

"Yes, sir. I mean, of course, sir."

"Fine, Charlie." Paul opened the door. "I'm going home."

5

They were fraternal twins, boy and girl, Jim and Sudie McCurdy, nineteen years old going on twenty. Sudie drove her little Fiat with almost professional competence; Jim beside her sunk low in his bucket seat. "Home's a drag," he said, "but the food is good."

"You look as if you could use some." Sudie shifted down, picked her opening, and gunned the little car across traffic to swing onto the bridge approach. She shifted back into top gear and resumed normal flow speed. "And a shave," she said. "If you're going to have a beard, go ahead and have one. But why try to look like that prick Arafat?"

Jim was amused. "You don't dig the PLO?"

"Why don't you wear a piece of striped toweling on your head?"

"And carry a gun?"

"Yeah."

Jim smiled and settled deeper into his seat. "How's your love life?"

"And what is that to you?"

"You're a good-looking chick—"

"Thanks a lot."

"Like they used to say, stacked; nice boobs."

"Is that all you think about?" Sudie slowed for the toll gate, paid her quarter, went smoothly through her gears gliding into traffic again.

"You know," Jim said, "you chicks are funny."

Despite herself she was interested. "In what way?"

They were over water now, and San Francisco rose clear like a fabled ancient city, moat-surrounded. Here and there a sail showed; shore lights were beginning to come on. "Take you, for instance," Jim said.

"What about me?"

"Like I said: nice boobs. No bra. So you're trying to show them off. But you act like you're insulted if I say I've noticed them. Now, does that make sense?"

Probably not, Sudie thought; but it was the way it was, and she wouldn't try to explain even if she thought she could, which she did not. She drove in silence.

"What about that jock, what's-his-name?" Jim said.

"You know his name."

"I don't read the sports pages. Or watch football on the tube."

"Maybe you should."

"Oskie wow-wow!"

Always he had teased her, and there had been, and were, times when she thought she hated him. But you can't hate part of yourself, she thought; or at least I can't. "Is there anything special about tonight?" she said. "I mean, you know, it sounded like a command performance. Alan's coming too."

"Our brother the doctor, as opposed to our brother the banker. Will Brucie-boy be there too?"

Sudie was smiling now. "Why don't you call him that to his face? Just once?"

"Because I'd probably get my ears slapped back. Is that what you wanted me to say?" Jim paused. "And maybe you'd like that."

"No."

"Because we shared the womb? That's pretty funny."

"You know," Sudie said, "you're a real shit sometimes." She turned to glance at him. "And the worst part is that you know it, and do it deliberately."

"And why, dear sister, do I do that?" He was smiling again.

"Because it's the only way you have of attracting attention."

"Like," Jim said slowly, "being a something-else quarterback like your jock?"

"Yes."

"Or waving a pair of boobs around like you?"

Sudie hesitated. They came down the ramp at the Broadway exit, missed the light, finally turned right toward North Beach. "Okay," she said at last, "maybe that's why I do it, to attract attention. But it's better than being a deliberate shit."

Jim smiled faintly. "Maybe you're right."

Alan McCurdy walked slowly from the hospital to his apartment, thinking about the spine fusion–laminectomy he had just watched with such attention. Enter a patient, he thought, with his low back in excruciatingly painful spasm. There is the beginning.

Sedation, probably traction, certainly bed rest until the spasm was alleviated. X rays, careful examination, maybe even a spine tap, results carefully studied, judgment made: operate.

The judgment was not a light one. That point had been hammered home. If the condition could be alleviated by conservative medicine, then conservative medicine it was; Dr. Steinem, chief of the university orthopedic service, wanted no knife-happy butchers among his students. But if exercise and the temporary use of a brace, mild sedation, and a bed board, all of the possible conservative means, would not in mature judgment bring about a satisfactory cure —then the knife it was.

But how different it was today from what he had heard of, say, thirty, forty years ago. It was like looking back to the Dark Ages. Two techniques then, the Hibbs and the Alby, both developed in New York. One relied on bone chips from the spinal processes to develop a callus for strength, fusing the two vertebrae; the other used a piece of bone transplant usually from the patient's shin. Both techniques worked—most times. But recovery was at least six weeks of absolute immobility in a brace, and during that time leg muscles began to atrophy, and when at last the patient was allowed out of bed he had to learn to walk all over again. Barbarous.

Today's patient would be on his feet and discharged from the hospital within ten days. A marvel, almost a miracle. And maybe one day, Alan thought, I will be making miracles too, helping people who could not have been helped if I had not been there.

"How's the orthopod?" A light voice, easy and familiar, at the apartment-house entrance—Nancy Wilson, M.D.

"Hi." Alan was smiling. "And how are all the little monsters muling and puking in their nurses' arms?"

"They, my friend, are our future. You're just trying to patch up our past." Nancy's voice altered subtly. "For the next eighteen hours, barring a major catastrophe, I am my own woman. How about that?"

Alan was smiling still. "I'm off too."

"Do you want to make something of it?" Nancy paused, smiling.

"Dinner at the family's. But," Alan said, and his smile was broader now, "they don't last forever, and if you're still in the mood, say about ten, ten-thirty, I'll stop by."

"Knock on my door."

"I will."

"But if there's no answer, don't persist." She paused, eyebrows raised. "I just might be—occupied."

She might be, Alan thought, as he trotted up the stairs to his apartment, but he doubted it. They had no formal understanding, no solemn vows of fidelity, or anything like that. They were friends, both immersed in, and devoted to, their studies of medicine, and they just happened to be male and female, a fact which gave scope to a rather broad and very pleasant relationship. Why strain it with promises, or even conventional ideas?

The plain fact was that for the next several years each was already married—to careful development in his career—and there was simply not room for anything else of a demanding nature.

Alan showered, and smiled to himself thinking that symbolically he was probably washing off the operating-theater atmosphere. Then he dressed—a light turtleneck, flannels, loafers, and a tweed jacket; no need for formality, God knew, not with that twerp Jim, who was likely to show up in jeans and sneakers and no socks with an obvious "take me as I am or don't bother to call me" set to his jaw.

As he went out to his car, Alan wondered what you were supposed to do with a kid brother like that. Jim's motive, of course, was protest, and God knew there were enough things in this world which deserved protest, things like hunger and disease, economic chaos, pomposity, and downright dishonesty, and so on. But the question was simply: what did Jim's kind of protest accomplish? And the answer was, also simply: nothing. It focused attention on Jim as a person, or perhaps would have if there hadn't been hundreds or even thousands looking just like him here in this benighted state of California. And so he did not even achieve individuality, he only aroused scorn. Maybe that was an end in itself, Alan thought, and immediately the picture that came to mind was of a little boy shouting obscenities from a safe distance.

Well, Jim was Jim, and Sudie did her own thing, too, whatever that happened to be at the moment, currently probably screwing the second-string 49er quarterback whenever she got the chance.

Bruce, now, was something else again, and the contrast between Bruce and Jim was laughable. They were a little over two years apart in age, and light-years apart in temperament and viewpoint. If Jim was still a little kid, Bruce was, and for too many years had been, an old man. There was a dictum Alan had read once: Take your work seriously, but never yourself. Bruce would have done well to frame that and hang it on the wall of his apartment in a prominent place.

Face it, Alan told himself, the dictum is one Dad could well remember too. Among other benefits, it might lengthen his life. Solemn, uptight men tended to be coronary-prone. On the other hand, with his fencing at the Olympic Club, his golf, skiing, swimming, and his daily fast walks to and from the bank, Paul was fit, far fitter than all but a few men of his age, so the matter of health was probably balanced.

His mother, Alan thought, appeared fit, but was not, and it worried him. She had always been a woman of will, of decision, and now she vacillated. It was the menopause, of course, which could be completely asymptomatic, but for some could also be both physiologically and psychologically distressing as it obviously was in his mother's case.

"Damn it, Mother," Alan had said once, "there is no need to put up with your symptoms. Stilbestrol, properly administered—"

"I will not take hormones, and that's that." There was a deep puritanical streak that sometimes showed itself. It was rare that Susan would even take aspirin.

His mind jumped—by association from ill health to death?—to his uncle's funeral down in Los Angeles. Should he have gone too? His father had said that there was no need, and probably from a logical point of view that was correct. There was no great closeness between the cousins. On the other hand, there was in all of them, even in Jim, a sense of family, and weren't relatives supposed to rally around at times of death? Turn the proposition around, he told himself: Would Marty have come north for a San Francisco death? I don't know; I just don't know. I have an idea, he thought, that we don't know Marty at all, and can't even guess what he would do in any given situation. He is a strange one.

6

At evening the lights of Los Angeles stretched endlessly to the south and east. To the west they ended abruptly where the land met the water; and gradually all detail except the lights disappeared.

Billy Gibbs's white Porsche was parked in the drive of the Stone Canyon house. Billy himself, still in business clothes, sat with Marty, drink in hand, on the broad porch. "Everything went all right today?"

"Sure. Great."

"Oh?"

"The arrangements were fine. Thanks for handling them. I wouldn't have known where to begin."

"Maybe I saved you a little money, that's all."

"It's the whole thing," Marty said. "That's what pisses me off." Molly Moto had turned on the lights in living room and study. By their glow Marty could see Billy's face. "I had a phone call this afternoon. A Beverly Hills salesman wanted to sell me a Rolls-Royce." He paused. "I called him a goddamn ghoul, and hung up."

Billy smiled without amusement. "Not all ambulance chasers are lawyers, friend. You're the target now." He sipped his drink slowly. "And what about the plant?"

"Walter Jordan called."

"And?"

Slowly, "I'm going to see him tomorrow. At the plant."

"And?"

"I don't know yet. You, my uncle—even, goddamn it, Joe's ghost—looking over my shoulder." Marty made a short, almost angry gesture. "I'll make up my mind."

"You used to talk about big things."

Marty shrugged.

"Maybe it was just talk." Billy's voice was carefully noncommittal.

"Maybe."

"Damn it," Billy said, "you used to be able to make up your mind in a hurry."

There was a vague sense of hostility between them. You asked him here, Marty told himself; remember that. "Go on, say it, whatever it is."

Billy took his time. "You know, I've always wondered about you. Everything you've done, you've done so damn well, and so damn easily. I've always wondered just how you'd perform if you ever came up against something that wasn't easy for you."

"You mean," Marty said, "would I fold?"

"Something like that."

"What am I supposed to say to that?" Marty said at last. "You asked me pretty much the same question once before."

"I remember." Billy smiled faintly, without amusement. "You busted me in the nose. That was then. This is now."

"I still might."

"You might. And you might even get away with it. But it wouldn't change matters." Billy stood up suddenly. He took quick steps toward the porch railing, turned, and walked back to his chair. "When you sail with a man, you think you get to know him pretty well. At least I did. But that's a different world. Decisions in a race on the water aren't the same as decisions that may affect the rest of your life. That may sound pretty pompous; I don't know. But it's true. When a man decides to go into a business, or go out of it, throw in the sponge and admit that he's licked—those are the kind of decisions that make you or break you because you're going to have to live with them a long time." He paused. "You're asking me what I think you ought to do. I don't have an answer because it isn't my problem and I wouldn't have to live with the decision. Make up your own mind, and then maybe I can help you."

Right up to you, Marty told himself, and found that he could smile. "You always were a serious bastard," he said. "All right, let's say I'm going to start running the plant. What ideas do you have about that?"

Billy walked around the chair and sat down again. "Now maybe we're getting somewhere." He picked up his drink. "The way I hear it, your father started that plant as a kind of rich man's toy. Anything to keep him close to airplanes. Right?"

Marty nodded.

"He wasn't greedy," Billy said. "He was an engineer, and he knew there was a need for a plant that could produce carefully engineered and carefully manufactured parts for major aircraft manufacturers. Right?"

Marty nodded again.

"But he wasn't really interested in setting the world on fire."

"No."

"And there," Billy said slowly, "is the difference. You don't like second best. You never have. You might even begin to believe your own talk about big things."

"Is that a warning?"

"I'm just trying to get a few things straight. Suppose you did take over, and suppose you did want to expand—how would you go about it?"

Marty took his time. "Contracts with major airframe manufacturers," he said at last, "for major assemblies, that kind of thing. Instead of fabricating small parts and subassemblies, go into the business of taking on, say, a whole empennage—an entire tail section. Or maybe the ailerons or flaps or landing gear. But a big part of the whole aircraft, not just a lot of little pieces. And work up from there." The idea was suddenly appealing. "Our own engineering staff. Our own tool shops, fabrication and assembly departments."

Carefully, "Doesn't that cost money? Lots of money?"

There was no argument about that. Marty nodded. "But there's a bank in San Francisco I think I own a piece of. And with contracts to show—" He spread his hands. "Their business is making loans."

"You make it sound easy."

"Maybe it is."

"Maybe." Billy paused. "For a McCurdy."

Marty was frowning now. "Does that bother you?"

"Some. Most of us have to fight our way."

There it was again. "And I don't?"

"You never have. Maybe this will be different." In the near darkness Billy's voice was remote, impersonal. "It may not be as easy as you think. I've been asking around a little, and it may take money, quite a bit of money, not to expand, but just to keep McCurdy Aircraft afloat."

"What do you mean?"

"There are rumors. There isn't any McCurdy stock on the market, I'm told, but I'm also told that if there were, it wouldn't be worth much. And only a few months ago it would have been worth a great deal." Billy paused. "Just rumors, as I said, but they are what push stocks up or down sometimes, and sometimes they are even accurate."

"Walter Jordan—" Marty began, and stopped. "What's he been doing?"

"Getting in a little deep with Coast, on their big air bus."

Marty stared out at the city lights unseeing. "He's supposed to take orders, not go off all by himself."

Billy said, "He's been there how long?"

"Twenty years, more or less. So?" There was no immediate answer, and Marty wanted one. "He took orders from my father. It looks as if he's going to have to take orders from me. Anything wrong with that?"

"Suppose they're not very good orders?"

"Then I'll take the blame."

Billy nodded and sipped his drink. It was the way the system worked, he told himself. What Walter Jordan might have invested in the plant in terms of effort, energy, and thought in the end counted nothing against McCurdy ownership. And if that seemed unfair, why probably it merely meant that the system, as Churchill once said of democracy, was the worst possible system—except all others. In the darkness he was smiling. "Okay," he said, "I'm for the sanctity of private property too. And for motherhood, and against sin—most sin."

"Maybe," Marty said slowly, "you'd better go with me tomorrow."

Billy hesitated. Then, in a different, less casual voice, "Maybe." He paused. "But there's something else maybe we'd better talk about first." He paused again. "Liz Palmer," he said.

Marty was frowning. "What about her? I didn't even know you knew her."

"Why shouldn't I? We were down there together." In the near darkness Billy's head nodded toward the lighted UCLA buildings. "We've kept up." His voice altered subtly. "And then you came along."

"Cutting in on your time, eh?"

"You might say that."

"Damn it, I didn't even know—"

"Would it have made any difference if you had? And there's another point. If I'm second best to anybody with her I'd rather know it now than find it out later. So maybe you'd rather find yourself another lawyer?"

Marty took his time. "No," he said at last, and his voice was definite. "If you come at me, it'll be from the front. Somebody else might go for my back."

They ate Molly Moto's good steaks with a green salad and a bottle of Zinfandel. Dessert was a cheese board. Liz was not mentioned again. "What time tomorrow?" Billy said, settling their relationship once and for all.

"I'm due at the plant at ten."

"I'll meet you there."

Marty laid down his napkin. "Coffee," he said, "with chess, gin, or billiards. Your choice."

Billy was grinning, suddenly loose again. "Hobson's choice," he said. "You'll beat me at any one of them. And one of the differences between us is that I know that losing doesn't break me up. You haven't had a chance to find out yet."

Over coffee on the glassed-in porch with the lights of San Francisco twinkling beneath them, shaggy Jim McCurdy said, "And was the funeral done Los Angeles style, a 'Rampart Street Blues' kind of performance?"

Susan said, "That isn't a very nice question."

"But typical," Bruce said. Like his father, he was dressed in sober gray, with a white shirt and a neatly patterned tie. "If there is a way for our Jimmy to be offensive, he usually finds it."

Paul, who agreed, said, "Enough. Fight out your differences elsewhere." He paused. "Your uncle was buried at Forest Lawn. It was a proper service, very well attended. He had many friends." That was Joe, he thought, friendly as a puppy, totally unlike himself, and, for that matter, Marty. Why were children so frequently so unlike their parents? "Marty—" he began.

"I think he's neat," Sudie said. "That time he was up here with that lovely boat. What does he do now?"

"Probably," Jim said, "the same thing he's always done—nothing."

"Maybe when you remake the world," Alan said, "you can find a way to put him to work."

Susan said, "Must we bicker?" She looked around the room. "We are together so seldom, and every time we are it seems that—that—" She was silent, close to tears.

Bruce said quickly, "I had a talk with Mr. Trent today." He was looking at his father. "He said he might be able to make a place for me in his foreign department."

"That would be nice." Susan was already recovered, now anxiously affable. She looked at Paul. "Wouldn't it, dear?"

How long Wally Trent was going to be in a position to make a place for anyone was a real question, Paul thought, but said merely, "Travel sounds like fun, I'll admit, but I think it gets a little boring after a time. You have a lot to learn right here in San Francisco." Do I sound pompous? Probably. It is something parents can't seem to avoid. He looked at Sudie and Jim. "And how is Berkeley?" Inane question, but what did you say to nineteen-year-olds, even if they were your own?

"Now, Daddy." Sudie was smiling. "Do you really want to know what I think I'm learning in econ?"

Paul felt better. "Frankly, no. Because whatever you're learning, you can find another economist who'll say it's wrong." He stood up. "If you'll excuse me, it's been nice, but"—he smiled apologetically at Susan—"Miss Soong had a briefcase packed for me. There is a special Loan Committee meeting in the morning."

"All those dollars," Jim said, "to keep the dirty wheels of industry turning."

Paul nodded pleasantly. "And to keep you living well, or at least as you choose." He smiled around the room. "Good night, all." He walked out in his brisk, buoyant fashion.

"Your father is worried," Susan said. She spoke to no one in particular, but to the family as a whole: to Alan, the surgeon; Bruce, the banker; the twins, Sudie and Jim, students. Not so long ago, in a time she preferred, she would not have been able to attach different labels to her children; to differentiate among them, yes, but not to separate them into categories. But they grew up, began to go their own ways, and the old, easy intimacies were no longer possible. And you began to feel alone, no longer needed, merely living out a pointless existence—and all you could do was smile, and feign calmness, and, to keep conversation alive, frequently make what probably sounded like inane remarks. "He has a great deal on his mind," she said.

Alan said, "He looks fine." And you do not, he thought. There are signs of strain around your eyes, and in them; too much rigid control in your manner. What I ought to say to you in private is that you *are* important, to me, to all of us; in your own way as important as you have ever been, and as Dad is. But would you listen? Or believe? "I don't know much about running the bank," he said, "but I imagine it is like keeping a lot of colored balls in the air, and that requires concentration."

Bruce said, "With interest rates where they are, which means tight money, inflation and recession at the same time, and all that OPEC money posing the threat that it does, I don't wonder that he's worried. I am too."

"When weren't you?" Jim said in a scarcely audible voice. Alan he could cope with. Alan was distant, almost Olympian in his calm, usually above bickering. From time to time, he had lost his cool, and even on occasion threatened to deal with Jim on a physical basis; occasions which Jim had always considered triumphs. But Bruce was another matter indeed.

Bruce was an exercise freak, for one thing. He boxed and he wrestled and he did karate or judo or whatever it was currently called; and he swam, and played tennis, and rushed off to places like Yosemite or Alpine Meadows to slide down mountains on skis. And he had a short fuse, and he would take just so much from Jim before, smiling, he would demonstrate one of those judo or karate techniques involving nerves that could be excruciatingly pressured or squeezed, and it was no triumph at all to be forced to your knees to beg for mercy. A hundred times Jim had thought of taking up judo or karate himself; and a hundred times nothing had come of it.

Sudie said, "If it's all the same to you, Mother, I think we'd better be getting back to Berkeley. Daddy isn't the only one with homework." If there were only the two of us, she thought, I would like to stay and try to capture again the ease and the sense of importance I used to feel when we were the women of the family together, sharing thoughts the men could not begin to understand. But it wouldn't work, because there are so many things in my life now that you do not know about and would not approve of, or even condone, no matter how hard I tried to explain them to you. To you what you would call morality was fixed a long time ago, and set in cement for all time. Boys can be expected to stray, but girls never. And that simply is not the way it is. "A delicious dinner," she said, "as always." Her mother did not cook; there was Felix, the Filipino chef, for that. But her mother could cook, and the chef knew it, and that was why things in the kitchen ran so well.

"Anytime you want, dear," Susan said, "we can watch Felix at work. He would love it." And so would I, she thought, and left the words unsaid. "Run along if you must. And thank you for coming clear across the Bay so we could all be together."

Driving back across the Bay Bridge in the cool, bright night: "Jesus, what a drag," Jim said. "We sit around and look at each other—"

"And you are just as shitty as you dare to be," Sudie said. "I'm really ashamed of you."

"The difference between us," Jim said, "one of the differences, is that I'm the same all the time, and you turn sweetness and light on and off like a neon sign. Why don't you say 'shitty' at the dinner table? Afraid you'd be sent to your room?"

Sudie drove in silence, both angry and embarrassed.

"And why don't you tell dear Mother about that jock you're screwing? Have you taken him home for tea yet?"

Sudie said, "If you want to get out and walk, just keep it up."

7

Alan parked his car on the street, front wheels carefully turned toward the curb. Strictly speaking, all-night parking in this area was illegal, but the police winked at it. But park without cramping your wheels, and you were in trouble. Too many unattended cars had rolled down too many San Francisco hills with sometimes disastrous results.

He got out of his car and looked up at the front of the apartment house. Nancy's windows showed light. Well, what else had he expected? She was a night person, as he was, and besides, it was only nine-thirty. The question all along had not been whether she would be awake, but whether she would still be in the mood.

He was. Sitting at dinner, listening to the family talking but not saying much, his mind had drifted again and again to Nancy and what might euphemistically be called her charms. As a youngster he had wondered if male doctors through overfamiliarity with the female body lost all sense of anticipatory delight, and if the sex act itself became merely a brief, almost perfunctory exercise. He knew now happily that it was not that way at all. Those horny surgeons in *M*A*S*H* were an accurate representation of at least what he, Alan McCurdy, felt.

When he was examining a patient or in the operating room there was no such thing as sex in his thoughts. But walking down the hospital corridors the sight of a rounded rump in a tight uniform or a pair of bouncing breasts could bring that scrotum-tightening sensation he had known since early puberty, and the fact that he saw nakedness during a fair share of his waking hours mattered not at all. Even tonight he had found himself looking at Sudie's breasts as they stirred gently, unencumbered by a bra; and that he had thought immediately of Nancy did nothing to alter the fact that it was the sight of his own sister's body that had turned him on.

He let himself into the apartment building and ran up the stairs two at a time. Nancy's apartment was just down the hall from his, which was handy. He knocked on her door, and placed himself in front of the peephole.

The door opened a few inches and Nancy's eyes looked out. The door closed again and there was the sound of the chain being removed. Then, at last, he could enter, hear the sound of the door closing behind him, and feel immediately that the world was shut out.

She was in a light wool robe and heeled slippers. She had been reading—the book lay face down on the end table beside her easy chair. But, then, when was a medical student or young doctor not banging away at the books? There was the wide, wide world of interrelated medicine to explore, and you had damn well better explore it carefully.

"I have some bourbon," Nancy said.

"No thanks. I had a snifter of the parents' brandy after wine at dinner. *Basta.*" Now that he was here, he thought, all sense of haste disappeared. It was as if, through desire intensified, time could be slowed, and the world, or at least that part of it concerning him now, put into sharper perspective. "How long do we have?" he said.

Nancy was smiling. "About three hours less than we did." She was a tall girl, slender, but well rounded at hip and breast; through her training and discipline, she had become confident without arrogance. "Was it a good dinner?"

"Do you mean, was it worth it not to be here? No. On the other hand—family. Symbolic gathering in a way. My father and mother buried my uncle in Los Angeles today. Tonight we gathered." He smiled suddenly. "Without solidarity, but I had to go."

"I understand. I even approve."

For the moment enough talk. Alan reached for her and she came to him, warm and pliable; and her lips were sweet. It was a long kiss, reluctantly ended. Alan stepped back. "What's under the robe?"

She was smiling, with her lips, with her eyes. "I thought you'd never ask. There's only me."

He watched her hands move with unhurried dexterity, loosening the belt of the robe, letting the ends fall. She opened the robe and slid it back and down on her bent arms. She was naked, smiling. With an almost imperceptible shoulder motion she shook her breasts gently. "Satisfied?"

"Wrong word. Convinced, but nowhere near satisfied."

She nodded then, smiling still, and turned toward the bedroom doorway.

She lay back on the bed, the robe discarded, and watched him undress. He had a lean, well-muscled body, broad through the shoulders, narrow at the hips. Man and woman, she thought; this is how we evolved: dissimilar bodies with built-in physiological need for each other; but with psychological need too, which may well set us apart in the animal world. In medicine you learned to analyze, to look for cause, to understand effect. But here, now, she thought, I am throwing analysis out the window.

Because I care nothing for effect, what may come after. Nor do I care to examine motives beyond the simple "what both he and I want at the moment" stage. Is this relationship permanent? I don't care whether it is or not—I tell myself. And that is enough.

Alan lay down beside her and took her warmly in his arms. "I've been thinking about you all night. About all of you."

She was smiling against his cheek. "Then show me how your thoughts were running," she said. "And don't hurry."

They lay quiet, spent, companionably close. "Someone," Alan said, "has probably invented a phrase for it and it's somewhere in the medical books: postcoital languor, or something." His smile was relaxed. "Somebody who didn't even know what it was."

"You mean," Nancy said, "like the male experts on childbirth?"

"Exactly."

"You're funny."

Smiling still, "I had hoped I was more than that."

"What would you like to be?"

"An orthopedic surgeon, a good one."

"Nothing else?" She too was smiling.

"Nothing I can think of at the moment."

"No." Nancy's smile held, but its quality had changed. "There is a difference, isn't there? I want to be a good pediatrician. But I want something else too. I want to make enough money so I don't have to worry about it. I want to pay back my parents for what my education cost them, and I want to be able to do a few things for them besides to make up for what they did without." Her smile turned gentle. "That's the kind of thing you don't even have to think about, isn't it?"

Slowly, "I guess. I never have thought about it." It was always uncomfortable to be reminded that through no doing of his own he had been born into this world with things already made easy for him.

"I grew up hearing about the McCurdys," Nancy said. "Maybe I should have told you before."

Frowning, "About what?"

Nancy was silent for a little time. Then, in a different voice, almost with an air of confession: "We weren't rich, but we weren't poor, either. I'm talking about my grandfather. Comfortable, I guess, is the word. The Depression caught him as it caught so many people." She was staring up at the ceiling. "Overextended, as they said. He—believed all the fine talk out of Washington about prosperity being just around the corner." She turned to look at Alan and her voice rose suddenly. "Did you ever read any of that?"

Alan put his hand on one full, firm breast and moved it gently. "This," he said, "is bed talk?"

Nancy was silent.

"Okay," Alan said, "go ahead, get it off this beautiful chest. Your grandfather—?"

Nancy said, her voice quieter now, "It's only that he lost what he had, his property, his house, *and* his savings through trying to keep what he could." She rolled her head again to look at Alan. "That's all."

It was a kind of sudden coldness that he felt, an emptiness and a silence in his mind. It was as if a chill wind had swept through the room. "The bank," he said, "is that it? Our bank?"

"I've always been told," Nancy said, "that the McCurdy National people were very nice when they foreclosed. They said they were sorry, but that was how things were. Nothing personal, they said. My father remembers. He was going to start college, but it didn't work out that way."

Alan started to remove his hand from her breast. She covered it with her own and held it firm. "Not your fault," she said.

"But you had to tell me. So it was on your mind."

"Silly, isn't it?" She was close to tears. "Aren't we taught to take the objective, dispassionate view? I—never knew my grandfather. He didn't have to, but he went off to war. He didn't come back. My grandmother told me once she was sure he had no intention of coming back. So it has nothing to do with me, does it? Or you?" She managed to keep the tears under control, and made herself concentrate on the hand on her breast. There, she told herself, was the reality; not in the past.

"I knew my grandfather," Alan said. "He only died six months ago. Ten years ago—" He shook his head. "He still went down to the bank every day. Walking. He had his desk on the main floor and he seemed to know by name half the people who came in, maybe more than half. He took me to lunch one day at the Pacific Union Club and asked me if I wanted to go into the bank like my father. He seemed to want to know. I was sixteen, and I took a deep breath and told him I wanted to be a doctor, a surgeon, and then I sat and waited for him to lower the boom, but he didn't.

"He said, 'All right, boy, go to it. Just one thing. Make goddamn good and sure you're the best surgeon who ever came down the pike. You hear?' I think the entire dining room heard." Alan paused. "That doesn't change things a bit, does it? In your eyes he's still a son of a bitch, and in a way I guess he was. And maybe some of it has rubbed off on me too. Maybe—"

"Shut up." Her voice was fierce. "Put your arms around me! Tight! I'm going to cry, and maybe that will—help!"

Dressed, his jacket over his arm, Alan walked down the hall and let himself into his own apartment. It was close to midnight, not as late as he had thought to stay, but somehow things were changed. Which was ridiculous, wasn't it?

He undressed again and put on a fine cotton yukata which he preferred to a robe. He rarely drank alone, but now a drink seemed necessary. He mixed it, bourbon and water, and sat down in his reading chair to stare at the bookcases he had had built against the far wall.

There in what had become a fair medical reference library was a good share of the accumulated knowledge of hundreds of years of medicine. Knowledge, but where was wisdom? Where was the ability to deal with the subtle barrier that now disturbed his and Nancy's intimacy?

We can expose a heart or a spine and do all manner of ingenious things, he thought. Through the miracles of X ray and other radiation we can diagnose and sometimes cure in a magical fashion. We have drugs to cope selectively with a spectrum of diseases. But do we know how to deal person to person with people? The answer was no; a disturbing concept. There were the books, but they held no answer.

So you play it by instinct, he thought; and maybe that was a subtle part of medicine too, the part the old family doctor used to play, part medicine man, part father confessor, part stern disciplinarian? Who never turned his back on a problem? Never admitted defeat until the end was final?

He put down his drink, picked up the phone, and dialed Nancy's number. The phone rang only once. Nancy's voice said, "Yes?"

"What are you doing?"

There was a short silence. "Just sitting."

"I'm sitting too, with a drink."

"I'm sorry," Nancy said. "I spoiled it."

"No. If anybody spoiled it, it was your grandfather and mine, which is silly."

"Yes."

"Something that happened more than thirty years ago, before either of us was born."

"Yes."

" 'The sins of the fathers,' and all that jazz."

"I know. I shouldn't have said anything."

"No. Sooner or later it had to be said. On behalf of my grandfather, I apologize—as he would never have done. That's probably silly too, but it makes me feel a little better. Okay?"

"Alan—"

"Apology accepted? Yes or no."

Softly, "Of course."

"Then let's try to forget it and get some sleep. You have your little bastards to cope with tomorrow."

"And you have bones to chip."

"Exactly."

"Good night, Alan." Her voice was gentle. "Until I spoiled it, it was—lovely."

"We must do it again. Soon."

There was no answer. The phone clicked dead.

8

Marty had known the plant since childhood, approached it a thousand times, but never quite like this. Being the boss's son was one thing; it was different now, no longer casual, almost a game on which he could turn his back at will. A childhood phrase came into his mind out of nowhere: I'm playing now for keeps.

Billy Gibbs's white Porsche was waiting in the employee parking lot. Marty parked beside it and got out.

"I've been doing a little snooping just to see where we stand," Billy said. "Old Max Wimple drew up your father's will and kept it in his office. He showed it to me this morning. Except for a few relatively minor bequests, you are it. The point of all this is that your father's stock in McCurdy Aircraft, and it is a majority holding, goes to you, so your position vis-à-vis Walter Jordan is firm. You can do what you want."

The overtones were plain. "And," Marty said slowly, "you don't think that is how it ought to be, is that it?"

"That depends on what you do with the clout you have. I'll be interested to see how you handle it."

Overtones remained. Marty said, "Let's get this straight. Where do we stand, you and I?"

Billy took his time. "I'll give you the best legal advice I know," he said. "And I'll back you as far as I can."

"Which is how far?"

"I told you," Billy said, "we aren't aboard *Westerly* any more. The Captain Bligh approach doesn't work too well on land."

Marty thought about it. "Okay." And suddenly he could smile, and mean it. "Let's go see what Jordan has to say."

It was a pleasant office, light and airy, and quiet, as the shop was not. Down in the fabrication department, Marty knew, would be the constant unholy cacophony of the clomp of shears, the scream of shapers, the thudding rhythm of punch presses, and the whine of hydros. In the assembly department the sounds would change, and the chatter of rivet guns would be dominant. Somehow this office seemed too distant.

Walter Jordan was a middle-sized man with slicked-down hair and rimless glasses. Marty had long wondered if Robert McNamara was his hero. "Sit down, gentlemen," Jordan said, and took his own place behind his large, uncluttered desk. "You're looking well, Marty."

As if I were still sixteen, Marty thought. "You said you had some things you wanted to talk about."

Walter Jordan took off his glasses and began to polish them with his breast-pocket handkerchief. He said, "Mr. Gibbs is—?"

"Among other things," Marty said, "my lawyer."

"I see." Jordan looked at Billy, question plain.

"Marty inherits," Billy said.

Jordan took his time putting the glasses back on. "I had hoped—" he began. "Never mind." He was looking now at Marty. "What do you intend to do?"

"I'm not sure yet."

"Your father," Jordan said, "left matters pretty much in my hands. I believe you are aware of that."

Marty nodded.

"It was," Jordan said, "an amicable and I think I can say successful relationship. The plant prospered. Your father was free to pursue his own interests, as you were, Marty, without worry about decisions or details. Your father was a very capable man when he chose to be, a very capable man—"

"He's dead," Marty said. "We buried him yesterday." Was he being callous? Maybe. But the point had to be made. "What happens now has nothing to do with him." He was conscious that Billy watched him, expressionless. The hell with it, he thought; I play it my own way. "Let's go on from there," he said.

"Marty," Jordan said in a reasonable tone, "I am twice your age—"

"Agreed. But whether that is benefit or handicap, we'll just have to see."

Walter Jordan was not used to being interrupted. He was silent for a few moments. "Your best course, Marty, is to leave matters as they are, as, if you will forgive one more mention, they were while your father was still alive. You know nothing of the business." He raised his hand to forestall another interruption. "Oh, you have your engineering degree, I know. But there is a great deal more than simple engineering to running a business of this complexity."

Billy, watching, listening, thought: you are taking exactly the wrong approach, friend. You are raising hackles, which is precisely what you ought not to be doing. He watched Marty and waited. Marty surprised him.

"You're probably right," Marty said, mildly enough, even smiling. "The world is full of things I don't know anything about."

"You are a very fortunate young man," Jordan said. "Most cannot avoid responsibilities. You can. You have your sailing and your—other pursuits."

"True," Marty said, again to Billy's surprise.

Walter Jordan smiled benignly. "I am glad you see it my way."

"The only trouble is," Marty said, "I don't think I do. Are you trying to keep me from having anything to do with the plant? Why? Aren't things going well? There are rumors that maybe we are in a little too deep with Coast Aircraft. What about that?"

"Rumors," Jordan said, and smiled again. He looked to Billy Gibbs for support.

Billy said nothing. He watched Marty.

Marty said, "The rumors aren't true?"

"Of course not."

"I'm glad to hear it," Marty said. "But so there won't be any doubts, maybe we'd better run a check, don't you think?"

Jordan said at last, "I don't know what you mean by that, Marty."

"Simple. It's called an audit, isn't it?"

The benign smile was gone now. "If an accounting is what you wish, Marty," Walter Jordan said, "I will be happy to have our accounting department—"

"No," Marty said.

Jordan smiled again, relieved. "I was afraid for a moment—"

"I think an outside firm," Marty said. He turned his head. "Don't you, Billy? Aside from my wanting to know just what I'm inheriting, won't we want an independent audit for tax purposes?"

Billy's face revealed nothing. He is smoother and smarter than I gave him credit for, he was thinking. He said, "It would probably be a good idea."

Marty said, "Do you have an accounting firm in mind? And can you arrange it?"

"Yes," Billy said. He looked at the man behind the desk. "If Mr. Jordan has no objections."

"I most certainly do."

The office was still. "Do you, now?" Marty said gently. "Let's hear what they are. Is there something you don't want me to find out?"

"Certainly not."

"Then what harm can an audit do?"

"I resent the implications." Jordan's voice was rising. "I will not be—"

"Wrong," Marty said. He spoke with slow distinctness. "You will do exactly what you are told. Is that clear?"

For as long as it might take a man to count slowly to ten Jordan didn't speak. At last he said, "And if I do not choose to?"

Marty's smile was crooked. "Don't ever try to bluff me," he said. "Because I'll call your bluff. If you want to stand up and walk out of here right now, go ahead."

"You can't—"

"Wrong again. I can, and if you push me, I will." He waited, but Jordan didn't say anything. "There will be an independent audit. It will begin tomorrow." He looked at Billy, and watched him nod. "Any lack of cooperation—I want to hear about it." Looking again at Jordan: "I will be happy to have you stay in your present capacity," he said. "But only on my terms." He stood up then. "I think that's all for now." He walked out, and Billy walked after him.

In the employee parking lot: "You're becoming a hard-nosed son of a bitch," Billy said.

"Any objections?"

"And you're a touchy son of a bitch too. No objections. I think he asked for it."

"Maybe," Marty said slowly, "I'm not doing things according to the book. I don't know. I've never read the book. I'm doing things my way."

"Haven't you always?"

Slowly Marty's shoulders relaxed. He smiled. "I guess I have at that."

"'Damn the torpedoes! Full speed ahead!' You may be heading for shoal water."

"I'll take that responsibility." He looked back at the plant buildings. "I guess in the end that's what it comes to, isn't it?"

Billy said unexpectedly, "Liz will probably be happy." His tone was carefully expressionless. "She is having lunch with me. Shall I tell her you're taking command?"

"Tell her," Marty said, "that she and you can watch and see if I fall flat on my face."

Liz wore a simple shirtwaist dress that on her, Billy thought, was something special. She also wore the inevitable dark glasses, and in a small gesture of intimacy she took them off and smiled at him as she slid into the Porsche. "Hi, counselor. How are the law books?" Exposure complete, she put the glasses back on.

Right from the start, Billy told himself; lay it right out. "I have a new client. Marty McCurdy."

"I am not surprised."

They were moving smoothly now, heading west toward the beaches. "I thought someplace where we could talk," Billy said. "In in places like the Bistro you can't hear yourself think." And then, "Do you want to explain how you figure everything out?"

Liz was smiling gently. "It's simple enough. He knows you, and when the going gets rough, he wants somebody he can trust standing behind him."

"He knows about you and me," Billy said.

Liz's voice was unchanged. "I never tried to keep it a secret. The subject just never came up. There was no reason why it should have."

"Now there is, or was, so I told him and asked him if he wanted another lawyer."

Liz was smiling. "Ethics?"

"You might call it that." Damn the girl; she had always had a way of getting to him.

"I'm glad," Liz said, thereby erasing the sting. "Ethics is a rare commodity these days." She paused. "I'm sorry I'm the cause. And flattered."

Billy's thoughts were off in a different direction. "You said when the going gets rough. Do you think it will?"

"Don't you?"

"All right. Tell me why."

"For the same reason you think it—Marty. If he has called for you, then he is coming out of his playpen. And from what I hear, whatever he does he does all the way."

True enough. He had said it himself.

"You are in for a sleigh ride, counselor."

"It's already begun." Billy smiled without amusement. "He had a message for you. He said you and I could watch and see if he falls flat on his face."

"You know," Liz said slowly, "it will be interesting."

They had lunch on the terrace of a small restaurant overlooking the sea. On the horizon a freighter trailed a line of smoke as it churned its way northward. A single tall sail, a sloop under main and overlapping jib, lay into its work close-hauled against a brisk westerly breeze. Billy watched it idly. He sipped his drink.

"Big ocean," he said. "Under spinnaker at night a thousand miles from any land it seems even bigger. And then one morning Diamond Head rises out of the sea like something you can't believe, and the race is over." He smiled at Liz. "You're both glad and sorry that it's over. Glad because you're tired; sorry because while you were doing it, pushing the boat, you felt you were really doing something. Kid stuff, I guess."

"Maybe." Liz had taken off her dark glasses and dropped them into her purse. Her eyes watched Billy steadily. "Did you and he ever fight?" The question came out of nowhere.

"We've had our arguments."

"That wasn't what I meant."

"A brawl?" Billy smiled. "Twice. Once when we were just kids. His round; two punches. And once when we were a little boozed up after a hard race. That one was a draw. No real damage. I don't even remember what it was about."

"Maybe you refused to take orders?"

Billy was watching the sailboat again. "No. He only gave the orders when we were sailing, and I never refused to take them. Sometimes afterward we argued about them, but not at the time."

"And now?"

Billy finished his drink as the waitress approached with their orders. "As you said, it will be interesting to watch."

They sat over coffee. "I'm playing hooky today," Billy said. "No rush. What would you like to do?" He paused. "Besides talk about Marty."

Liz said slowly, "Not very nice of me, is it? I'm sorry."

"Some people," Billy said, "have a way of getting into conversations even when they aren't there."

"I said I was sorry, Billy. Let's talk about you."

"And you?"

Liz smiled quietly. "If you like, but there isn't much to say about me. I think you know where you are and what you want to do, and you are doing it. For you there is a pattern to fit things into. I haven't found my pattern yet." She produced the brilliant smile.

"Until maybe today," Billy said, "Marty hadn't found his pattern either."

"We weren't going to talk about Marty, remember?"

"You know," Billy said, "the hell of it is that he's right here with us. I think if we went to bed together he'd be there too, damn him." He was silent for a few moments, conscious of the question in Liz's mind, unspoken, unspeakable. "No," he said at last, "don't worry. I won't sabotage him. I'll give him the best I can, and if and when I feel I can't do it any more, I'll tell him to go find somebody else."

9

Paul McCurdy came out of the Loan Committee meeting with Helen Soong following. In the outer office the girl who manned Helen Soong's desk during meetings said, "Mr. Waldo called from New York, Mr. McCurdy," and stood up to relinquish her place.

Paul nodded his thanks. "Call him back," he told Helen, and went on into his own office.

Helen Soong was thirty-five, unmarried, with a B.A. in economics from the University of California, secretarial skills dating back to high school, and a knowledge of banking procedures and banking law from University of California night school extension courses. She was a fifth-generation Californian, born in San Francisco's Chinatown.

The Waldo call went through quickly, and Helen buzzed it into Paul. "Good morning, Ted," Paul said.

"Morning, hell. The sun has been over the yardarm for an hour back here."

There was lightness in the voice, and, Paul thought, there would be a smile on Ted's face. "Sorry I'm breaking into your lunchtime drinking," he said. Thank God he could treat it lightly; Ted, unlike some Paul could name in the banking world, had no drinking problem, probably because Ted had not yet reached the dead end so many senior bankers did. Maybe he never would.

"The word here," Ted said, "is that Citibank will lead with a quarter-point drop in their prime, and Chemical will probably follow. I thought you ought to know."

"Quite right."

"It will be announced after market close today."

Paul nodded. "Good man." Ted *was* a good man, affable, gregarious, careful, and accurate; word from Ted was to be believed. It was very pleasant to have men around like Ted who could fit in just about anywhere and do a job. As a matter of fact: "Ted," he said, "anything urgent on your hands right now? Say for the next few days?"

No hesitation. "Two dinner dates. One private, one public." The smile in the voice was plain. "I'll miss the private one, but I'll live. You want me out there?"

"Yes." Paul hesitated. "A matter of some—delicacy. Make it your idea, Ted. Just a routine report back to the home office."

"Got you. I'll be in first thing in the morning."

"Now go have your martini and lunch."

Ted chuckled. "Are you saying what the bank chairman is supposed to have said to his senior VP's about three- and four-martini lunches?"

"I don't think I know that one," Paul said.

"He told them that from now on the martinis would be made with gin, not vodka. He wanted customers in the afternoon to realize that the VP's were drunk, and not just think they were stupid."

Paul hung up smiling. Board chairman, he thought, and tried to imagine how Charles Goodwin, his own chairman, would handle a situation like that one. Probably profanely; Charles Goodwin had a lot of Joe McCurdy in him, which was only natural after all their years together.

The smile faded. Ted Waldo for Wally Trent? Why not? If

Wally had lost his touch, then a change would have to be made, wouldn't it? And I will be the son of a bitch, Paul thought, to break Wally's heart by putting him out to pasture. He sat up and buzzed Helen Soong. "Mr. Waldo will be here in the morning. Give me thirty minutes with him."

"Yes, sir." Helen Soong consulted notes. "Mr. Simpson of Latour Vineyards is on his way."

"I'll see him as soon as he arrives."

"And Mr. Goodwin would like you to call him."

"Call him back." Paul leaned back in his chair. Speak of the devil, he thought, and smiled. Whatever the board chairman wanted, it would not have to do with four-martini lunches.

It did not. "I am sorry about your brother, Paul," Charles Goodwin said. And then, without waiting for response: "What is this I hear about our foreign operations? Have you let Wally Trent stray off the reservation?"

So word of the audit had leaked out after all. "I am looking into it."

"I should hope so. I want a report."

"You shall have it." It was not always easy to hold your temper in the face of Goodwin's demands, Paul thought, but it was far better not to cross him. Technically, Charles Goodwin was almost in retirement. Practically, he could still muster his forces and raise considerable hell if he felt something was being handled incorrectly, or not in the old way. There was no point in asking for trouble. "I will see that you are kept informed," Paul said.

Helen Soong buzzed to say that Mr. Simpson had arrived. Paul stood up as the door opened and walked out from behind his desk to shake hands. "Good to see you, George." They sat in two of the leather visitor's chairs.

"I'm worried, Paul." Simpson was a short, wiry, sandy man in his late sixties, with what looked to be a perpetual sunburn. "That's a hell of thing to tell your banker, I know, but there it is."

"I've heard problems before," Paul said. He was smiling. "Sometimes they've been pretty bad, and sometimes they've blown away when you looked at them. What's yours?"

"Cabernet Sauvignon." Simpson saw the faint frown appear between Paul's eyes. "I know, I know," he said, "we've done well with it, very well. And this looks to be a tremendous year. The trouble is that maybe we've done too well, because everybody and his jackass brother in the whole Napa Valley has planted Cabernet Sauvignon, and in a year, two, the bottom is just going to drop out—and we'll still be owing you money."

"Your credit is good, George. You know that." Paul smiled reminiscently. "If I heard it once, I heard it a thousand times that my father would lend a million dollars to a man of character but he wouldn't lend a goddamn cent, no matter what the collateral, to a man he didn't trust. That still goes."

Simpson produced a faint smile. "You make me feel some better."

"But you're still worried?"

The smile spread. "I'm a worrier. Your father knew it. The wife says if I don't have something to worry about, I worry about that." He paused. "Price, for one thing. Good, solid California wine, Cabernet Sauvignon, Sauvignon Blanc, damn good wine, with color, nose, taste, but still domestic—selling for four, five dollars a bottle, in stores, not in restaurants. I don't like it, Paul. We can price ourselves right out of the market. French wines—"

"After that false-labeling scandal," Paul said, "Bordeaux isn't exactly in good repute right now."

Simpson said, "Between you and me, damn few people can tell the difference between a good wine and a great one. Damn few. Between pure horse piss and a good wine, yes, but that's about it. And I'm not so sure that even the best of the French clarets is a damn bit better than some of our Cabernet Sauvignon, for example. But people have been taught that it is, just the way they've been taught that a dress made in Paris, no matter what the hell it looks like—and if I caught the wife dead in some I've seen, I'd divorce her on the spot—they've been taught that it's better than anything the ILGWU turns out. It doesn't make sense, but it's true.

"And so if we start competing in price with French wine—" He shook his head. "Not yet. Maybe someday, but not yet."

"You've come a long way since 1933," Paul said.

"Thank God for the banks that helped us after Repeal. Thank God for your father. And you."

"And I think you're solid," Paul said. "Latour in particular." He smiled quickly. "What else are you worrying about?"

"You know Miller? That goddamn fortuneteller, meteorologist, whatever the hell he wants to call himself? Well, six weeks ago he predicted two weeks of rain this month. If we get half that, that beautiful goddamn crop of grapes will be finished, or near enough. Or, almost worse, if we catch a heavy frost—and Miller's talking about that too." He grinned suddenly, ruefully. "See what it's like in the outside world? And all you have to do is sit here and count your money."

"Something like that," Paul said, smiling again. "No problems here."

Simpson stood up. He held out his hand. "I guess all I wanted was to get it off my chest. A banker, a good banker is kind of like a holy man or a good family doctor: you go to him with your troubles."

"And," Paul said, "we don't even charge interest for listening." He shook Simpson's hand. "I'm glad you stopped by."

Simpson said suddenly, "Oh, shit!" He shook his head in annoyance. "The wife will give me pure hell. 'You go see Paul McCurdy,' she said, 'and he'll cheer you up. But the first thing you say to him is how sorry we are about his brother, you hear?' Well, hell, I get so wrapped up in my own problems I forget everything else. We are sorry as hell, Paul. First your father, then your brother, it's tough. Both Joes were good guys." He grinned suddenly. "Different as hell. Old Joe was as tough a son of a bitch as ever came down the pike, and Bud just plain nice. I liked them both, and I'm sorry as hell they're gone."

Paul walked to the door with the older man. They shook hands again. "In the current vernacular," Paul said, " 'not to worry, George.' And thanks for the condolences."

He went back to his desk and sat down heavily. He felt tired today and he could not have said why; and the sense of fatigue was compounded because on days like this problems took on a larger-than-life proportion.

He found himself thinking back to last night's dinner, the entire family assembled, squabbling as usual. Jim and Sudie—what if anything was he to do about them? They were strangers, as Alan and Bruce had never been, going their own sometimes merry, sometimes bitter way in God only knew what directions.

He had heard rumors about Sudie and that 49er quarterback, what was his name? Pete Mankowski? A big, blond, shaggy-haired kid from, he thought, Pennsylvania, the coalfields, via an athletic scholarship, All-American status, and the NFL draft; by all accounts what was called a swinger, and, if rumor was correct, not a trustworthy guy.

And what did a father do about that in this day and age? Make a fool of himself by a confrontation with Sudie, who was probably behaving no better, but certainly no worse, than her nineteen-year-old contemporaries?

If asked, he knew Susan would say yes, have a good long talk with the girl; that was what my father would have done.

But these days, Paul thought, we wait it out and hope for the best with some awful examples in mind. As far as he knew, Sudie was not into hard drugs, which was damn small consolation, but at least something he could cling to. Well, maybe after all a little chat with the child would not be entirely out of the question. Damn it, he told himself, when I talk most people listen; why shouldn't my own daughter?

The phone buzzed discreetly. He picked it up. Helen Soong's voice said, "A Mr. Walter Jordan is calling from Los Angeles. He is connected with McCurdy Aircraft."

"I will take it," Paul said, and punched the phone button. He knew the man only casually. "Yes, Mr. Jordan?"

"I hesitated to call you, Mr. McCurdy," Jordan said, "but I am uncertain how to deal with my—problem."

Were there overtones of something deeper than uncertainty in that dry, pedantic voice? "What is it?" Paul said.

"Your nephew, Marty McCurdy."

Paul leaned back in his chair and stared at the far wall. "Maybe you had better tell me about it," he said, and listened quietly.

It was a tale of threat and intimidation, of outright bullying, a scene Walter Jordan could not forget and which had upset him considerably.

"And what," Paul said, "was the cause?"

"There was no justification, none. The young man even brought his lawyer." Jordan paused, and his voice altered. "For a time I feared physical violence."

"Mr. Jordan," Paul said carefully, "I am handicapped by distance. I am also somewhat baffled. What was Marty's purpose? What did he hope to accomplish?" He paused. "What did he want from you?"

"Subservience. Total submission."

Now we are getting somewhere, Paul thought. "To what?"

There was hesitation. "To his outrageous and insulting demand."

Why, Paul thought, this man is desperate. "You will have to tell me more than that," he said.

There was more hesitation. Then, "There are rumors, Mr. McCurdy. There are always rumors, as you well know."

Frequently, Paul thought, but not always. Let's hope that we don't have them too. "What kind of rumors?"

"That we, McCurdy Aircraft, have invested heavily in engineering, planning, and tooling for component assemblies to be furnished to Coast Aircraft for their air bus."

"And have you?"

"Under the late Mr. McCurdy's orders, yes."

"Then," Paul said mildly, "the rumors are true, aren't they?"

"To a certain extent, yes." Jordan's voice held appeal now. "But you can appreciate that in Marty's present frame of mind everything will be exaggerated."

" 'Will be,' " Paul said. And then, "I see. Marty wants an accounting?"

"Yes." The word came out with slow reluctance.

"Isn't he entitled to it?"

"Mr. McCurdy, I offered to have our accounting department—"

"I see," Paul said again. "But he insists on an outside audit, is that it?" As I insisted with Wally Trent. Good for Marty, he thought; I would not have given the boy credit. "I see nothing wrong with that. In his place I would do the same." He paused for emphasis. "I don't see that there is anything I can do, do you?"

There was a long silence. "I had hoped—" Jordan began. "I mean, the family, Mr. McCurdy. You are the older man. I am sure you have influence with Marty."

"The family," Paul said. He was annoyed now. "One of the things the family has always prided itself on, Jordan, is keeping noses out of others' business. McCurdy Aircraft was my brother's affair. It is probably now Marty's. If he asks me for advice, I will be happy to give it if I can. Until then, he is on his own.

"And," he added, "from the sound of things he's starting out rather well." He hung up.

So obviously Marty was taking over. Well, Paul thought, that is his right. He is young for the job, inexperienced, but we shall see. He found himself looking around the big office which had been his father's. Come to think of it, he told himself, Marty is no younger than my father was when he took over the bank, is he? And in many ways they are the same kind of men. He smiled. I can appreciate Jordan's fright.

10

1918–1923

Joe McCurdy was twenty-eight at the time of the 1918 Armistice, and in full control of the McCurdy National Bank. He had wanted to go off to war, but his elders, including the governor of California, had persuaded him to stay put.

"We're going to be drawn into this war, young fellow," Hiram Johnson said; this was in 1916 during the campaign that would send Johnson to the U. S. Senate, "and you'll probably paw the ground and want to go. Stay here. We need you. Your father is dead and you're running the bank, and the bank is a vital part of this community. Wars, modern wars anyway, are fought on the home front too. You hear me?"

"Yes, sir." Peppery Hiram Johnson was one of the few men Joe McCurdy treated with great deference. "I hear you, but—"

"No buts. You can do a hell of a lot more good for the country here than you ever could in the trenches. Why do you think I'm taking time out from running this state and campaigning to come down here if I didn't think it was important to talk to you? You're a money man, and damn few are, and we're going to need all the sane money handling we can get before this thing is finished. And afterward."

And so Joe McCurdy sat the war out in San Francisco, something he never quite forgave himself for.

He was valuable; there was no doubt about that. And McCurdy National, if not essential, was certainly an important part of the local war effort. There were ships to build, and bank money went out to finance the yards that built them. There was food to be grown, processed, and shipped. McCurdy National loans went out to growers, packers, shippers.

War was a bonanza. By 1918 the cash value of California's field crops, fruits, vegetables, and livestock alone totaled more than

$680,000,000, and McCurdy National held notes on its share of this bounty.

Mary Pickford and Douglas Fairbanks promoted Liberty Bonds. Joe McCurdy led the way in setting up automatic bond purchases for bank customers.

There were speeches to be made, but Joe stayed away from that. In 1917 and 1918 a large, obviously healthy twenty-seven-year-old did not appear in public urging patriotism. The word "slacker" had come into common usage, and tempers could run high as the casualty lists from France grew.

"I hated every goddamn minute of it, boy," he once told Paul in a much later time. "But I guess I had a job to do right here, so I stayed. But I sure as hell understood your brother's attitude. I'm just glad that you're too young for this new war."

Joe Jr. was born in 1919, and the following year Joe built the big comfortable house at Pebble Beach where the family began to spend a good share of their summers, Joe coming down from San Francisco for long weekends.

California was booming. Local banks sprang up. "Some of them," Joe told Martha, "run by damn fools. Giannini makes branch banking look easy because he knows what he's doing. And we've done fine so far ourselves. But some of these morons are going to get themselves in so deep they'll never get out without help, and those of us who are sound will have to throw them a lifeline."

"I don't understand why," Martha said. "I thought you were competitors."

Joe nodded. "Up to a point we are, but beyond that point we're tied together like Siamese twins because the essence of banking is confidence, and if one bank goes under, all banks are suspect."

"But there are bank examiners." Martha smiled. "You're always swearing about them. How can a bank be allowed to come close to failing?"

"Honey, when you're dealing with things as volatile as agriculture and human nature, almost anything can happen. Down in the San Joaquin, raisins are riding high right now, and loans to growers, dry yards, and dehydrators safe as can be. But a grape crop could fail disastrously, and then the picture would be entirely different." Joe paused. "Almonds are good, but there have been early frosts to ruin an entire year's crop. Oranges, lemons—" He spread his large hands.

"We make the best judgment we can when we approve a loan, and then sometimes we still have to take a deep breath and hope for the best."

Industry began to grow in northern California, and the state became less and less dependent on the East with its "prices slightly higher west of the Rockies" attitude which so infuriated Westerners.

"One day," Joe told Martha, "we're going to be the biggest state in the Union. We can't miss. Climate, for one thing. For another, the way those Los Angeles people are scrambling, hauling themselves right up by their bootstraps. By rights Los Angeles ought to be no more than a few inland orange groves and a dusty plaza, but they don't believe it. Why, hell, they don't even have enough water, so they're reaching up to Owens Valley in the Sierra Nevada over two hundred miles with that big aqueduct of theirs. They aren't going to be stopped."

The State Superintendent of Banks walked into the McCurdy National one day in late 1923. Joe was at his main-floor desk. He stood up to shake hands. "Sit down, Harry, and tell me what we're doing wrong."

Harry Watson sat down. "I wish," he said, "that all banks in California were doing as right as you are. I'd sleep better nights. That damn Valley National in Fresno—"

"I've heard about that." Joe shook his head. "Giannini and the Crocker and the Pacific Southwest in Los Angeles may be involved. We aren't. We aren't into Fresno."

"I'm aware of that, Joe. But you are into Caloro. You're the biggest bank in town."

Joe leaned back in his chair. He said quietly, "And?"

"And Floyd Robinson's in trouble at the First."

Joe took a deep breath and let it out slowly. His stomach hurt. "I don't feel very good, Harry," he said. "Something I ate. And you aren't making me feel any better." He pushed back his chair and stood up. "Let's go upstairs where I can maybe swear a little without shocking customers."

They rode the elevator to the twelfth floor in silence, and walked down the corridor to the executive offices. To his secretary, Emily, Joe said, "No calls," and closed his office door. He indicated one of the leather visitor's chairs and took the other himself. "All right,

Harry," he said, "let's have it. What has that horse's ass Floyd Robinson been up to?"

"Pretty much the same thing as Mitchell in Fresno. When the bottom dropped out of raisins this last summer, he was left holding a lot of paper that wasn't worth much."

"We took a licking too," Joe said, "but it didn't cripple us."

"You're a banker, Joe, a money man. Floyd Robinson was a wholesale butcher when he decided to go into banking. He should have stayed in butchering."

The big office was quiet. Through the open windows sounds of Montgomery Street traffic reached them faintly. Down on the embarcadero a freighter gave one long whistle blast indicating that she had cleared her berth. Joe said at last, "How bad is it?"

"I have examiners there now. So far the word isn't out. And there's been no hint of a run."

Joe heaved himself out of his chair and walked to the windows. There was the Bay, ferries plowing their way to Sausalito, Oakland, and Berkeley; ships berthed along the embarcadero. It was a sight he loved. He turned from it. "This is just forewarning, Harry?"

"I thought you'd better know."

Joe sat down again. "You may have to close the Caloro First National? It's that bad?"

"I may have to."

"And then," Joe said, "the panic begins. There'll be a run on us."

"Yes."

"And the poor bastards with money in the First will be lucky if after the dust settles they get how much of it back?"

"Probably damn little, Joe. The time ought to have passed when a bank should fail in California, but that is exactly what we're looking at." He paused. "Unless you take over the First."

"What the hell do I want with it?" His voice had risen. Damn his stomach, anyway, he thought; this was no time for a kid's bellyache. He made himself speak more quietly. "I know. I know, Harry. I've said it myself: confidence in the community makes us or breaks us. But, goddamn it, saying it and looking right at it are two entirely different things. How would you feel—? Never mind."

"I'm sorry, Joe." Watson stood up. "We set up rules and regulations and we police them as best we can. But in the final analysis it all depends on somebody's judgment how well the system works."

"And some people," Joe said, "don't have the brains God gave a titmouse." He too stood up. "All right, Harry. I'll think about it, and you keep me posted."

Watson nodded. They did not shake hands. At the door Watson hesitated, his hand on the knob. "I don't need to say that this has to be kept quiet, Joe."

"You think I'm going to—?" Joe stopped and lowered his voice again. "You don't need to say it, Harry." He went back to his desk and sat down heavily. He buzzed for his secretary and she came in immediately. "I want Mr. Barker, Emily." And he waited quietly, staring out the windows until Barker arrived.

"Close the door, Frank. Sit down." Joe paused. "We've got a little problem in Caloro. I want some cash, lots of cash, sent down there immediately."

"'We don't need to send actual cash, Mr. McCurdy. We—"

"Frank, I usually say what I mean. I want actual cash sent down there, and I want it in the bank's vault by the time the bank opens tomorrow morning. Is that clear?"

"Yes, sir."

"And," Joe said, "I don't want any questions asked, and I don't want any talk. *Any* talk. Is that clear?"

"Yes, sir. An armored car—"

"How you do it is your business, Frank. Just do it and keep it quiet."

Barker took a deep breath. "About how much cash, Mr. McCurdy?"

"At least a million dollars. In small bills and silver. Gather it up however you can."

Barker swallowed. "Yes, sir." He stood up. He had reached the door when Joe stopped him.

"By the time the Caloro branch opens its doors tomorrow, Frank," Joe said.

"Yes, sir."

It may not be necessary, Joe thought, but how long it will be before word gets out and a run starts is anybody's guess.

He told Martha about it that evening. "We'll have to wait and see what the examiners say. Then it's up to Harry to decide what he's going to do."

"And what will you do?"

"I don't know yet. I'll want to see some figures." He made a vague hand gesture of annoyance.

Martha studied him quietly. She knew him well. "Is something else wrong, Joe?"

Joe smiled, mocking himself. "I've got a bellyache. Isn't that ridiculous? Kids get bellyaches."

Martha said, "Dinner—"

"I don't think I want any dinner."

"Shall I call Dr. Burns?"

"For a stomachache?" Joe shook his head.

He was a stubborn man, this husband of hers; Martha knew it well. "Maybe a cup of hot tea," she said. "I'll see to it."

At quarter past eleven that night: "I think you'd better call Jim Burns," Joe said in the darkness. "This isn't an ordinary bellyache." He was sweating and in great pain, and when Martha got out of bed and turned on the light she was shocked by the sight of his drawn face. She hurried to the telephone.

Dr. Burns came. He wasted no time. "Hospital for you, Joe. Appendicitis as ever was."

Weakly, "You just want to use your goddamn knife."

Dr. Burns smiled. "I've been waiting for years for a chance to start carving on that big carcass of yours. Martha, call this number. We want an ambulance. I'll give you a shot, Joe, for the pain."

At two o'clock Dr. Burns operated and removed a badly distended vermiform appendix. "Just about in time," he said to his assistant. "Another little while and we'd have had a real mess on our hands."

And to Martha outside as they wheeled Joe down the corridor to his room: "It's all right, Martha. We caught it in time. He's going to be an unhappy fellow for a couple of weeks, and we'll have our hands full keeping him in bed, but he's strong as an ox and there won't be any real problems." He sighed. "Now home to bed for what's left of the night."

"We are grateful to you."

"It's part of my life, Martha, and I chose it. Joe was smarter. He doesn't have crises to deal with." This was early Thursday morning.

Saturday morning at nine o'clock Harry Watson called the McCurdy National and asked to speak to Joe. "Why, he's in the hospital, Mr. Watson," Emily told him. "They operated on him two nights ago for appendicitis."

There was silence on the line.
"Can anyone else help you?" Emily said.
"Maybe God." Watson hesitated. "Which hospital?"
Emily told him.

They had installed a telephone in Joe's room over Dr. Burns's objections. "You are supposed to rest and recover, damn it," Dr. Burns told Joe. "I cut right into your belly and messed around with your basic organs, and that is not to be treated lightly."

"You can take your pick, Jim," Joe said. "A telephone here in the room where I can reach it from my bed, or I walk down the hall to find one when I want to make a call, or when I get one."

"Nobody is that important."

Joe grinned wickedly. "In my business I am. Now get out of the way and let the man do his work."

Now on the phone Harry Watson began, "I just heard about the operation, Joe. How do you feel?"

"That," Joe said, "is as silly a question as I'm likely to hear for some time. My belly is sore, goddamn good and sore. What else is on your mind?" Joe listened to silence for a few moments. Then, in a different voice: "The Caloro First? You have the examiner's report?"

"It's bad, Joe. I wouldn't be bothering you, but there isn't—"

"Never mind that. How bad?"

There was more heavy silence.

"Speak up, damn it," Joe said. "How bad?"

Watson said slowly, "The bank won't open Monday morning. I'm closing it at noon today."

Joe said slowly, "Jesus wept." He paused. "And I'm lying here in this shimmy shirt."

Martha appeared in the doorway, and Joe waved her into the room. "You're at your office, Harry? Good. Then stay there. I'll call you back within the hour." He hung up, and leaned back against the pillows, handed Martha the telephone.

Martha put it on the bedside table and bent to kiss him. Her face was troubled. "Harry Watson? The Caloro bank?"

"He's closing it."

Martha sat down in the visitor's chair. She made herself fold her hands in her lap and speak quietly. "And what happens now, Joe?"

"A lot of people lose a lot of money. Some of them lose just about all they have."

Martha closed her eyes. As Mrs. Joseph Martin McCurdy, she had the world now, she thought, anything she chose, but it had not always been so. Her family had scrimped to send her to Berkeley. No sorority, no frills, but somehow she had met Joe McCurdy, and that was it: ease, comfort, and security with this restless giant of a man other men listened to and trusted to the hilt with their treasure. But she remembered what lack of money could mean, and how close to the edge so many peopled lived, and for them to have their savings wiped out would be a catastrophe almost too great to bear.

She opened her eyes and said slowly, "And you could help, Joe?"

"Not from this bed."

"Couldn't Mr. Giannini—?"

"He isn't in Caloro. We made an agreement on that. And he is not in the business of saving banks that aren't in his territory. Besides, my guess is that he and Stern down at the Pacific Southwest are going to have their hands full with the Fresno situation." Joe took a deep breath and pushed himself to a sitting position. "Help me up, Martha."

"Joe!"

"Damn it, help me."

"Please, Joe!"

"Martha, if you won't help, I'll have to do it alone." He threw back the covers and very slowly moved his legs over the edge of the bed. The room tilted and then slowly came level again. He looked up. "Well?"

"Joe—" she began. And then quickly, as he began to move: "No. Wait! I'll help."

His legs seemed overlong, and his belly muscles agonized with the lifting motion, but he stood erect with Martha's help and waited until the suddenly retilted floor was level again. He took one step, two—

"What in the hell do you think you're doing?" Dr. Burns from the doorway. "Get back into that bed, and stay there!"

Joe took the two steps back and lowered himself to the edge of the bed. He breathed deep. There was sweat on his forehead from the pain.

"Of all the damn fools," Dr. Burns said. "What are trying to do, show how tough you are?"

"I'm leaving tomorrow morning, Jim," Joe said, "and I'm not

going to argue. Somebody will drive me down to Caloro. I'll come back here late Monday."

"You will do nothing of the sort. I forbid it."

Joe wiped his damp forehead with his fingertips in a weary motion. "Have you ever seen a bank panic, Jim? Do you know how people react when their money is in danger? Well, I do, and if I can help it, it isn't going to happen. Get on the telephone, Martha. Call Harry Watson. Tell him I'll drive down with him tomorrow morning, and I want that horse's ass Floyd Robinson and his whole board of directors waiting for us in the bank, and I want figures here today. Then we'll see what we can work out."

Dr. Burns said, "Martha—"

Martha shook her head. "It won't do any good, Jim." There were tears in her eyes as she picked up the telephone.

Harry Watson drove. Joe sat beside him in the front seat of the black V-63 Cadillac touring car with the diamond-E license plates and the seal of the state of California on the door. Martha rode in the back seat alone.

"There is no need for you to go," Joe had said.

"I'm going. You can't stop me." And that was that.

Even this late in the year the San Joaquin Valley by late morning was hot; heat waves shimmered like water on the pavement ahead.

"Walters will meet us there," Watson said. Walters was attorney for the Superintendent of Banks. "And they'll have their people, of course." He paused. "How is it, Joe? Are you all right?"

Joe ignored the question. There was pain, but pain he could bear. "They're going to listen," he said. "They're not there to foul things up further with their rotten ideas."

"You've seen the figures," Watson said.

"I've seen the figures and they stink. When we get this straightened out you're going to want to call in the U. S. Attorney. I'm not a lawyer, but I think there will be some criminal angles to follow up. What I'm concerned with," Joe said, "is the bank and the people with their money in it. And, incidentally, my bank branch too. If we have a run—"

"Dear God, no!" Watson said.

"I think we can stop it," Joe said. "There's over a million dollars in cash in the McCurdy branch vault. I had it sent down after I talked to you Wednesday."

Watson opened his mouth and closed it again in silence.

Despite an overhead fan, it was hot in the board room of the Caloro First National, and voices seemed to echo into the large empty main floor outside. Joe, Watson, and Walters sat on one side of the table; Floyd Robinson and three others across from them. Martha sat in a corner.

Robinson said, "What is your proposition, Mr. McCurdy?"

Joe laid it right on the line. "It isn't a proposition. It's an ultimatum."

"Well, now, we can't just take that."

Joe sat straight, ignoring the pain in his belly. His voice was strong and steady. "You'll take it," he said, "or I'll stand up and walk out. And I'm your last hope. Your doors don't open tomorrow"—he looked at Watson, who nodded—"unless I say so. And I will say so only under my own conditions. Is that clear?" He looked from face to face and saw resignation. So far, so good.

Robinson moistened his lips with his tongue. "And what are your conditions?"

"You're out, all of you. That's the first thing." He saw the shock, the incredulity in every face, and he waited, but there was no audible protest. He said, "What the U. S. Attorney may have to say to you later is his business, not mine. I've seen your books, and if it weren't for the people here who've put money into your bank, I wouldn't touch any part of the situation with a ten-foot pole. It is going to cost me the better part of half a million dollars to cover your depositors, and that's assuming we can get something for your physical assets. But there isn't any other way out."

Robinson took a deep breath. "There are—ah—other directions we can turn, Mr. McCurdy."

"No, there aren't. I spent some time yesterday on the telephone. You've tried San Francisco, and you've tried Los Angeles, and everybody has turned you down. The only reason I'm doing anything at all is because I have a branch in this town, a stake in it, and with that goes a responsibility." He paused. Then, looking straight at Robinson: "Which you wouldn't understand."

Robinson said, "There isn't any call for insults, Mr. McCurdy."
"I'm not even beginning to say what I really think."
There was silence. One of the men on Robinson's side of the table said hesitantly, "What do we get, Mr. McCurdy?"
"You're lucky to get out with your whole skins."
"But our equity—"
"You lost your equity a long while back. If you've bothered to look at the books, you should know that."
"Then," Robinson said, "what you're saying is that we just walk out, and don't come back to the Caloro First National?" There was a trace of belligerence in his voice. "This is our bank—"
"It was," Joe said. "And you played fast and loose with it and lost it. The Caloro First National will cease to exist. It will become part of McCurdy National, and it will disappear."
Walters the lawyer stirred. "I'm afraid there's been some talk in town," he said. "These—gentlemen haven't been as discreet as they might. Some telegrams went out through the local Western Union, which wasn't a very good idea." He paused. "If the doors open tomorrow morning there will be a run."
"There will be a run on my bank whether these doors open or not," Joe said. "That's one of the reasons I am here. There is cash in our vaults. Enough cash, I hope." He looked around the table. "Any further questions?" In the silence he stood up slowly and braced himself on the back of his chair. "Harry," he said, "you and Walters can handle what has to be done."
Watson nodded. "Permission from Washington, for one thing. We'll take care of it."
Joe said, "Before the doors open tomorrow morning, we'll transfer half a million dollars in cash from my branch. I'll be here when the doors open." He paused. "If you need me in the meantime, I'll be at the hotel. Come on, Martha." He walked out on Martha's arm.

Bank doors were due to open at ten o'clock. By eight o'clock lines had already formed in front of both banks. This was agricultural country, largely grapes on fair-sized holdings; word did not spread as rapidly as it might in a city. But by nine o'clock the streets were lined with cars and pickup trucks, and the lines at the bank doors stretched far.
From the window of his hotel suite Joe studied the street without

expression. Harry Watson beside him said, "They could turn ugly, Joe."

"We'll just have to see that they don't." Joe had spent the night lying naked on his back, sweating in the valley heat, and from time to time Martha had risen from the bed to sprinkle water on the sheet; its quick evaporative cooling helped some. By early morning the room had cooled off and Joe slept for a few hours. Martha slept not at all, alert for the first signs of open distress, which, happily, did not come.

Walters knocked on the door and came in, closing the door carefully behind him. "They're transferring the cash from your branch now," he said. He smiled grimly. "Down the back alley."

"Shades of the 1906 earthquake," Joe said. He smiled reminiscently. "I was sixteen. The bank was ten years old. I went down with my father, and we loaded everything we could, cash, silver, gold, into a wagon, covered it with a tarpaulin and took it down to the embarcadero and loaded it aboard a small boat. 'Just go out in the Bay,' my father told the boatman, 'and stay there. Don't let any other boat come near you. What's in those boxes—'

" 'I sure as hell don't want to know what's in them, Mr. McCurdy,' the boatman said, and that was it. I went with him."

Watson said, "Giannini—"

"Giannini," Joe said, "loaded the Bank of Italy's treasure into a wagon, covered it with oranges, and took it down to San Mateo. Same idea. As a matter of fact, it's more or less the same thing we're trying to do here—protect depositors' money. What time is it?"

Walters wore a wristwatch. "Nine-thirty," he said.

Joe nodded. "We'll wait another fifteen minutes. The mayor—"

Walters let his breath out slowly. "I—don't think he's coming, Mr. McCurdy. He's not what you might call a ripsnorter of a mayor, and all these people scare him half to death."

"Then we'll do without him."

Martha said, "Why don't you sit down, Joe. You have a little time to rest."

Joe shook his head. His eyes were still on the street. "I want to watch, Martha. They're good people, just plain people, most of them, and I think they'll listen to reason. But there are likely to be some sons of bitches too, troublemakers, and I want to see who they are."

Watson said, "The line is shorter at your bank, Joe. So far, that is." He got no comment; he had expected none.

"When we go down, Martha," Joe said, "you stay here."

"I will not."

"Now, Martha—"

"My mother," Martha said, "walked to California from Missouri beside a covered wagon. There were Indians, among other things. She didn't hide under the covers, and neither will I."

Time passed. "Quarter till ten, Mr. McCurdy," Walters said.

Joe put on his hat. "Let's go."

Down the stairs, past the desk, through the lobby, and out the etched glass doors. Martha and Joe led; Walters and Watson together right behind. As they stepped down from the sidewalk and started across the street, "I don't know about you," Walters whispered, "but I'm scared pissless."

Watson nodded, his lips pressed tight.

The line in front of the First National buzzed with talk that carried clearly down the street. The buzz diminished and then stopped altogether as Joe and Martha approached, and all faces turned toward them.

Joe left Martha's arm and walked alone, neither slow nor fast; steadily. The line opened in silence to let him through, and he took his stand at the doors.

He raised his voice. "I'm Joe McCurdy," he said. "That is one of my branch banks down the street. Until yesterday this was the competition, the Caloro First National. We've taken it over. You have heard rumors. Some of them are true, some probably false. But what I am telling you is not rumor; it is fact: This is now part of the McCurdy National Bank of San Francisco, with assets in excess of a quarter of a billion dollars. Your money is safe."

"How do we know that?" It was a loud voice, deliberately raised. It came from a large sunburned man standing number three in the line. "That bastard Robinson said our money was safe too and earning interest. How the hell do we know what you're telling us is any different?"

There was a murmur along the line, a growing note of concern.

"Because I say so," Joe said. "And because I will prove it." He waited while the murmuring died away. "There is over a million dollars in hard cash in these two banks. I had much of it sent down here last week. We will honor your withdrawals, all of them. And you can take your money home and put it under the mattress and hope nobody steals it." His voice and his manner flayed them. "Let's get on with it." He knocked on the doors. One door opened promptly. To the guard who stood inside, "Let the first four through," Joe said. "We will have order."

The first four, including the sunburned man, hurried through. The crowd waited in silence. The four returned one at a time, clutching greenbacks. Their expressions were a mixture of satisfaction and embarrassment.

"Did you get it all, Henry?" someone asked the sunburned man.

"Yeah, I got it." He held the sheaf of greenbacks in his hand as if he did not know what to do with them. He looked at Joe.

"Next four," Joe said. "Let's keep the line moving."

Watson stood next to Walters off to one side. "He's gambling," he said. "Five hundred thousand won't cover the deposits by a long shot. He's running a bluff."

"Next four," Joe said.

Walters was studying the crowd as he would have studied a jury, weighing Joe's words and his manner and trying to calculate their effect. As each four came out with money in their hands, the odds shifted slightly, he thought, but it was not something he would have bet on. You never knew how a jury would behave when the time for decisions came.

The line moved slowly, four steps at a time.

"That's seventy-two people," Watson said after a time. "If the average withdrawal was two thousand dollars, they've taken out a hundred and forty-four thousand already."

"Next four," Joe said. He was very tired, but it did not show. He stood straight and tall, totally unconcerned. Sooner or later the break would come. It had to.

"Next four," he said.

The line did not move. The man at the head of the line was small and scrawny, wearing a collarless shirt with sleeves rolled up on his tanned arms. There was a chew of tobacco tucked into one cheek. He said, "I'm Jake Simmons, mister. I got me a thousand acres of Thompsons, and twenty thousand dollars in this bank."

Nothing changed in Joe's face. "You are a fortunate man, Mr.

Simmons. I wish you safety and luck with your money." Inwardly, he held his breath.

Simmons turned his head and shot a stream of tobacco juice into the gutter. "I ain't goin' to take her out," he said. "I'm leavin' her right where she is." He paused. "Can I trust you, mister?"

The question hung shimmering for all to hear. There was silence along the line.

Walters was smiling. Watson watched almost in awe.

Gravely Joe nodded. He held out his hand. "You have my word, Mr. Simmons," he said.

Simmons nodded, and gave Joe's hand a single pump. "That's good enough for me," he said. He stepped aside. "Go on in," he said to the crowd. "Me, I'm goin' home." He walked off up the street, strutting a little, conscious that all eyes followed him.

Joe looked at the crowd. They looked now at him. There always came a time in any transaction, he thought, when you shot the works, put it all on the table. Call it bluff, if you would; it was part of business practice. Over his shoulder he said, "Open both doors. Let them all in." He turned aside as if uninterested in the result.

The doors opened wide. There was a surge, but it had no momentum. A few went in; many did not move.

"Mr. McCurdy." It was the large sunburned man, still holding his sheaf of bills.

Joe turned, looked at the man, and waited.

"Jake Simmons," the man said, "is a lot smarter than he looks, a lot smarter. He didn't get a thousand acres of grapes and that much money by guessing wrong very often."

Joe produced a faint smile and a nod of acknowledgment.

"I guess maybe I was some hasty," the man said. He raised the fistful of money. "Will they take this back?"

Nothing changed in Joe's face. "We will be delighted to reopen your account," he said. And then, to Watson, Walters, and Martha:

"I think we are finished here." He walked back to the hotel on Martha's arm.

Dr. Burns stood in the doorway and looked at Joe, who lay back in the bed, relaxing. "Well," Dr. Burns said, "did anything happen?"

Joe smiled faintly. He rolled his head on the pillow. "Nope."

11

Marty drove over the pass into the valley to the sprawling Coast Aircraft factory. On the field beyond Final Assembly, four Coast supersonic fighter-bombers waited in what he assumed was final check-out; lethal-looking monsters, designed to carry two men and more explosive power than was dropped on the entire European continent during World War II.

A single giant Coast transport swarmed with men. Its rear loading ramp was down, a broad highway into the cavernous interior.

Over by a smaller building were three shiny Coast Executive models, sleek twin-engined aircraft such as his father had flown. He stared at them thoughtfully before he turned away and went into the main lobby.

"Mr. Granger?" the receptionist said. "Is he expecting you?"

"No. My name is McCurdy, and I think he may see me." He walked over to look at the pictures that decorated the walls, a record of Coast aircraft past and present. He admired them, but they had no power to turn him on as they had had with his father.

"You have your passion for sailboats," Bud McCurdy had told him once. "Mine is for airplanes." And he smiled, and added, "One of the differences between us. There are quite a few." Had there been a wistful quality in the words, an unexpressed wish that father and son were not quite so dissimilar? Or had Marty been reading into the words something that was never there?

"Mr. McCurdy?" A bright, brushed-up young woman at his elbow. "Mr. Granger will see you." She smiled. "We'll have to give you a temporary pass. The process is painless."

And quick. Marty tucked the pass into his breast pocket, its upper half showing, and they walked down a gleaming corridor, through a reception area and into a large paneled office. "Mr. McCurdy," the girl said, and disappeared.

George Granger came out from behind his desk to shake hands. He was a large fleshy man in a carefully tailored lightweight plaid suit. His handshake was firm, and he wore a practiced smile. "Sit down, young man." He took his own desk chair. "First off, I am most sorry about your father. I knew Bud rather well. I was at the funeral."

And what was there to say to that? Marty merely nodded.

"The FAA is interested in the crash, of course," Granger said, "as we are. We are particularly interested since your father's aircraft had come out of our shops from a complete overhaul only one week before the crash."

Marty said slowly, "I didn't know that."

Granger nodded. "I didn't know it either until I began looking into the crash at your request." He seemed uncomfortable.

"And what else have you found?"

"The tower operator's story is quite clear," Granger said. "The port engine burst into flame. Bud immediately went up on his starboard wing and started to turn for the floor of the valley. The plane exploded in mid-air." His voice was expressionless. "Those are the facts as we know them."

Marty said, "Fuel leak?"

"There is that possibility. It is remote, but it is there." Was his manner too expressionless, unnaturally so?

"What are the other possibilities?"

"Your father kept the aircraft at his own plant, isn't that so?"

Marty nodded. "There is a runway there."

Granger leaned back in his chair. "I'll be frank with you. There is no doubt that there was an explosion. The cause is what we are trying to pin down."

So we read between the lines, Marty thought, and what do we come up with? The answer was plain, and he sat quiet, unbelieving, contemplating it. And yet what other explanation was there? "What you mean," he said slowly, "is that you haven't ruled out the possibility that something was—planted in the aircraft?" He made himself put words to the unthinkable: "A *bomb* of some kind?"

The office was still. Granger, looking uncomfortable again, said, "As I said before, you do come on strong. A bomb is a very serious accusation."

"Against who?"

"Against anyone. And we can't be certain yet just what caused the explosion, as I said."

Either you faced up to things, or you turned your back—and then they were liable to take you by surprise. Long ago Marty had learned that. Or maybe, strange thought, the knowledge was somehow carried in the McCurdy genes. "Have you ever had this problem before with an Executive model?"

Granger shook his head. He seemed reluctant to speak.

"And you've sold a lot of them, haven't you?"

A barely perceptible nod.

"Then," Marty said, "I don't see why you're pussyfooting around the possibility that somebody did something to the aircraft, no matter how far out it sounds." He paused, studying Granger's face. "Unless," he said, "you're afraid an investigation might show hanky-panky in your own shops."

Granger's face was stiff. "You do believe in saying what is on your mind, don't you?"

By now he was prepared to accept the possibility. "Damn it," Marty said, "either we have a bomb, or we don't have a bomb. If we don't, then there was something wrong with the aircraft—almost immediately after a complete overhaul in Coast shops. If we do have a bomb, then where was it planted, and how—in the Coast shops, or elsewhere? It's as simple as that." And, he thought, as devastating. But have I been thinking all along that there might have been something funny? Is that why I called Granger in the first place? "Well?" he said.

"You like things black and white, don't you, young man?"

"I like things out in the open where they can be seen," Marty said. "And this one is going to be. I want to talk to whoever is actually in charge."

"The Executive model project engineer." Granger seemed relieved.

The same smiling young woman guided him through labyrinthine corridors, through a mahogany door marked ENGINEERING and into a huge open room filled with drafting boards and men and women perched on high stools under brilliant fluorescent lighting. There was a quiet murmur of voices and a sense of contemplative haste. Distantly, sounds of the vast Coast fabrication and assembly shops provided a background of urgency.

The Executive project engineer had his own glassed-in office large enough for his desk and chair and two straight visitor's chairs. His name was Tom Chambers, and he was no older than Marty. "What we've got," Chambers said, "is a pile of pieces, a lot of questions and damn few answers. It was a mess."

At least this one was not afraid to show some feeling, Marty thought. "Bomb," he said, "or fuel leak, we can take our choice, is that it?"

Chambers picked up a pencil, looked at it for a time, and then set it down. He showed no surprise. Obviously the bomb possibility had been discussed. "That's about it," he said. "Something started the fire, and that wing tank blew." He spread his hands. "I'm not sure we'll ever really know."

"What's your guess?" Marty said. "Or are you under wraps?"

Chambers merely looked at him, for the first time vaguely hostile.

"Granger," Marty said, "had a hard time even admitting that there had been a crash."

Chambers relaxed, and even smiled a little. "Over in Sales and Service," he said, "they are so goddamn full of public relations they don't like to admit that any airplane can ever crash. Bad for business. What's my guess? Only a guess right now." He paused. "Something exploded in that port-engine nacelle, ruptured a fuel line, started a fire behind the firewall. Fumes in the wing tank did the rest. You know what gasoline fumes can do?"

Marty knew. He had seen what was left of a forty-foot cabin cruiser down at Newport after someone failed to run the blowers to clear the bilges of fumes before he pressed the starter button: the explosion had rocked the harbor.

He stood up then and held out his hand. "Thanks."

Chambers had risen too. "I wish I could be more help. Maybe we'll find something conclusive."

"You'll keep looking?"

Chambers nodded. "I want the answer too. If it was caused by something inherent in the aircraft design or construction, we'd damn well better find it and change it."

Another young woman, this one from Engineering, escorted Marty down to the main lobby, where he turned in his temporary pass and went out into the sunlight. He walked slowly to the guest parking lot.

Maybe this, maybe that, he thought: pure guesswork. But, he told himself as he unlocked the door of his car and got in, there is one question for which we don't even have a guesswork answer: if the explosion *was* planned, what in the world was the motive? Who would have it in for Joe McCurdy, a man who loved everybody?

He drove back over the pass, dropped down to Sunset, and headed for Stone Canyon. There was a little smog today; not enough to bother your eyes, but enough to cast a haze over the mountains, blurring their sharp outlines. It had not always been so, and Marty knew older men who had grown up in Los Angeles who could remember when day after day you could look up through orange groves at snow on Baldy or Mount Lowe, and the air you breathed had no taste. Depressing thought.

His father's car, a Mercedes 280SE sedan, was in the garage where Marty had had it driven from the plant parking lot the day after the crash. On impulse he went to it and got in behind the wheel to look around.

There was a neat folder of maps in the left door pocket; a small first-aid kit in the right. In the glove compartment there were a five-year flashlight, a folder of gasoline credit cards, a pocket altimeter, a small notebook and pencil, and a round tin of lemon drops. No clues there.

Beneath the driver's seat, Pliofilm-wrapped, was a hand spotlight which would operate from the cigarette lighter. Again, nothing. The seat was too far forward for Marty's legs. Another of the differences between us, he thought: he got out of the car and went into the house.

Molly Moto appeared in her soundless way. She handed him three slips of paper. "Telephone calls." She started away.

Marty stopped her. "We haven't talked, Molly." There are a lot of things I haven't done, he thought, and felt a measure of guilt that it was so.

"I haven't wanted to intrude." Molly stood solid and patient, waiting.

By rights, Marty thought, she should have hated his father, all the Joe McCurdys of this world, because while they had gone gaily off to flight training and overseas heroics and exchange of signatures on short-snorter bills, she and hers, citizens and aliens alike, had been herded like cattle away from their homes, out of their own state, interned for the duration of World War I in a godforsaken corner of either Arizona or New Mexico, Marty had forgotten which, just because of the shape of their Japanese eyes. "You were with my father a long time," he said.

"Twelve years." She watched Marty quietly. "And now? Do you wish me to stay?"

"The house couldn't run without you."

Molly smiled, acknowledgment, no more. "Then I will stay." She turned away again.

Marty walked into the study and sat down at the desk. He looked at the telephone messages. Call Billy at his office. Call Liz. Call Lester Peters, telephone number given. Lester Peters? Marty had no idea who he was. What was the motto of Kipling's Rikki-tikki-tavi? Run and find out. He picked up the phone and dialed the number.

First a secretary. Then, "Lester Peters, Mr. McCurdy. Thank you for calling. I am, I was your father's accountant, and in a sense business manager. We took care of his bills and handled any larger than ordinary expenditures he wished to make. The purchase of a new car, for example, or additions or changes to the house." The implied question was left hanging.

"Then I suppose," Marty said, "that we'd better keep it like that for now. I'm still—finding my way." Too true, he thought.

"Understood, Mr. McCurdy." There was satisfaction in the voice. "Your housekeeper holds all household bills and all charge-account bills and we collect them and pay them once a month. If there is anything else you would like us to do, please let us know."

Marty hung up. This is the way I live now, he thought, taken care of on all sides. And, aside from being born, what have I ever done to deserve it? Now where did that question come from? He put it aside unanswered, unanswerable, and dialed Billy Gibbs's number.

Billy said, "We have your father's will. Your grandfather's will is still in probate up in San Francisco."

"Speak English."

"Your grandfather left a will, of course, but it hasn't been given final court approval. That is, the estate hasn't yet been settled. Your father's death may change things a little. I don't know yet. You aren't going to be turned out into the street, if that's what you're thinking."

"I was worried."

"I'll bet."

"How did your lunch go with Liz?"

"We talked about you, you bastard." And then, in a different tone, "The accountants are at work on the plant audit. Jordan is unhappy, but offering no resistance. I've told them that if they come up with anything that looks out of line they are to let us know at once and not wait for the entire report."

"Right." Marty hesitated. "I've been out to Coast Aircraft." He told Billy what both Granger and Chambers had told him. "What do you think?"

"Jesus!" Billy said. "That's my immediate comment. Are they continuing the—investigation?"

"Chambers is as anxious to know as I am—for a different reason," Marty said. "I don't see anything to do now but sit and wait, do you?"

"No," Billy said, "but if I think of anything—" He left the sentence unfinished. "Back to your grandfather's will. It affects you directly now. Do you want me to go north and see precisely what's going on? Or do you want to sit tight and let your uncle and his attorneys handle everything?"

Marty thought about it. "I think I want you up there," he said. "I'm not mistrusting anybody, but I think it will look a lot better if we are showing interest."

"My thinking too," Billy said. "If you need any legal advice while I'm gone, John Carrington here will take care of you. And I'll tell the accountants to report directly to you."

Marty was looking at the message to call Liz.

It was as if Billy were reading his thoughts: "And you'll make hay with Liz while I'm gone," he said.

"It was your idea."

"You'll only get the chance because I'm a conscientious idiot." Billy's tone changed. "Right," he said. "I'll keep you posted from San Francisco."

Marty hung up slowly and sat looking at Liz's name on the phone message, feeling for the first time a sense, not of guilt, but of unease, as if what he intended to do was not wrong, but neither was it wholly right.

For one thing, it was Billy Gibbs, his lawyer and friend, whose territory he was invading. But even that fact only a few short days ago would not have made all that difference. Billy was able to take care of himself, and he had no lien on Liz Palmer, so the game was open.

But now what gap there might have been between him and Billy had widened enormously as a considerable amount of power, wealth, leverage, call it what you would, had suddenly come into his hands. And so, he thought, you looked at things a little differently.

Still, it was Liz who had made the first move, wasn't it? He picked up the phone and dialed her number. She answered almost at once, and Marty said easily, smiling, "You've been sitting by the phone waiting for my call?"

"Of course, pining away."

That would be a day, Marty thought, and the smile widened. "How are things?"

"How are things with you? I saw you at the funeral. You looked uncomfortable. I guess that's an odd thing to say."

"I don't know. Probably." Marty found himself looking at the framed picture of his mother. Was I taken to her funeral? "I didn't even know you were there."

"I wanted to watch you."

"That is an odd thing to say."

"I spend quite a bit of time Marty-watching. Was that your uncle Paul, the banker? He looked as if he was used to sitting at the head of the table."

"Himself. And Aunt Susan, the proper Bostonian."

"You sound—isolated."

That was precisely the word, Marty thought. "I am," he said. "I'm trying to sort things out. Look, today is no good, but how about tomorrow afternoon? I'll pick you up, bring you out here. We'll have a swim, lie around—"

"I wasn't hinting."

"I don't care if you were or not. It's you I want to see." There was a relief in the admission. "I want to look forward to seeing you."

"I've never been there," Liz said. "There's a pool?"

"How could you hold your head up in these parts," Marty said, "if you didn't have a heated pool? You aren't thinking, woman. Tomorrow, about two." He hung up without waiting for an answer.

Liz lived in a small house high up in the Hollywood hills. "It is a drag fighting the freeways all the way down here," she had told Marty once in Newport, "and I suppose I could just as well live here as up there, but I have a horror of turning into a female-type Ginger

Ted, a conscious character. Besides, I enjoy my privacy, and there isn't any down here. Just a wall doesn't do it."

"You don't mind living alone?"

"I have Hans. And a shotgun."

Hans was a large German shepherd, and the first time Marty had seen him, he had understood why Liz felt secure in his custody. Hans barked twice when the doorbell rang, and then, when the door opened, Hans stood squarely in the doorway with what Marty later described as a contemplative look on his face, "as if he was making up his mind which one of my arms he was going to take off if I turned out to be the wrong fellow."

"He's friendly, Hans," Liz had said, and the dog had taken one more good look and then turned away.

He barked twice now when Marty pushed the doorbell, and when Liz opened the door, Hans without hesitation seemed to nod, satisfied, as he turned away. "One day," Marty said, "he's going to let me pet him."

"He would now if you pushed it."

Marty shook his head. "In his own time." Damn, she looked good, he thought. "I've missed you." He took her arm and squeezed it gently. She had a small canvas beach bag, and he took that.

"Take care of the house, Hans," Liz said, and closed the door.

It was a sports car Marty drove, a Mercedes 350. He wondered if Lester Peters, that voice on the telephone, had actually written the check for it. He had never thought much about it before.

"Thinking deep thoughts?" Liz said.

"Thinking confusion." And then, because the words had to come out, "I've sent Billy to San Francisco."

She understood at once. "And it bothers you?"

"In a way."

"I'm a free agent, Marty. Billy understands that."

They wound down the hill, the little sports car swooping into the curves. "I've set things in motion," Marty said. He was thinking of the audit at the plant, the investigation of the crash, and now Billy headed for San Francisco to look into legal matters; all new, unknown territory. "And so you look at things a little differently."

"From your isolation?"

She saw deep, he thought, maybe uncomfortably deep. "Something like that."

"Scott Fitzgerald said that the very rich were different," Liz said. "And Hemingway said, 'Yes, they have more money.'" She was watching Marty's face. "It is different now, isn't it?"

Marty drove in silence. They were on Sunset now, and suddenly through the Strip, in effect breaking out into the open, past the businesses and buildings cheek by jowl. "It is different," he said, "and that is ridiculous, because I haven't touched anything, held anything in my hand, but I know it's all there, and in a way it scares me."

"I've never seen you scared."

"Stick around and you will. Scared of a lot of things. Scared of making a wrong decision—"

"But you will still make them."

"Probably." Marty paused. "Scared of throwing my weight around too much in the wrong directions."

"Does that bring us back to Billy?"

Marty turned to glance at her. "It does."

"I told you, I am a free agent. And I have some say in the matter, Marty. Remember that."

Up the Stone Canyon road and then in through the massive pillars; Liz watched the house appear, and the view. She got slowly out of the car and looked around. "A nice little pad you have here," she said. "Where are the slave quarters?"

12

Ted Waldo was waiting in the outer office, obviously deep in easy talk with Helen Soong, when Paul came in. "We'll have lunch," Ted said to Helen Soong, and followed Paul into the inner office.

Paul closed the door and indicated the two leather chairs. He shook his head smiling as he sat down. "She has been my secretary for eight years," he said. "I still call her Miss Soong, and I wouldn't dream of taking her to lunch."

Ted raised his eyebrows. "Objections?"

"None at all."

Ted nodded then. "She's an interesting female. Fifth-generation Californian, did you know that? How many are there?"

"Very few." Paul smiled again. The smile faded abruptly. "It's

Wally Trent, Ted. That's what I wanted to talk to you about. We're doing an audit on his operation." The words seemed to hang in the air.

Ted whistled soundlessly. He said slowly, "I've always thought of Wally as a pillar of the community. Well, not quite that, but entirely dependable, and, yes, honest of course."

"We're not questioning his honesty," Paul said. "At least not at the moment. We're just looking into the results of his judgment. Foreign-currency speculation in particular."

Ted said, "Not a Franklin National kind of mess!"

"I hope it's nothing like that. I can't think that it is." I hope, he thought. "But we'll see when the auditors are through." Paul was choosing his words carefully. "What it boils down to is that I'm afraid Wally has lost his touch." There, he thought, I've said it. In a sense I have signed the death warrant for Wally's business career. He's finished, through, and from now until his retirement he will merely be serving time, dying slowly. Is this how a hanging judge feels?

Ted sat silent, lips pressed together. He was a large, jolly man, somber now. "A friend dies of cancer," he said presently. His smile was grim. "But you think it can't happen to you. The hell it can't." He looked at Paul. "Now what?"

"I don't need to tell you," Paul said slowly, "that something like this *is* like a cancer. Word gets out. Rumors start." And Charles Goodwin will react like a firehorse when the bell sounds, he thought; he won't be able to keep his hands out of the—mess. "The one thing we have, the one thing that any bank has or ought to have, is the confidence of the financial community and of its depositors. The Caesar's wife bit. And with times as they are, something like this could shake that confidence right down to the ground." His voice was quiet, uninflected. "Particularly if there is even the faintest suspicion of hanky-panky."

"Do you think that Wally—?"

"I think nothing, Ted." It was possible, of course, that Wally for God only knew what reasons had indeed been trying to feather his own nest with bank funds; when something like this happened there was always that possibility. But until there was proof, or even some kind of indication, you assumed the best, not the worst. "I'm just pointing out the danger to the bank," Paul said. And, of course, the possible danger to me—if Charles Goodwin thinks this is basically my fault. "Do you think you can handle Wally's job?"

Ted thought a moment, smiling. "Modesty has never been one of my outstanding faults. I think I can handle it. I'll need a little time to get acclimated, but basically banking business is pretty much the same, whether it's here or abroad. Lending money for higher interest than you pay on it—that's what it all cooks down to."

Paul said, "Probably at least one trip with Wally to see the places, meet the people, learn something of the local ground rules."

"Jesus, Paul." And then Ted smiled again and nodded. "You're right, of course. It's just that—would you tell him first?"

"Either way, he would know. In his place, wouldn't you?"

Ted nodded slowly. "Right again. I'm glad I don't sit in your chair, Paul. What do you want me to do now?"

He had thought about it, of course. "Spend a day or two here. You can find things to look into."

"Lots of them. There are things that can't be handled on the phone or by letter. And the trust people want to pump me about what may be happening in Washington."

"Then after a day or two," Paul said, "go back and sit tight. And of course keep this under your hat."

Ted nodded. "Will do."

When he was alone Paul walked to the windows and stood looking out at the Bay; the graceful swing of the two suspension bridges; a single freighter leaving a white wake, outward bound; a blue-hulled yawl under main, mizzen, and overlapping jib, showing her bottom as she lay over, close-hauled, making probably for the St. Francis Yacht Club around on the Marina.

This business of Wally Trent's depressed him more than he cared to admit. Never mind Charles Goodwin's probable reaction; it was Wally himself Paul worried about. Why would a man of Wally's ability suddenly falter? That was the question.

They would probably never know the complete answer, he thought. "No matter what the head shrinkers say," his father had said once, "I don't believe you can look inside a man's skull. All you have is your own judgment based on what he does. Some men are predictable; some aren't. And some you thought were predictable suddenly go off the deep end for reasons that don't seem to make sense. Then you've got problems, because it's people you're dealing with from this office, not just figures on paper and money in the vaults. Remember that."

That hit the nail right on the head, Paul thought. Wally Trent, for reasons unfathomable, blotting his copybook, as the British would say. It was a sad thought.

Something else his father had said also applied. "There is a lot of crap written about how lonely it is when you're in command. Of course it is. What the hell else could it be? All decision making is a lonely business unless, God help you, you make decisions by committee—and those aren't decisions, they're a vote, usually a bad one. But if in this office you ever start feeling sorry for yourself because of that loneliness, then you'd better start looking for somebody else to take over."

He turned back to his desk as the phone buzzed, and picked it up. Helen Soong said, "Mr. Waters is here. You asked for him."

Charlie Waters came in, young and bright and eager. All business school graduates seemed to bear a stamp, Paul thought; decided that he was making another of his probably erroneous generalizations; and then hid a smile when it occurred to him that he would have to include himself in the category. It had been so damned long, he thought, he tended to forget. "Sit down, Charlie." He took a chair himself. "George Simpson was in yesterday," he said. "He is worried, but he is a worrier. Cabernet Sauvignon—"

"It is the top of their line, Mr. McCurdy, and very good it is too." Charlie prided himself on his palate.

"I am aware of it, Charlie. Just listen." Paul paused. "It is Latour's success with the grape, and of course the success of some others, Paul Masson, Inglenook, I don't need to name them. George tells me that the Napa Valley is now quite possibly overplanted with Cabernet Sauvignon and that in a year or two the grapes may be a glut on the market."

Charlie said merely, "Oh."

"I want you to look into it. Then have a look at our loans to growers in the area and get some idea of their thinking. Then I want a report. We are in pretty heavily, I'm afraid, and I want to see what our prospects are."

"Yes, sir."

As the door closed after Charlie, the telephone buzzed again.

Helen Soong said, "Mr. McKenzie is on the line."

Paul punched the button. "Yes, counselor? Do we have legal problems?"

"I don't know, Paul. There is a young man in my office up from Los Angeles. He says he represents your nephew, Joseph Martin—"

"McCurdy the third. I know his name, John." Paul was smiling. "As a matter of fact, I am his godfather. This young man *says* he represents Marty?"

"I have no doubt that he does. He is young Gibbs from Gibbs and Carrington. A very reputable firm."

"Well?"

McKenzie's voice was solemn. "He is asking to be brought up to date on the details of your father's will. He is, for example, unaware of the trust the will establishes. I gather that your nephew knows very little either."

But he sent his lawyer up here to find out what we are doing, Paul thought; and was both annoyed and approving. "As far as I know," he said, "Marty is my brother's major, if not sole, heir."

"He is." McKenzie paused. "The young man brought a copy of your brother's will."

"Then," Paul said, "Marty has just as much right to know about my father's estate as I have, doesn't he?"

After some hesitation, McKenzie said, "I can't deny that."

"But you don't like it. Tell me why."

There was a smile in McKenzie's voice. "A lawyer's natural caution. It's a required course in all law schools."

Paul too was smiling. "All right, you've demonstrated it. Now give young Gibbs what he's asking for." He paused. "Wait a minute, John. I'd like to meet the young man. Is he there? Let me talk to him."

The voice that came on the line was strong, confident but deferential. "Billy Gibbs, sir."

"Paul McCurdy. You already know that. Are you free for lunch, young man? I would like to meet you."

"Yes, sir."

"The Pacific Union Club. Twelve-thirty. John McKenzie can tell you where it is."

He hung up and leaned back in his chair. It will be interesting, he thought, to find out just what Marty has in mind. And, remembering John McKenzie's lawyerly caution: why do I feel the same reluctance? Because Marty is Marty, what my father used to call a take-charge guy, totally unlike his father? "You are the older, the more experienced," Susan had said. But sometimes, Paul thought, they come out of nowhere, and age and experience don't count much against them. Ridiculous thought. Or, was it?

The Pacific Union Club is in what was once the Flood mansion, on top of Nob Hill. Paul walked through the front door and into the lobby beneath the dome at precisely twelve-thirty. He wondered if Billy Gibbs would be as prompt. He was.

He was waiting; a big man, Paul thought, even a little larger than Marty, broad without fat, tanned, exuding health. He shook Paul's hand almost gently as if quite aware of his own strength and accustomed to using it carefully.

"I like punctuality," Paul said. He smiled. "The only quotable quote attributable to Louis XVIII that I know is: *'L'exactitude est la politesse des rois.* Punctuality is the politeness of kings.'"

"I didn't know that," Billy Gibbs said.

And he admits it, Paul thought, as he led the way to the bar. Good for him. Standing at the bar, "Your tipple?" he said. "I like a martini myself."

Billy smiled. "I'll join you."

While they waited for their drinks, "The martini is supposed to have been invented here in San Francisco," Paul said. "Maybe yes, maybe no."

"I didn't know that either," Billy said. "Martinis have just always been there."

Paul raised his glass. "Cheers." He sipped and set the glass down. "Is John McKenzie giving you what you want?"

"Yes, sir. He's been very cooperative. He had a copy of the will made for me. And a copy of the trust. And he gave me an office to study them. This afternoon he's going to bring me up to date on the probate."

Paul said, "You're a friend of Marty's as well as his lawyer?"

"Yes, sir. We pretty much grew up together." Billy smiled. "The first time I met him, he broke my nose. We've gotten along together ever since."

Paul could not help asking, "On that basis?"

"Not always."

No, Paul thought; I will wager that there have been times when this one asserted himself. He was beginning to like young Billy Gibbs. "Another drink?"

"No thank you, sir. I have a lot of listening to do this afternoon."

Another plus, Paul thought, and led the way to the dining room.

They were shown to a table for two. "What are Marty's plans?" Paul said. "When I saw him right after the funeral he was uncertain."

"I wouldn't be sure," Billy said. "He keeps things pretty much to himself."

"I had a telephone call from Walter Jordan." Paul's voice was expressionless.

"Marty twisted his tail a little," Billy said.

"Was it necessary?"

"Marty thought so."

Loyalty, Paul thought approvingly. All in all, young Billy Gibbs was scoring high marks. "I know very little about McCurdy Aircraft," he said. "It was my brother's project."

"But you, that is, the bank provided financial backing, didn't it?"

"On a merit-loan basis."

Billy hesitated. "Marty didn't tell me to ask," he said, "but would you consider further financing if it seems necessary?"

First the audit Jordan had complained about, now this question, Paul thought. "On a merit basis," he said. "Money is tight now, as you know."

"I'm not a financial man, Mr. McCurdy."

Paul smiled. "Just a simple lawyer, is that it?"

Billy grinned. "That's about it."

They were a different breed from himself, this one and Marty, Paul thought. They seemed open and frank in their breezy way, but they were actually playing their cards close to their vests. As a banker, he approved; as more or less head of the McCurdy family, he was not so sure that he liked the possible implications. Marty and I are tied together, he thought, by more than bloodline; but money is a powerful force which can divide as well as unite.

"You studied both the will and the trust which the will established?"

"Yes, sir." Billy paused. "Your father tied it up pretty tight. You, your brother, and the bank's trust officer as trustees controlling the whole thing."

"Now it will be Marty, the trust officer, and myself."

"That gives you a built-in majority, doesn't it, Mr. McCurdy? I don't imagine the bank's trust officer would be anxious to spit in your eye."

Paul smiled faintly. "The trust officer is a man of integrity."

"I'm sure he is. I was just wondering—" Billy stopped.

"Wondering why my father set it up the way he did?" Paul said. "He didn't explain his reasons. He rarely did. But I can guess. I don't think highly successful men ever believe that their sons are as capable as they are. And so they hate to let go completely. Hence the trust, keeping the actual estate out of our hands. He probably had another reason too. Trying to divide his estate equally between my brother and me would have been an enormously difficult job, and it might have led to at least some bitterness or feeling of unfairness between us. Keeping the estate intact in trust and dividing the income probably seemed simpler, and safer. I'm telling you this so you can explain it to Marty if he asks."

A generous gesture, Billy thought, and said so.

"Are you married, Mr. Gibbs?"

"No, sir. Since law school I've been pretty busy learning my trade." He grinned suddenly. "But I'm not a celibate, any more than Marty is."

Was there something in the boy's tone? Paul wondered. "A particular girl?" he said. "Or do you, as we used to say, play the field?"

The grin was gone. "There is one girl, Mr. McCurdy. It just happens that Marty has his eye on her too. And Marty is rough competition." Billy's smile was rueful. "The McCurdy name carries clout. I'm sure you know that."

"I am aware of it," Paul said, "but I try not to abuse it. Does Marty?"

"No, sir." Billy was unsmiling. "He just can't help it. In many ways Marty is the best man I've ever known. And his name just happens to be McCurdy too." He grinned suddenly. "So I get the feeling sometimes that I am just spinning my wheels."

"I doubt if you are, young man," Paul said truthfully. "I doubt it very much."

Outside in the bright, crisp San Francisco day, a breeze sweeping in from the ocean: "Shall we share a taxi? I don't want to keep Mr. McKenzie waiting."

"You go on," Paul said. "I'll walk. I enjoy walking. I sit enough in the bank."

They shook hands. "Thank you, sir. I enjoyed the lunch. And the visit. Maybe one day in Los Angeles I can—retaliate." Billy was smiling.

"My pleasure," Paul said. "Tell Marty for me that I think he is in good hands." He turned away and began to walk at his fast pace. They are a formidable pair, he thought, young and inexperienced though they may be. Let's hope the money unites, rather than divides, us.

13

In a string bikini, Marty thought, Liz was something else. Enjoying the view, "How do you keep those little pieces on?" he said.

Liz looked down at herself. "You probably haven't noticed," she said, "but I stick out here and there, and that's what does it."

"Do you want to swim?"

"Not at the moment."

"A drink?"

Stretched out on a chaise, Liz waggled her head in denial. "I like it just like this."

Warm autumn sun, only a hint of a breeze, privacy, and the city spread beneath them. The pool was rectangular, designed for swimming; its tiled bottom showed clearly through the filtered water. Eucalyptus trees grew up the hillside above them, their long leaves stirring gently.

"I have a job offer," Liz said. She rolled her head to look at Marty. "Berkeley, the radiation lab."

"Good God. Why do you have to go as far as Berkeley?"

Liz smiled faintly. "I *am* supposed to be a physicist, you know. And I get tired of the lotus life."

He knew really very little about her, Marty thought; he had merely taken her way of life for granted. "You don't have to work?"

Liz shook her head again. "I have a little income." Her gesture included the pool and the house. "Nothing like this, but with frugality, enough. But that isn't the point, is it?"

Marty sat up and swung his legs to the deck. He wore brief nylon trunks, and his body, sharply muscled, was deeply tanned. When he moved, the muscles seemed to flow. "What is the point?"

"A number of people," Liz said, "spent a great deal of time and effort educating me. It seems only proper that I should put that education to work. Does that sound silly?"

"You were the one who said that the only reason for having a mind was so you didn't have to worry about it."

"Consistency is not my main interest. Circumstances change."

"Berkeley," Marty said, "is four hundred and fifty miles away."

Liz smiled. "So I understand. Maybe that's for the best."

Marty stood up. He took a single step, launched himself into a flat dive, and swam the length of the pool and back at a furious pace. He hoisted himself out of the water and to his feet in a single long motion to stand dripping quietly.

"Impressive," Liz said. She was shading her eyes, smiling. "Now give Tarzan's call."

"You pushed me toward the plant," Marty said. "I thought you'd stick around to see if I fall on my face."

"You won't."

"Maybe Billy can prop me up."

"You don't need props. And you don't need a cheering section."

Marty sat down again. His hair, cut short, was plastered to his skull. He shook some of the water from his hands and rubbed at his face. "You're saying," he said, "that I don't pay any attention to what people think, is that it?"

Liz smiled faintly. "I haven't noticed that you worry too much about public opinion. You go pretty much your own way."

"This," Marty said, "is the damnedest discussion. It—tucks its tail in its mouth and rolls like a hoop. What are you trying to say anyway?"

"That's my come-to-the-point guy." Liz was smiling again. "Maybe I don't really know what I am trying to say."

"Except that you're dissatisfied with things as they are?"

"I guess so."

"With me?"

Liz considered it. "Maybe just with me," she said.

"Looks," Marty said, "body, brains, the whole package."

"Why, thank you, sir. If I were standing, I'd curtsy."

Marty stood up again, picked a towel from one of the umbrella-shaded tables, and began to rub at his head and arms. "What are you looking for?" he said. "They write whole books about jerks who walk around in circles worrying about what they call their identity crises. I never believed it."

Liz smiled again. "No, you wouldn't. I envy you."

"There are advantages to being a clod."

"That wasn't what I meant. You don't doubt yourself. Most people do. I do."

"With everything you have going for you?" Marty shook his head. "Incredible. You—" He stopped there as Molly Moto came out of the house and walked toward the pool. Marty went to meet her.

"Telephone," Molly said. "A man named Chambers, Tom Chambers."

Marty nodded. "Be right back," he called to Liz, and walked over to the glassed-in poolside dressing-room-playroom-bar building to pick up the telephone extension. "Marty McCurdy," he said.

"We've done a little chemical analysis," Tom Chambers said. "On some pieces of that nacelle behind the firewall, there are traces of substances that haven't any business being there. I'm not a chemist, so the report is mostly gobbledygook to me. But the conclusions aren't."

"Go on," Marty said.

"Dynamite was somehow involved."

Marty closed his eyes, and opened them slowly.

"Are you still there?" Chambers said.

"Still here."

"That would account for the sequence," Chambers said. "A triggered explosion and fire. A ruptured fuel line spreading the fire. Fumes in the wing tank taking it from there."

"You're sure? Good and sure? Because," Marty said, "what you're talking about is murder. The police, and God knows what all." Murder, he thought; it couldn't have been. Damn it—

"There was dynamite," Chambers said. His voice was quietly emphatic. "The rest is conjecture, except that the wing tank did blow. Two facts."

Marty was silent for a long time. "Okay." His voice was suddenly weary. "I'll—see if I can find out what to do about it. They'll probably want to talk to you."

"I'm here every day with my nose to the grindstone."

"Right," Marty said. He started to hang up.

Chambers' voice stopped him. "I'll add only one thing." He paused. "I'm sorry."

"Right," Marty said again, hung up, and walked back out to the pool. He sat down heavily and took his time before he spoke. "It seems," he said, "that the plane crash was no accident. The plain truth is that apparently somebody deliberately killed my father, mister nice guy who never hated anybody."

John Carrington, of Gibbs, Carrington & Gibbs, was cordial on the phone. "Billy told me that I might have a call from you, Mr. McCurdy. What can I do for you?"

"I don't know which way to go," Marty said. "I'd better begin at the beginning." He told of asking Granger at Coast Aircraft to look into the plane wreckage. "I had nothing specific in mind," he said. "But my father was supposed to be a good flyer, and I think a careful flyer. He used to say he had gotten the hotshot-pilot ideas out of his system during the war. So the crash didn't seem to make sense. Maybe I had a weird hunch. I don't know."

John Carrington said quietly, "And?"

Marty told him of Tom Chambers' call. "All I know is what he told me," he added. "He seems sure of the dynamite. And there was an explosion. Two facts, as he says. So what do we do now?"

"I am not very well acquainted with police procedures," Carrington said after a moment, "so I think we will start with the District Attorney. You are where?"

"Stone Canyon." Marty gave the address and the telephone number.

"Wait there for a call," Carrington said.

Marty looked up from the desk. Liz, still in her bikini, was standing watching him. "I'm sorry," Marty said. "I've fouled up our afternoon."

"Hardly your fault."

"Molly could drive you home." He could smile faintly, at the same time wondering how a smile at this time was even possible. "She isn't the world's best driver, but I'm sure she could manage."

"Do you want me to go?"

Marty smiled again, this time mocking himself. "No. But I don't think it is going to be a very pleasant operation from here on, and—"

"Then I'll stay." There was quiet decision in her voice.

It was relief that he felt, solid and warm. The mocking smile relaxed. "Thanks." He stood up, and the smile spread. "But get back into some clothes. That way you are too—distracting."

The telephone call came within a few minutes. "Mr. McCurdy? Howard Carter, DA's office. John Carrington has told me a little. I'd like more from you. I'll come to Stone Canyon, if I may."

"I'll be here," Marty said, and hung up thinking that this was probably no ordinary treatment he was getting; and feeling a mild sense of guilt that it was so.

Liz, dressed again, was in a club chair watching him.

"A man from the DA's office," Marty said, "coming here."

The telephone rang again. Marty picked it up and spoke his name.

"John Carrington, Mr. McCurdy. Howard Carter is coming to see you. Do you want me present?"

"I—shouldn't think so. I mean, why?"

There was a short silence. Then, "Murder," John Carrington said, "is a messy business. It spreads, and you never know whom it will stain. If Billy were here, I would advise him to go to you at once. But I don't want to thrust myself upon you."

"Oh," Marty said. "In that case, maybe you'd better come out, if you will."

"I'll be happy to."

Marty hung up shaking his head. "I'm not used to this, being nurse-maided, protected."

"What I understand from reading mysteries," Liz said, "is that the first person the police look for in a suspicious death is somebody who benefits. You're the obvious somebody."

"That," Marty said, "is ridiculous."

Liz nodded solemnly. "You know it, and I know it, but the man from the DA's office may not be so sure."

Howard Carter from the DA's office was short and stocky, and there was about him a no-nonsense air that was almost belligerent. "Is John Carrington coming?"

Marty nodded.

"Then we'll wait for him. I don't want any—protests."

"Are you thinking, Mr. Carter," Liz said, "of using a rubber hose?" Her smile was innocent.

Carter looked at her, opened his mouth, thought better of comment, and closed his mouth again. He walked to the wall and stood looking at the framed short-snorter bills. To Marty: "My father had one of those. Probably some of the same signatures. He was ETO too." He looked then at Liz. "European Theater of Operations," he said.

Liz's smile reappeared. "Thank you."

John Carrington drove up in a long gray Continental and parked beside Carter's Nova. Marty met him at the door. They shook hands. "Thank you for coming," Marty said. "I am beginning to learn how things are done."

Carrington was tall and trim with white hair and deeply tanned face and hands. "We try to look after our clients." He smiled faintly. "I know Carter. And I am leery of short men who walk on their toes." Together they walked into the study.

Liz rose. "I'll leave."

"Stay," Marty said, and made introductions. He sat down. "Shoot," he said to Carter.

"I'd rather hear it from you first."

Marty leaned back, and began at the beginning with the telephone call from Walter Jordan telling him of the crash, through his identification of his father's remains, his call to Granger at Coast, his visit to Coast and his talk with both Granger and Chambers, and finally the telephone call from Chambers. "That brings it up to date," he said. "Chambers and his people will have to tell you the details."

"You were down at Newport when you heard of the crash," Carter said. "Had you been in Los Angeles earlier, say within a day or two?"

"No."

"Can you verify that?"

"Probably not. I took *Westerly* out single-handed one day. Another day there was a good surf running and I did some body surfing at the Wedge. I did some work on *Westerly*, some varnishing, a little engine work—" He shrugged. "The kind of things you're always doing around a boat. Nobody notices, or remembers." He looked at Liz. "You came down."

"The day before the crash," Liz said. She looked at Carter. "And I was there when the telephone call came."

Carter gave no indication that anything he had heard was of importance. "That telephone call," he said. "How did Walter Jordan hear about the crash?"

"The plane was registered as belonging to McCurdy Aircraft," Marty said.

"Did anyone other than your father fly it?"

"Not to my knowledge."

"Where was the aircraft kept?"

"At the plant. There's a runway there and a wind sock. It was handy."

"On plant property?"

Marty nodded.

"Is there security?"

"I'm not sure how tight it is," Marty said. "Walter Jordan could show you."

Carter said, "You inherit?"

Marty nodded.

John Carrington said easily, "Now you aren't going to draw hasty inferences, are you?"

"I'm going to keep an open mind."

"Splendid." Carrington was smiling benignly.

"One thing," Marty said. "I didn't know it, but the plane had been through a complete overhaul at Coast less than a week before the crash." He spread his hands. "I don't know if that means anything at all, except that a malfunction was probably unlikely."

Carter said, "Is there anyone you know who might have wanted your father dead?"

"That," Marty said, "is what makes no sense at all. He was—mister nice guy, a rich man's son who flew his sorties in France and Germany and, I think, hated it because it meant hurting people." He had never thought of it that way before, but it seemed clear now. "Maybe he spent the rest of his life trying to make up for it. I didn't know anybody he disliked, or anybody who disliked him." He looked around the study walls. "He had a framed collection of his decorations, but he never displayed them. I think they're in a drawer somewhere."

Liz was watching him steadily. She showed no expression.

"If there was dynamite in that aircraft," Carter said, "and if no one but your father flew it, then somebody wanted him dead, isn't that so?"

Carrington said mildly, "That calls for a conclusion from the witness, wouldn't you say?"

"This isn't a trial."

Carrington nodded. "Let us not make it one." He looked at Marty. "Mr. Carter's logic seems impeccable, don't you think? If there was dynamite in the aircraft, then the crash was hardly an accident, and someone intended it to happen. I think that is a safe assumption."

Neat, Marty thought; the point is dealt with without my having to say a word. He looked at Carter and waited.

Carter looked at his notebook. He closed it with a little snap, and stood up. "All for now, I think. I will call in some help from the police lab, and we'll have a look at what Chambers has at Coast Aircraft. Then we will want to see the McCurdy plant—" He looked at Marty.

"I'll tell Jordan to expect you," Marty said. He too was standing. "And just to clear up the point," he said, "I'll be around and available if you have any more questions." He tried to make it light, even facetious. "If I happen to be out in *Westerly*, I suppose you could have the Coast Guard pick me up."

"If we want you, Mr. McCurdy," Carter said, unsmiling, "we won't hesitate." He nodded shortly to John Carrington and walked out. The front door's closing was audible.

John Carrington smiled at Marty. "You were right: you didn't need me."

"But I'm glad you were here. I'm just beginning to learn that it isn't a black-and-white world."

Carrington smiled again. "Gray is the color we lawyers deal with. Billy will be calling probably late this afternoon. I'll bring him up to date." He paused again. "May I suggest that you do the same with your uncle in San Francisco? There will be newspaper headlines and reports on television concerning suspicion of foul play."

"Can't Carter keep his mouth shut?"

"He has no reason to. In his way he is a very able man in an ill-paying job, and a certain amount of prominence by publicity doesn't hurt him a bit."

"Everybody," Marty said, "has his angle, is that it?" His tone was bitter.

Carrington's smile was easy. "That is probably more often true than you may think. Miss Palmer. Mr. McCurdy." He raised his hand in a gesture of denial. "No. Please don't bother. I can find my way out."

Marty walked around the desk and sat down. He looked at Liz. "Quite a performance, wasn't it?"

"You looked pretty good."

"That," Marty said, "is the best word I've had today." He reached for the telephone and began to dial.

In San Francisco, Helen Soong took the call from the bank switchboard operator. "Mr. McCurdy is in conference," she said, "but if it is important?"

"I'm afraid it is," Marty said, and when Paul's voice came on the line, "There are probably going to be newspaper stories and TV news reports," he said, "saying that Joe's crash was no accident. Sorry about that. I stirred it up."

Paul said slowly, "And are the reports true?"

"They seem to be." Marty went through the entire story, as he had for Carter, and Paul listened quietly. "The DA's office," Marty added, "are bringing in the police, county, state, city, I don't know which ones, I don't think it matters, the whole thing is out in the open now."

Paul took his time. "Your young lawyer friend had lunch with me today. He is still up here. Do you have other legal advice available?"

"Billy's senior partner is holding my hand."

"Good. Do you want me to come down?"

As at the funeral, Marty thought, the family closes ranks. It was a not uncomfortable thought. "I don't think there's any need."

Paul said quietly, "Have you any idea who might have—done this?"

"At the moment, none. If and when I do have—"

"I hope you will go to your lawyer and take his advice."

Marty smiled. " 'Vengeance is mine,' and all that?"

"I have found it a good dictum to follow," Paul said. He was sounding stuffy, he was aware of it, and it annoyed him. "Don't do anything foolish, Marty." Was that too damned—avuncular? "And keep me posted, please."

"Will do." Marty hung up. Liz was watching him. "Shall I take you home now?"

"Do you want to?" She saw the negative answer in his face. "What do you want to do?"

"I'm damned if I know. Maybe sit in the sun. Or go for a walk."

Liz was smiling now. "Then let's do it. And maybe go back to the pool. And see what happens after that."

14

One day, Bruce McCurdy had always assumed, he would succeed his father as head of the bank. But what had seemed easy and natural enough from a distance had now become through familiarity an awesome prospect.

For one thing, there was tradition, and it was beginning to weigh heavily upon him. Hanging in the board room on the twelfth floor were portraits of Amos McCurdy, the bank's founder, and old Joe, his son, and from time to time Bruce could not resist walking into the room and looking up at them. Or, rather, letting Amos and Joe look down at him. He was pretty sure that what they saw did not impress them. From his father down, the bank was filled with men, and women, who were prepared to make hard decisions, and abide by them. What was it Bruce had read once about Harry Truman—that he faced his enormous problems, said "This is how we'll do it," and then went to bed and slept like a baby? Not Bruce.

When he made a decision, he agonized over it. Had he said the right thing in the right way, or would a mistake come back to haunt him, or, worse, cause his father to frown and shake his head and wonder what was wrong with the boy? In many ways it was not easy being the boss's son.

Charlie Waters, a close friend, was fond of saying, "Anytime you want to trade, chum, I'll take your place as a McCurdy, and one day sit in that big office on the twelfth floor."

"And you'd love it, too, wouldn't you?"

"Wow! Would I!"

Charlie was no brighter than he, Bruce told himself, no better educated, no more willing to work. The difference was that Charlie was instantly willing to undertake any job and do it well without nagging self-doubts about his ability; which was probably why Charlie was Paul McCurdy's personal assistant, privy to the large affairs of the bank, and he, Bruce, was constantly shuttled from spot to spot as if he were playing a game of musical chairs.

He was currently in the trust department, a very junior member of the group which administered God only knew how many millions of customers' dollars, largely inherited wealth, dealing in bonds and stocks and commercial paper with the kind of cautious care that meant financial security for a large number of people.

And beyond the mere financial transactions, the trust officers, Todd Markham, senior vice-president and trust officer, in particular, seemed to feel that they had an obligation to advise their customers on almost any subject under the sun.

Old Mrs. Brooks, for example, was forever lurching in, her no-nonsense hat not quite square upon her head, and her reticule—there was no other word—clutched firmly in both hands, probably containing a half-pint bottle of brandy.

"My dear Mr. Markham," she said one day in a voice that carried throughout the office, "I am going East to visit my granddaughter. I have always traveled by train. But the service has deteriorated badly. Do you think airplanes are safe?"

Todd Markham thought that commercial airplanes were quite safe.

Mrs. Brooks was pleased with the information. She said, "When I travel by ship, I take pills to prevent seasickness. Should I do the same for airplanes? Do they jump around?"

Todd Markham thought that pills would do no harm. Privately he thought that Mrs. Brooks's constant load of brandy would take care of any possible airsickness, but he would not for the world have said so.

"Thank you, young man. I trust your judgment." And then, some of the old lady's considerable shrewdness showing, "Short-term commercial paper is not returning the interest it was. You are bearing that in mind?"

Todd Markham assured her that they were bearing it very much in mind. He walked with her to the elevator, punched the button, and waited until the door had closed after her before, expressionless, he walked back to his office.

Polly Wright at the desk next to Bruce's said quietly, "Old folks' ward. On the other hand"—she gave her quick smile—"I shouldn't knock it. She and others like her pay our salaries."

They had not spoken much before. "How do you like it here?"

"The chairs are nice. And it's quiet."

"You're business school, aren't you?"

"Guilty."

Polly, red-headed, medium height, with a tiny waist, curving hips, and large breasts, was friendly as a kitten. "You know," she said, "it can't be all sunshine being the boss's son, can it?"

Bruce could smile. "Sometimes up; sometimes down." Strangely, with her he was at immediate ease as he was with few people. Suddenly bold: "Why don't I buy you a drink after work and tell you about it?"

She had a trick of lowering her head, wrinkling her brow, and studying you. Suddenly the smile appeared. "Done," she said. And as she turned back to her work: "But if you change your mind, I'll let you off the hook."

They eyed a booth in Henry's Bar around the corner from the bank. "I think a lot of the bank people come in here," Polly said. "Do you mind?"

"Why should I?"

Polly smiled. "Up to you." They sat down. She ordered a scotch and soda.

Bruce ordered bourbon. He toyed with it. "What are you trying to say?" he said at last. "That I shouldn't be seen with you? Why?"

Polly's nose wrinkled when she smiled. "You're serious, aren't you? I mean, most times."

"I guess I am." Bruce paused. "Maybe pompous is the word."

"Don't run yourself down. I like you the way you are." Polly took a small sip of her drink. "And probably you shouldn't be seen with me. I mean, suppose your father walked in?"

"What if he did?"

"You wouldn't mind?"

"Why in the world should I?"

Polly studied him quietly. "I guess you mean that," she said slowly. "Do you go out with many girls whose families don't know your family?"

"I don't know. Does it matter?"

"Maybe I'd better shorten it," Polly said. "Do you go out with many girls?"

He could not begin to explain the sense of ease he felt with her. The answer came so easily. "No." He made himself smile. "But I'm not gay, if that's what you're thinking."

"I know that." Polly paused. "Just—lonely?"

He had never really thought about it before, and it came to him now with the force of revelation. "I guess I am." He could smile suddenly. "Pretty silly, isn't it?"

"I told you not to run yourself down. I think you're a nice sweet guy and you haven't any business beating yourself over the head."

Warm words. He savored them. "You," he said, "are something else, something very special else."

Polly shook her head, unsmiling. "I'm a girl from Modesto. I've never been to college. My—"

"It doesn't matter. None of that matters at all."

"Maybe. But I think it does. And maybe sometime I'll tell you the story of my life. Why? I don't know."

"Maybe because you've been needing to tell somebody." Loneliness to loneliness, Bruce thought; in a way they were two of a kind. Perhaps that was what made for the ease between them. Strange. He finished his drink. "Drink up," he said. "Let's go."

"Where?"

"I don't know. Let's just walk for a little while. Then maybe we'll stop and have another drink. Maybe dinner somewhere."

They walked in the city. When he thought back to it later, as he often did, Bruce could never remember where they walked; it didn't matter. They went up and down a few hills, but, then, anywhere you walked in San Francisco you would sooner or later find a hill, so that didn't mean anything. It just didn't matter.

Talking was almost compulsive. "I have an older brother," Bruce said. "He's an orthopedic surgeon—almost. A younger brother and sister, twins. I guess you'd say swingers. They think I'm just plain stuffy, and maybe I am."

"I won't tell you again," Polly said. "Stop running yourself down. You can be anything you want to be—"

"I used to think that."

"It's true!" Her voice was urgent with conviction.

They walked in silence for a time. "What about you?" Bruce said.

"I don't know a thing about you except that you're something special—to look at, and to be with."

"I'm just—ordinary."

"Now who's running who down? Whom?" He was smiling, free and easy as could be.

"All right." Polly produced an answering smile. "I can type and take shorthand. I know my way around a desk calculator and the stock-quote pages in the *Wall Street Journal*. I took a night school course in Spanish once because I thought maybe I'd go to Mexico someday. I never have."

"You will."

"I keep telling myself. But sometimes it's hard to listen."

"Keep listening," Bruce said. "And tell me more."

Somehow their hands had come together. They clung firmly now. "I learned to swim in irrigation canals," Polly said. "I earned money baby-sitting to buy my first good swimsuit. It was a two-piece and I almost died when I first went to the canal in it."

"I'll bet the boys almost died too."

"They whistled."

I'll bet they did, Bruce thought; one look at that body in a two-piece suit and there would be a lot of bare feet pawing the ground. "I don't blame them," he said.

"I can't help it. I just grew this way."

"But you can enjoy it."

Polly smiled faintly. "Sometimes I do, and sometimes I don't."

Bruce's hand squeezed hers. "What else?"

"I like pizzas, and the smell of the Bay in a fog."

"Carmel?"

Polly smiled again. "I was there once. It was nice, but it was too cold to swim. And the boy I was with—" The smile turned rueful. "Well, he came on a little too strong with some ideas I didn't like. I took the bus back to San Francisco from Monterey."

Bruce thought of the big comfortable McCurdy house on the Seventeen Mile Drive next to Carmel overlooking the Pebble Beach golf course, where he and Alan and the twins had spent summers for as long as he could remember, golf, tennis, swimming in any of half a dozen pools, horseback riding, easy living through long, uncluttered days. He said nothing.

"I like the view from Coit Tower, and the wind on the Golden Gate Bridge." She looked up at Bruce. "And walking with you."

Never in his life, he thought, had he felt quite so—so loose. Talking to this girl was like talking to himself, only better. With her, he thought, a man would not be afraid to dream dreams aloud, or speak nonsense, discuss the infinite or the infinitesimal, or just enjoy companionable silence. He squeezed her hand again, and felt her answering pressure. "Tired?" he said. "We've been walking quite a while."

"Have we?" Polly paused. "Whatever you want."

"We'll find a pizza. That means North Beach."

Past the topless and bottomless bars and the neon lights, they found a small restaurant with pizzas and red wine, and they smiled at one another across the table as they ate. "You were going to tell me about being the boss's son, remember?" Polly said.

And how do you begin? he wondered. "I guess," he said, "you grow up used to it. There was always the bank. And my grandfather, big and sometimes loud, dominating any group. My father isn't loud, and he isn't as big, but—"

"I've seen him," Polly said. "When he talks, people listen."

"He expects—" Bruce began, and then stopped and shook his head. "I don't really know what he expects from me. He's never said. I just keep being shuffled around because maybe nobody really wants me in his department."

Polly laid down her fork. "I think you're wrong," she said. She planted both elbows on the table and rested her chin in her hands. "You're learning it all, the whole bit, everything that makes the wheels go around. Then when you sit in that big office up on the twelfth floor and somebody wants to talk to you about the trust department, or loans, or how we handle foreign transactions or anything else, you'll know exactly what he's talking about because you've been there with your nose right in it. That's why you're being shuffled."

"I wish I could believe that."

"You'd better believe it because it's so. Do you think your father was born with all the knowledge he has? I wasn't there, but don't you think your grandfather gave him the dirty chores just so he could see what they were like? You won't hear them because your name is McCurdy, but there are all kinds of stories in the bank about your father and your grandfather, and how sometimes you could hear your grandfather all the way down to the trust department making some kind of point when he didn't think your father had done something right."

It was a totally new concept: that his father had in his youth been fallible. If he had ever thought about it, he would have known of course that his father, like everyone else, had had to grow up, and growing up almost by definition involved many mistakes. But that there existed living legends of the times when his father had been found wanting in bank affairs was something he had never imagined and found even now difficult to believe.

Polly straightened in her chair and picked up her fork again. Almost offhandedly she said, "Do you like the bank?" She kept her eyes on her pizza for some little time before she looked up.

"Why, sure. I mean, I guess I do. What else?"

Polly smiled then, wrinkling her nose. "Name McCurdy, college, business school, what else than the bank, is that what you mean?"

"I guess it is."

"Did you ever like anything else?"

He smiled then, deprecating the very idea: "I thought I wanted to teach."

"Did your father object? Or didn't you ever tell him?"

Bruce hesitated. "I never told him, but I don't think he would have objected. He's read more history than most."

Polly put down her fork again and leaned forward, elbows on the table, chin in her hands. "That means what?"

"About families." Suddenly he was uncomfortable. Whatever he said was going to sound so damn—snobbish.

"Tell me about them." Polly's face and her voice were serious. "My family begins with my father and mother as far as I know, and it hasn't won any prizes, so I wouldn't know what you mean."

"It—isn't important." But she was silent, somehow intent, watching his face, and he had to go on. "Well," he said, "somebody—starts something, something different, and that's the beginning. My great-grandfather started the bank."

Polly nodded.

"Then my grandfather took over, and expanded the thing into what it is now. Do you see what I mean?"

"I think I'm beginning to."

"It could have ended there," Bruce said. "Lots of times it does.

Two generations build something up, and the third generation has no interest. It almost did end there. My uncle, Joe Jr., had no interest at all. He flew airplanes and eventually killed himself last week down in Los Angeles. But my father did take interest, so the third generation took over."

"You're saying," Polly said slowly, "that he would understand that the odds are long against the fourth generation having anything to do with the bank, is that it?"

He was pleased with her quick perception; and much of his discomfort had disappeared. "Right."

"You've thought a lot about it, haven't you?"

He had. What he supposed was conscience had haunted him for years. He had no desire to be merely a dabbler, a dilettante, a rich man's son like some he knew. And the way in the bank was open to him; there was little doubt that if he chose one day he would sit in that big twelfth-floor office at the pinnacle of power. But when he thought of those two fierce old men whose portraits hung in the board room, and of his father, quieter, less fierce, but still a major force to be reckoned with, one question repeated and repeated itself in his mind: was he worthy?

"Do you know what I think?" Polly said. Her chin was still in her hands, a small, square, determined chin. "I've watched you ever since you came into the department. You're already the best man there. Mr. Markham knows it, and I think he thanks God you aren't bucking for his job because it wouldn't be long before you got it. I think you're the best man anywhere, and after you've been around a little longer and seen how more departments operate, I think your father is going to see it too, if he hasn't already."

Bruce smiled, embarrassed. "I appreciate—"

"Look," Polly said, "I've told you what I am—not much from nowhere. But you, you've got it all, and you've got to believe it!" She sat up straight again and seized her fork. "Let me finish my pizza, and then take me home." She began to eat.

Outside the restaurant, "We can walk," Polly said. "It isn't far." They did not hold hands, and they walked in silence.

"You're angry at something," Bruce said.

"No, I'm not."

"I haven't changed my mind." His voice was quiet in the near darkness. Their footsteps seemed overloud. "I still think you are something very special, and I'm sorry if I've said anything that—upset you."

"You haven't. Here we are."

It was a three-story stucco apartment building that had seen better days. Bruce stood quiet in the tiny vestibule while Polly out of habit opened her mailbox. It was empty. She said nothing until she had unlocked the door. Then, "I live on the top floor," she said.

"I'll see you to your door." They climbed the stairs in silence.

"Here it is," Polly said. She smiled. "Rear apartments are cheaper." She unlocked the door, opened it. "Come in. I can't offer you a drink."

"I don't want one." He followed her inside. The door closed after him. "It was a lovely evening," Bruce said, and meant it. "I'm in your debt." He smiled suddenly, deprecatingly. "I can't believe all the things you said, but—"

"Damn it!" Her voice was quiet, but almost angry. "You've got to."

His smile faded. "If you want me to, I'll try."

"I want you to." Her voice was quieter now, and the near anger was gone. She watched him steadily. "I've never called you by your name," she said, "have I?" She smiled quickly. "Before today I suppose I would have said: Mr. McCurdy."

"I hope you won't."

Her smile was not quite steady. "I won't, because I'm going to ask you a question, Bruce. I don't know how else to say it."

He shook his head, uncomprehending.

"Do you want to make love to me?" The words were quiet. The unsteady smile remained. "I know you now, and I want to know you better."

15

Billy Gibbs, back from San Francisco, drove the white Porsche out Sunset and up the Stone Canyon road. Behind him Owen Waterson in his own car, attaché case on the seat beside him, followed reluctantly.

"I would rather have waited until we completed our audit," Waterson had said, "but you were insistent." He said it several times. He wanted the point made plain.

"We're stepping in cold," Billy had replied, and found himself somewhat amused by his use of the plural. "Marty has to know as soon as possible what the situation is. You can see that."

Waterson sighed. "I like to dot the *i*'s and cross the *t*'s," he said. "I will admit it. I have a horror that unless we do a thorough job, any conclusions we might reach could be overturned by further facts."

"But this time you are sure."

Waterson sighed again. "As sure as I can be." He hesitated. "What kind of man is young McCurdy?"

"That," Billy said, "is a question you'll have to answer for yourself."

"The McCurdy name has a certain—connotation."

"Exactly."

Marty met them at the door, shook hands, led the way to the study. He took his place behind the desk.

"I told you on the phone," Billy said, "we may very well have something." He looked at Waterson.

Waterson began to open his attaché case. Billy stopped him. "I think just generalities first," Billy said. "Evidence later, when we need it." He looked at Marty, who nodded.

"Very well," Waterson said with visible reluctance. He gave the impression of a man who was uncomfortable without papers in his hands. "You commissioned my firm to conduct an audit of McCurdy Aircraft. We are doing so. You asked that as soon as we found anything extraordinary, if we did, we notify you right away." He was speaking to Marty.

Marty nodded. "Right."

Waterson said, "For a number of years a considerable amount of the assets of McCurdy Aircraft have been held in readily convertible form, bank accounts, Treasury notes, in effect liquid reserves which could be called upon immediately. I am given to understand that this was your father's wish in order that new contracts for fabricated parts or subassemblies could be put in train at once with ample funds available for the initial outlays for matériel, tooling, planning, and the like. McCurdy Aircraft was, if I may say so, a very conservative operation, living well within its means. Since more than a controlling interest was held by your father, it was not necessary that he attempt to satisfy any other stockholders' desires for larger dividends. It is my understanding that he ran the operation in accord with his own conservative wishes."

Billy was watching Marty.

"And now?" Marty said. "Those reserves—?"

He doesn't need a diagram, Billy thought; he sees it just as clearly as I do.

Waterson said, "The—ah—reserves have been liquidated, Mr. McCurdy."

"And where have they gone?"

"I was told that they have been spent in engineering, tool planning, and tooling time, and for matériel. I have no reason to question that, but our continuing audit will clear up the matter."

Marty looked at Billy. "What do you think?"

"I think," Billy said carefully, "that maybe some of the rumors concerning the plant's overinvolvement with Coast Aircraft's air-bus project are true."

Marty thought about it. To Waterson: "You're used to this kind of thing. I'm not. What does the present lack of reserves mean?"

Waterson hesitated. "Until our audit is complete—"

Marty interrupted. "I'm not asking you to stake your life or your reputation on your answer. I want a best guess. You need money, cash money to run a business. You can't pay wages with tool plans or tooling. Are we too low on cash for comfort?"

Waterson sighed. "In a word," he said, "I would say yes. But," he hurried on, "further facts our audit may turn up could prove me wrong."

"I doubt it," Marty said. "I doubt it very much." He looked at Billy. "Have you talked with Jordan?"

"No." Billy hesitated. "But Jordan called your uncle. I got the impression he was asking him to get you off his back." He smiled faintly. "I told him you had twisted Jordan's tail a little."

"Then I guess another little talk is in order," Marty said.

Waterson was busy with his attaché case again. "I have—ah—preliminary figures." He looked hopefully at Marty.

Billy smiled to himself, and was immediately surprised by Marty's answer.

"Fine," Marty said. "I'll look them over." He stood up and held out his hand. "Thank you for coming to us so promptly," he said.

"You keep on with your audit, and we'll handle the rest of it. If we need you, we'll shout."

He sat down again when Waterson was gone, looked briefly at the pages of figures, and pushed them aside. "So," he said, and looked at Billy. "What have we got? Who do you think made the decision to go that heavily into reserves? Joe, or Jordan?"

Billy said nothing.

"I don't see Joe changing his spots," Marty said. "If he'd played it safe all this time, why wouldn't he keep it up?" He pushed back his chair and stood up. "Don't answer that. Jordan will say it wasn't his idea, of course. But maybe Coast can tell us something." A long shot, he thought, but just maybe it would pay off. He opened the door to the cantilevered porch. "Let's sit outside. How about a beer?"

Molly Moto brought them Mexican beer in cold pewter steins and peanuts. "How was San Francisco?" Marty said.

"Fine." Billy's voice was noncommittal. "And how was it here?" He watched Marty for reaction.

"Liz?" Marty said. His smile was faint, and humorless. "She was here."

Billy nodded, expressionless. "I heard. John Carrington filled me in."

Marty said mildly, "Do you want to know more?"

Billy hesitated. "Yes, I guess I do."

"Okay." Marty paused. "She spent the night. No apologies. While you were off on my business, Liz spent the night with me. If you asked her, I'm sure she would tell you herself."

"That is the hell of it," Billy said. "She would." He had a long swallow of beer, set the stein down gently, took a few peanuts and began to eat them one by one. "All right," he said, "what about your father, the dynamite, the DA's man? Carrington gave me only the broad picture."

Marty talked. Billy listened, while a part of his mind stood off and watched. Outwardly, he thought, we are lawyer and client, together studying a problem. Actually we are two bull elks in rut, at the moment peaceable, but not for long. Liz will color everything we do, and sooner or later, and probably sooner, something has got to give.

He ate peanuts and drank his beer, showing nothing. And in the end he said, "Not a very good situation. So far the newspapers and the TV newscasts have treated it gently. But that won't last."

"That was your John Carrington's prediction." Marty's tone was faintly bitter. "Actually, I don't give a damn whether they play it up or forget it. Publicity doesn't change anything. We want to find out who did it, and why."

"Any ideas?"

"None."

"Have you done any looking?"

"Where?"

Billy waved one hand. "This was your father's house. Have you gone through his things, his papers, that desk? Did he have a safe-deposit box? We can get an order to open it. These are things you usually do immediately, but I'll admit, matters have been a little—screwed up."

"And what do we expect to find? A signed letter with a threat in it?"

All because of Liz, Billy thought, they were close to open hostility. "Get that chip off your shoulder," he said, "or get yourself a new lawyer. I'm trying to keep Liz out of this. If you can't too, we might as well give up."

There was a long silence. Marty stared at the ocean. He said at last, "Okay, you're right." He grinned suddenly. "I'll—behave." He stood up and walked to the porch railing, turned and went back to his chair, sat down. "Suppose you talk with a guy named Carter, Howard Carter—"

"I know him. A feisty little bastard."

Marty nodded. "And find out what's going on. I'll have a talk with somebody at Coast, and go through the desk and anything else I can find. If there is a safe-deposit box, there ought to be a key."

Billy said, "And Jordan?"

Marty's smile was not pleasant. "Let him sweat. He went running to my uncle. Now he'll have to come to me." He studied Billy's face. "What's wrong?"

"You're a heartless son of a bitch."

"I'm learning." Marty made a brief gesture of dismissal. "Now what did you come up with in San Francisco—besides lunch with my uncle? And where did he take you, the PU Club?"

"Nice place," Billy said. "Quiet."

"Not always, when my grandfather was alive." Marty smiled at his memories of the big, outspoken old man, then settled down to listen. "Make it simple."

"It isn't simple," Billy said. "It's complicated because your grandfather's estate spreads out in all directions—real property, stocks, bonds, an interest in this and an interest in that wholly aside from the bank's interests—" He spread his hands. "He built that bank from maybe a hundred million when he took over to well over a billion that it is now, and in the process made himself one of the richest men in northern California."

Marty sat listening.

"His own personal interests," Billy went on, "go all the way from lumber and fishing and canning up in Humboldt County, through manufacturing and transportation and agriculture including viniculture in the Bay area and the San Joaquin, to real estate development and some oil leases down south here and beyond. You name it; if it was in California he was a part of it. It's going to take another six months at least before the whole thing can be tied up in any kind of package the court can understand and approve."

Marty said, "You're leading up to something. What is it?"

Billy said, "You're a shrewd enough bastard when you put your mind to it. What it boils down to is this: Aside from some more or less minor bequests—one or two of which I don't understand—aside from them, your father and Paul McCurdy are heirs to the bundle. But it is in a trust which the will establishes, and the trust has three trustees: your father—now you—your uncle Paul, and the trust officer of the McCurdy National Bank." Billy stopped and studied Marty's face.

"You think that's important," Marty said. "Why?"

"There's no problem about income," Billy said. "Under the terms of the trust, you and your uncle would have as much as you can possibly spend, probably more."

"Go on," Marty said. "What's bothering you?"

"Any major decisions concerning the corpus of the trust, the body, take a majority vote of the three trustees."

"So?"

Billy said, "Let's say you need capital to put into McCurdy Aircraft to replenish those reserves Waterson says are depleted. Maybe you *have* to have the money to meet payrolls. But two of the three of you—Paul, the trust officer, and you—have to agree before you can have money from the body of the trust—before you can invade the principal."

Marty stared out at the ocean. "And if Paul says no, then the trust officer will say no too, because he takes orders. Is that what you're thinking?"

"That," Billy said, "is the way I see it. And as your lawyer, I don't like it."

Marty looked out again at the ocean. There would be a breeze offshore, he thought, enough to set *Westerly* romping through her paces, lying into her work, sending water hissing along her sleek sides. Out there, firmly braced against the lee cockpit coaming, eyes fixed on the luff of the jib watching for telltale flutter, the wheel alive in his hand, feeling the surge and drive of the boat, hearing the myriad working sounds of the hull and the towering rigging, the clean, fresh salt air in his face—out there all these land-based intricacies and worries would be wiped away, forgotten, left for landlubbers to wrestle with. And the temptation was strong. He looked at Billy. "Why does everything have to be so goddamn complicated?" He paused—"Don't answer that"—and deliberately turned his head so the ocean was hidden from even his peripheral vision. "Go on."

"If we could," Billy said, "it would be to everybody's advantage if we could inject you as one of the two major heirs, in place of your father, into the probate proceedings. Frankly, I don't know if it can be done. It's going to take some study and thought."

Inactivity was suddenly no longer tolerable. Marty heaved himself out of his chair. "Okay," he said. "That's your bailiwick. Mine is Coast Aircraft and Joe's papers. Let's get to it."

Billy too had risen. "I kind of thought you'd head for Newport."

"I'm tempted. Believe me, I'm tempted." Marty studied Billy's face. "Would you go along, wherever we wanted to go in *Westerly*—the way we used to—if I paid the freight?"

Billy was smiling still as he shook his head. "No."

Marty nodded. "I thought not. Can you tell me why?" And then quickly, "Never mind. Maybe I'm beginning to understand."

16

On the telephone Helen Soong said, "I'm sorry, Sudie. Your father is in conference, a very important conference. He ought to be free in about forty-five minutes. If you could call back? Or perhaps I can help you?"

"He—" Sudie began. "Daddy." She was silent, angry. "Oh, never mind! I'll come over." She hung up, went outside, jumped into the little Fiat, and sent it scudding down the quiet Berkeley street toward the water and the Bay bridge.

He was such a horse's ass! she told herself, thinking of her brother Jim. No sense at all, merely a big grin and charm he could turn on at will to get himself out of trouble. It had always been so.

Less than a year ago, for example, that silly girl, whoever she was, letting herself get caught—and how in the world could a girl today be that stupid? Jim, of course, was responsible. And his allowance already spent, needing money from his sister for the girl's abortion. Sudie could remember the scene vividly.

"For a sister, even, God help us, a twin, you aren't bad."

"What are you bucking for?"

"Now, is that nice? The steely eye and the quick shaft when all I'm doing is telling you what a slick chick you are?"

"Come on! What is it?"

The grin that could be so appealing, and the sudden boyish admission of helplessness. "Okay. I've blown it. I've come up losers, and unless you bail me out, the sheriff's posse—"

"What are you talking about?"

The appealing grin held steady. "There is this chick. You know about chicks. You were the one who told me they like to screw just as much as guys do. At first I didn't believe it. But it's true."

"Oh, no!"

"So there it is. She's still, like they say, in the first trimester—I've been looking in books. So something has to be done, right? I thought of hitting brother Alan—"

"For an abortion? Have you flipped? He's an orthopedist."

"And I thought of putting the arm on brother Bruce." Jim shook his head sadly. "It would shatter his illusions." The grin returned. "So that leaves you. Or, of course, the august parents."

Since the nursery, Sudie thought, you had learned that grown-ups were the the last ones you went to when there were problems. It didn't mean that they wouldn't listen, or that they were either too strict or too permissive; it was merely that grown-ups were a different breed, and you stuck with your own and settled things in your own way if you possibly could. Why? Sometimes she wondered, but there it was; the rule was set.

Now, "Great," she said, "you could ask Daddy to okay an abortion loan. How much?"

"Two-fifty."

She was tempted to say that she didn't have it, and why should she not? Jim was never very reluctant to lie to her if it served his purpose. But something in her objected, however ridiculous that might seem. "That'll wipe me out until next payday." Miss Soong saw to the prompt mailing of allowance checks.

"Still in the first trimester," Jim said. "The books say that's the best time. The only thing is, time doesn't wait."

"Who is she?"

The grin turned faintly mocking. "You might know her. Wouldn't that be a gas?" And then, unsmiling now: "Look, I'm trying to do right by her. What do you want me to do, marry her? She says I'm the one. Okay, maybe I am, and maybe I'm not too. Here I am busting my ass trying to be a little gentleman, and my own true womb mate—"

"Oh, stop it!"

"Okay. But how would you like to find yourself in the same fix? You're too smart, sure, but think what it would be like."

And there was the trouble: she was thinking what it would be like, and she was tempted to cry. As Jim damn well knew, she thought, which merely added to the angry sense of impotence.

"Look," Jim said again, in a "now let's be reasonable" tone, "I'll pay you interest. How about that?"

"Oh, shut up! I'll let you have the money. I'll probably never see it again—"

"You will, you will. Solemn promise."

Well, she thought now, she hadn't seen the money so far, but maybe, just maybe he would come through yet. But that wouldn't help a bit in this present situation, not a bit.

She took the elevator to the twelfth floor of the bank and walked down the corridor to the executive offices. The receptionist phoned in her name and Helen Soong came out immediately.

"Your father is free now, Sudie," Helen Soong said. "I told him you were coming. He has a busy morning still ahead of him."

"I can't help it," Sudie said, walked past into the big corner office and closed the door.

Paul stood up, and smiled. "Hello, honey." He kissed her lightly. "What can I do for you? A loan until the next check?"

She was close to tears, and she would not allow herself to cry.

Maybe later, but not now. "It's Jim," she said. "He's—he's such a jerk!"

When she was young, Paul thought, he would have taken her in his arms and told her that everything would be all right. Now? I don't know the ground rules, he thought helplessly. "What has he done?" he said with as little inflection as he could manage. "To deserve the title, that is?"

Sudie took a deep breath. She kept her voice as steady as she could. "He's in the slammer."

"What?"

"Jail! He's in jail." And then the tears did come, and without even knowing how it happened she was in her father's arms, and he was patting her back as if she were twelve years old and saying over and over again the old meaningless words that nevertheless still had the power to bestow vast comfort and relief.

The tears subsided at last, and Paul said, "I think a drink of water," he said, and poured from his desk carafe. "Do you want Miss Soong to bring you some Kleenex?"

"No." Her own wad of Kleenex was sodden, but it would suffice. "I've told him and told him, Daddy, but he is such a—horse's ass!"

Paul winced slightly. "Is that the language they teach—? Never mind. Why is Jim in jail?"

"He was busted. Last night." Sudie spoke angrily. "Grass, of course. Maybe something else too, I don't know. Some of the guys went down to Tijuana over the weekend. They think it's cool to bring the stuff back." She stopped. "You do understand what I'm saying, don't you?"

Paul kept his face expressionless. "I think we are back in communication," he said. "He was arrested last night. Why haven't I been notified?"

"Because he says his name is John Doe, and they can't make him say different." Sudie took another deep breath. "Don't you see? He knows what a hassle there'd be with James McCurdy in the slammer, so he, you know, won't say anything." Impatience took over. "But he thinks of it afterward! Why doesn't he think of it *before?* That's why he's such a horse's ass!"

In a way it was pitiful, Paul thought, in a way admirable. Maybe much human behavior contained both qualities. He smiled gently. "I guess most of us are—horses' asses at times," he said. "Sit down, let's see what we can do."

She had never really seen her father in action before, and she sat quietly, impressed, watching, listening.

To Miss Soong, Paul said, "I want to speak to John McKenzie. Interrupt him if necessary." He did not raise his voice, but the force of command was plain. He closed the intercom, picked up a pencil, and pulled a yellow pad into position. "The Berkeley jail?" he said.

Sudie nodded. "He'll kill me for coming to you."

Paul smiled faintly. "We'll chance it." The telephone buzzed quietly. He picked it up, listened, and punched a button. "John," he said. "Sorry to bother you, but we have a problem. My son Jim is in the Berkeley jail on a drug charge. He calls himself John Doe."

Over to you, Sudie thought. He expects answers and action, and he will get them. The realization came to her with almost stunning force. This is the way things are done when you have reached this—position of importance and power. She looked slowly around the big office. I never thought of it that way before. I always just—took it for granted. It was a belittling thought.

Paul was listening now. "I think an East Bay lawyer might be best," he said. "But I don't need to say, John, that I am available anytime." He paused. "I am aware of it. The media would find it hilarious. But if I am needed, I want to be called. He is my son." A pause. "Very well. Keep me posted." He hung up.

Sudie said slowly, "I'm sorry, Daddy."

Paul nodded soberly. "So am I. So will your mother be." He picked up the pencil again, looked at it, and set it down. "Understand me," he said. "I don't condone this. I deplore it. And it may prove embarrassing to us all." He made a small deprecatory gesture with his hand. "I can't even say I understand it. On the other hand, I have the feeling that there are a lot of things you may take for granted that I don't understand. Why that should be so, I don't know, but I think it is."

"Did it used to be different, Daddy?" It had been a long time since she had been able to talk with him like this. Strange. Maybe in a time of crisis you were drawn together; maybe that was it.

"I don't suppose it was much different," Paul said. "My brother did things my father didn't approve of. I did too."

"Like what?"

Paul smiled. "Joe lied about his age and took flying lessons nobody knew about. He crashed and it all came out. He had nothing but a broken arm, but the plane was—as you would say—totaled. Father paid. And made it known that he was not amused. Oh boy, did he make it known."

Sudie said softly, "And what did you do?"

Paul hesitated. Then he smiled again. "I spent one Big Game night, what was left of it, in a Berkeley jail. The charge was drunk and disorderly. Stanford was the underdog, and we won the game. Father didn't approve on two counts, one of them being that he was a Cal man."

Sudie was silent, thinking hard. She said at last, "But the difference is that the rest of the time you were straight, is that what gets you?" She paused. "And Jim—and I, we don't play by your rules much of the time at all?"

"Maybe it is something like that." Paul nodded. "Our standards, Joe's and mine, and my father's, were pretty much the same. When we—transgressed, we knew that we were doing it. Transgression wasn't a way of life." He smiled suddenly. "At least it didn't seem so to us."

Sudie said, "I'm glad you told me, Daddy." Her smile mocked herself. "Probably you and Mother have told me before, lots of times, but this time I dig it."

He was about to take unfair advantage in a moment of contrition, Paul told himself. "And now that you—dig it," he said, "is it going to change anything?"

She had been a little girl for a number of minutes. Instantly now she was a woman grown, wary and evasive. Her face was guileless. "What do you mean?"

"What is his name? Mankowski, Pete Mankowski?"

"What about him?"

Her guard was up, Paul thought, the transparent shield in place, and frontal assault was futile. "I could say," he said slowly, "that there are rumors, many rumors. But you could say that there are always rumors, couldn't you?"

"What kind of rumors?"

So by this much she was willing to face the subject. Paul approved. "That you are sleeping with Mankowski."

Sudie had not expected bluntness. Maybe, she thought, she was learning more than a little about her father today. "Do you believe the rumors?"

"Should I?"

Nor had she expected subtlety, and it occurred to her that maybe the man who sat behind the big desk in this office would be far more used to verbal sparring and negotiation than she was. She sat silent.

"Unlike Jim," Paul said, "I don't think you have ever lied to me. Have you?"

"No."

He was being merciless, he knew, and he disliked himself for it. Still. "Are you going to lie to me now?"

She faced him squarely. "No, Daddy. If you ask me the question, I'll—tell you the truth."

Paul nodded. "I think you've already answered the question. So I'll ask one more. Do you think there is any future in it?"

There was open defiance now. "I don't care."

The telephone buzzed quietly. Paul picked it up, listened, and punched the button. "Yes, John?"

McKenzie said, "A young lawyer in a very reputable East Bay firm will take care of bail, Paul. The young lawyer"—a smile came into McKenzie's voice—"wears his hair long, I am assured. There will be no curiosity about his appearing in a drug case." The smile disappeared. "Do you want Jim sent over here?"

Sudie was watching him, and suddenly Paul was weary of what amounted to posturing, putting on a front he did not believe in. "If he'll come, John," he said. "If he'll come. Thanks." He hung up.

Sudie stood up. "I'll go now. You coped. I knew you would."

The chasm had opened again between them. Paul stood up. He made himself smile. "Back to your own world," he said. He nodded, and bent to kiss her lightly. "Good luck, honey."

17

Marty put his call through to George Granger at Coast Aircraft as the only place he knew to start. Granger came on the line almost immediately. "I have talked with Tom Chambers," he said, "and I am distressed by what he has found. If there is anything I can do to help, you have only to ask."

"Thanks," Marty said. The man might be pompous and windy, but the offer sounded sincere. "You can tell me who to talk to about McCurdy Aircraft's involvement with your air bus."

There was hesitation. Granger said at last in a different voice, "The purchasing agent would be the proper man. His name—"

"No." Marty was definite. "His boss. Or maybe his boss's boss. I want some policy answers."

Again the hesitation. "I believe I said before that you come on strong, young man," Granger said. "Vendors customarily work through channels."

Marty waited and said nothing.

"Very well." Granger's voice made no attempt to hide his exasperation. "The vice-president of matériel," he said, and then with heavy irony, "or perhaps you would prefer the general manager?"

"Why not? Does he have a name?"

Granger said slowly, distinctly, "The general manager's name is John Black. He is a very busy man. He—"

"Did he know my father?"

The hesitation was longer this time. "Probably," Granger said. His voice was resigned. "In fact, I know he did."

"Thanks." Marty hung up, and redialed the Coast number.

John Black's secretary was cool and unhurried. "May I ask what you wish to speak to Mr. Black about?"

"I'm Joe McCurdy's son, and I want to talk to him about my father's death before the police do."

There was a pause. "Police?" And then, "Just a moment, please."

There was another short pause. "This is John Black," a new voice said. "What's this about the police?"

"My father's crash," Marty said, "was no accident. That's been settled. Ask your project engineer. What hasn't been settled is whether you're going to get some of the parts and assemblies you need for your air bus."

Black said slowly, "Are you tying the two together?"

"I don't know. Maybe you can help me."

"I'm confused," Black said after a moment. "I knew your father personally for a number of years. I was very sorry to hear of his death. I don't like hearing that the crash wasn't an accident. But what business your father's firm did with us was strictly routine—"

"Through channels," Marty said. "Yes, I know. But maybe this time it wasn't. That's what I want to talk to you about."

"Perhaps," Black said, "you had better talk first with a man—I believe his name is Walter Jordan. You must know him."

"He's been told," Marty said flatly. "Now I want to find out what he's been up to."

"I see." There was a pause. "And so you come to me?"

"If you don't know the answers, you can get them."

There was a smile in the voice now. "I must say your approach is —refreshing," Black said. "On the other hand—"

"Are you really that busy?" Marty said. "Somehow I've never believed all those stories about big executives."

"You have the guts of a burglar, young man," Black said. The smile was still evident in his voice. "How soon can you get here?"

"Forty minutes."

"Give your name at the main lobby." Black hung up.

The routine was as it had been before: the temporary pass issued in the lobby; a smiling, brushed-up young woman to guide him down the shining corridors. But once Marty entered Black's outer office the atmosphere was changed.

There was a no-nonsense air of quiet efficiency, two secretaries at their widely spaced and uncluttered desks, at work, not at gossip. Only one, the secretary on the left, looked up when Marty came in. She stood. "Mr. McCurdy? Mr. Black will see you." No hesitation; no delay. She tapped twice on the inner door, opened it, and held it wide.

John Black was a stocky man with heavy shoulders and heavy hands and the same quiet air of command, Marty thought, that Paul McCurdy exuded. They shook hands. "Sit down," Black said, and resumed his own chair.

There were papers in a neat pile on his desk. He ignored them for the moment. "Chambers," he said, "verifies what you told me—the crash was no accident." Anger showed, under tight control. "Aside from my personal feelings, everything like that that happens concerns everyone in the industry whether they realize it or not. Your father's aircraft underwent a complete overhaul in our shops. I have told our own security people to go into that carefully. I am sure the authorities will cover the other possibilities—particularly where the aircraft was kept."

"They will have complete cooperation," Marty said. He liked this stocky man who obviously had asked questions and received answers and issued his orders without unnecessary motion. There seemed to be no doubt who ran giant Coast Aircraft.

Black tapped the neat pile of papers. "Here I was wrong," he said. "McCurdy Aircraft's business with us is not strictly outside production routing, minor parts and subassemblies, as I thought. McCurdy has contracted to supply us with major components for our air bus, control assemblies for both wing and empennage. I was unaware of it. Presumably you were not?"

"I was guessing," Marty said. "All I know is that we have gone in deeper than we ever have before in engineering, planning, and tooling, and what you tell me shows why."

Black sat quietly. "Can you deliver?"

"I don't know. But I intend to find out."

Distant and almost imperceptible, the life sounds of the vast factory blended in a constant subdued murmur. Other than that there was no sound. Black said at last, "I appreciate your frankness. I want to know what you do find out. And I will be frank with you. We have had problems with the air bus, some of them our own doing, some from causes beyond our control. Engine design changes, engine delivery delays—you may have read of some of the complications."

Marty nodded.

"So," Black said, "we are not in a position to be magnanimous even if we chose to. We will hold McCurdy Aircraft to its commitments." He paused for emphasis. "You understand that."

Marty nodded again in silence.

"I am not sure we were wise to place the contracts with McCurdy," Black said. "I intend to go into that further. But the contracts were placed and it is too late now to put them elsewhere."

Marty said, "Somebody approached your purchasing people." He paused. "Do you know who it was?"

"Walter Jordan. Speaking for your father, which by inference meant McCurdy financial backing." Black was silent for a few moments, studying Marty's face. "Do you have reason to think otherwise?"

"No."

"Because if you do," Black said, "if you need financial assistance and you are not in a position to get it, then I see considerable unpleasantness ahead. I knew your father," he said, "and I liked him. Once upon a time we were young together. In France. Over Germany." He paused. "But my responsibilities are to Coast Aircraft, young man, and to our stockholders, and sentimentality has no place in business."

Marty stood up. "Okay. You've warned me."

Black pushed back his chair, stood up, and came around the big desk. He held out his hand. "I am sorry about your father," he said. "I will be even sorrier if we—run into difficulties on your contracts. I hope you understand that."

"I'm learning," Marty said. "We're playing for keeps."

Black nodded. He was smiling faintly. "We are indeed. All of us."

Marty turned in his temporary pass in the main lobby and walked out to the parking lot. Movement and sound caught his attention and he turned to watch one of those deadly-looking Coast fighter-bombers scud down the runway, lift, tuck its gear into its underbody, and with a bellowing roar of afterburner reach for the sky at an impossibly steep climbing angle trailing a faint dark smudge to mark its passage. He watched until the aircraft was only a tiny speck over distant mountains, and its sound had long since died away.

He looked then at the multiple buildings and the vast area of this, merely the Coast home factory, one of a number, and compared it with McCurdy Aircraft. We could put our entire plant in this final-assembly hangar, he thought, and still leave room to move around in. So? Was mere size important? The answer seemed to be yes.

A gigantic enterprise such as Coast Aircraft was so woven into the fabric of the country, its defense and its economy, that it simply could not be allowed to collapse. Witness the government loans to Lockheed, to the Penn Central Railroad, and probably to others he had never heard about. The giants could not be allowed to die.

But the same rule did not apply to something the size of McCurdy Aircraft. It could fail, disappear, and go unmourned except by those immediately concerned. And who would lift a finger to prevent it in the first place?

He was in a thoughtful mood as he got into his car and started back to Stone Canyon. Up to now there had been almost a sense of unreality about the plant, Walter Jordan, the possibility that something was amiss. Now Black had put it all into sharp focus with his blunt warning that what they faced in all probability could be summed up in one word: failure.

And what was it Billy Gibbs had said to him that night after dinner? "And one of the differences between us is that I know losing doesn't break me up. You haven't had a chance to find out yet."

To hell with it, Marty thought. We aren't going to lose. We've just begun, and there is a long way to go.

There was a note on the desk in Molly Moto's neat hand saying that Walter Jordan had called. I'm not ready for you yet, Marty thought; and when I am it won't be on the phone. He tossed the note into the wastebasket. Then he settled himself and began to go through the desk drawers.

First the file drawer. He took out a pile of file folders and lined them up on the desk top. They were labeled, but not arranged, he noticed, in any kind of alphabetical order, which probably merely meant that his father had not been a very good file clerk. Or perhaps he kept the folders in order of importance.

The first was labeled "Temperatures," and it contained hand-drawn bar graphs of daily maximum and minimum temperatures by the month, with a summary sheet covering the entire year. Interesting, but not immediately important.

The next folder was labeled "TBA," and Marty puzzled over the label briefly and then smiled and nodded—of course, To Be Answered, he thought; and looked inside. There were three letters: one from Paul in San Francisco suggesting a weekend in Pebble Beach and some golf. "I haven't played much recently," Paul wrote, "but I'll still give you four strokes. You pick the date, and I'll try to fit it. We have a few things to talk about."

What things? Marty wondered; and told himself it was probably none of his business. Or was it? Face it, he thought, at best this is a ghoulish business, going through a dead man's private papers—even if he was my father. So the questions deserve to be asked.

The second letter was brief, merely a note: "Joe dear, it was lovely and I was sorry that it had to end. When I am back from Palm Springs, if you are still in the mood we might play a repeat performance? Love, Val."

Marty crumpled the note and tossed it into the wastebasket.

The third letter was from someone named Pete, handwritten, with a Chevy Chase return address. It read in part, "Thanks for the congratulations. They will be the last. Two stars is as far as I go. You might have gone farther, if you'd wanted to. They had their eyes on you even then . . ."

Air Force, Marty thought; a major general. And his father might have gone that far, or farther? I know so damn little about him. Strange, it had never mattered before.

There was an entire folder labeled "Paul." It contained sporadic correspondence going back some years, none of it, as far as Marty could see, of any great importance.

There was a folder labeled with his own name filled with newspaper clippings—*Westerly* in the Acapulco race, at the Mid-Winters, Newport-to-Honolulu. Somehow all those triumphs seemed very distant now. He put the folder aside, and then pulled it close again and reopened it.

He had sent none of these clippings to his father. Joe himself must have found them and cut them out, tucked them away in this folder. Parental pride? Marty had never even thought about it before. There are a lot of things you have never thought about, friend, he told himself, and closed the folder again.

In a folder marked "Peters" there were bills: from gas company credit cards, Bullock's, the Mercedes garage, the Sunset Liquor Store, an insurance premium notice—all of them current; no doubt to be picked up and paid by Lester Peters.

In a folder labeled "Cal Tech—Stanford" (an odd juxtaposition, Marty thought) there was a paper-clipped sheaf of correspondence from and to each college culminating in the establishment of a total of four $4,000-a-year four-year scholarships for needy and worthy students to be chosen by the respective college deans. Letters of appreciation were clipped at the bottom of each sheaf.

Stanford, Marty could understand; his father had gone to Stanford. Cal Tech—of course, of course; because of me. He never bothered to tell me.

In the largest folder of all, marked "Personal," was a hodgepodge of newspaper clippings, old letters, invitations, and a marriage license dated August 12, 1945, issued to Joseph Martin McCurdy, Junior, and Mary Elisabeth Davis. Stapled to the license was a folded newspaper clipping with a two-column picture of Marty's mother, and a lead that read: "Mrs. Joseph McCurdy, Junior, Victim of Hit-and-Run." The date was June 8, 1949.

So that was what had happened to his mother. He looked at the silver-framed picture on the desk. It smiled back at him. You don't leave much behind when you go, he thought: a marriage license, a newspaper clipping, and a few pictures, maybe some memories in others' minds, and that is about it. He closed the "Personal" folder, pushed it aside, and leaned back in the chair.

Nothing so far that told him much of anything. There would be other files, of course, no doubt a number of them at the plant. But the plant could wait. Before he went there again he wanted as much information as he could gather. He sat up and began going through the other desk drawers.

He found the safe-deposit box key among the paper clips and rubber bands in the partitioned trough of a top drawer. It bore merely a number, but the printed checks in the checkbook in the same drawer carried the name of the Bank of America branch in Beverly Hills. Good enough. He put the key in his pocket, and went on with his search.

He found little more, and nothing of consequence, and at last he closed the desk drawers, got up, and walked out on the cantilevered porch into the sunshine.

Standing there, looking at the city and the ocean beyond, he had the odd feeling that forces were gathering. At sea sometimes the feeling was the same, a falling glass, a subtle wind change, swells beginning to lose their smooth monotony, and clouds altering shape and texture—at times like that you did well to pause, to think, to adopt a what-if? attitude and make sure that your preparations were in order.

18

Susan McCurdy sat on the board of the Children's Hospital. She was also involved with the Opera and the Symphony. These were obligations one accepted and discharged faithfully, just as one gave generously to charity. She was aware that to some her views were anachronistic, but they were hers, and she clung to them.

On this day the last thing she wanted was a board meeting, at least an hour and a half of tedious, repetitive chatter, in which the "Oh, that's what you meant? I thought you meant . . ." syndrome of confusion was sure to figure heavily.

She could, of course, plead illness. But I am not ill, she told herself; it is all in my mind. Years ago I faced and settled the "why am I here and where am I going?" questions; and it is ridiculous that they should creep nagging again into my mind now, at my age.

In her robe, standing in front of her walk-in closet, she found it difficult, if not impossible, to decide what to wear. Blue was her favorite color, but today the sight of the blue suit depressed her. Lightweight tweed would be appropriate for this brisk fall day, and if a walk in the country were what she had in mind, there would be no question. But for a board meeting? Well, there was the tailored off-white of which she was very fond, but it was revealing, and although neither her scales nor her mirror gave credence, today she felt just plain *big!*

And San Francisco itself depressed her. She knew that it was one of the world's most liked cities, and it had been good to her as she hoped she had been good to it. But it faced the wrong way, toward the Far East, which she mistrusted, rather than toward Europe, where she had always felt at home.

San Francisco boasted of its restaurants, and she had to admit that she was fond of Jack's and Bardelli's and the Ritz Old Poodle Dog, but the names that kept running through her mind these days were Locke-Ober, Durgin and Park, and the Old Union Oyster House; and instead of sailboats in the Bay, her thoughts turned to single sculls and eight-oared shells in the Basin, the swan boats in the Common, and the tang of real Fall in the air.

In the New England countryside the leaves would have turned by now, scarlets, clear yellows, and salmon pinks against the evergreens; and the snow would come soon to muffle sound and create the Currier and Ives kinds of scenes she remembered from childhood.

Ridiculous, maybe, but there it was.

And on days like this, and recently they had been more and more frequent, small annoyances piled up and decisions seemed to come at her from all sides. Discussing today's menus with Felix this morning, for example, had been inordinately difficult: Beef, or lamb? Broccoli with hollandaise, or asparagus vinaigrette? A cheese board for dessert, or would Paul also prefer a fruit cup? For herself, Susan could not have cared less.

And then today she was to have met Paul in town for lunch, but at ten-thirty Helen Soong had called to say that Paul had been called out of town on urgent business, and would have to cancel. Where had he gone? Over to Berkeley, Helen Soong said, and did not elaborate. Questions, Susan thought, but no answers.

As a child she had been spoiled—she admitted it. Her world had revolved around her personal axis. In those days one *came out,* and the event was splendid, all those nice boys from Harvard, and some even home for the party from Yale or Williams or Amherst, herself the absolute center of attention, savoring every moment.

And then, strange thing, that summer at Pebble Beach where she had met Paul; and almost imperceptibly Boston had receded in her mind, and it seemed that in the fresh young California atmosphere she began to bloom as vegetation bloomed in this mild climate; and a new sense of freedom filled everything that she did. Where had those feelings gone now?

This house of which she had always been so fond seemed empty and echoing now with the children gone most of the time. Sudie and Jim would be on their own shortly, they almost were now, and what then? Should she and Paul find a smaller house? Even an apartment? She had never discussed the matter with Paul, but probably it was something she ought to bring up. Another decision to face.

It was not fair, although that was a silly way to think, but Paul had his bank, friends and associates, responsibilities and authority, recognition. She, Susan Webster McCurdy, had only reflected glory, if that was the word. And it was not enough.

As she dressed automatically (in the blue suit; bother the depression!) she told herself that tonight she would have a long talk with Paul, because dissatisfactions ought not to be hidden, ought they? And then she would see. Perhaps what she needed was a vacation in Boston to drench herself in familiarity as in a hot soothing tub. Just the thought cheered her up. As she hurried down the stairs and out to her car to drive to the board meeting, a new thought struck her: What if I don't come back from Boston? The question echoed and reverberated in her mind like a jingle phrase that would not be stilled.

The young East Bay lawyer's name was Robert Story, and as advertised, Paul thought, he did wear his brown hair long, well over his ears and his collar. But his shoes were polished and his white shirt was immaculate, and if the cut of his plaid suit was a trifle too flamboyant for Paul's taste, he was altogether quite presentable. And he displayed surprising deference when they met in Berkeley.

"Sorry to have to bother you, sir," he said. "I had hoped to take Jim over to the city as you asked. Short of force, no way, I'm afraid. It was hard enough just to get him to accept bail."

"I see," Paul said. He did not see, but he assumed that explanation would be forthcoming. It was.

"He argued," Story said, "that through no doing of his own he was in a position to put up bail when others could not, so he didn't think he was justified in taking advantage of it."

Paul's face was expressionless. "And what is your thought on the matter?"

Story smiled. "From a strictly moralistic point of view, sir, he is possibly right. But from a practical point of view, I have never seen anything to be gained by starving myself just because I knew there were people in the world who were going hungry. I doubt if many would."

Paul nodded. His thoughts exactly, and if from time to time he had small nagging feelings of guilt that he was healthy, well fed, clothed, and housed when others were not so fortunate, he could remind himself that it was futile to bleed to death for the world's ills, and that by and large only those misfortunes or lacks within his immediate sphere were within his power to alleviate. "You drove him to his—apartment?" Rabbit warren, Paul thought, would be a better description. He had been there only once, and left as soon as he felt he could.

"Yes, sir." Story paused. "And I told him I would report to you."

"I can imagine what he said. Never mind. Thank you for attending to the matter."

"Do you want me to go with you, sir, to see him?"

Things had come to a pretty pass, Paul thought, when a father needed someone with him when he visited his own son. And a lawyer at that. Still. His slow smile was weary, mocking himself. "Probably you speak his language," he said. "I am not sure I do. I would appreciate your company."

It was a redwood shingled house among the eucalyptus trees in the Berkeley hills behind and above the campus. The view of the Bay, San Francisco, the Golden Gate, Sausalito, and the mass of Tamalpais was spectacular. Paul wondered fleetingly if any of the young people who lived in the house, or came and went, even bothered to look at the view, or whether their attention was wholly directed inward upon their own personal vistas with their problems and their triumphs, their dreams, or would the word be fantasies?

A girl answered the door. She wore jeans and an oversized cotton flannel shirt, tails out. She was barefoot. She smiled at Story. To Paul she said, "Jim? Yeah, he's here. Let me guess. You're the parent. I'll tell him." She held the door wide.

Paul was standing with his back to the living room admiring the view when Jim came in. "At first," Jim said behind him, "you have the feeling that all those people over there across the Bay are looking at you." His tone was conversational. He waited until his father faced him. Then, "The upstairs john has this big window and no curtain," he said. He shook his shaggy head, smiling broadly. "You wouldn't believe how many people, chicks particularly, get all tight-assed and constipated just sitting there looking across at the city."

Story watched Paul and said nothing.

Paul said, "And having delivered yourself of that crudity, are you ready to talk now about your situation?" Wrong approach? He didn't know, but it didn't take much of Jim these days to provoke him into comment. "You are out on bail."

"Through the generosity of your friendly McCurdy National Bank."

Paul ignored it. He looked at Story. "What now? Must there be a trial?"

"I haven't talked to the prosecutor yet," Story said. "A lot will depend on just what all they picked up in the raid." He looked at Jim. "Just grass? Or was there hard stuff too?"

Jim shrugged. "They'll say there was whether there was or not, so what difference does it make?"

"Is it really necessary to point out," Paul said, "that we are in your corner, trying to help you?"

"Big of you."

Paul was fighting down angry words. In the end he said, "You're enjoying this, aren't you, Jim?"

"Punks always do, Mr. McCurdy," Story said unexpectedly. His tone was quiet, even deferential, but there was biting contempt in the words. "I moonlight in what they call a storefront operation. We take cases without a fee, lots of them just like this." He looked coldly at Jim and then back to Paul. He smiled without humor. "You might say that my acquaintance with punks is extensive. The phony attitude is all they have, and they cling to it."

Jim said, his voice all at once not quite steady, "Then if you feel that way, why bother to help them?"

This time the cold contempt was even plainer. "I could explain it to you," Story said, "but you wouldn't even begin to understand." He turned to Paul. "I will talk to the prosecutor, and see where we stand. If it is only marijuana, it may not be too bad. If hard drugs are involved—" He made a small gesture of uncertainty. "We'll have to see. That is, if I am still representing your son?"

Paul looked at Jim. "Well?"

Jim hesitated. "I don't have any choice, do I?" A measure of defiance remained, but much of the bravura had disappeared.

"That," Paul said, "is no answer."

Both Paul and Story watched Jim steadily. "So okay," Jim said at last, "I guess he's still my lawyer."

"I'll be in touch," Story said, and turned away.

Jim turned to his father. "Okay, lay it on me."

Paul shook his head. "I don't even feel anger any more," he said. "All I feel is shame." He too turned away and walked out to his car, where Story waited.

For a few minutes they drove in silence down the winding hill road. Then, "Maybe I shouldn't have popped off like that," Story said. "I'm sorry."

"Maybe you shouldn't have," Paul said, "but you only said what was in both our minds." He glanced at the young man. "And it undoubtedly had more impact coming from you." He hesitated. "Can you explain it?" There was the pain of admitting his own insufficiency by the question, but personal feelings were less important than the reality. "I am speaking of course of his attitude."

Story said slowly, "I'm a square, Mr. McCurdy, straight arrow—although I haven't heard the phrase in a long time. Maybe there's something lacking in me. I don't know." There was a sense almost of apology behind the words. "I went to UC on a baseball scholarship. Most of the guys who were any good had ideas of playing pro ball. I didn't. Oakland offered me a tryout. I turned it down. All I wanted was law school. I—managed."

Paul watched the road in silence. "You're saying, are you," he said, "that you didn't have time for—defiant antics?" He glanced again at Story's face.

Story's smile was apologetic. "Maybe that was it. Maybe if I had had time I would have been into all sorts of things. Maybe I'm doing a kind of penance in the storefront operation now because I didn't even feel the need to step out of line myself." The smile spread. "It's pretty hard to tell what might have been."

It was indeed, Paul thought, as he headed back across the Bay alone. Maybe if he had handled Jim, and Sudie, differently from the beginning? Did that make sense? As far as he knew both he and Susan had treated all four children pretty much alike, and Alan and Bruce had turned out like young Robert Story, as different from the twins as day from night.

Maybe as a parent, he thought with some bitterness, I am a good banker. Come to think of it, parenthood was the one occupation most people moved into with absolutely no training, with only a blithe conviction that they could do the job satisfactorily. And I wouldn't even hire a bank messenger on that basis, he told himself.

Helen Soong followed him into the inner office. "I called Mrs. McCurdy and canceled your luncheon engagement."

Paul nodded as he sat down. "Maybe it would be nice to send her some flowers."

"I have, potted chrysanthemums." Helen Soong hesitated. "Did you have lunch, Mr. McCurdy?"

"I won't starve." Paul looked at the notebook in Helen Soong's small hands. "What do we have?"

There was no need, but Helen Soong opened the notebook anyway. "Mr. Goodwin would like you to call him. So would Mr. McKenzie. Mr. Trent would like to see you. Mr. Waters would like to see you. Mr. Simpson called. He merely wanted to leave a message that there is a heavy frost warning for the entire Napa Valley tonight. He said you would know what he meant."

"Poor George." Paul smiled without humor. "Unfortunately I do know what he meant." And there is nothing I can do about it, he thought, except to wish him luck—for us as well. How much money was riding on this year's wine-grape crop? Charlie Waters should have some figures by now. "McKenzie first," he said. "Then Mr.

Goodwin. Then Waters." He paused. "Tell Mr. Trent maybe tomorrow. We will call him."

He sat quiet and very much alone after the door had closed. Sounds of traffic reached him faintly from Montgomery Street. Out in the Bay a freighter sounded its whistle in two angry blasts, and there were two answering blasts from a whistle of a different tone. A starboard-to-starboard meeting, Paul thought idly, and went back to his concern over Wally Trent.

I am letting him hang motionless, he thought, and he has no way of knowing why I am doing it. I merely want the figures pinned down before I brace him with them, but to him it may very well look as if I am using suspense like a Chinese water torture. Paul could remember vividly how heavy the weight of suspense could be.

He was thirteen, and for the Christmas holidays acting as office boy for his father at a salary of a dollar and a half a day. He smiled now, thinking of it. That white rat he had bought at lunchtime—a white mouse had been too expensive—and proudly brought back to the bank to show to his chum Joe Stein, head teller. And the rat had gotten away, on the main floor of the bank, and it would be forever before Paul forgot the scene of pandemonium, secretaries up on their chairs and desks, screaming, an elderly guard having no idea what was going on with his gun in his hand trying to look in all directions at once, ground-floor vice-presidents shouting orders—and Joe Stein and Paul chasing the white rat with a money sack, finally catching him, and both being bitten in the process.

For days Paul waited for Joe McCurdy to lower the boom. Young Joe, knowing the story, watched in glee. The blow never came; the matter was never discussed, but for the rest of his life, Paul thought, he would remember the near terror of waiting. Maybe if he called Wally Trent—

The telephone buzzed, and John McKenzie was on the line. Wally Trent forgotten, "I met young Story," Paul said. "I'm impressed."

"A very good man, I think." McKenzie's voice held overtones. "I called you about something else, Paul. We may have made a considerable error. An oversight. Maybe it is important; maybe not. I certainly hope not."

Paul was smiling. "You are being unusually evasive," he said. "What's up?"

McKenzie's tone was dry, pedantic. "At the time of your father's death," he said, "your brother was still alive."

"Yes."

"You and he were the two principal heirs of your father's will. When the will went into probate, both of you should have been notified. *You* were."

Paul's smile was grim. "Constantly."

"But your brother was not."

Paul frowned. "I talked with him half a dozen times. We were going to meet at Pebble Beach to talk everything over. He knew what was going on."

McKenzie's voice sounded quiet, grave. "The customary procedure is a registered letter, some correspondence to show, if necessary. I have had our files searched. We have nothing."

Paul thought a moment. "Two questions," he said. "Why have you thought about it just now? And what difference can it make?"

"Both questions have the same answer," McKenzie said. "Your nephew's lawyer was here, which means that your nephew, who is now the other major heir, is interested in the probate proceedings. By failing to notify your brother we may have left an error which could be seized upon by your nephew's attorney—if he wants to make a fuss."

Paul was frowning again. "Why would he want to make a fuss?"

"Wills are sometimes challenged, Paul."

"Why would Marty want to challenge?"

"I don't know."

"He has more money than he can possibly spend."

"I repeat, I don't know."

"Laywer's caution again, John?"

"Perhaps. But I thought you ought to be told."

Paul hung up, sat back in his chair, and swiveled it around to face the windows. The sky was cloudless, a beautiful San Francisco fall day. And yet—the thought struck him with sudden force—heavy frost warnings had already been issued for tonight in the Napa Valley, which meant that hidden forces were at work. All you could do was wait to see how they coalesced.

Frost depended on two factors: temperature and humidity. *If* the dew point was reached (that percentage of humidity at which the air would give up its moisture on contact) *and* if the temperature fell below freezing, frost would result.

There was a parallel, however farfetched, with Marty. *If* his need, or avarice, reached the point at which he might be tempted to secede from the northern California branch of the family, *and* if the means of that secession were at hand, trouble might result. And, Paul thought, there is nothing I can do now to prevent it, just as there is nothing I can do to prevent a heavy, perhaps a killing frost tonight.

The telephone buzzed. Paul picked it up and winced at the sound of Charles Goodwin's voice. Charles said, "The more I think about it, the more concerned I am about this Walter Trent matter. Your father would never have allowed this to happen. It reflects on your judgment."

"I haven't seen the figures yet, Charles," Paul said, "but I have already taken certain precautions, and matters are in hand."

It would be useless to point out that his father had made errors, Paul told himself, or that in an operation as varied and complicated as running a billion-dollar bank there were bound to be matters that went temporarily astray. The fact was that in Charles Goodwin's judgment there could never be anyone who could adequately fill Joe McCurdy's shoes, and so he magnified any error into a near crisis.

Still, the Trent affair was dangerous. And Charles, only a short time from retirement, was chairman of the board of the bank and was quite capable of creating dissension which might be hard to control.

"And now," Charles Goodwin said, "I understand that we are perhaps faced with problems in some of our agricultural loans in the wine area."

I'm going to have to tell Charlie Waters to button his lip, Paul thought grimly. The board chairman had a right to know what went on, but only after a more complete financial picture was available. Given Charles's volatility, piecemeal information could produce near chaos. "As father frequently pointed out, Charles," Paul said, "crops are always subject to the whims of weather. But we are watching the situation very carefully. Charlie Waters reports directly to me on that. Was there anything else?"

There was. "I have had inquiries made in the Los Angeles community. Your brother's aircraft plant seems to be in questionable financial circumstances. Are you aware of that?"

"I was not aware of it," Paul said. "We have no financial interest in McCurdy Aircraft at present—no loans outstanding. And it is understood that we would only make a loan on a merit basis."

"I trust you will keep it that way. If the plant needs financing, we are probably the bank your nephew will turn to. And I for one would be against allowing any family sentiment to influence how we invest the bank's money."

"Charles—" Paul began, and stopped. There was no point in confrontation over nothing. "I'll keep it in mind," he said, and hung up.

Almost immediately the intercom buzzed. Helen Soong's voice said, "Mr. Waters is here."

"Send him in, please." And when Charlie Waters was in his chair, "I have just had a call from Charles Goodwin," Paul said. "He is chairman of the board, but you are my personal assistant, and the orders I give you are for you alone. Is that clear?"

Charlie swallowed. "Yes, sir." He seemed deflated.

"All right," Paul said, "now we'll forget it. What do we have?"

"Uh—Cabernet Sauvignon," Charlie said. He took a deep breath. "You were quite right, sir. The acreage planted to that grape has increased approximately three hundred per cent in the last eighteen months." He had figures, and he read them. Paul did not even try to remember them. "Sales of that wine," Charlie said, "have been increasing, but not at nearly the same rate. By projection—" More figures, and a neat graph. Charlie laid it on Paul's desk.

Paul glanced at it, wondering if there was anything in the world which could not be reduced to the stark lines and impersonality of a graph. "So what it adds up to," he said, "is that given normal harvests and wine production, in a year or two, as George Simpson predicted, Cabernet Sauvignon will be a glut on the market?"

"It looks that way, sir." Charlie paused. "For the rest, how heavily we are involved, it is a little difficult to hit it exactly because some of our loans cover multiple varieties of grapes and wines, and even—"

"An approximation, Charlie."

Charlie took a deep breath. "In the entire area of viniculture, well into seven figures, sir. And it might even go to eight."

"Enough to think about."

"Yes, sir."

"Get on to the branches involved," Paul said. "Let's have each loan reviewed. I want local assessment of each situation. Do they know in Los Gatos what they are doing in Napa? That kind of thing. See if you can pull it all together."

"Yes, sir." Charlie hesitated. "There is a heavy frost alert in Napa for tonight."

Paul nodded and thought again of his maybe not so farfetched parallel. "I heard."

"I was there this morning," Charlie said. "I didn't really know before how they go about trying to protect the grapes. It's—pretty fascinating."

Young enthusiasm not to be dampened, Paul thought. "I don't know very much about it. Tell me."

"Well, sir, they don't smudge any more. I mean, they don't call it that, but it looks like pretty much the same thing with burners set around the vineyards and sometimes propellers mounted on towers to keep the air moving. But some of the burners use propane, not kerosene and oil the way they used to, so I guess it is a lot cleaner. But that isn't really the fascinating part. Some of the growers use water."

"Maybe you'd better explain that. Doesn't the water freeze?"

"That," Charlie said, "is the really strange part. The water does freeze. Mr. Simpson at Latour showed me pictures in a book of vines absolutely coated with ice, you know, like trees you've seen pictures of back East after one of those ice storms?"

Paul nodded.

"But the vines are somehow protected that way. I don't pretend to understand it, but it's so. But there's one thing. Once you start spraying the vines you can't stop until the frost danger is past. And that means an awful lot of water. If you run out of water, you're dead, and Mr. Simpson says not many growers have that much water, so they have to go the burner route. Anyway," Charlie said, "they're pretty uptight about the warnings. There's a lot of money riding on the grapes in that valley."

Paul smiled again. "And a good share of it is ours. All right, Charlie. Thanks for the report, and the—instruction."

Charlie said, "I didn't mean to—"

"I mean it," Paul said. "I learned something."

After the door was closed he again swiveled his chair and looked out at the clear sky. Over in Napa Valley the growers were braced as for an attack, a siege, their preparations already under way if not yet completed.

And what of us? he thought. Specifically, what of me? Is some kind of attack coming from the south, as John McKenzie with his lawyer's caution fears? Marty and his bold young lawyer friend? If so, why? Is it the plant? Or could it be just plain desire for independence, a severing of the family umbilical cord by this new generation?

And Joe's death—no accident. The full realization of that was just now beginning to make itself felt. Incredible, he thought, and yet there had to be a cause, and once the cause was known, incredibility faded, did it not?

I'm tired, he told himself, and depressed by Jim and Charles Goodwin. Too much. He pushed back his chair and stood up. In the outer office, "I am leaving for the day," he told Helen Soong. "I'll be at the Olympic Club for a while if there is anything urgent. After that, home."

Riding down alone in the elevator, he found himself thinking again of the siege concept. Farfetched? Maybe; maybe not.

19

Billy Gibbs, the branch manager, and a third man were waiting for Marty in the Beverly Hills bank. Billy introduced the branch manager. "And this is Mr. Reynolds," he said of the third man, "from the state tax people. To make sure that the box isn't full of undeclared money."

Reynolds was not amused. "It has happened," he said.

Marty produced the key. "Let's have a look."

It was one of the smaller safe-deposit boxes. Marty carried it into a cubicle, set it on the table, opened it, and began to go through the contents. Reynolds and Billy Gibbs watched.

Four passports, three of them outdated; his father's birth certificate and discharge from the USAAF; a gold pocket watch with the initials JMMcC on its back, his grandfather's, Marty decided; a plain gold man's-size wedding ring which he had never seen on his father's finger; the pink slip for the Mercedes in the Stone Canyon garage.

"I came prepared," Billy Gibbs said, and took a plastic bag from his attaché case.

Reynolds watched in silence as one by one Marty stowed the items from the box. "I had my job to do," he said at last to Billy, turned away, and walked out.

Marty hefted the bag. "Not much help," he said. What had he expected? he asked himself; and found no answer.

They walked together out to the bank parking lot. There in the hazy sunlight, "Anything new on the crash?" Marty said. He was very conscious of the plastic bag in his hand, and the little it contained of his father. And again that thought: you don't leave much behind when you go. "Carter had nothing?"

"Nothing new."

So for the time being put that out of your mind, Marty told himself. "Okay," he said, "so what do we do now?"

"You're the boss."

"I am?" Marty smiled. "I guess I am." Liz had said the same in a different way. Decisions were his to make. "I think the plant," he said, "and Jordan."

"You don't need me."

"Wrong. I want a witness." Marty turned to his car. "Follow me."

They parked side by side in the plant parking lot, and together walked to the front gate. There was a breeze from the ocean, and the wind sock beside the runway stood straight out. Marty looked at it thoughtfully.

"What's on your mind?" Billy said.

"I don't know." Something was scurrying around, he thought, like a name not quite remembered, or a word that would not reveal itself. "Let it go," he said. "I may think of it later." He led the way into the plant.

There was a subtle change in Walter Jordan; he seemed no longer quite so sure of himself. "I telephoned you," he said to Marty.

"I know."

"The police have been here."

Marty nodded. "I told them you would cooperate."

"Of course." Jordan took off his glasses, looked at them and put them back on. "And Waterson," he said, "has been a constant—annoyance." He waited, but Marty said nothing. "I resent the audit," Jordan said.

"So you said." Marty paused. "And you called my uncle to tell him too."

"I thought it best to keep him informed."

"Maybe," Marty said. "But don't do it again. If there is any calling to San Francisco to be done, I'll do it."

Billy watched and listened. From now on things will be done his way. What was it Liz had said? "You are in for a sleigh ride." Well, as long as I stay with him, I am, for sure. There was both satisfaction and resentment in the thought.

"I've seen John Black at Coast Aircraft," Marty said. "Wing and empennage control assemblies for their air bus. A pretty big bite to take. Black thinks so too."

"We have the capacity."

"I'll want to see about that."

Jordan took off his glasses again. Without them his eyes had an uncomfortable peering look as if they stared out from a dark place. "You know nothing about manufacturing," he said, "nothing. Even your father knew very little." He put the glasses back on. "And that is why he left the running of the plant entirely in my hands."

"Including negotiating contracts such as these with Coast?"

Jordan hesitated. "I consulted with your father."

"I wonder."

Jordan took a deep breath. "Are you calling me a liar?"

"If I think it's necessary, I will. Did you consult with my father about using up our cash reserves?"

"He knew about it."

"And approved?"

"He made no move to stop it."

"Again I wonder," Marty said, "but at the moment it doesn't matter. Let's get down to cases. How deep are we in, and how much help do we need?"

"What makes you think we need any help. I told you—"

"I've talked to Waterson."

"He's only an accountant. He's not—"

"Let's be frank," Marty said. He did not raise his voice, but the emphasis was clear. "If you are going to continue to sit behind that desk, you're going to give me straight answers to any questions I want to ask. Is that clear? Now how deep are we in, and how much help do we need? I'll get the information eventually from Waterson, but I want it now from you. For the record, Black is not going to let us off the hook. He made that clear. We're going for broke, and I mean broke, your job as well as all the others."

"I have a contract," Jordan began.

"Which isn't worth the powder to blow it to hell if we go into bankruptcy. Now let's get some facts and figures in here where we can look at them."

Jordan looked at Billy, and found no solace there. He looked again at Marty and seemed about to say something, and then thought better of it. Reluctantly he sat forward and flipped the switch on his intercom. "Ask Mr. Roberts to come in, please." He closed the switch and leaned back again. "Our treasurer," he said. "He can give you what you want. He could have done it before without Waterson's—interference."

Marty's smile was not pleasant. "But maybe we wouldn't have believed him," he said. "This way he knows he's being watched."

It was more than two hours before Marty and Billy Gibbs walked back out to the parking lot. "I think Stone Canyon," Marty said. "We've got some talking and thinking to do."

"We." Billy said the word without special inflection.

"I thought we settled that."

"I'm a lawyer."

"Once upon a time," Marty said, "you were also a friend. I can pay you for legal advice. The other part doesn't have a price tag." He paused. "Suit yourself."

Billy hesitated. "I'll follow you," he said, and walked to his car.

They sat on the cantilevered porch in the mildly hazy sunshine, steins of Mexican beer at hand. The ocean sparkled. "What do you think?" Marty did not turn his head.

"You shook him up. But good," said Billy.

Marty turned then to search Billy's face. "Was it justified? Or is he right in maintaining that everything is going to be all right, maybe a little close to the bone, but still copacetic?"

Billy said at last, "The figures—I'm a lawyer, not a business school type. It looks to me as if interpretation of the figures could go either way. But, as I said, I'm no kind of judge."

"That," Marty said, "makes two of us." He took a long pull at his beer, sighed, and wiped his lips. "So we need an expert."

"Jordan will flip. You've already put him down."

"Jordan will do what he's told. We need an expert," Marty repeated, "not an accountant who comes up with the figures, but somebody who can evaluate them and tell us whether we're heading for trouble or not." He looked at Billy. "What does that add up to?"

He is ahead of me, Billy thought, because the question almost supplied its own answer. "A banker," he said.

"Exactly," Marty said. "One of my uncle's bright young boys." He studied Billy's face. "You don't agree?"

"You're taking a chance."

"Why?"

Maybe I see some things more clearly than he does, Billy thought, and took a measure of comfort from the concept. "If you need financing," he said, "where will you go?"

"McCurdy National. Obviously. So?"

"But you won't know whether you need financing until someone from McCurdy National has done an analysis. And suppose his analysis shows that you would be a bad risk? Your uncle said he would only provide financing on a merit basis."

"You asked him?"

"I did. But I also told him you had not asked me to."

"So we're putting ourselves in their hands," Marty said at last. "It's either that or fly blind."

Billy said, "There is an alternative."

Marty looked at him, and waited.

"Walk away from it," Billy said. "Let Jordan stew in his own juice. Sell your stock for whatever you can get, cut your losses, and forget it."

"Maybe a week ago," Marty said slowly, "I would have thought about that. Now—maybe it would be good business. I don't know. But it isn't the way we're going to do it."

"Do you mind telling me why?"

"Are you just asking, or do you want to know?"

Billy said nothing.

"Okay," Marty said, "I'll try. I'm not one for waving the flag, but that plant's got my name on it, and that's one reason." Maybe it was just as well to get it all out in the open, he thought, and try to get his reasons straight in his own mind.

"In other words," Billy said, "you just don't want to lose."

"You could say that. You could also say that if I walk away from it all right now, I'll never have some answers I want. That's another reason." He stood up. "Dynamite isn't part of a normal installation in Coast aircraft. I want to know who put it there. And why he wanted to kill my father." He started for the doorway, stopped, and turned. A new thought had made itself felt.

"What if something happens to me?" he said. "Who gets my share of the trust? I don't have any heirs that I know of. And I've never made a will. Does it go, then, to Paul?"

Billy said, "Your next of kin would almost certainly inherit. Are you accusing your uncle?"

"Somebody is responsible for that dynamite." Marty turned away again and walked into the study, and Billy could hear him dialing the phone.

Maybe I am, by nature, more cautious than he is, Billy thought, or maybe it's my training; it makes no difference. He is willing to take the risks, and I am not sure I would be. When we were kids, it was different; we thought we were indestructible. He has that feeling still, and I do not. He sat quietly in the hazy sunlight, working on his beer and feeling suddenly, unaccountably old and staid.

Marty came out of the study and sat down again. "All set," he said, and grinned. "You know who he's sending down? My cousin Bruce. Stanford Business School, the bank, the whole bit. Jordan is going to think he is ass deep in McCurdys." He paused. "We'll get straight talk, no gobbledygook."

Still feeling old, staid, and conservative, "I just hope the straight talk is favorable," Billy said.

Marty's quick grin reappeared. "Why, so do I, friend, so do I."

"And if it isn't?"

"Then," Marty said, "we'll lay out a new course."

20

Bruce was at his desk in the trust department, very conscious of Polly Wright only a few feet away, when he got the message from Todd Markham himself, who walked out of his office to deliver it. "Your father would like to see you in his office," Markham said, hesitated, seemed about to say more, and then turned away and walked back into his office.

Polly looked a question. Bruce lifted his shoulders and let them fall. He made himself smile and even attempted levity. "I am summoned to the presence. If I don't come back, don't mourn for me."

"Come back," Polly said. She returned to her typing and tried to concentrate on it. It was difficult.

Riding up in the elevator, Bruce tried to put Polly from his mind. That too was difficult; she had been very much in his thoughts these last few days. Every afternoon after work they had met, not at Henry's Bar, where so many of the bank people were likely to stop in, but at a smaller, more distant bar called Gino's. It was not, Bruce told himself, that he was ashamed to be seen with the girl, but, rather, that there was no point in causing gossip. Polly agreed.

And there was both the pleasure and the pain in their relationship: Polly was agreeable. Not in everything, but in all important things. Like walking, and talking, and making love in that tiny apartment of hers with the let-down bed.

"I like what you like," she was fond of saying, lying naked in his arms, red hair lose, lips and eyes smiling.

Bruce was not without carnal experience with girls, but Polly was something else. What was that old joke about the difference between dignified acquiescence and enthusiastic cooperation? Well, that about covered it. He had never really believed what they said about red-haired girls being more passionate, but he was prepared to take it as dogma now.

All of this added up to the pleasure. The pain was another matter.

Once, lying close, relaxed, spent, "There isn't any future for us, you know that, don't you?" Polly said. With her forefinger she traced idle circles on his broad chest. Her eyes watched him steadily. "I mean, there is just—this. So let's make the most of it."

"I don't think I want it that way."

She was smiling now. "You're just being a nice guy. You don't have to be. I—enjoy all this just as much as you do, probably more. And I love our walks, and a drink at Gino's, and dinners in little places. That's enough for me."

"No."

She watched him quietly. Then she smiled again. "Okay. Let's not talk about it if it bothers you. Let's just—enjoy ourselves. Here." She rolled on her side, raised herself, and pressed his face between her warm breasts. "Let's—think about something else. Like this."

The pain, Bruce supposed, was what you called conscience, and it was a constant nagging pain. Because I am getting everything, he thought, and she is getting nothing. Maybe, probably, that was an old-fashioned concept, and there were some, his brother Jim came to mind, and even Sudie, who would break up laughing if they heard him expressing it, but there it was. I am a square, he thought, and that's that.

To the twelfth-floor receptionist whom he did not recognize he said, "I am Bruce McCurdy. My father sent for me." For what, he had no idea; and he was beginning now to be apprehensive.

"Yes, sir." The girl smiled and pressed the door release beneath her desk.

Bruce walked in. Helen Soong said, "Your father is waiting. Go right in." She too was smiling. As they had smiled in Paris watching the tumbrils go past?

Bruce knocked twice, and went in. He closed the door behind him. "You wanted to see me, sir?"

Paul had been facing the windows. He swiveled his chair now. His face was expressionless. "Sit down, Bruce. I have a—job for you. In Los Angeles." In a quiet voice he began his lucid explanation.

Bruce listened with growing wonder. He said at last, "You mean me? Alone?"

Paul produced his faint smile. He nodded.

"But—"

Paul interrupted. "If I didn't think you were competent," he said, "I wouldn't send you. I am not in the habit of sending the wrong men to do jobs. Sometimes I make a mistake." Wally Trent was very much in his mind. "But if I made too many of them I wouldn't be sitting here."

Bruce swallowed. "Yes, sir."

"There is a team of outside auditors in the plant. They will work with you. You can believe their figures."

"Yes, sir."

"You have spent time working with the loan officers downstairs. You have done loan analyses on your own. Quite competently, I'm told."

So maybe Polly had had it right that first evening after all. Maybe he had been shunted around in a training program that was for real, not just a myth fed to the boss's son. "I didn't know you—kept track," he said.

Paul smiled. "My father knew everything that went on in this bank and in all of its branches. He told me I had damn well better know too. I try."

Bruce was silent, vaguely shamed.

"There is another reason I'm sending you," Paul said. He paused, choosing his words. "This is in a sense a family matter, and I would just as soon not bring in outsiders. You and Marty—"

"We hardly know each other."

Paul smiled again. "That's all right. You wear the same name. I think that is beginnning to mean something to Marty. I hope it does to you." As it rarely does to Jim, he thought with some bitterness.

"It does, sir." He was thinking again of Polly. That is exactly what we're up against, he thought: the McCurdy name.

Paul leaned back in his chair. "Markham tells me he can spare you. I think there is need for a certain amount of haste. I want you to be thorough, but I don't want you to waste any time. When you have your conclusions, bring them to me."

Bruce said, "And Marty?"

"I'll talk with Marty." If lines are to be drawn, Paul thought, they will be between Marty and me, no one else. "I want to know first," he said, "whether McCurdy Aircraft as it stands is solvent. I don't think it is, but I want your judgment backed by figures."

"Yes, sir."

"I want to know second," Paul said, "if it does need financial help, how much does it need?" He paused. "And I want to know third if in your judgment a loan would be a sound risk." He watched Bruce quietly.

"Yes, sir." And then with a new sense of confidence, "I mean, I guess that's the kind of thing I'm supposed to be able to do, isn't it?"

"If it isn't, you're in the wrong business." Paul's smile took some of the edge from the words. "And we wasted some money down in Palo Alto, which I do not think is the case."

"Well." Bruce stood up. "I guess I should say thanks. For the chance to work on my own, I mean. I'll do the best job I can."

"I'm sure you will." Paul made no move to stand. "Sit down.

Maybe there is something else we had better talk about." He waited until Bruce was seated again. "Do you know what it is?" Paul said.

So here it is, Bruce thought; right up to you, son. "Polly?"

Paul nodded. "By and large relationships within the bank are not good. There are exceptions, of course, but they are rare. But most that are called office romances merely end unpleasantly with a bad taste that lingers."

Bruce began, "Polly—"

"You're of age," Paul said. "Your private life ought to be your own and to a large extent it is. But if it begins to impinge on the bank, interfere with your work, or threaten a scandal of any kind, then I am going to have to step in. Is that clear?"

He wanted to stand up and say: you can shove it; Polly and I have a right to ourselves. Instead, habit of obedience strong, "Yes, sir. I think I—understand."

Paul nodded soberly. "Then good luck in Los Angeles. Call me whenever you want." He got out of his chair, shook hands briefly, and sat down again. He did not look up as Bruce walked out.

When the door closed, Paul thought, I am a son of a bitch, interfering in what is essentially none of my business. He leaned back in his chair and stared at the far wall. The best you can do is call them as you see them, isn't it, use your own better judgment which is based on experience to point out pitfalls the young are not likely to see?

Then—and the question echoed and reverberated in his mind—why didn't you do the same with Sudie, put the pressure on her too to give up what is obviously a more unsuitable relationship than this one between Bruce and the girl in the trust department who, for all you know, is a perfectly decent young woman who will do the boy no harm? Well?

And the answer, admit it, was that he could put pressure on Bruce and make it stick, whereas with Sudie all he would do was antagonize openly. So aren't you by default shirking your responsibilities as a parent?

The phone buzzed softly. Helen Soong's voice said, "Mrs. McCurdy is calling."

Paul punched the button. "Yes, dear?"

Susan's voice said slowly, "I wanted to talk to you last night. And the night before." The words were coming faster. "And, oh, so many nights. But always there has been something—" Quieter now. "And it never worked out."

Paul's voice was gentle. "About what?"

"Me. Isn't that silly?"

Paul hesitated, and said at last, "I don't think I understand."

"That is the trouble. There—isn't anything to understand. Not really. I am simply dissatisfied. With me. That's all it is."

"Susan." Paul stopped. There were strange sounds in the background, and he frowned as he listened to them. "Where are you calling from?"

"The airport."

"Susan," he said again, and stopped. Very carefully, "Why are you at the airport?"

"I'm flying to Boston. My plane leaves in—ten minutes. So I have to go now. I'll be staying at the Copley. You can reach me there. Felix and Teresa will take care of you." The words were coming faster even than before. "I've gone over menus with Felix. You will be all right. You will be fine."

"Susan." Paul hesitated. "What in the world—?"

"Goodbye." The line went dead.

Paul hung up slowly. He shook his head as if to clear it. From your pinnacle, he told himself, you looked down and told Bruce what to do, Bruce and a girl you have never even spoken to. All right, now use that great experience and judgment to decide what to do yourself—if you can.

The phone buzzed again. Susan? He seized it quickly. Helen Soong said, "Mr. Waters is on the line."

Paul hesitated. Again that headshake so reminiscent of a boxer in his corner trying to clear the mists. "All right, I'll speak to him." He punched the button. "Yes, Charlie?"

"Two things, sir. First, the audit of our foreign—transactions is complete."

"Have you seen it?"

"Yes, sir. It—isn't good."

"Bring it up." Susan for the moment was forgotten.

"If you don't mind, sir, could we wait until maybe tomorrow?"

"Why?"

"Mr. Simpson called from Latour. He is quite—upset. The frost damage is much greater even than he feared and he wants me out there to see it, and I thought—"

Paul took a deep, calming breath. "Go out to him," he said. "Hold his hand." He had completely forgotten the frost warnings, and he was annoyed with himself for the lapse. "Tell him we will sort it out. It is not the end of the world. We have loans to other growers in the valley?"

"Yes, sir. We've invested heavily in this year's crop."

"Then spread yourself, Charlie. Work through the Napa branch, but make it known that you come from the home office. Clear?"

"Yes, sir."

"And you'd better send the audit figures up to me. I'll go over them myself." He hung up and sat back. And then, remembering, quickly pulled up his sleeve and looked at his watch. Ten minutes, Susan had said. Well, she was airborne or close to it by now, beyond reach. He leaned forward again and punched the intercom button. "Arrange for some flowers, Miss Soong, to be delivered to the Copley-Plaza Hotel in Boston to Mrs. McCurdy's room, please. With a card, of course."

"Yes, sir." Helen Soong's voice held nothing. "Any message on the card?"

Paul hesitated. What was there to say? Helpless question; with no answer. "I guess just my name," he said.

On the telephone Bruce said, "I'll have time for a quick drink at Gino's before I go out to catch my plane. Will you meet me?"

"Of course." Polly hung up and went back to her typing. It was even more difficult to concentrate.

He was waiting in the back booth they liked, two drinks, both bourbon—Polly had switched her tastes—already waiting. He stood when she came in, and waited until she was seated. Men had rarely stood for her before. It was just one of many different things. "I have maybe a half hour," Bruce said. He raised his glass. "To you."

"How long will you be gone?"

"It depends. There are already some figures, and maybe they're all I need. If they are—"

"You're excited, aren't you?"

He could smile. Always with her he could smile. "I guess I am." He paused. "On my own."

"Yes. And you'll do it well." Polly held her drink in both hands. The cold glass was a steadying force. She smiled. "I'll miss you."

"I wish you could come with me."

"No." She shook her head gently. "That's your world, the world you belong in."

"Look." Bruce's voice was gentle. "It's no big deal. I'll do this and then I'll be right back in the trust department. You'll see."

"No, you won't." Her quiet voice was positive.

"What do you mean?"

Polly set her glass down. She turned it around and around on the table, watching it intently. At last she looked up. "Why do you think your father is sending you?"

"Easy enough." With her he could even be light. "I'm the brightest fellow around, as you've been pointing out, and he wants the job done right. Simple as that. And there is one more thing."

"Yes?"

"Well, I'm—family, and he would rather—" What he saw in her face stopped the words. "Oh, no," he said. "What you're thinking just isn't so. He wouldn't send me to Los Angeles just to get me away from you. That's—silly."

"Is it?" She shook her head. She was smiling, but her eyes were bright with tears. She slid out of the booth in a single quick movement, and stood up. "I have to go. I'm sorry. Please don't—come after me." She turned and walked quickly away.

She had caught him entirely by surprise, and for a moment he did not react. Then he wriggled himself out of the booth, walked quickly to the door, and looked both ways on the sidewalk. She was already out of sight. He looked at his watch. Almost time to go.

His first reaction was quick anger. Damn it, what am I supposed to do now? She'd put him in a fine fix, hadn't she? He walked back to the booth and sat down to finish his drink.

By the time he was on his way to the airport the anger had died. Polly was wrong, of course, in what she thought, but under the circumstances maybe it was only natural. She had such a thing about being Miss Nobody and he being a McCurdy that maybe she tended to see everything in that light. It was like one of those old-fashioned novels in which families kept interfering and keeping kids apart, when all the kids had to do was say the hell with it and go their own way, didn't they? Well?

He seemed suddenly to be standing off looking at himself, and not particularly liking what he saw. You had your chance to stand up, didn't you, buster? Right there in the old man's office. And what did you do? You crawled.

Well, hell, the old man hadn't said anything specific, just a lot of if-this and if-that, and what was there in that to fight about?

But maybe that was just the reason parents usually came out on top; because they went at it gradually, subtly, never giving you something definite to hassle until before you knew it the ground had been chopped right out from under you.

Anger returned, but no longer directed at Polly. Well, it wasn't going to be like that this time. Maybe sending him to Los Angeles actually was, as Polly thought, a first subtle step to pry them apart. Come to think of it, the old man's reputation was for subtlety, wasn't it, rather than the direct confrontation Bruce's grandfather had been noted for?

He stood in the waiting room and watched passengers file through the doorway to the waiting plane. I could turn right around and go back to the city, he thought, see the old man first, and then go to Polly and tell her nothing is changed.

He could, but he wouldn't, and he knew it. So, all right, I'll go down to Los Angeles and I'll do a job that will make the old man's eyes bug out, and then I'll come back and lay it right on the line with him. Polly will wait.

He took out his ticket and boarding pass and walked through the doorway.

21

The restaurant, called Peter's, was small, quiet, and the food was unassumingly good. Billy had given considerable thought to the choice of locale.

He held Liz's chair for her and then walked around to his own. Their knees did not touch beneath the table, but her physical presence was almost palpable, overpowering. She was smiling across the table. "How are you?"

"I'd be embarrassed to tell you."

The smile spread. "I'll take that as a compliment."

"That's the way it was meant." He looked up as the waiter approached. "Two martinis on the rocks with a twist." And for the moment he was back in San Francisco standing at the Pacific Union Club bar with Paul McCurdy. To Liz: "Did you know that the martini is supposed to have been invented in San Francisco?"

"There is that tale," Liz said. "A cold day, Martinez Strait—legends."

"You," Billy said, "are too damned smart. You always were." He paused. "Looks, body *and* brains."

Marty had said the same out by the pool before that telephone call that changed everything. Or had it? Liz had not yet decided.

Their drinks arrived, and Liz sipped hers slowly, then set it down. "How was San Francisco?"

"Busy." He paused. "Do you really want to know?"

"If you want to tell me."

"Strangely enough, I do."

"Then I'm listening."

A woman of many moods, no, of many facets, Billy thought: sometimes frivolous, even flighty; other times quiet and thoughtful, as now; always quick and alert; rarely despondent; wholly desirable. "I met a very cagy lawyer named John McKenzie," he said. "And I met what I expect is his principal client, Paul McCurdy. I had the feeling that I was playing in the major leagues."

"I doubt if you struck out."

Warm praise, and he savored it. "We weren't really competing."

Liz studied him thoughtfully. "But you expect to?"

As always, Billy thought, she saw deep. "Just a possibility," he said. "I don't think Marty's seen it yet. Or maybe he has. He's already surprised me more than once."

"We're talking about Marty again."

"Yes, damn it," Billy said suddenly, "because, like a mountain, he's there. The trouble is that his head isn't in the clouds. He's turned out to be a lot more practical than I would have thought."

Liz said, "I saw him while you were gone."

"He told me."

Liz watched him quietly. "Say it," she said.

It had to be said, he thought; he could not escape it. "He said that you spent the night with him."

"Yes."

Billy picked up his drink and finished it. "Shall we have another and then order?" He beckoned the waiter.

"I am very fond of you, Billy." Her voice was quiet, even gentle.

"But?"

Liz shook her head. "I attached no conditions. The statement stands. I liked you when we were in college. I like you better now." She paused and smiled. "For what that's worth."

"It's worth a great deal."

"Once upon a time if you had asked me to marry you, I would have said yes."

"And now?"

Liz shook her head. "I think not. But not for reasons you might guess. When I was in college and even graduate school I was very sure of myself. In the phrase, 'the world was my oyster.' I would have thought myself ready for marriage then. But not now."

"Tell me why."

The waiter brought fresh drinks. Liz played with hers, studied it for a few moments. Then she looked up. "I came out of graduate school with my bright shiny doctorate, and I looked around, and suddenly I began to wonder just what I thought I had been aiming at all those years. It was like having made a long journey to a strange land, and then looking around and asking yourself what you had found so appealing in the idea in the first place." She paused, smiling. "*La donna è mobile*, Billy, the lady is fickle."

"I doubt that."

"You like what you're doing, don't you?"

"Practicing law? Yes."

"And I think Marty is beginning to like what he's doing."

"He's going at it with both hands."

"I envy you both. Not because you're men. I enjoy being a woman. What I don't enjoy is—uncertainty."

"Maybe you need someone to tell you what to do."

"No, Billy, that isn't it. We were going to order, weren't we?"

They came out of the restaurant into the soft night. Billy held the car door for her and then walked around and got in on his own side. He just sat, his hands motionless on the wheel. "What now? What would you like?"

"I'm content. No, that isn't exactly the word. What would you like to do, Billy?"

"A number of things." All of them having to do with you, he thought, and involving intimacies I will probably never know.

"Then," Liz said, her voice quiet in the darkness, "why don't we do them?"

He hesitated. "What I meant—"

"I know what you meant, Billy. Let's go home."

Hans barked twice and met them at the door. He studied Billy, and then turned and nuzzled Liz's hand. She pulled his ears gently. "There is a fire laid," she said to Billy. "How are you at playing Boy Scout? I'll get drinks."

They sat on the sofa facing the fire, its flickering, dancing light the only light in the room. Hans lay quiet in a corner. Billy put his arm around her and drew her close. She came willingly. It was a long kiss, tentative at first, and then with deep urgency.

Liz bent forward. Her voice was not quite steady. "Unzip me." She sat back against his arm once more, and watched him, smiling, as slowly he drew her dress and her brassiere from her shoulders and arms and down to her waist, baring her splendid breasts. "You see, Billy, I told you there were no conditions. I meant what I said, I am very fond of you."

She went with him to the door in the early pre-dawn, a light robe around her shoulders merely for warmth, no attempt at concealment. They kissed lightly. "Thanks for the dinner."

"Thank you—" he began, and then stopped, kissed her again, and walked quickly away.

At his apartment he undressed, set the alarm for an hour and a half, and got into bed. Pictures of Liz flowed through his mind, naked Liz, passionate, loving Liz, always smiling.

Then sleep, and with it wild, kaleidoscopic dreams, himself struggling for he knew not what. When the alarm sounded he clawed his way up into consciousness, feeling as if he had not rested at all.

There was a message for him to see his father when he arrived at the office. He went immediately to the big, old-fashioned, book-lined room where as long as he could remember his father had held forth. "Sorry I'm a little late," he said.

"Frolic with the owls and then try to fly with the eagles," his father said. He was smiling. "Never mind. At your age it can be done occasionally. Sit down, Billy. Bring me up to date."

Billy sat down. "The crash is still under investigation."

"There is nothing to be done about that." Henry Gibbs was well into his fifties, hale and fit, unflappable. His mind worked in orderly fashion. "I have taken the liberty of speaking with the District Attorney, as well as with John Carrington, and we are all agreed that until the official probing is finished, we are impotent. Your client understands that?"

"He has put it in my hands." And left me alone about it; I'll have to give him that.

"I am more concerned with the other matters," Henry Gibbs said. "The will you gave me to read. And the trust agreement." He paused. "What are your thoughts about them?"

"Knowing Marty," Billy said, "I'd say the trust agreement is an invitation to a fight."

Henry Gibbs nodded. "I am inclined to agree." He leaned back in his chair. "I knew old Joe McCurdy casually. In many ways he was—I hesitate to use the word, but it does apply—a great man. He had a vision, and"—he smiled, and shook his head slowly—"as we used to say, more guts than a tennis racquet. There are very few men who are prepared to back their considered judgment clear to the hilt, no hedging. He was one of them. When he had made his decision, he pushed the big bet right out into the center of the table, and you matched it or you folded; and while you thought about it, in the back of your mind was the knowledge that Joe McCurdy was seldom wrong and that he rarely bluffed. There is a tale of a bank failure up in Caloro. A legend, rather, but I am inclined to believe it is based solidly on fact."

Billy sat quietly, waiting; there would be a point.

"I am rambling, Billy," Henry Gibbs said, "but with a purpose. That was the kind of man old Joe McCurdy was. And I can see that that was precisely why he established the trust and tied up his estate—because he didn't think that Paul and young Joe were quite capable of carrying on by themselves." He paused. "Fathers rarely are sure of their sons' capabilities, I'm afraid."

"I get the message," Billy said. He was smiling.

"Maybe there are exceptions," Henry Gibbs said, and produced a smile himself. It quickly faded. "Under normal circumstances," he said, "I think Joe McCurdy's—autocratic ideas would have been harmless. Paul McCurdy is not an avaricious man. He has more money than he needs; and power, recognition, status if you will. I can't see him challenging the status quo."

"I had lunch with him," Billy said, "and neither can I."

"And," his father said, "young Joe, Bud, was easygoing, not in the least aggressive. Now comes the grandson." He watched Billy and waited.

"Who is a very different kettle of fish indeed," Billy said. "He goes for broke."

His father nodded. "As old Joe McCurdy did. But would he just out of contrariness try to find ways to break the trust and take his share of the estate into his own hands?"

Billy had thought about it. "I don't think so, sir. But he's taking a gamble right now, with McCurdy Aircraft, and if that loses, he has a big choice to make." He explained about Marty's phone call to San Francisco; about Bruce McCurdy's being assigned to an analysis of the plant's financial condition. "I asked him what he would do if the report was unfavorable. He said we would set a new course."

Henry Gibbs leaned back in his chair again. "You have been thinking about it, no doubt, considering possibilities?"

"Yes, sir."

"One or two things occur to me," Henry Gibbs said. "No doubt they have occurred to you too, but I'll say them anyway."

"I hope you will. I'm sure there's a lot I haven't thought of."

"Young Joe McCurdy," his father said, "was not a business type. He left detail to others. I know that he felt his brother in San Francisco was far more competent in financial matters than he was. The point I am making is: Was Joe Jr. even notified officially of the probate of his father's estate, or did he just assume that Paul would handle everything?"

"I don't know, sir."

"If he was not notified," his father said, "and if it could be shown that by the oversight he was in some way hurt, then there might be a handle with some leverage."

"I hadn't even thought of that," Billy said. He smiled. The old man was sharp. "Point one. Point two?"

"The old gentleman himself," Henry Gibbs said, "old Joe McCurdy. Maybe you have gathered from the little I've said about him that it was damn the torpedoes, full speed ahead? He didn't give a damn what most people thought of him, and he never bothered to explain why he did what he did. Those in the know, who counted in his world, usually understood his motives, and usually admired his courage and his ingenuity. But to some people, a lot of people, he seemed like a financial madman. The line between eccentricity and madness is a very shadowy one."

Billy was smiling. "I am beginning to see point two," he said. "A will made by one of unsound mind—"

"Exactly." Henry Gibbs paused. "And there is one more possible direction for investigation. No, two. The first: while as far as I know there was no estrangement between old Joe McCurdy and young Joe, I think there is little doubt that Paul, the successor at the bank, even though considerably younger, was the closer to his father, and might have exerted some influence on the making of the will. Whether that influence was undue, I have no idea, but it is a matter to think about."

Billy was smiling again. "Yes."

"And then," Henry Gibbs said, "there is the trust itself. Opinions differ here, but at times it has been held that when the trustees and the beneficiaries are one and the same, there exists no legal trust. Here we have a third trustee who is not a beneficiary, the bank's trust officer, and that might alter the situation. Still I think the point is worth pursuing."

"Yes," Billy said. "I've got a lot to learn."

"Merely things to think about against the possibility," Henry Gibbs said. And then, smiling once more, "With the client you have, I think you are going to do a great deal of learning out of necessity."

"Yes, sir. In more ways than one."

Billy went back to his own, smaller office, sat down at his desk, and stared at the far wall with thoughts of Liz again crowding his mind.

If in their lovemaking last night she had been merely doing what she had denied, giving him her body as a kind of consolation prize, then she was an actress without peer; and that he doubted. There had been an urgency in the way she held him, clung to him as if out of need, that belied sham; and the look in her eyes this early morning when she had seen him to the door was not the look of a woman who was glad the night was past. He was sure of that. Then, he thought, why do I have to keep reassuring myself?

He roused himself as the phone buzzed. It was Marty. "Cousin Bruce arrived," he said. His voice was matter-of-fact, holding no overtones that Billy could detect. "I picked him up this morning at his hotel, brought him here, gave him my father's car, and went with him out to the plant."

Billy put thoughts of Liz aside. "And Jordan?"

"I thought he was going to have apoplexy." Marty paused. "And now there is nothing to do but wait. Unless you have ideas?"

"Things to think about, but nothing to do." Many things to think about, only some of them legal.

Marty surprised him. "Have you given thought to what we do if Bruce's report is bad? Like taking a good hard look at that will and the trust just in case we need money, and think we want to take a run at them?"

"I have some ideas in that direction. They're going to take study."

"*Bueno*. Carry on."

"Marty." Billy hesitated. He leveled with me, he told himself; I owe him that, even if it did hurt. "I saw Liz last night." Pause. "I took her to dinner."

There was silence on the line. "And?" Marty said.

He could not bring himself to put into words what had happened there in Liz's small house. The fact of the matter was that he still found it almost unbelievable. He sat silent.

Marty's voice said, "I see." The line went dead.

22

Paul sat in his study with after-dinner coffee and a pile of papers on the desk in front of him. He had placed a call to the Copley in Boston, but Mrs. McCurdy had not yet arrived. Yes, her reservation was firm, and flowers had already been delivered to her room. Traffic through the tunnel into town from the airport, the deskman said, was sometimes impossible, and that was probably the explanation. He would see personally that Mrs. McCurdy had the message.

Paul sat now, waiting for Susan's call, wondering what he was going to say, and all the while staring at the pile of papers and digesting the facts they contained.

Wally Trent had gone right out on a limb, of that there was no doubt. And the West German bank's closing its doors with no warning had cut the limb right off at the trunk. It was what came from playing in the other fellow's yard, in this instance wheeling and dealing in, of all places, Europe.

"Never bet a man at his own game." How often had he heard old Joe McCurdy say that? "I've done it once or twice, and I've been goddamn well burned each time. Stick to the rules you know, and then your edge is that maybe you're a little smarter than the other fellow. Or maybe you're willing to hang in a little longer when the going gets rough. If he knows you aren't going to quit, ever, you've already won half the battle. But if you get in a strange game, you don't know whether you're being a damn fool or not by hanging on, and then the advantage is all to him."

Well, here in these figures was the proof of the old man's predictions.

It had looked good for a while. Trading through Switzerland, switching back and forth between currencies, turning a point gain here and a point gain there, the operation Wally Trent had conducted had looked good. Better than good. But the West German bank had closed its doors unexpectedly right in the middle of a business day with McCurdy National funds in it and no way to get them out immediately, if ever.

They hadn't been the worst hit. A bank up north was caught with over $22 million in that same German bank, more than double the McCurdy loss. But that was small consolation.

My fault, Paul thought. I let Wally operate on too loose a rein. I was thinking of too many other things, father's death for one, and the details of starting to settle his estate. But that is no excuse. There is no excuse. All credit and all blame in the end lands on my desk, and here it stops.

And now? Paul knew what his father's reaction would have been; he could almost hear the words. "All right, so you fell on your face. Not Wally Trent—you're responsible for what the troops do. So the only thing to do is pick yourself up and go ahead. No point in denying anything. It's all there for anybody who can read a balance sheet to see. McCurdy National got taken. But provided you don't blow a few more like that, it isn't quite the end of the world. It just seems like it."

But what would Charles Goodwin's reaction be when he saw the figures and knew the true extent of the problem? That was the question. Paul reached for the phone as it rang.

"The flowers are lovely," Susan's voice said. "Miss Soong has good taste."

Should I have tried to choose them myself? Paul asked himself. I don't know one from another. "I hoped you would like them." Inane comment. "How was your flight?"

"Fine, just fine."

"Look—" Paul began, and then stopped, wondering what he had thought to say. He was not usually at a loss for words, and the feeling was uncomfortable. "Do you think you'll find what you are looking for?" he said. It was the first sensible bit of conversation he had managed.

"I don't know, Paul."

Here at least was a beginning. "Do you know what it is?"

"No. Maybe just—peace."

"You don't find peace here?"

"You are—maneuvering me into saying things I'm not sure of."

"I'm sorry." He stared at the papers and tried to put their information from his mind. "It's quiet here. Dinner was a lonely meal."

"I'm sorry."

"Both of us sorry," Paul said, "doesn't it seem we ought to be able to do something about it?"

There was no reply.

"If I could," Paul said then, "I'd come to Boston."

"I think I would like that." For the first time her voice held animation. "We could rent a car, drive up through New England, see the colors. They are beautiful now. They—"

"Susan, I can't. I'm sorry, there is too much here I have to deal with. More than usual. Please try to understand."

"Is there no one else? Must it always be you?"

"This time I'm afraid there is no one else." Aside from Wally Trent and Charles Goodwin, he thought, there is Jim, and what Bruce is doing down in Los Angeles, which means Marty; all things that demanded personal attention. I could tell her about Jim, he thought; and that would bring her back; the twins' troubles have always made her drop whatever she was doing. He rejected the thought. It wouldn't be fair. "Maybe in a little while," he said, "when some of these matters are cleaned up, we can get away."

"The fall colors will be gone."

"Mexico," Paul said, "or the islands. And there is always Pebble Beach. You haven't played much golf lately. Neither have I." He waited but there was no answer. He was, he thought, floundering in darkness. "Damn it, Susan, what is it you want?"

Another long pause. Then, slowly, "I'm sorry, Paul. Good night." The line went dead.

Paul hung up and sighed. So what do we do now? His eyes were still on the papers. Wally Trent I can deal with, he thought; and one way or another Charles Goodwin and Jim will be dealt with. Even Marty, if it comes right down to it. But your own problems are the ones that defy solution, maybe because you look at them from the inside, like a man in a cage, and your view of the whole is incomplete. Maybe—

The telephone rang and he picked it up quickly, hope rising. But it wasn't Susan. "It's Alan. I have a problem for which I can't find an answer in the medical books. Can you spare a little time, or are you and mother—?"

"I'm here alone." Strangely, the words came easily. "I'd welcome company."

He had one more look at the papers before he locked them into his attaché case. Tomorrow Wally Trent, unpleasant chore which could not be avoided.

I could fire him, Paul thought, and that would obviously be punishment. Instead, I'll find a place for him where he can do no further harm, let him down as easily as I can. And yet, where was the difference? Either way I'm branding him a failure, destroying once and for all the bright hopes and dreams he probably started with, pushing his face right down into the dirt.

He stood up wearily and pushed the desk chair back into its place. So be it. There was no other way, and no one else to do the executioner's job. And after that job was done, there would be Charles Goodwin to deal with. He went to a cupboard and took out the brandy decanter and two balloon glasses. He had been honest when he had said he would welcome company.

Alan wore a turtleneck, a light wind jacket, flannels, and loafers. He stretched out in one of the visitor's chairs and cupped the brandy glass in both hands. "It's been a long time since I came running for help, hasn't it?" He wore a wry smile. "Rhetorical question. No answer required." He came straight to the point. "I have girl trouble. She is a pediatrician, and we have been having a thing." He studied his father's face. "What used to be called an affair."

Paul permitted himself a tight little smile. "Yes."

"The only problem," Alan said, "is that my name is McCurdy, and neither of us can forget it." He paused. "My grampa lowered the boom on her grampa, and isn't that silly? Like a mountain feud. What do you do about that?"

"Do you want an answer?" Paul said. "I haven't the faintest idea."

Alan sniffed his brandy, tasted it, set the glass down. He said at last, "I guess I expected—omniscience." Again that wry smile. "You grow up having the idea in the back of your mind that there is an answer to every question, and that your parents have it."

Could he remember the same? Paul asked himself. And the answer was yes. Old Joe McCurdy was always there, looming large, with what seemed infinite wisdom to resolve all problems. But I am not like that, he thought; I am not cast in the heroic mold. I have my own problems, for which I can't find solutions either. "Sorry to let you down," he said. And then, "What's her name?"

"Nancy. Nancy Wilson."

"And obviously this—thing means a great deal to you. Does it to her?"

"I thought so." Alan studied the floor. "I still think so." His head came up suddenly and he looked again at his father. "Is that what you're saying? That if it means enough to both of us, then the other bit doesn't matter?"

It wasn't at all what Paul was saying, but it seemed to make sense, and it amused him that he was willing to take the credit. "Could be," he said.

Alan's face had brightened. "You may be right," he said. "Perfectly simple, even obvious, but I looked right past it and I guess she did too. Thanks." He looked around. "Where's Mother?"

There was no point in evasion. "In Boston. She flew there this afternoon."

Alan sat quiet, their roles suddenly reversed. He watched his father's face. "I see a patient," he said slowly. "He has a problem or he wouldn't have come in. But he doesn't tell me the whole problem, because he's afraid it might turn out to be serious and he's afraid to find that out." He paused. "Wasn't this a sudden trip? She didn't say anything about it."

He ought to have resented the questioning, Paul supposed, but he did not. Instead what he felt was a measure of relief that the matter could, in fact now had to, be brought out into the open. "Very sudden," he said. "I found out about it when she telephoned me from the airport. Her flight left ten minutes later. I have no real idea why she's gone."

Alan picked up his brandy glass again and held it in both hands. "I have." He looked up. "The menopause. Some women aren't badly affected. Others have one hell of a time and do strange things. Mother—Dr. Williams could prescribe for her. He probably has. I doubt if she even bothered to have the prescription filled. She thinks meddling around with body chemistry is—immoral. I wish I could help."

"So do I," Paul said.

He thought of calling Susan again after Alan had left, and decided against it. If I could go there, he told himself, see her face to face, talk to her, maybe even that trip up through the fall colors, just the two of us with no telephones, no problems . . . But the fact was that he could not. Not now. And maybe later would be too late. He hoped not. He would just have to wait and see.

He turned out the lights and went upstairs to bed in a despondent mood.

He was in his office early the next morning. To Miss Soong: "Mr. Trent now, please. And no interruptions." He walked into his own office and closed the door.

It was, he thought, a hell of a way to start a day, but postponing unpleasantness never helped either. His father had made that point clearly:

"Make a list of the things you don't want to do but have to, and do them first," the old man had said. "Otherwise they're going to keep nagging at you and interfering with your judgment in other matters. There is nothing worse than putting off the inevitable."

When there was a knock on the door and Wally came in, Paul

made no move to rise from his desk. No false friendliness; this was going to have to be strictly business. "Sit down, Wally. You don't look very good. A cold?"

Wally's smile was wan. "Maybe that's it." It was not; it was hangover pure and simple, and why couldn't he say it right out? Because I know what's coming, and I don't want to make it any worse than it is by admitting that I've been drinking too much these last few days. "Lots of colds around," he said.

Paul had the pile of papers from his attaché case on his desk. "Here's the audit, Wally. You probably know what it shows. If you don't, you should." He tried to keep his voice quiet and almost matter-of-fact. It was uphill work. The man had been damn reckless, and that was all there was to it.

"If it hadn't been for that German bank—" Wally began.

"That," Paul said, "was what pulled the trigger, but you had been loading the gun for quite a while. Just on the odds, sooner or later something was likely to happen."

Wally was not going down without a fight. "Currency trading is done all the time. You know that, Paul. And through Zurich we had the best advice available. We showed good profitability at first and for some time. The figures show it—and then the roof fell in. I have to admit that."

"We were outsiders, Wally," Paul said. He ignored the word "profitability," which he detested. "How many Swiss banks were caught with funds inside when Herstatt closed its doors right in the middle of the day? Or German banks? As far as I know, none. But we were. And Seattle was."

"Things happened pretty fast."

"We were playing in a fast game," Paul said. "And I'm not sure all the cards were always on the table."

"You okayed our going through Zurich."

"So you say. It doesn't matter. The blame is not the important thing," Paul said. "I'll take that. All of it. What is important is the lack of judgment these figures demonstrate." He pointed with his forefinger at the pile of papers.

It was going to be just as bad as he had feared, Wally thought; and there was an unpleasant empty feeling in his stomach. Hangover or not, he should have choked down some kind of breakfast. With a little sustenance inside, you didn't feel so—lost. "Okay," he said, "I called some wrong. It happens. I'm not Jesus Christ. I make mistakes. So I'll play it a little more by the book from here on out. Is that what you want?"

Was the man actually misunderstanding, Paul asked himself, or was he being deliberately dense just to make matters more difficult? Or stalling?

He heaved himself out of his chair and walked to the windows that looked out over the lower part of the city. Sounds of traffic reached him faintly; people going about their everyday affairs, oblivious, of course, to what was happening up here. And even if some had known, would they care? Foolish question; man does ask, and only idly at that, for whom the bell tolls.

He turned to face the office again. "There isn't going to be any 'from here on out,' Wally," he said. "I think you know that." In the silence he walked back to his desk and sat down.

That empty feeling threatened to turn into nausea. "No mistakes allowed, is that it, Paul? All hits and runs; no errors?"

"You know better." Paul's voice was flat. "It is, and it has always been, a matter of percentage. For a long time your percentage of good calls to bad was high."

"Thanks."

In a way, Paul thought, Wally's reaction was not unlike Jim's. For the same reason? Resentful defiance arising from a knowledge of guilt? Perhaps. But it made no difference at the moment. "But that percentage has been slipping, Wally. You know it as well as I do. And now this. What would you do if you sat here at this desk?"

Wally took his time. He said at last, "What I would do if I sat there doesn't matter a fuck, Paul. All that counts is what you are going to do. You're the one with the clout." That feeling of nausea was growing.

What was it his father had said? "When you come down to the bone, boy, the only thing to do is lay it right out in the plainest language you can so there is no misunderstanding, because the man you're putting down is going to look for loopholes he can hope to crawl through, and that only makes it worse. That's no time to try to let him down easy."

"What I am going to do, Wally," Paul said, "is call Ted Waldo in from New York to take over our foreign operations. When he goes out the first time, I'll want you to go with him, introduce him around. In the meantime—"

"Yes," Wally said, "there's always the meantime, isn't there?" The blow had fallen as he had known, but never believed, it would, and for the moment he was stunned and angry. The real reaction would come later.

"In the meantime," Paul said as if Wally had not spoken, "we have our problems in the wine country. I want you to get together with Charlie Waters and see what those problems are. He's a bright young boy, but I'm afraid this case may get over his head, and he'll need your kind of experience to guide him." There, it was done. Now the protests, maybe the recriminations—well, he could stand them.

Wally surprised him. He got slowly out of his chair, and said, his voice not quite steady, "I don't suppose there would be any use in—making a plea?" He shook his head, answering his own question. "No. You said it yourself. The McCurdys are born sons of bitches. Okay. Is that all? Well then, have a good day," he said, and walked out the door without a backward look.

Paul sat quiet for a long time, and at last sat forward to open the intercom switch. To Miss Soong he said, "I want to speak to Mr. Goodwin, please." It was better, far better that he make the advance; it was going to be difficult enough regardless.

Charles Goodwin's voice was expressionless. "Yes?"

"I have the figures on the foreign operation we discussed," Paul said. "They aren't good. I have relieved Wally Trent, and I am bringing Ted Waldo in from New York to take over. I promised to keep you informed."

"I see." There was still nothing in Goodwin's voice. "I think we had better have a talk, Paul."

"As you like. Perhaps lunch?"

"I don't think so. I think we'd better have our talk in private. Let me see the figures and look into one or two other matters. Then I'll come to your office."

23

When Walter Jordan walked in, Bruce was in shirt sleeves, necktie loosened and sleeves rolled up, working away at a desk printing calculator in the small office he had been given. Jordan stood for a few moments watching. Then, in as offhand a manner as he could manage: "How is it going?"

Bruce leaned back in his chair. "It marches." The job was easier, really, than he had anticipated. Owen Waterson and his people knew their business, and in the time they had had, the information they had accumulated and digested was both comprehensive and immense. It remained for him merely to fit it together and make his judgment.

"I think I could tell you what you are going to find," Owen Waterson had told him in his dry way with no resentment at all. "But you were sent down here to see for yourself. In your father's position, I would do the same, send a man I could trust rather than take the word of strangers. I think you will find all you need, but if you do not, do not hesitate to call on me." He even smiled. "I am happy to be of service to McCurdy National."

Now Jordan said, "Everything you need?"

Bruce smiled. "All I could ask for." Jordan seemed like a nice enough guy, maybe a little stiff and formal, but, then, Bruce could think of a number in the San Francisco home office who also walked around wearing self-important frowns, and considered what they did as of far greater urgency than anything that could possibly happen on, say, the old man's twelfth floor.

And he, Bruce, could see that Marty would not take to Jordan's kind. Marty was probably used to more freewheeling types who tended to let themselves go. As a matter of fact, Bruce thought, I rather like this Jordan guy. He is in a spot, and that alone could make him as uptight as he seems to be.

Jordan sat down on a straight chair, took off his glasses, and with the always present clean breast-pocket handkerchief began to polish them. He did not look at Bruce as he talked. "Marty's father's death was—ah—unfortunate." He did look at Bruce then. "Your uncle, of course." He put the glasses back on and tucked the handkerchief away. "His death precipitated this—flurry of, shall I say, concern?" He seemed to wait for comment.

"That could be the word," Bruce said.

"Marty," Jordan said, "knows little or nothing of the manufacturing process. I have told him so. He's familiar with the shop, I'll give him that. Since he was only a boy he has had the run of the plant. But never any of the responsibility, and accordingly none of the understanding that goes with it."

Bruce said nothing. He had seen his father do the same, just sit and let the other fellow talk himself out. It was a useful ploy.

"Marty," Jordan said, "can be quite—forceful, even blunt. I think that when the rough edges wear off, he may be quite useful here—if he doesn't tire of routine, as his father did, and go off in his own somewhat frivolous directions." Jordan smiled. "Sailing," he said, "and, I understand, swimming in the ocean, that kind of thing. You, I understand, went directly into the bank from business school?"

Bruce smiled. "More or less."

Jordan nodded approvingly. "The fourth generation of the family. There are not many who can say the same. Have you seen Marty?"

"Not since he brought me out here the other day." Bruce paused. "I'm having dinner with him tonight."

Jordan stood up. He said casually, "Of course you will bring your report to me when you have finished."

So that was it. "Sorry," Bruce said. "The report goes elsewhere."

Jordan stiffened. "I am the general manager here, young man."

"So I understand."

"Then?"

"The report goes elsewhere." He said it without emphasis.

"I must insist—"

"You're wasting your time, Mr. Jordan." Bruce sat up in his chair. "Excuse me." He swung the chair back to face the desk, presenting Jordan with his broad back. He began again to punch the keys of the desk calculator, with his left hand turning page after page of Waterson's neat handwritten and Xeroxed figures.

Jordan took a deep breath. "Now, see here—" he began.

Bruce's chair swiveled with astonishing speed. Bruce looked up, and for a moment the McCurdy temper showed. "Get lost. I'm busy," he said.

Jordan swallowed once, twice, turned and left.

Owen Waterson came to the small office in late afternoon. He laid papers on Bruce's desk. "Final inventory figures," he said. "Manufactured parts and assemblies, and raw materials on hand. You may find them—ah—interesting."

"In what way?"

Waterson hesitated.

"Sit down," Bruce said. He leaned back in his chair. "Maybe you'll tell me what's on your mind. As a favor."

Waterson sat down slowly. "I am reluctant to make judgments. I was asked to do an audit, not to evaluate it."

"But?" Bruce tapped the new papers. "These, for example?"

"It is only," Waterson said carefully, "that the inventory seems—excessive."

"Do you mean," Bruce said, "too much capital tied up in inventory for a plant this size?"

Waterson acknowledged the point with an almost perceptible nod. "That is—part of it."

"And the other part?"

Waterson sighed. "I have a friend at Coast Aircraft," he said. "He is head of their planning department." He produced his tight little smile. "We have a golfing foursome every Sunday, weather permitting." It seemed important that he dot every *i* and cross every *t*. "I happened to ask him some weeks ago what Coast's production schedule for the air bus might be after the aircraft is in full production. He said that with the orders they hoped to get, they might reach a production rate of one aircraft every two weeks." He was silent, waiting to see if this young man representing one of the large banks in California could put fact and inference together.

Bruce could. "And the inventory of parts, assemblies, and raw materials for Coast is out of line with that rate of production?"

Waterson stood up. "There is what amounts to a five-year supply of some assemblies already completed," he said. "I would consider that excessive."

As did Marty that evening over dinner in the Stone Canyon house. He set down his knife and fork, looked the length of the table at Billy Gibbs, and then back again at Bruce. "You're sure?"

"If Coast's production schedule is as Waterson understands it, yes." Bruce had gone out into the plant to see for himself. "One of the assemblies," he said, "are required two-per aircraft. A production rate of one air bus every two weeks is twenty-six aircraft a year; fifty-two assemblies required. There are two hundred and fifty assemblies already completed."

"Jordan," Marty said after a moment, "has lost his mind. Even allowing for spare parts, that's far too many. Engineering changes, and there are always changes on a brand-new plane, could obsolete the whole lot."

Billy said, "That didn't quite come out in the figures we were shown." After his telephone talk with Marty, and the fact of his night with Liz understood between them, he had been surprised to be asked here for dinner tonight. Now, he thought, he understood; it was not purely a social occasion. "Maybe we didn't ask the right questions."

"That," Marty said, "is why we have the expert." He looked again at Bruce. "What else can you tell us?"

First Jordan, now Marty wanting to see his report. "I'd rather you got it from my father," he said.

"I'd rather get it now." Marty paused. "In a sense, you're working for us."

Jordan had implied the same. Bruce smiled and shook his head. "The bank pays my salary," he said.

"Damn it—"

"He's right, you know," Billy said.

Marty looked at them both and then smiled suddenly. "Okay. We wait for the word from Montgomery Street." He tasted his wine. To Bruce: "What else can you tell us about Jordan? Has he been giving you a bad time?"

Bruce smiled again. "No trouble."

"And how about the San Francisco family? Bring me up to date."

Bruce left early in Joe McCurdy's car. "Come by here tomorrow," Marty said. "Leave the car and I'll drive you to the airport." They shook hands. Marty walked back to the study, where Billy waited, and sat down. "Now," he said, "let's have our talk."

He might have known, Billy told himself; sooner or later the subject of Liz would be laid right out on the table. He found himself eager to get to it. "You are talking about Liz, I suppose," he said.

"I am." The evening's ease was gone.

"All right," Billy said, "make your point. Your case isn't a particularly good one. I've known her a lot longer than you."

"That doesn't matter."

"True." Billy kept to a reasonable tone. "When you want something, nothing matters, not even that I was in San Francisco when you made your play. Some people would say that was sneaking in the back door."

"I'd have done the same if you'd been here."

"Granted. Just as you were here when I took her out the other night. So what's your beef? That you don't like the idea of her—being with me? That's tough. I don't like the idea of her spending the night with you. That sort of makes us even, doesn't it?" Showdown, he thought.

Marty surprised him. All at once the tenseness disappeared, and Marty was smiling. "You have a point. Maybe I am too used to getting my own way." He stood up. "Let's have a drink." The smile returned. "I don't like it. But then there are a lot of things these days I don't like."

Billy too was standing. "I said it before," he said. "Do you want to get yourself another lawyer?"

"When I want you to quit, I'll tell you."

Billy nodded. "That's good enough. But just remember—it works both ways."

Bruce used the time on the airplane handwriting his report on a yellow legal pad. There was need for a certain amount of haste, his father had said. Well, he could see the reasons now, even if he could not foresee what would happen next.

He took a taxi from the airport to the bank, winced at the fare even though the bank would be paying it, and went straight upstairs to the twelfth floor.

Miss Soong said, "Your father is tied up at the moment."

"I don't need to see him yet." Bruce dropped papers on Miss Soong's desk. "I expect these ought to be typed before he sees them. Then he can call me when he's had a chance to look them over."

And now Polly, who had never really been out of his thoughts. A drink at Gino's. Dinner somewhere. He was back, and it would be as it had been before. Never mind that scene the afternoon he left.

Polly's desk was empty. Not just unoccupied, somehow *empty*. Bruce set down his bag and attaché case and walked into Mr. Markham's office. "Where is Polly Wright?" No preamble; no by-your-leave.

"Miss Wright has left us." Markham paused. "You are stepping a bit out of line, aren't you, barging in like this?"

"You fired her?"

"As it happens, I did not. She left of her own accord. You—" Bruce left him talking to himself.

He stopped at his own desk, picked up the phone, dialed for an outside line, and then dialed Polly's apartment number. There were rings, a number of them, before a recorded voice cut in: "The number you have dialed is not in service."

Bruce hung up, aware that everyone in the large outer office was watching him; he could not have cared less. He picked up attaché case and bag and walked out.

Charles Goodwin was past the sixty-five-year bank retirement age, but Paul, among others, had not yet brought himself to a firm suggestion that Goodwin step out; Goodwin remained the sole link to the bank's legendary past.

Now, sitting in Paul's office, cigar in hand, "This Wally Trent business is distressing," Goodwin said. "I have made the point before, and I would not make it again if it were not for the implications. A loss of this magnitude—"

"We have taken losses before," Paul said. "That isn't to say that I like them. I don't. But I believe we can cover this one. Wally will be put in a position where he can't make any more serious mistakes, and I will keep a careful eye on Ted Waldo."

"And of course you will explain to the board."

"Yes."

"Will you also explain our problems with our wine industry commitments? We are obviously going to take a big loss there too."

"If it's necessary, I will." Easy, Paul told himself.

But Goodwin was far from through. "Even though you do control your father's bank holdings, I'm amazed that you seem to expect no real protest or even criticism from others of us in management. I am —disappointed."

"Charles—"

Goodwin gestured with his cigar. "I'm not a doddering old fool, Paul. I look over your shoulder, as I probably shouldn't. But I helped your father build this bank up, and we made it right through the Depression, the war, and all the nonsense in this country and in the world since. I wouldn't criticize honest mistakes. Everyone makes then, even your father."

Exactly what I told Wally, Paul thought; but it sounds different when you are on the receiving end.

"Someone with the quality of leadership," Goodwin said, "inspires confidence. Your father had it. Even when he was wrong, he inspired confidence. But your handling of this Wally Trent affair, and the wine industry problems, and others—I am afraid I detect a growing lack of confidence in your leadership, and that affects McCurdy National itself, because you are one and the same. This kind of thing often produces insidious side reactions—a loss of momentum, then perhaps a retrogression with unpleasant implications not only for the bank but for the economy of this entire region."

The office was still. "Lack of confidence is epidemic," Goodwin said, "as contagious as the plague, and McCurdy National is woven right into the fabric of this part of the country. The bank's health, good or bad, affects everything and everybody."

Goodwin stood up then. Paul stood with him. Goodwin said, "I would not like to see Joe's son cause a loss of confidence which would hurt what Joe, and in a far lesser way I, built up. I would have to force a confrontation if that happened, Paul. I still have some clout, and if I feel forced, I will not hesitate to use it. Even if it means airing the bank's dirty linen in public."

24

Paul studied Bruce's neatly typed report, and glanced through the sheets of Xeroxed handwritten figures which supported it, while Bruce sat quiet in one of the leather club chairs, trying not to appear to be watching. Paul looked up at last. "It seems conclusive."

"Yes, sir."

Paul produced his faint smile. "An analysis carried out in accordance with best business school methods." He nodded approvingly, and the smile disappeared. "They are in trouble." It was a statement; no question, but it asked for comment.

"They are in too deep," Bruce said, "and they've gone too far and in ways I don't understand. Neither does Marty."

"What do you mean?"

Bruce told about the five-year supply of the one particular assembly. "But that's only part of it. Marty seems to think Jordan has gone in for what he calls gold-plated tooling too."

"Go on."

His father was a good listener; it was a quality Bruce had always envied and tried to emulate. And for a good careful listener you tried to choose your words with care. "Marty explained to me that building airplanes isn't like building automobiles, for example. When you put a new model of Chevrolet into production, say, the tooling you design and order has to be able to produce hundreds of thousands of parts, if not millions, that are all alike. That takes expensive tooling. He mentioned steel dies, that kind of thing."

"I am beginning to see, but go on."

"But if Coast builds, say, three hundred air buses before they change models, that will be a lot," Bruce said. "And if one of the parts McCurdy is manufacturing for them is used only one per aircraft, that's only three hundred parts over the life of the contract, plus spares. It just doesn't make sense to order expensive steel dies to turn out only three hundred or so parts. There are other, cheaper ways of doing it."

"But in some instances Jordan has ordered steel dies? Is that what you are saying?"

"That seems to be it."

"Has he been asked why?"

"I think," Bruce said, "Marty will take care of that."

There were overtones. Paul said, "You think Marty is serious about the plant?"

"That was the impression I got. And Waterson seemed to think so too." Waterson in one of their talks had been emphatic.

"I can only guess what has been going on here," Waterson had said, "but if anyone from Jordan on down has been out of line, I would not like to be in his shoes. Young Marty McCurdy, your cousin, has blood in his eye."

"Marty," Paul said gently now, "has always been something of a playboy. Has he changed so radically?"

"I can only tell you what I think, sir."

"Yes." Paul stood up. "A good job, well done." High praise indeed. "I'll take it from here."

Bruce too was standing. "Yes, sir." He took a deep breath. "Polly Wright has left the bank."

"I heard." The boy, Paul thought, was teetering right on the brink of open rebellion. Have I handled him wrong? "I think I told you," he said, "that I made it a matter of policy to keep informed. For the record, Bruce, I had nothing to do with her leaving. You may believe that."

"She's left her apartment. And no forwarding address."

Paul hesitated. "I am sorry about that."

Bruce took another deep breath. "One question," he said. "Did you send me to Los Angeles to get me away from her?"

Hesitation would be a mistake. "I sent you to Los Angeles, Bruce, to do a job for the bank and for me. You have done it very well." Was that an answer? It would have to suffice. "And now—"

"Okay," Bruce said, "I'll run along." His tone said that he might be back.

Paul sat down again and stared at the typed report. There was about this entire matter, he thought, an inexorability that wrote its own script. From that day on the porch of the Stone Canyon house after the funeral to here and now, events had moved almost with a pattern that could have been foreseen—toward what? I am sidestepping the answer because I know it full well. It is one word: confrontation. With Marty, or with Charles Goodwin, he told himself, still remembering vividly that scene.

He roused himself and leaned forward to open the switch of the intercom. To Helen Soong, "I want to speak to Marty McCurdy in Los Angeles," he said, closed the switch, and sat back again to wait. The siege is about to begin, he thought, and we had better look to our defenses.

It was as before, Marty and Liz in *Westerly*'s cockpit, hatchway opened, sail covers removed, when the waiter came down to the slip with word of a telephone call. "Long distance," he said. "I think she said San Francisco."

Marty smiled at Liz. "Here we go," he said, and headed for the clubhouse.

He was gone for some time. When he returned he stepped down into the cockpit, expressionless, and said, "We wait. Billy's coming down to go out with us."

Liz frowned faintly.

"I called him and told him to come," Marty said. The actual words had been, "Haul your ass down here. We're going sailing and we've got some talking and thinking to do."

"Maybe you don't want me," Liz said.

"You're here. Stay."

Liz hesitated. "Billy and I—"

"I know."

"Okay. I just didn't want to be sailing under false colors. I'll go below and make some coffee."

Billy came aboard in his office clothes. "There're some shorts and topsiders that will probably fit in the hanging locker," Marty said. He started up the engine blowers. "You'll have time to change before we cast off."

They backed out of the slip, swung and powered down the bay, out the channel past the bell buoy that rolled to the long swells and tolled their number. The breeze was up, out of the west, and Marty headed *Westerly* into it and throttled down. To Liz: "Take the wheel. Keep her on the wind." He and Billy went forward along the deck.

Liz watched them, big strong men both, working together with an ease of years of practice. First the big jib, hoisted, sweated taut, left luffing. Then the main, and last the jigger. Marty dropped down into the cockpit. "I'll take her now," and Liz relinquished the wheel.

"Starboard tack," Marty said, and put the wheel over, switched off the engine. Billy handled the jib sheet and the coffee-grinder winch clattered harshly. "Okay," Marty said, "an easy reach. We want to talk." He busied himself with the main sheet, trimmed it to his satisfaction. Billy came aft and trimmed the mizzen. He dropped down into the cockpit.

It was quiet, only the faint thrumming of the rigging and the hiss of water along *Westerly*'s sleek sides. The boat heeled at an easy angle and laid into her work. Marty tucked himself comfortably against the lee coaming, one hand resting lightly on the wheel. "We have the report on the audit," he said. He smiled without amusement at Billy. "You guessed what it would be—bad. I think we both saw it coming."

Liz watched and listened.

Billy said, "How bad?"

"We're top-heavy on inventory, and we've gone in deep on some of that tooling. Coast is having its own problems, so they may be reluctant to accept all that we've already done. We're talking about needing, about a million or so, my uncle says—for starters. *If* we try to keep McCurdy Aircraft afloat."

"And he doesn't think you should try?"

"Paul didn't say that," Marty said. "He leaves that up to us. All he said was that he couldn't see his way to a loan. Money is tight. He says he has some problems of his own. And he doesn't see McCurdy Aircraft as a good risk, period."

Liz thought, I don't think I have ever seen him truly angry before. He is seething now. I can feel it. And yet his touch was light, even gentle on *Westerly's* helm, and his voice had not risen.

Billy, against the weather coaming, long legs braced, said, "Is there more?"

Marty nodded. "Yes. The trust. You called it 'invading the corpus,' didn't you? Letting me take out a piece of my share?" He shook his head. "No dice. I don't think Paul will go for it, and if he doesn't, the trust officer sure as hell isn't going to stick his neck out for me and buck the boss."

"If your own bank turns you down," Billy said thoughtfully, "the chances of getting a loan elsewhere are not very good. I assume you've thought of that?"

"I have." Marty was looking off to windward where a tall sloop sailed on a parallel course. He watched it for a few moments in silence.

"I've given it some thought too," Billy said, "and I don't particularly like the only answer that comes up."

Marty's eyes had gone to the tall sloop again. All at once she had hardened up and was pointing higher now, her lee rail down; and as Marty watched, the man at the wheel gave a light, mocking wave of his hand.

"But it's your decision," Billy said. "Your money. Your family."

Marty said, with a sudden release of the anger he felt, "There is a smart-ass sloop over there asking for a lesson. Get on the jib, Billy. We're going to give it to him."

Liz spoke for the first time. "What can I do?"

"Just stay out of the way."

Billy worked the coffee grinder, Marty handled main sheet and jigger. Close-hauled, *Westerly* took on a sharp heel, and her lee rail began to slam into the swells. Spray flew aboard. Marty, braced against the coaming, squinted at the luff of the big jib, holding the boat as high as she would go and still move well. "Another notch, Billy! Harden up, damn it!"

Liz watched the muscles in Billy's back as he strained against the winch handle. The tiny looseness in the jib disappeared.

Liz turned to look at the tall sloop. She was closer now, trying still, but unable to stay with *Westerly.*

"Have you got one more notch?"

Again those big straining muscles, one more ratchet tooth, another tiny change in the jib's tautness. Spray, heavier now, blurred Liz's vision. She wiped her eyes with the back of her hand. Billy was grinning at her. Why? She had no idea. And then, of course, she did, and she turned to look at Marty.

His face was set, eyes squinting, hands light and sensitive on the wheel, feeling, anticipating *Westerly*'s needs and whims. There was only himself, the boat and the tall sail they were overhauling, all else blocked out.

I understand it, him, now, Liz thought suddenly. It is not in him to give up, ever. She remembered what the waiter had said the day of the phone call telling of Marty's father's death: "He worked our ass off. Him and Billy Gibbs between them . . . what I mean, they were sailing to win."

Always, she thought, in whatever he does, even in as unimportant a contest as this. She turned again to look at the sloop, and as she watched almost unbelieving, the boat came about, and on the port tack paid off, the mast came more erect, and on an easy reach the sloop sailed off—giving up the contest.

"Let's ease off a little, Billy," Marty said. In victory he was still unsmiling.

Billy paid out the jib sheet, cleated it again, came aft and dropped into the cockpit, breathing deeply, but not hard. He watched Marty in silence.

"Paul could lend us the money," Marty said, as if there had been no interruption. "He won't. He could agree to let me take it out of the trust. He won't. We might have to break away from the San Francisco branch of the family, and fight for the money."

Billy said slowly, "You know what that means? It means attacking your grandfather's will which established the trust in the first place." Billy's voice was grave. "It means a dirty, knock-down, drag-out family contest, butting and kneeing in the clinches. It probably means trying to show that your grandfather wasn't playing with a full deck of cards when he drew the will." Billy paused for emphasis. "In short, it means dragging your family right through the mud. Is that what you want?"

"If we go," Marty said, "we go to win."

Liz watched them both. I am forgotten, she thought; there are only two of them. Out of the corner of her eye she saw the sloop, now a mile or more away, sailing off in defeat.

"Your decision," Billy said. "Do we go?"

Marty nodded. "We go."

II

THE TRIAL

25

Susan, still in Boston, saw the item in a column forwarded from the San Francisco *Chronicle*. "McCurdy versus McCurdy," the item began, and went on with scarcely concealed glee to speculate that the prominent McCurdy clan was coming apart at the seams. "The old lion is gone, and now the hassle over the remains of the feast begins."

But there was more too, careful innuendo. "It has also been reported on good authority that McCurdy National, not alone among American banks, took something of a beating when Herstatt closed its doors in Germany. And the recent killing frost in the wine country has not added to the bank's fiscal health. McCurdy National has always been heavily involved in the California wine industry. All in all it would seem that the problems of the world are not confined to distant Washington."

Susan called Paul. "What does McCurdy versus McCurdy mean?" She ignored the rest. The bank was and had always been Paul's bailiwick.

"It means," Paul said, "a bloody and unpleasant fight right out in front of everybody." He tried to keep the bitterness from his voice, and was aware that he failed.

"Is it Marty's fault?"

"Yes. No. The answer probably is maybe." He was trying to be fair, he told himself, and was not entirely sure he was succeeding. A phrase kept repeating itself in his mind: the inexorability of events; and where in that context could blame properly be laid?

Susan's voice changed. "I went to the symphony last night. It was lovely. Schubert, Glazunov . . ." She closed her eyes. Exactly suiting my mixed-up feelings, she thought, and was suddenly furious with herself for no reason at all.

"I can't come to you," Paul said. His voice was gentle. "If you came back here, we could talk."

Susan was silent.

"Have you found your—peace?"

"That isn't fair." The vehemence in her tone was startling.

Paul said slowly, "Perhaps it isn't." He hesitated. "Maybe you are not being fair either. Had you thought of that?"

There was a short silence. "I have thought of it," Susan said. "Good night, Paul." She hung up.

John McKenzie said, "We'll try for Judge Geary. We can expect no favors from him, but at least he won't be prejudiced from the start against you as head of the bank and, in effect, head of the family, Paul."

They were sitting in McKenzie's mahogany-paneled office with its dark walnut and leather furniture; its fine, rich Kermanshah rug on the floor; and the large Fritz Scholder painting on the far wall bringing the wild reds and yellows and purples of the Southwest into the quiet dignity of the otherwise conservative surroundings.

"You call the shots," Paul said. "Marty and I are the principals, but you lawyers are the ones on stage."

"Not exactly." John McKenzie took his time, choosing his words and his thoughts with care. "You and Marty are important, yes. But you aren't the principals. Your father is the main character in this drama, Paul. Everything will revolve around him, and he is going to be very much in evidence in the courtroom."

Paul studied McKenzie's face. "You are worried about what?"

"I am afraid," McKenzie said, "that there is a lot I don't know about your father. I have an idea that there is a lot only a very few people know."

"Such as?" Paul's voice was expressionless.

"I hoped you could tell me."

"What are you getting at, John?"

McKenzie shook his head. "I don't know. Old Joe McCurdy was a flamboyant man. All San Francisco, all California knew that. He didn't seek publicity, but it came to him just because he was the kind of man he was. He said what he thought often and not quietly. You tend to think that you, the public, have seen all there is to be seen of such a man, that he has no secrets, no private life, nothing at all to conceal."

"Go on," Paul said.

"But I don't believe it," McKenzie said. "Not for a moment. Your father was a very complex man, and I think the world saw only as much of him as he wanted the world to see." He was waiting.

"And you think," Paul said, "that in his private life there are matters that could be—embarrassing?"

"Matters," McKenzie said, "that might alter the picture of the man whose will we are going to try to defend. If there are such matters, I don't want to face them for the first time in the courtroom. If you know anything I should know, now is the time to tell me about it."

Paul was reminded of Alan talking about the patient who did not tell his doctor all of his symptoms for fear of finding that they were serious. Not the same thing, of course, but there was a parallel. "I can't help you, John."

McKenzie sighed. "All right. I have to accept that." He drew a yellow legal pad to him, picked up a pencil. "Now here is what we can anticipate, the points upon which they will mount their attack, and the arguments and testimony we will use in rebuttal."

Marty, Billy Gibbs, and Billy's father sat in the father's large office in downtown Los Angeles. "I think your case is coming together," Billy's father said. He smiled. "A case on paper and the same case in a courtroom can turn into two entirely different things, of course, but that is the risk any lawyer takes when he goes to court. Don't underestimate John McKenzie."

Billy shook his head. "No, sir. No way."

Billy's father looked at Marty. "I understand you have worked with Billy on his preparation?"

"I knew the old boy," Marty said. "My grandfather, I mean. I liked him. But if we're going to have to make him look off his rocker, and the facts are there, then that's the way it has to be. The funny thing is that I don't think he'd mind a bit." He smiled suddenly. "He was an arrogant son of a bitch, and I think he would have been the last to deny it."

Billy said, "I had Marty go over both the will and the trust. There isn't anything in the trust that seems odd to him, except that built-in two-to-one majority."

His father said, "But in the will there is?"

Marty said, "A couple of the people mentioned—legatees. I'm learning words." His smile faded. "I never heard of them. Maybe that doesn't mean a thing."

"But we're looking into it anyway," Billy said.

His father nodded. "Better too much information than too little." He was silent for a few moments, obviously with something in mind to say. The younger men waited. The father said at last, "I am going to make an obvious point, because from time to time in the excitement of a trial, a contest, obvious points can be overlooked. The point is simply this: In a will contest, compromise is not a dirty word. Unlike a criminal trial, you are not trying to prove someone's guilt or innocence. Nor are you, as in, say, a suit for damages, trying to prove that negligence was involved. You are dealing with the motives and decisions of a dead man, and while some points can be decided as a matter of law, most will be entirely a matter of judgment. And your goal, as I understand it, is simply to free a sum of money from that trust, not necessarily to destroy the trust itself, although that may be your only course."

Marty, listening, looked thoughtful.

"If you can win your objective without total victory," the father said, "then I think you might do well to give it long and careful consideration. Unconditional surrender has a fine, brave-sounding ring to it, but it is rarely the most sensible solution, particularly in a family-will contest." He smiled. "So much for platitudes. You will fight it your own way. If I can, I'll be happy to help."

Marty drove again out to Coast Aircraft, received his temporary pass, and was escorted to John Black's office. There in the quiet with only the murmuring voice of the great factory reaching them, "I promised to keep you posted," Marty said. "I'll lay it on the line. We're in trouble, and for the present we're not going to get any help from San Francisco."

"I warned you that Coast Aircraft cannot afford to be magnanimous."

"Understood." Marty paused. "But you need what we are producing and are about to produce, so maybe you'll take a small gamble."

Black sat quietly. "Maybe," he said. "I make no promises. What do you want?"

"One of your men, a good one."

"To do what?"

"Run my factory while I'm in San Francisco prying loose the financing we need."

Black raised his eyebrows and smiled faintly. "A little unusual." He paused, smiling no longer. "Your man Jordan?"

"He'll stay for the present, but I want him controlled." Then, for emphasis: "For the record, we have a five-year supply of one of your assemblies already completed and in our stockroom. Does that make sense to you?"

The faint smile reappeared. "Go on."

"There are going to be some layoffs," Marty said, "some tightening up. We're going to have to concentrate on the essentials, which means the things you need most. Your man can see to that. He'll have a free hand. Jordan will do what he's told."

Black leaned back in his chair, looking thoughtfully at the far wall. He said at last, "You are a very trusting young man, in effect putting your factory in our hands."

"Okay," Marty said, "so I'm gambling too. But when you make a decision, do you hedge it around with a lot of ifs and buts that can only get in the way? I'm not asking Coast to take the responsibility for my factory. I'm responsible for it. What I am asking is some competent help so I can turn my back and attend to other things. You'll be helping me, and yourself." His quick smile appeared. "Isn't that the test of a good bargain?"

Black said, "I never met your grandfather, but I gather this was his style too." He nodded and leaned forward to open the intercom switch. "You have a deal. A young man named Hopkins, Jerry Hopkins. You can explain to him what you want, and make sure that your man Jordan understands."

"Jordan will," Marty said. "He'd damn well better."

He walked out to his car, unlocked it, got in, and then just sat for a few minutes staring at the vast Coast plant.

It represented power, the Establishment—as did Paul, secure in his big office above Montgomery Street. Am I being sensible, Marty wondered, in trying to deal with the one and challenging the other? Wrong word. Am I right? That was the question. And the answer had to be yes, or he had no business going on. Think about it, he told himself.

Okay, he was my father, and his crash was not an accident. Privately, Marty had always thought Hamlet's motivations pretty shaky. He saw them differently now. When what had to be murder happened to one of yours, whether it was sensible or not you were involved. It was a gut reaction.

And then there was the factory, which his father had started, for a time built up, and then largely ignored. But it remained his, with his name on it, in a sense his monument just as truly as the McCurdy National Bank was old Joe McCurdy's monument. A vast difference in size, but the principle was the same.

So it was a matter of pride, but you simply did not turn your back and let the whole thing go down the drain carrying with it all traces of its founder. Those pitifully few bits of memorabilia in the safe-deposit box came to mind. Did one live an entire life and depart leaving only those insignificant proofs that he had ever existed? No, if it was at all possible, and he was prepared to do everything necessary to see that it was possible, Marty was determined to keep McCurdy Aircraft a going concern.

So then: Money that could easily be freed at no cost to Paul was nevertheless being withheld. Why? By what right, other than the whim of an old man now dead, did Paul even have the power to control the purse strings? Didn't that deserve testing?

A vicious-looking Coast fight-bomber scudded down the runway, lifted suddenly with a bellowing roar of afterburner, and, tucking its gear into its belly, tore off into the clear sky. Marty watched it until its faint smudge trail had disappeared. Somehow just watching its smooth performance settled matters in his mind.

Okay, he thought, the answer is yes. I am right to fight this. As I told Billy aboard *Westerly*, we go, and we go to win.

As he drove out of the parking lot and started back toward the pass and Stone Canyon he felt looser, easier in his mind than he had in a long time.

Miss Soong's call caught Marty as he was walking out the door of the Stone Canyon house. "Your uncle would like to speak with you. A moment, please."

Paul's voice was uninflected. "I hoped to catch you."

"I'm just leaving. I'll be up there tonight."

"In time for dinner? That's an invitation."

"Billy Gibbs and I are driving up together."

"You alone, Marty. If we fail, the lawyers will have their chance."

"We're pretty far along to stop things now." Too far, Marty thought.

"Do you read history?" Paul's voice was quiet, unemphatic. "Because there is a distinct possibility that World War I could have been avoided, and was not, because all plans were made for launching war, and none for preventing it. I don't believe a talk would do any harm. If you do—" He left the sentence hanging.

"Are you daring me?" Marty was smiling grimly now. "Okay. Where, and what time?"

"My house. Seven o'clock."

"I'll be there."

Going north, Interstate 5 bears left, branching from California 99 just beyond Wheeler Ridge, and runs almost straight up the west side of the flat Central Valley into the Bay area foothills where it joins Interstate 580 for the final run through Oakland and across the Bay Bridge into San Francisco. From Los Angeles the total distance is 381 miles.

Marty drove; Billy sat relaxed in his passenger bucket seat. The soft top was lowered and stowed, and the rush of wind past the Mercedes had a high, triumphant sound, matching Marty's thoughts.

"You're looking forward to it, aren't you?" Billy said.

"Dinner with Paul?"

"That, and the trial." Billy was smiling. "A contest," he said.

"I'm glad the shadowboxing is over, if that's what you mean." Marty turned his head for a quick glance. "Aren't you?"

"Next landfall Diamond Head," Billy said. "That's the way you look at it, isn't it? We've cleared the jetties and almost crossed the starting line and before dark we'll be out of sight of land. Twenty-four hours of working to windward, and then a spinnaker run, or at least a broad reach with the big jib and mizzen staysail all the way to Honolulu." He was smiling still, but the smile held even a touch of sadness. "It isn't going to be that way, clean salt air and mostly sunshine. It's going to be dirty fighting in a dark alley."

"Okay. It'll be just as tough on them as it is on us."

"Granted."

Marty turned his head again for another brief glance. "Then what's your beef?"

Billy's smile spread. "No beef. I'm just being philosophical."

"But you don't like it."

Billy said at last, "To put it bluntly, what we're trying to show is that your grandfather was a loony, and your uncle was a conniving son of a bitch. Do you like that?"

Marty was silent.

"We've got people snooping around into your grandfather's past," Billy said, "going back well before the time when he made out the will. Tomorrow I'll find out what crawled out from under the rocks they've turned over."

"Do you know any other way?"

"No."

"Then that's it, isn't it?"

Billy was silent for a long time. "That's it," he said at last.

Near Lost Hills they stopped for gas. "Take over," Marty said.

"Aye, aye, sir." They grinned at one another as Billy walked around the car and slid in beneath the wheel.

In the passenger seat Marty stretched his legs and leaned his head back against the headrest. "Liz," he said, "will be in Berkeley." His tone was noncommittal. "She's taken that offer at the radiation lab." He looked at Billy. It was their first mention of Liz.

"She told me," Billy said.

"Did she tell you why?"

Billy kept his eyes on the flowing road. "She's—searching. Just like you."

Marty thought about it. "Maybe," he said. "But not you?"

"I think I've found my niche."

"And you're content?"

"I don't know about that, but I'm not unhappy with what I do. Sometimes I think some people have a built-in itch. They can't reach it to scratch, but they keep on trying."

Marty smiled. "You're talking about me?"

"Maybe. When you play to win—"

"Is there any other way?"

"Some people think so."

"And they," Marty said, "are the ones who lose."

They stopped again near Gustine to top off the tank, and switch drivers again. Under way once more, "You said your grandfather was an arrogant son of a bitch," Billy said.

"He was."

"Then you come by it honestly, don't you?"

Marty grinned. "I don't think I'm illegitimate." The grin faded. "Or unreasonable," he said. "Granted, I didn't do a damn thing to earn my share of the old boy's estate, but it comes to me anyway, and does that make it any less mine?"

"If I thought so," Billy said, "I wouldn't be representing you in what would amount to attempted theft."

Marty nodded. "Fair enough. So all we are trying to do is get what is rightfully mine, no? But because an old man now dead thought he could look ahead and know best, we have to fight for it. Okay. So we fight." He glanced questioningly at Billy.

"I signed on," Billy said. "I told you I'd let you know when I'd had enough. But as your counsel, my advice is that you listen to what your uncle has to say tonight, instead of going in with your mind already made up."

"Okay," Marty said. "That's fair enough too. I'll listen."

Marty parked in the street outside Paul's house, and remembered to turn his wheels toward the curb. He went up the steps two at a time. Felix's wife, Teresa, answered the door and held it wide with a large smile and a display of gold teeth. Paul appeared in the study doorway. He and Marty shook hands. "I thought drinks in here," Paul said, and led the way to a portable bar stand.

Marty took bourbon on ice with a little water; Paul a martini on the rocks. They sat in club chairs flanking the fireplace, where a small fire gave off its cheery glow. "Once," Paul said, "they burned coal in the fireplaces and in the furnace in the cellar. My grandfather, your great-grandfather, had a Chinese steward named Sam."

"In this house?" Marty had never before thought of four generations living in this house.

"In this house," Paul said. "It was rebuilt after 1906, but it is the same house." He paused, smiling still, guiding the talk, setting the tone. "Sam was an operator, as well as a very good steward. My grandfather found out that Sam was buying coal for nine dollars a ton and charging the house accounts eleven dollars. He braced Sam with the fact. 'Sure,' Sam said, 'I charge you eleven dollars. You buy coal yourself, it cost you twelve-fifty. I make money, you save money. Good business?' "

Marty found that he was smiling too. "And?"

"Grandfather was a banker," Paul said. "He could compute profit and loss as well as the next man. The arrangement continued. I never knew my grandfather. He was dead before I was born, before your father was born." He paused. "My father took over the bank when he was younger than you are now. It was just before we got into the First World War. I am not waving the flag, Marty. I am merely stating facts."

He was smooth, Marty thought, smooth and easy, setting up nothing that could be challenged, and yet making the point of family continuity, solidarity implied. It was a neat maneuver. "For a youngster," he said, "he did all right."

Paul sipped his drink and set it down. He offered a bowl of salted almonds, took one himself, and chewed it thoughtfully. "He did indeed," he said, "not only for a youngster, for a man of any age. If I am ever in his league, I'll be very proud."

Two could maneuver, Marty thought. "From what I understand," he said, "you haven't exactly gone backward since you took over."

"I have made mistakes," Paul said. Wally Trent came to mind; Wally was never very far from his thoughts these days. Or Charles Goodwin. "And I have done some things that were perhaps—questionable. Decisions have to be made, sometimes without hesitation, quick decisions are more likely to be wrong."

He was leading up to his point, Marty thought, and sipped his bourbon in silence while he waited.

"Something that is generally not understood," Paul said, "is that any fair-to-large-sized business runs itself most of the time. The bank is no exception. We have our routine which copes with most of our business, and decisions from me are not required." He stared into the fire. "And then," he said, "the matter turns up that will not fit into the routine." He looked at Mary and smiled in a deprecatory way. "And as my father said, 'That, boy, is when you start earning what the stockholders pay you.' He was right, of course. He was right more often than not."

"And," Marty said, "I don't fit into the routine?"

"You could," Paul said, "but you don't. Let me explain. If one of our loan officers had gone down to Los Angeles to have a look at your books, any request for a loan from you would automatically have been denied. McCurdy Aircraft in its present condition is a very shaky risk, and we are not that hungry for business. The matter would never even have come to my attention."

Marty said, "Go on."

"But because it is a family matter," Paul said, "I sent Bruce. His report is no different from the one a loan officer would have given, but instead of going into routine for automatic denial, it came straight to me."

"Is there a difference?" Marty smiled. "You've turned it down."

"I have. I was prepared to stretch a little, but I cannot justify this much. I think it was astute of you to have the outside audit made. I think you did the sensible thing in asking us, me, for our judgment on the basis of that audit. You have it. Pouring more money into McCurdy Aircraft would be a mistake." And if I were to become involved in any way in doing it, he thought, it would only be more ammunition for Charles Goodwin.

It was a bitter thought, but one that could not at present be ignored. Rumors—really more than rumors, stories of fact—about the bank's recent losses were already abroad. An open confrontation between the chairman of the board and the president, who was also chief executive officer, could trigger additional speculation about the bank's internal strength. And that could only lead to chaos.

"You think," Marty said slowly, "that I'm just being stubborn?"

Paul smiled. "Apparently you like your answers unvarnished. I am afraid I think you are just being stubborn. The facts are there. Take your audit to any competent financial man, and I am sure you will get the same answer that Bruce came up with."

"Okay," Marty said. "Spring loose some of the money in the trust, my money, and let me go to hell in a hand basket in my own way. Only I won't. There are a lot of things I don't know, but there are parts and assemblies to be made and we can make them and Coast will buy them, and the rest is not important. It was a going business. It can be again."

Paul stood up. He took Marty's empty glass and his own to the bar stand, busied himself with ice and bottles. With his back to the room, "I cannot justify that, either," he said. "A trust is precisely what the word implies. I have a duty to administer the body of the trust to the best of my ability." He turned from the bar stand, walked back to his chair, handed Marty his fresh drink, and sat down. "The size of the trust makes no difference. Money wasted is money wasted, and I cannot be a willing partner in a wild gamble." Logical enough, but of course not the whole reason.

The room was still. "So," Marty said, "we're right back where we started, aren't we?"

Teresa appeared in the doorway. Paul looked up. "Telephone for you," she said. "A Mr. Trent. He says it's urgent."

Paul nodded and stood up. To Marty, "Excuse me," he said, walked to the desk, picked up the phone. "Yes, Wally?"

"I want to talk to you, you son of a bitch."

"Are you drunk, Wally?" Paul said. "Sleep it off and we'll talk tomorrow."

"Okay, I'm drunk. But tomorrow I'll be sober and you'll still be a son of a bitch. I want to talk to you tonight when that Chinese girl of yours can't put me off."

"I've got guests, Wally."

"Send them away."

"I'll see you tomorrow." There was a tone of command evident now. "Make an appointment with Miss Soong." Paul hung up, stood for a few moments looking down at the phone, and then walked back to his chair by the fire. "I'm sorry," he said. He paused, and then answered Marty's question as if there had been no interruption. "I had hoped," he said, "that we were not quite back where we started, or at the least that we could find room to compromise before we actually go to court."

"Tell me why."

Damn Wally Trent, anyway; he was making it as difficult as he could, and it was hard to put him out of mind. Paul said slowly, "I could give you half a dozen reasons, some of them real, some probably specious, but they all come down to one reason and its ramifications." Not quite true, but it would serve. "Two generations of our family built up that estate, and passed it along with definite instructions for its use. Those instructions ought to be honored, not challenged, and in the challenging dragged through the mud. My father—"

"I have said," Marty said, "that he was an arrogant son of a bitch. I don't think you can deny that."

For a moment it was anger that he felt, and then the anger disappeared. "No," Paul said, "I can't deny it." He smiled without amusement. "And there is a great deal of him in you."

"Fair enough," Marty said. His own sudden smile was loose, relaxed. "Then let's say that the old boy would understand perfectly what it is that I'm doing. He might not approve entirely, but I'll bet he'd be interested to see how it all comes out."

26

Judge Geary, in his chambers, was in shirt sleeves and deep in what he called his thinking chair. He looked around the room, at Paul, John McKenzie, Marty, and Billy Gibbs. "I am taking some liberty," the judge said, "and this gathering is strictly unofficial." He looked at Billy. "For your information, Mr. Gibbs, I am acquainted with both Mr. McCurdy and Mr. McKenzie. It would be difficult to find someone on the bench in this area who is not acquainted with both, at least by reputation."

"Yes, sir."

"But," the judge said, "it goes without saying, or ought to, that our acquaintance will not interfere with the conduct of this trial"—he paused and looked at them all—"if trial there must be."

Billy opened his mouth, thought better of it, and closed it again. They all watched the judge and waited.

"I am not going to discuss the pros and cons of this matter," the judge said. "I am not yet sufficiently conversant with the facts. But what I will say, and again let me emphasize that this is both informal and unofficial—what I will say is that I deplore the fact that it has been felt necessary to bring action at all. Not, I hasten to add, because I have any preconception that the action is unjustified, but simply because I would far prefer to see the matter settled in private, away from the glare of publicity, amicably if possible, between the members of this distinguished family." He looked directly at Paul, and seemed to be awaiting comment.

"Marty and I have talked," Paul said. "Our differences, I am afraid, seem to be—irreconcilable."

"Irreconcilable differences, Paul," the judge said, "are frequently the result of just plain stubbornness. There is such a word as compromise. You should know that. All of you should."

"I have heard of it," Paul said.

The judge looked at Marty.

"We talked," Marty said, "as he said. We didn't get anywhere." He disliked being in effect lectured to, even if it was by a judge. He was conscious that Billy was watching him, and the message Billy was sending was clear: this is no time to argue. "We look at things in different ways," he said.

"People frequently do," the judge said. His tone was dry. "But the essence of civilization is accommodation. Otherwise there is anarchy."

For God's sake, Marty thought, platitudes yet! He said nothing.

"I gather," the judge said, "that you two were alone when you talked, Paul?"

"I thought it best." Paul hesitated. "Maybe I was wrong."

"There are no wars as vicious as civil wars," the judge said. "And the same principle applies to will squabbles, families tearing themselves apart." He stood up, and took his jacket from the coat rack. "I am going for a walk. I will be gone perhaps an hour. I leave you four here. When I come back, I hope—it is only a hope, mind you, but a fervent one—that you may have found some ground for compromise." He nodded to them all as he walked out and closed the door behind him.

John McKenzie looked around the office. "A wily bird, our Steven," he said. He sighed. "And I agree with his sentiments, even if I haven't been asked for my views." He looked at Paul.

"Do you think I want a fight?" Paul said. He felt on the defensive, and he resented it. He also felt hampered, unable to maneuver as he might like because of the things that had been happening at the bank. Wally's shenanigans, those unfortunate crop losses in the vineyards, and particularly Charles Goodwin's self-appointed-watchdog attitude had all conspired to limit at least for the present his freedom of movement. Now, in front of these witnesses, he felt like a man in shackles beneath a bright, white light. "Because I don't want a fight," he said. But neither can I compromise.

"Then give me what I need," Marty said.

"You don't know what you need. That's the trouble."

McKenzie said, "Let's slow down. You are both McCurdys. It doesn't show quite as often with Paul, perhaps, but the temper is there. We get nowhere this way."

"It seems to me," Billy said, "that Mr. McCurdy is standing firm on what he considers a matter of principle." He and Marty had discussed the pre-dinner talk of last night. He looked at Paul. "Am I right?"

"You are."

"Compromise is not a dirty word, Paul," McKenzie said. "You have always been a reasonable man."

He was clinging hard to his temper; it was uphill work. And why did thoughts of Susan, the children, as well as Wally Trent and Charles Goodwin, have to intrude themselves at this time like jingles that would not be stilled? He tried to ignore them. "I will say it one more time," he said. "I will not lend the bank's money in a bad-risk cause. And I will not be a party to what amounts to wasting money my grandfather and my father worked hard to accumulate merely because of someone's—whim." He was looking straight at Marty.

"Then we're back to that standoff," Marty said. "I'm willing to settle for only part. You aren't willing to give any at all. You accuse me of being stubborn. What are you?"

"Accusations aren't going to help either," McKenzie said. He looked at Billy. "Do you think you and I could work out some kind of compromise?" He shook his head. "Forlorn question."

"There is something else," Marty said. "Don't I own part of the bank?"

"You do," Paul said. "Or you will when the estate is settled. But your share is part of the trust."

"And the trust is under your control." Marty nodded shortly. "Neat."

Tempers were rising, John McKenzie thought, and he could find no way to prevent it. Paul's attitude puzzled him. It was unlike Paul to take a stand and refuse to budge. Did he realize what his intransigence was going to bring on, the nastiness of a back-alley brawl conducted in open court, splashed through the press?

Marty said unexpectedly, "I'll make one more try," and had their immediate attention, but he ignored the other two and spoke directly to Paul. "At least part of your worry is that my actual manufacturing experience is limited, isn't that so?"

Paul's faint nod was mere acknowledgment, no more.

"I think you're wrong," Marty said. "But let's assume that you do have a point. Then suppose I were to hold still for putting in charge, complete charge, an experienced manufacturing man you would approve of? What then? Would you either lend us money or approve of my dipping into the trust? As a matter of fact, there is a manufacturing man in charge now. I borrowed him from John Black of Coast Aircraft to mind the store while I'm up here."

"A fair proposition worth considering, Paul," John McKenzie said.

Paul understood now how the man under the bright lights must squirm beneath questioning; and how easy it would be to lose self-control. "How often do I have to say it? I consider a bank loan unsound. And as a trustee of my father's will I do not consider that allowing invasion of the corpus of the trust for this purpose is a sound move." Was he sounding pompous? Probably. It was either that or a show of open anger.

Marty said slowly, with unexpected shrewdness, "You've got your back up. So have I." He stood up. "Let's go, Billy." He looked at John McKenzie. "You can tell the judge we tried."

Paul and John McKenzie shared a cab back to Montgomery Street. "Go on," Paul said, "say it. I can almost hear your thoughts."

"You are defensive, Paul, intransigent. Why? I don't think it is merely that Marty strikes sparks."

"Let's just say that I have my reasons."

"Maybe it would help if I knew what they were?"

Along with everything else it was loneliness he felt now. Susan, he thought; damn it, Susan, I need you. Can't you understand that? "I don't think it would help a bit, John," he said.

He left the cab in front of the bank, avoided the open main floor where for all those years his father had maintained a desk, and took the express elevator to the twelfth floor. Miss Soong followed him into the large corner office. "You told me to expect a call from Mr. Trent," she said.

The sooner, the better, Paul thought. He had been too easy on him in their last meeting. "I'll see him whenever he calls."

"He didn't call." Helen Soong paused. "So I checked downstairs. He didn't come in this morning."

Paul sat down at his desk. There were overtones in Helen Soong's usually noncommittal voice. "Go on," Paul said.

"I called his apartment. His housekeeper is in near hysterics." The overtones were even clearer now. "Mr. Trent was ill when she came in this morning. He—couldn't speak, and she called his doctor and then an ambulance. He was in convulsions by the time the ambulance arrived."

Paul said quietly, "Do you know which hospital?"

"University." Her voice was expressionless.

Paul nodded. "Get my son Alan. I want to speak to him." And when the door was closed he sat staring at the far wall, vaguely aware of the sounds from outside. When the phone buzzed he snatched it up and quickly pressed the button. "Wally Trent is in your hospital, Alan," he said. "He—"

"I know. I saw his name, and asked a few questions."

"Well?"

"He'd been drinking," Alan said.

"He had. When I talked to him last night before dinner, he was already—drunk."

"And apparently he took a sleeping pill," Alan said. "Maybe a couple of them. Sometimes you get away with that, and sometimes you don't. Alcohol and sleeping pills—there can be a synergistic effect. Apparently this time there was. He is in a coma and listed as critical, which means it can go either way."

Paul closed his eyes. He said slowly, "Is there anything I can do?" ("You are responsible for the troops." How often had he heard old Joe McCurdy say that? How often had he reminded himself and others concerning those in their command?)

"Not unless you think prayer might help." Alan paused. "I am not being facetious. There are those who believe in it. We see lots of them."

Something else he had never thought about, Paul told himself; his son seeing raw aspects of life that he sitting here in this lofty office had never encountered, grief, agony, despair, life and death in their basic forms stripped of the pretense and polish which his world thought of as sophistication. "Thanks, Alan," he said. "If there is anything I can do, or if there is any definite word—" He left the sentence unfinished.

"I'll see that you hear," Alan said. "I know he's a close friend of yours."

Paul hung up. He was a close friend, he thought, but well before last night's angry telephone call, that was finished. Whose fault? It was a pointless question; the fixing of blame no longer mattered. In his drunken way Wally was asking for help last night, Paul told himself, and I turned my back on him. I will not be able to forget that, no matter what happens.

Marty and Billy Gibbs sat over pre-lunch drinks at a window table overlooking the water and the boats in the crowded slips at Fisherman's Wharf. Out in the fairway a freighter, riding high in the water, swept by outward bound, and Marty watched it idly. Under the great red bridge, through the Gate, and then where? Hawaii? The Philippines? Or more likely Japan for a fresh cargo of automobiles. Her name was probably something-or-other-*Maru*.

"Lines drawn," Billy said, referring of course to the meeting in the judge's chambers. He paused. "Your uncle almost blew his cool. He doesn't like being told he might be wrong."

The freighter steamed out of view. Marty turned back to the table. "Who does?"

"Some less than others. I've made the point before, haven't I?"

"You have."

"And your uncle is going to like even less what we're going to have to say about your grandfather."

"It can't be helped."

Billy picked up his drink, studied it, and set it down again. "We have our nuts down in Southern California," he said, "lots of them. They have them up here too. You've heard about Emperor Norton; Norton I, Emperor of the United States and Protector of Mexico?"

Marty smiled. "Vaguely."

"Twenty years here in San Francisco," Billy said. "He issued his own paper money and his own proclamations. The city loved him."

Marty set his own drink down. "What's the point?"

"By the time we finish," Billy said, "Joe McCurdy is going to be in Norton's class, a lovable old boob not really playing with a full deck of cards. I saw it more clearly this morning in the judge's chamber."

"And you don't like it?"

"Do you?"

"I made an offer to Paul. I've made several. How far do I have to go?"

Billy shook his head. "There isn't any answer to that. You and your uncle are both right, and you're both wrong. It's a funny thing to say, but I think John McKenzie and I could change places without feeling a bit uneasy about it."

"Then look at it as pure exercise. I don't expect fanaticism, just a good workmanlike job of lawyering."

Billy nodded. "You'll get it."

27

In shirt sleeves in his chambers, Marty thought, the judge had seemed ordinary and merely pompous. Now in his anachronistic black robe looking down from the bench, he seemed somehow larger than life, a stern, unyielding representative of a power that was awesome in its magnitude, ubiquitous and omniscient. That all-seeing eye in the Great Seal of the United States seemed to be watching. If Billy Gibbs felt the same, he did not show it.

All during the laborious process of selecting a jury, Marty had watched the judge, hearing only vaguely Billy's and John McKenzie's questions to each venireman going to the matter of prejudice: Was the name Joseph Martin McCurdy familiar? Had newspaper accounts of the impending trial in any way influenced their thoughts concerning the matter at hand? Were there other factors which might influence a prospective juror and render him or her incapable of dispassionate judgment? And so on.

And the judge had exhibited infinite patience, occasionally putting a question himself, but for the most part remaining silent, and attentive. How he did it, Marty could not imagine. For himself it was an effort to sit still, waiting for the action to begin. Even Paul at the other table, he noticed, seemed relieved when at last the jury was seated.

And then the judge's charge to the jury, and Billy's and John McKenzie's opening remarks, to which Marty paid no attention at all, except to watch the twelve faces and their reactions, some open, some scarcely discernible. Like any group of strangers with whom you were thrown in contact, he thought, they would begin to sort themselves out as the days went by, and there was no point in trying to keep them straight in his own mind now. The action was in Billy's hands.

The judge rapped gently with his gavel, and the courtroom was hushed. "You may call your first witness, Mr. Gibbs."

Billy rose. "Thank you, your honor." His voice was clear and strong. "I call Dr. James Burns."

The doctor was well into his seventies, still erect and active, with a shock of white hair and bushy, almost forbidding eyebrows. He took the stand, was sworn in, seated himself, and faced Billy. There was in his attitude not so much antagonism as a clear expression of wariness.

"You are," Billy said, "a doctor of medicine?"

"I am." The doctor had been on witness stands before. "My degree is from the University of California Faculty of Medicine. I am also a Fellow of the American College of Surgeons, and of the American College of Physicians." The doctor paused, smiling faintly. "That is, I was. I'm retired."

"When you were in practice, what was your field?"

Again that faint smile, tinged now with obvious pride. "I was in general practice, what might be called a family doctor. I even made house calls."

There was a faint stir of amusement from the audience. It died quickly.

"And," Billy said, "was the late Joseph Martin McCurdy one of your patients?"

"For the better part of fifty years he was. As was his wife and their children."

"Would you say that you knew Mr. McCurdy well?"

John McKenzie started to rise in objection, and Billy said quickly, "I will rephrase the question, Doctor. Was your association with Mr. McCurdy purely that of doctor and patient?"

"Hardly. I was a guest many times at their Pebble Beach house. Joe McCurdy and I played cribbage perhaps once a week. Occasionally I sat in poker games with him." The doctor paused. "Not often. It was not financially healthy to play poker with Joe McCurdy."

There was again that murmur of amusement. Judge Geary looked around the courtroom, and the murmur died away. The jury, he was pleased to see, was attentive and unsmiling, obviously impressed with the importance of their task. The black man in particular—what was his name? Jensen—wore a look of fierce concentration, and his eyes, following question and answer, went from Billy to the doctor, ignoring the rest of the courtroom. Jensen, the judge remembered, was a postal clerk, a solid family man.

"Was Mr. McCurdy a man of robust health, Doctor?"

"In layman's language," the doctor said, smiling, "I would say he had the constitution of an ox. In almost fifty years I attended him professionally only twice."

"And what were those—occasions, Doctor?"

"The first time was for an acute attack of appendicitis. I performed an appendectomy. After three days he got out of bed and drove down into the San Joaquin Valley—" The doctor stopped. "That is another story. The second time I treated him for a hairline fracture of his right hand. I believe he had broken it—"

"Objection, your honor," John McKenzie said, rising. "The conclusion is at best hearsay."

Judge Geary nodded. "Sustained." To the court reporter: "Strike that portion of the answer. . . . You may continue, Mr. Gibbs."

Paul whispered to John McKenzie, "One of the gardeners at Pebble Beach, probably high on drugs, ran amok. Father clobbered him. That's how he broke his hand."

John McKenzie nodded faintly. In character, he thought.

Billy Gibbs said, "In all those years that you were the McCurdy family physician, you treated Mr. McCurdy on only those two occasions. Remarkable." He smiled as he consulted his notes. He looked up slowly. "Does the date August 23, 1973, have significance for you, Doctor?"

The doctor sat quietly for a moment. "Unfortunately," he said at last, "it does."

There was a small stir in the courtroom, and the judge noticed that the jury moved forward a little in their chairs as if afraid they might miss a word. It was at times like this, the judge thought, that the drama inherent in any trial came to the surface. There would be many such moments as the trial progressed, and given any kind of skillful maneuvering by opposing counsel, it would be an insensitive dullard indeed who would not find himself caught up in the case as in a novel or a play. The Chicano juror, Mr. Leyba, the judge noticed, wore an expression of almost eager anticipation, as if he were watching the throw of the dice, or perhaps the moment of truth when the matador went in over the horns for the kill.

"Will you tell the jury what happened on that date, Doctor?" Billy said.

"I had already retired from practice," the doctor said. "I received a call from one of my younger colleagues. Joe McCurdy had suffered a stroke. He was in the hospital."

"Why were you called, Doctor?"

"Because Joe wanted me. His speech was impaired, but he managed to make his wants plain. To put it mildly, he was a man of strong will, and he had given the attending physicians to understand that if they wanted his cooperation he wanted me on the scene. Hospitals, to one unaccustomed to them, can be places of mystery and apparent impersonality. Joe wanted someone familiar at hand."

Four of the jurors nodded, the judge remarked. He was tempted to nod himself.

"And did you go to the hospital, Doctor?"

The doctor looked at Billy with near contempt. "Certainly."

"Of course," Billy said, and watched some of the near contempt disappear. He is a touchy old boy, he told himself; take it easy, you don't want to get his back up. He took his time consulting his notes. "Will you explain to the jury, Doctor, please," he said, "just what is meant by a stroke?" He paused. "In layman's terms, if that's possible."

"In general," the doctor said slowly, "a stroke is a vascular accident in or about the brain or brain stem, resulting in the shutting off of the blood supply to a portion of the brain. There is almost always paralysis and coma, both of which may be short-lived or of considerable duration." He paused. "A stroke may, of course, be fatal."

Billy waited for the explanation to be absorbed, understood. "Obviously," he said then, "Mr. McCurdy's was not, since he lived a reasonably active life for almost two years after the event."

The doctor merely nodded.

"You mentioned paralysis, Doctor," Billy said. "Could you enlarge on that, please?"

The courtroom was still. At his table with John McKenzie, Paul watched and listened, understood full well what was coming, and could see no way to prevent it. He looked at McKenzie. McKenzie shook his head faintly, and the message was clear: hear him out; there is no other way.

"The paralysis," the doctor said, "is a hemiplegia—that is, a loss of motor power of the muscles on one side of the body. The face, tongue, arm, and leg are involved. At first the paralysis is usually complete, but with physiotherapy, and determination, unless the brain damage has been too extensive and severe, at least some muscle power can be made to return."

"And in Mr. McCurdy's case, Doctor?"

The doctor shook his head slowly, smiling in memory. "I don't believe that Joe knew the meaning of the word 'can't.' He was going to walk again and he was going to regain use of his left arm and he was going to stop mumbling his words." He paused. "He did. I watched him early on in his recovery. The therapist wanted to hold his arm as he tried to walk without other support. Joe would have none of it." The doctor smiled again. " 'Get the hell out of my way,' is what he said, and he made it by himself clear across the room. 'Now you can give me a hand back,' he told the therapist. 'I'll take a little breather and we'll try that again.' "

To Marty, Billy's careful step-by-step questioning was producing only a picture of an indomitable old man who knew, and would always know, precisely what he was doing, which was not at all what he had expected. You're building him up, he thought; and you should be tearing him down. How in hell—? He stopped the thoughts and listened carefully.

Billy was saying, "Are there other effects than paralysis, Doctor? Mental effects, perhaps?"

Here it is, John McKenzie thought, and there is nothing in the question I can object to.

The judge listened quietly. Young Gibbs was handling it well, he thought, and almost wished that it were not so. The implications of the question were not lost on the jury; that much was clear. Ms. Carstairs, for example, pursed her lips and nodded faintly, and her expression seemed to say that of course there were mental effects, as any fool would have understood. Ms. Carstairs, small, trim, unsmiling, did not suffer fools gladly, the judge decided. Again he looked at both Paul and Marty, damn fools that they were; it would be a pleasure to knock their stubborn heads together.

"There may be mental changes," the doctor said. His voice held reluctance.

"What manner of changes, Doctor?"

The doctor hesitated. "They may be transitory or permanent."

"Yes, sir. But what kind of changes are they?"

The doctor glared at Billy. Billy watched him steadily. "There may be apparent diminution of intelligence," the doctor said at last, "and loss of memory. But as I said, the changes may be only transitory. In Joe McCurdy's case—"

"Thank you, Doctor," Billy said. "I think that will be all." He nodded to John McKenzie. "Your witness."

In the jury box, black Mr. Jensen settled back in his chair. Mr. Leyba watched still with his almost eager look of anticipation. Ms. Carstairs sat stiff and straight, awaiting fresh developments. Already they are beginning to sort themselves out, the judge thought.

John McKenzie rose slowly, and walked toward the witness stand in a leisurely, almost reluctant manner. "This must be painful for you, Doctor, to speak clinically and as dispassionately as you can of an old, close friend."

Billy was on his feet. "Objection, your honor."

McKenzie turned, smiling. "I believe that you successfully established the friendship, did you not, counselor?"

Judge Geary said, "I believe you did, Mr. Gibbs. Objection overruled. Proceed, Mr. McKenzie."

"If that was a question," the doctor said, "the answer is yes. Joe McCurdy was probably the finest man I ever knew, and—"

"I am afraid, Doctor," McKenzie said, "that we can't very well have eulogies here in the courtroom—which is perhaps a pity. Let us go back a little in your testimony. I believe you said that a stroke is a vascular accident almost always accompanied by paralysis *and* coma?"

"That is the classic definition."

"In Mr. McCurdy's case," McKenzie said, "there was paralysis. You have so testified. Was there coma?"

"I wasn't present. I arrived some time after the event."

McKenzie paused to consider. "How long after the initial seizure, would you say, did you first see Mr. McCurdy?"

"Objection, your honor," Billy said, on his feet again. "The time has not been established. The question calls for a conclusion from the witness—"

Judge Geary said, "Under the circumstances, I believe we can allow this question. I take it, Mr. McKenzie, that you are not pressing for a precise length of time?"

"No, your honor. Merely an approximation."

The judge nodded. "Proceed."

"Was it on the order of a half hour, Doctor?" McKenzie said. "An hour? Longer?"

"From what I gathered from the attending physician and the medical reports," the doctor said, "it was less than an hour from the time of the seizure until I was on the scene."

McKenzie nodded. "And how long before that had you received the telephone call summoning you?"

"Maybe twenty minutes. Maybe thirty. I didn't time it."

"Of course not. At a time like that the hour of the day isn't very important, is it?" McKenzie smiled. "So let us take the shorter time, twenty minutes. If the total time elapsed before you saw Mr. McCurdy and the actual seizure was less than an hour, and you had been telephoned, *at his request*, no, *his demand*, at least twenty minutes earlier than that—" McKenzie paused for emphasis, and glanced at the jury before he continued. "Then it must follow, must it not, that if indeed there was coma, it must have been of very brief duration, only a matter of a few minutes?"

Marty looked at Billy. Billy gave a faint shrug. Nothing to do, the shrug said; for what it is worth, his point is sound.

"Quite brief," the doctor said, "yes."

McKenzie had done his homework. "And is not the length, the duration of coma something of an indication of the severity of the stroke, Doctor?"

"It may be. It frequently is."

"The longer the coma persists," McKenzie said, "the less chance there tends to be for full recovery, that is, the greater chance there is for permanent damage to result?"

"By and large, I would say that is correct."

"Particularly for mental damage to be overcome?"

"That is a pretty broad question," the doctor said.

McKenzie smiled. "Then I withdraw it." He took a few paces away from the witness-box railing, turned to glance at the jury, and came slowly back. "But would it be fair to say that since the coma was of quite short duration, if indeed there was coma at all, which has not been established, then we might tend to believe that what mental damage there may have been was slight?"

"That," the doctor said, "is another broad one. There is that possibility, yes, perhaps even probability. Beyond that I can't say."

"Nor shall we ask you to," McKenzie said. "But we can deal with more tangible evidence, can we not? You testified, and I believe I quote, 'He was going to walk again and he was going to regain use of his left arm and he was going to stop mumbling his words. He did.' Is that not correct, Doctor?"

"That is correct."

"I realize," McKenzie said, "that these matters are not susceptible of measurements as precise as, say, the cost today of a certain stock on the New York Stock Exchange, or the price of butter in a Safeway store. But judgments by qualified personnel can be made. What percentage of recovery would you say Mr. McCurdy made in restoring his legs, his arm, and his tongue to their previous levels of strength and dexterity?"

"The percentage," the doctor said, "was very high. I should say on the order of ninety per cent at least. What disability remained was almost unnoticeable."

McKenzie nodded. "Would it not be logical then," he said, "to assume that his recovery from mental damage, *if indeed there was any mental damage at all,* would have been at least as great?"

Billy was on his feet again. "Objection—" he began.

"Then," McKenzie said, smiling, "I withdraw the question, and I have no further questions, your honor." He walked back to his and Paul's table and sat down. He picked up a pencil and appeared to make a note on a legal pad. "The best we could do, I think," he said. "To go farther might land us in a mare's nest."

"I see your point," Paul said, "but, damn it, his mind was as clear as yours or mine. Maybe clearer. He was making judgments—"

"What kinds of judgments?"

Paul hesitated. "They are neither here nor there," he said, "but he was making them."

McKenzie looked up. Billy Gibbs was on his feet again, and clearly undecided. He said at last, "With the court's permission, it may be necessary at a later time to recall this witness, your honor, but I have no further questions now." He sat down.

"You may step down, Doctor," Judge Geary said. "Thank you." He looked at the wall clock. "I think we might break for lunch now. The court will stand in recess until two o'clock." He rose, and the court rose with him.

28

The restaurant booth was set for three.

"I asked Liz to meet us here," Marty said. He smiled. "Objections?"

"It's your money. For the lunch, and for my time. I thought we might talk."

"Why can't we?"

"You want to talk shop in front of Liz?" Billy shrugged, and suddenly smiled. "I've sat in restaurants in London," he said, "and heard British at the next table talking about the damnedest most personal things as if they were entirely alone in the whole world, nobody near enough to hear what they were saying." He smiled again. "Same thing, I think. You just don't care, do you?"

"Do we have something to hide? It's all going to come out in open court, isn't it? Marty slipped out of the booth as he saw Liz approaching. "And I enjoy her company," he said.

Liz sat between them. "First day," she said. "How did it go?" She looked at Billy. He shook his head, smiling faintly. She looked at Marty.

"I thought," Marty said, "that buster here had struck out." He paused. "It seems he knew what he was doing after all."

"We may have scored a few Brownie points with the jury," Billy said. "Hard to tell. Thank the Lord it is a jury trial. If we were just before old Ironpants alone on the bench, we'd have far rougher going."

Liz said slowly, "And now what?"

Billy picked up his water glass, looked at it, and set it down again. He looked at Liz. "We start laying the groundwork to show that after his stroke the old boy no longer had all his marbles," he said. "And even, if we can get it in somehow, demonstrate that he was never quite the pillar of virtue he was supposed to be, although how

I can manage to make his wild oats germane to the case, I haven't figured out yet."

Liz looked at Marty, her question plain.

"It seems," Marty said, "that I have an illegitimate uncle. He's only four years older than I am." He smiled suddenly. "We wondered about a couple of those bequests in the will: Mary and Richard Harlow. That's what turned up, an illegitimate uncle And his mother, old Joe's mistress."

Liz closed her eyes briefly. "When you're dead," she said, "you are defenseless, aren't you? That's obvious, but I never thought about it before."

"If it isn't grave robbers or muckraking historians," Billy said, "it's lawyers. You can't talk back from your grave."

Marty beckoned a waiter. "On that uplifting note," he said, "let's order. I don't think Ironpants would appreciate our being late."

Liz walked with them back to the courthouse. On the sidewalk outside she and Marty paused while Billy hurried on. "What do I say?" Liz asked. "Do I wish you luck? Or is this like opening night of a play, and is 'Break a leg' more appropriate?"

"I'll meet you," Marty said, "in the St. Francis bar at five o'clock."

Liz shook her head. "I'm a working girl. I took a long lunch hour, but that's it. Back to Berkeley."

Marty nodded. "Then I'll come to you. Make it five-thirty."

Slowly Liz nodded. "Five-thirty," she said. "If you can find the house."

"I'll find it." He too turned away to follow Billy up the steps.

At their table in the courtroom Billy whispered, "Here we go. This is the one who has to stand up." He rose. "I call Millicent Potter," he said.

She was tall and angular, with large hands and feet, and she wore her gray hair pulled tight in a bun beneath a squarely positioned no-nonsense hat. She examined the proffered Bible as if questioning its authenticity, laid her hand gingerly upon it, and swore to tell the truth, the whole truth, and nothing but the truth. Then she sat down and gave her name and a South San Francisco address. She glared at Billy as he approached the witness stand.

"It is *Miss* Potter, is it not?" Billy said.

"It is, and it has always been." Her tone said that no males had ever needed to apply.

In the jury box, Ms. Carstairs showed approval.

"You are no longer employed, Miss Potter?"

"I am not. I have my Social Security and the money I saved. I take no charity."

Billy smiled. "Self-reliance—" he began.

Miss Potter sniffed. "I need no lectures, young man."

Ms. Carstairs seemed on the point of applause.

Billy nodded gravely. "What was your most recent employment, Miss Potter?"

"I was housekeeper at the Joseph McCurdy residence."

"How long were you in that position?"

"Eleven years. I went there right after Mrs. McCurdy's death and I stayed until the old gentleman died." She paused and glanced in Paul's direction. "Then I was—retired."

"By 'the old gentleman,'" Paul said, "do you mean Joseph Martin McCurdy?"

"Who else? Himself."

The courtroom was still. Someone coughed; the sound seemed overloud as in church. The juror of Japanese ancestry, Mr. Sato, the judge recalled, had said, yes, the name Joseph Martin McCurdy was familiar to him; no, he had no prejudice either for or against the gentleman, it was merely that he had read the name from time to time in the newspapers, as who had not? In the jury box now, Mr. Sato's face showed only interest.

We are getting down to the meat, the judge thought. Thank heaven here, unlike many trials, the preliminaries can be brief.

"As housekeeper," Billy said, "what were your duties, Miss Potter?"

"To run the house, the servants, keep the house accounts, make sure that no one cheated or shirked, to order what was needed and see that it was right when it came, when things needed doing, to see that they were done."

From her expression, juror number five, Mrs. Beatty, housewife, was impressed by the list of Miss Potter's duties, the judge thought. Did it follow that she would accept her testimony without question?

"In short," Billy said, "you were in charge, is that correct?"

"No. Mr. McCurdy was. It was his house. I just ran it for him so he didn't have to bother himself with details."

Rebuked again, Billy thought, and managed to stifle a smile. "You mentioned servants," he said. "How many were there?"

"Cook. The maid. The chauffeur. The gardener. Myself." Pause. "And after his—affliction, the nurse."

"They all reported to you?"

Miss Potter's lips were a thin straight line. "Cook and the nurse and I—cooperated." The word had an obviously bitter taste. "The rest did what I told them."

"And you in turn reported to Mr. McCurdy, is that correct?"

"Yes."

"How often?"

"How often what?"

"Did you report to Mr. McCurdy frequently?"

"Once a week. Sundays, before I went to church. He was a busy man. Unless there was something that couldn't wait, I kept everything for Sunday."

"But you saw Mr. McCurdy more often than that?"

"Of course. Every day."

Billy walked to the table where Marty sat, and pretended to consult papers. Then he walked back to the witness stand. "In the early years of your association with Mr. McCurdy, Miss Potter," he said, "did he have any hobbies, golf, perhaps, or fishing? Or did he, for example, take an interest in the garden?"

John McKenzie stirred in his chair, but did not rise.

Paul whispered, "You see the direction he is going, don't you?"

McKenzie nodded. "And he is within his rights, unless he goes too far."

Miss Potter was saying, "Hobbies?" She shook her head. "Like I said, he was a busy man. There're some who play golf and such." She sniffed and glanced again in Paul's direction. "But the old gentleman wasn't one to waste his time in fribbles." She even managed a thin smile. "And as for the garden, why, he couldn't tell one flower from the next. And the only fish he liked came from the Wharf."

There was a murmur of amusement. The judge let it die away of its own accord. He glanced again at the jury. They are listening, he told himself, and a little relaxation will do no harm.

McKenzie rose. "This is all very interesting, your honor," he said, "but I don't see that it is either relevant or material."

You are throwing up smoke, John, the judge thought; you know perfectly well where counsel is heading; but none of the thoughts showed. He said, "Mr. Gibbs?"

"It is our contention, your honor," Billy said, "and we intend to show that after the seizure Dr. Burns described and explained, and despite apparent recovery, Mr. McCurdy was never the same man again."

"That he was not," Miss Potter said. Her chin was up and her voice firm.

"The witness," the judge said, "will only respond to questions. Gratuitous opinions will not be tolerated." He waited for a few moments while the order sank in, and then nodded to Billy. "You may proceed along that line of questioning, Mr. Gibbs."

"Thank you, your honor." Billy turned to the witness stand again. "No interests outside the bank at all, Miss Potter? Is that what you mean to imply?"

"I didn't say that."

"Then perhaps I misunderstood?"

"Like I said," Miss Potter said, "no fribbles, golf and the like. But he liked to entertain. He was a sociable man. Maybe too sociable."

Gently, "What do you mean by that, Miss Potter?"

There was an obvious bad taste in Miss Potter's mouth again. "Cards," she said. "Whiskey. In the morning smoke in the study so thick you could cut it with a dull knife. Up until all hours, but down he would come for breakfast as usual, and off he would go to the bank just as if he'd had the eight good hours a body needs. It's no wonder—"

"We will come to that in good time, Miss Potter," Billy said. He glanced at the jury. On three faces, reaction to Miss Potter's comments on cards and whiskey was clear: Mrs. Beatty, ample and motherly, wore a faint tolerant smile; Ms. Carstairs' expression indicated that men were like that; and one of the four male Anglos—was his name Smith?—grinned broadly, probably out of pleasant recollection of evenings at poker with quantities of beer at hand.

Billy turned again to the witness. "I think it would help, Miss Potter, if we established the routine of the McCurdy residence during those years before Mr. McCurdy's unfortunate—seizure. I take it there was a routine? You mentioned 'breakfast as usual.' "

"Seven o'clock sharp. He was an early riser. He listened to the news upstairs while he shaved and dressed. At the table tomato juice with Worcestershire sauce, lemon, and a touch of Tabasco. Then one six-minute egg, a piece of whole-wheat toast, and one cup of coffee, black. He read the morning paper while he ate."

"Seven o'clock?" Billy said. "So early?"

Miss Potter was not to be interrupted. "Seven-thirty he walked out the door. On all but very bad days, rain and the like, he walked. Real bad days Tim Allen drove him. Tim was the chauffeur, but until the old gentleman's affliction, there wasn't really enough for him to do just chauffeuring, and the Devil finds work for idle hands, so I saw to it that he kept busy. Heavy cleaning, and floor waxing, and window washing and the like." She paused for breath.

"Back to Mr. McCurdy," Billy said. "He walked to the bank, or was driven. He did not come home during the day?"

"Sometimes. His secretary would call. Miss Wood, that was. 'Mr. McCurdy will be bringing three guests, or two, or maybe even five, for lunch.' Usually at twelve-thirty. I'd send Tim down to pick them up." Miss Potter sniffed. "And the cocktail tray would be set out in the study. Always at least one cocktail before lunch." She sniffed again. "And wine with. It was business. Always business. 'Too many ears in town,' the old gentleman told me once. 'Here in this taut ship you run'—whatever that means—'we can talk without thinking about being heard. I am grateful to you.' " Miss Potter paused. "That's how it was." There was a wistful quality in her voice. "Before, I mean."

The judge glanced around the courtroom to the jury box. No one stirred or whispered. They are listening to a legend, he thought, from someone who watched it up close. For as long as any of them could remember, longer, the McCurdy name had been as much a part of California as the missions and the beaches, the Golden Gate and the Sierra Nevada. And now they were hearing firsthand about the home life behind that name, the home life of Joe McCurdy himself.

The judge wondered if the jury members were going to like what they would be hearing later. He knew that he would not. Legends ought to be left untouched, unsullied, he thought.

Billy was saying, "And in the evening, Miss Potter?"

"Same as morning. Unless the weather was real bad, he would walk home. Up and down those hills, no matter, it was all one to him. And his secretary, Miss Wood, that was, would always call me mid-afternoon to say whether he was dining in or out. Considerate, he was." She paused. "Before, I mean."

There was a little silence. "Weekends?" Billy said. "Sunday morning, you have told us about. You made your reports."

"Before I went to church." Miss Potter nodded.

One gathered, the judge thought, that after her report, in a sense a cleansing operation, she went off to worship her God with an easier mind.

"Did Mr. McCurdy go to church?"

"Him?" Miss Potter's tone was incredulous. "Never." Her mouth snapped shut. It was clearly a sore point.

"Tell us about the rest of the weekend routine," Billy said. "Did he rise as early as during the week?"

"Breakfast at seven o'clock sharp," Miss Potter said. "Some Saturdays he would go down to the bank again. Not often, but sometimes. Usually he stayed in and worked until lunch over the papers he always brought home in his briefcase. 'Banks used to be open Saturday mornings,' he told me once. 'It's hard to break the habit.' Saturday afternoons he did different things. If there was a football game either over to Berkeley or down to Palo Alto, he'd be pretty sure to go to that. Or maybe baseball at Candestick Park."

"Alone?"

"I told you," Miss Potter said, "he was a sociable man. He had lots of friends, all kinds. He liked young people. Sometimes we would have a buffet lunch at the house before a football game—maybe eight, ten guests. He loved that." Miss Potter nodded toward Paul. "Sometimes he would come over, young Mr. McCurdy. With his wife. And they would go to the game with the old gentleman. Like that," she summed up.

"Go on, Miss Potter."

"Almost always he had an engagement Saturday night, a dinner, a party, a concert, the opera, and if there was a play in town he was sure to see it. He—lived!" she said.

Billy's voice was gentle. "I think we are beginning to understand that." He hesitated, not certain how to proceed. "Mr. McCurdy was a bachelor—" he began.

"Widower." Miss Potter's voice was firm.

"Of course," Billy said, "widower." It was somehow easier now. "Did he have feminine companionship, Miss Potter? Ladies invited to the house?"

"Never. His wife was dead. Cancer, it said in the papers. There were couples invited to the house, but the old gentleman himself never looked at another woman. 'I'm a lucky man, Miss Potter,' he told me once. It was when I walked into his study not knowing he was there, and he was standing by his desk with her picture in his hands. 'We had a good life,' he said. He never mentioned her again, and I wouldn't have dreamed of it. I just saw to it that her picture frame was kept polished and the glass dusted. Out of respect, you might say."

It was rare, the judge thought, that a courtroom filled with people maintained this degree of attention and quiet. True, Billy Gibbs asked his questions in a clear voice, and Miss Potter's answers were easily heard, which was not always the case. Many lawyers spoke only to the witnesses, and many witnesses tended to mumble as if afraid their answers would actually be heard. How many times had he had to admonish witnesses on behalf of court reporters or jurors unable to catch the testimony? Not with Miss Potter. With faith in the Lord and in her own rectitude, he judge thought, Miss Potter spoke out fearlessly, let the chips fall where they may. The judge envied her her self-confidence.

"Aside from your reports," Billy Gibbs was saying, "was Sunday any different from Saturday in routine? Breakfast, for example—?"

"Seven o'clock sharp. Cook used to grumble sometimes. She liked her bed, she did. But she knew as well as I did that on the stroke of seven the old gentleman would walk into the breakfast room and sit down to his tomato juice and the paper. And when he rang, he expected his toast and egg and coffee." Miss Potter smiled grimly in memory. "So, grumble or not, Cook had them ready." The grim smile spread thinly. "Sometimes with the curlers still on her head," Miss Potter added.

Marty, listening quietly, decided that Billy was doing the first-rate lawyerly job he had promised, setting the background with care, giving no impression of guiding the witness, merely asking the right questions and letting her say it all in her own way. And she was convincing, of that there was no doubt. Marty stole a glance at the judge, and decided that he could tell nothing from his expression. Sitting in a poker game with the judge would be a frustrating experience, he thought. He looked again at Paul and could tell nothing from his expression either. In a way they were two of a kind.

There was emerging for the jury's benefit, Marty thought, a clear, if somewhat overflattering picture of old Joe McCurdy, a portrait without the warts. Well, that was good; the contrast with the old boy's later irascibility would be all the more vivid.

He found himself thinking of old Joe's wife, his grandmother, Martha. He remembered her; he had been, let's see, sixteen when she died. And it was cancer; the newspapers had had it right; breast cancer unnoticed until it was too late, spreading out of control. But when you were sixteen, something happening to someone two generations removed meant very little, and cancer was merely a word. And he had not known his grandmother all that well either.

He did remember a few things about her. She was, for example, probably the only older person he could remember who did not open an attempt at conversation with "My, how you have grown!" Kids were supposed to grow, weren't they? Then what was all the fuss about? Martha—strange, he always thought of her by her first name—had understood that.

She was in no outward way a forceful woman. In old Joe McCurdy's presence she spoke little, but when she did speak, even Joe listened. Once, during one of Marty's rare San Francisco visits: "I don't really think Marty is all that interested in banking practices, dear." Gently interrupting the old man in full flow. "I have an idea he would rather run down to the yacht club and have a look at some of the boats moored there, wouldn't you, Marty?"

Old Joe McCurdy sighed. "I suppose you're right. I didn't give much of a damn about money either when I was your age. Beat it. Just get back for dinner."

And one day at Pebble Beach, Marty remembered too. Martha had taken him, Alan, and probably Bruce too, but not the twins, who were too small; and they had driven to Point Lobos. Martha had brought a bag of peanuts, and the squirrels who had staked out the parking area for their own gathered around and made their small daring dashes to snatch a nut right from your fingers. Marty liked that.

And then they walked out to the point to watch the sea lions sunning themselves on the rocks or frolicking in the waves that slammed against the cliffs, and Marty thought of the Wedge, and decided that he and Billy Gibbs and even the best of the body surfers were pretty feeble specimens compared to these magnificent animals who were clearly enjoying themselves in their total mastery of their environment. He hated for that day to end. He could have stayed, admiring, forever.

Fragmentary memories of a strong, gentle lady, and it came to Marty now that old Joe McCurdy must have lived in a hell of loneliness after she was gone. So? We are here and now, Marty thought, and that is what counts. He made himself concentrate again on what Billy was saying.

On the bench the judge listened patiently, only occasionally injecting himself into the proceedings. Young Gibbs was moving along, drawing a picture the jury could follow, the judge thought, which was exactly what was wanted, and the judge had no intention of needlessly interrupting the process.

From time to time the judge glanced at the list of jury names before him, and then glanced at the jury box to try to fit name to person. Some he had already identified: Jensen, the black postal clerk; Sato, the Japanese American; Wang, the Chinese, who was the foreman; Ms. Carstairs; Mrs. Beatty; and Leyba, the Chicano; which left six, four men and two women, not yet sorted out.

One of the men, in windbreaker, with a beer drinker's belly lopping over the waistband of his denims, was Smith, the judge was pretty sure. A truck driver.

And the one with small, pinched features, wearing rimless glasses, was the bookkeeper, Harwood.

The rest would have to emerge as individuals in their own time.

Juries were usually a mixed bag, the judge thought, and if you merely looked at them casually you might very well ask yourself if it was at all logical or even reasonable to expect that from them might come a sensible verdict. Well, the fact of the matter was that juries were not infallible; sometimes their findings made no sense at all. But often enough they did, and there was the heart of the matter.

When he pondered the weaknesses and strengths of the jury system, the judge often thought that most men and women tended to rush to either/or judgments, black-and-white, good-or-bad, honest-or-crooked. In the judge's experience more often than not the choice was rarely that clear-cut, which was why purists often found themselves either embittered or confused.

In voting for a candidate one seldom found a saint on the ballot; the choice was almost inevitably between comparatives.

Most laws had sound arguments both for and against.

The system of trial by jury sometimes failed, true; but often enough, by what the judge viewed as an inexplicable emergence of collective judgment far greater and grander than the sum of its parts, it triumphed, and in so doing vindicated itself.

That beer drinker Smith or, for that matter, angry Ms. Carstairs could be a functional part of that process seemed unlikely in the extreme, but the judge would almost have been willing to wager that they would.

And while the voices droned on, Billy's questions, Miss Potter's firm answers, they were accumulating, the judge thought, a vast amount of minutiae at considerable taxpayers' expense, and when all the arguments and testimony were finished this jury would have its opportunity to vindicate its existence—or to fail. Either way, the judge asked himself, would the matter at issue be settled for good and all? The answer was no. Not then. Probably not ever. There was the depressing thought.

Billy returned once more to the table to glance at his notes. The judge seized the opportunity. "I assume, Mr. Gibbs," he said, "that your questioning of this witness will go on for some time?"

"There is a considerable amount of ground to cover, your honor."

The judge nodded. He glanced at the wall clock. "I think we might start fresh again tomorrow." He tapped his gavel gently. "Court will stand in recess until nine o'clock tomorrow morning."

29

Paul let himself in the front door of the big quiet house, and walked directly to his study, where he put his briefcase on the desk, looked at it with distaste for a few moments, and then turned away. Teresa appeared in the doorway.

"You will be dining in tonight?"

He had not even thought about it. He nodded. "Something simple, please." He walked to one of the club chairs flanking the fireplace and dropped into it.

There would always be times like this, he knew, when vague depression would set in and ordinarily unimportant matters would tend to take on distorted significance.

Sitting in the courtroom and listening to Millicent Potter's sometimes acid testimony, it had been as if he were hearing talk about a total stranger instead of about his own father, and how could that be? The concept aroused vague feelings of guilt.

True, the Potter woman had lived for eleven years under this roof, seeing the old man daily, and perhaps in her spinsterish way understanding the depth of the sense of loss that had followed Martha's painful death, while he, Paul, with Susan and the growing children, had lived their own separate lives in their comfortable, but not grand, house on Russian Hill. Had that been a mistake?

After Martha's death it had been suggested, very tentatively, that Joe McCurdy might want family around him, but the idea had been flatly vetoed. "Three generations under one roof," Joe McCurdy had said, and shaken his head. "No. You're happy where you are. I'm well taken care of here. The sensible thing, of course," he had added, "would be for me to move out of this big place and turn it over to you and your family, but I'm not going to. Let's say I'm too selfish."

It was Susan who had said, "I don't believe that for a moment." She smiled gently at the old man. "You could, and I'm sure you would if you thought it was the thing to do, leave all the *things* in this house." Her smile was tinged with sadness and understanding now. "But there are memories too, aren't there? And I don't blame you a bit for not wanting to give those up."

"Anyway," Joe McCurdy said, maybe a little too quickly, abruptly switching the direction of the conversation, "you were good to suggest it, but we'll just let the matter drop. Now I think one more drink before dinner. I understand Cook has extended herself tonight. *Coq au vin*, I believe. She does it well."

Now Teresa came into the study with the cocktail tray, set it on its stand, and bent to touch a match to the already laid fire.

"Thank you," Paul said, and after a time rose to mix himself a martini. Back in his chair again, staring unseeing at the growing flames, thinking of Susan and wishing she were here, he asked himself what it would be like if suddenly he knew with certainty that

Susan was never coming back. Nonsense. Or was it? He turned in his chair to look at the telephone on the desk, and as he looked, it rang. He made himself wait, the cocktail at his elbow untouched.

Teresa appeared again in the doorway. "It is Dr. Alan," she said. Having known him as a child, she could not bring herself to say Dr. McCurdy, nor, now that Alan was grown, could she feel right using only his given name. A difficult choice.

Paul heaved himself out of his chair and went to the phone. It had been too much to hope that the call was from Susan. "Yes, son?"

"Are you busy?"

The empty house, the lonely cocktail, the vague sense of depression after the day in court, Paul could even smile mocking himself. "No," he said, and forebore elaboration.

"Will you give me a drink if I come around?"

"I think that might be arranged. In fact, if you want to come soon, I'll tell Teresa to plan for dinner." Paul hoped the answer would be yes.

There was hesitation. "I was thinking of bringing someone," Alan said. "I sort of wanted you to meet Nancy. Would the dinner stretch to three?"

"It will." Very happily, Paul thought. And then, with a sudden sense of guilt that this thought had actually been repressed all day by other matters, forgotten: "Any word on Wally Trent?"

Alan said slowly in a different voice, "I'm afraid so. I was going to tell you when we got there. He didn't make it. He never came out of the coma, and he died this afternoon. I'm sorry."

Paul closed his eyes. "Yes," he said. "Thank you." Later, he thought, as had happened before, he would actually begin to realize the fact of death, feel the loss, the sadness, even the grief. Now all he felt was a curious numbness compounding the sense of depression, and of guilt. "What was that?" he said.

"I said, do you still want us to come?"

"Now," Paul said, "more than ever." And when had he last humbled himself to ask for aid and comfort?

He hung up slowly, punched the bell for Teresa, gave his orders for dinner almost without thought, and started back to his chair. The ringing phone stopped him and he walked back to pick it up without waiting for Teresa to answer in another part of the house.

"Paul?" Susan's voice.

"How are you?" Paul said. "I've been—thinking of you."

It was as if he had not spoken. "The trial started today, didn't it?" Susan said.

He felt rebuffed. "Yes."

"Was it—bad?"

"It will be worse."

"I'm sorry."

"That helps." A little; not much; but in his present mood he accepted small comfort eagerly.

"Is something—wrong?"

He had not realized how close he was to frustrated anger until the words tumbled out now of their own accord. "Yes, something is wrong, lots of things are wrong! Damn it, I want you here!"

There was silence on the phone.

"I need you," Paul said. His voice was overloud. The hell with it. "Can you understand that?" He waited, but there was no answer. "Damn it, answer me! Can you understand that I need you?"

"I'm—not sure. I'll—try." The line went dead.

Paul hung up and walked back to his chair and the untouched drink. He felt tired, even somewhat drained. Need, he thought; there was a word. It reverberated in his mind. I am not the independent entity I thought myself. Perhaps nobody is? No matter. I'm not, and at this moment that is all that counts. It was a new concept springing spontaneously into being, and he was still considering it when Alan and Nancy arrived.

She was a large, calm girl; that was his first thought. Attractive too, and when she smiled she was almost beautiful.

"I am sorry about your friend." They were her first words.

"You have seen death before." Now where had that thought come from?

"Yes," Nancy said, "and so has Alan, but I don't think you ever get used to it, and so I mean it when I say I am sorry."

"Thank you." He roused himself then to become host and father, with a role to play that should not include breast beating and lament for the dead. "I have here," he said, "a very tired martini which I intend to replace." He smiled at the girl. "What is your pleasure?"

They sat with their drinks by the fire. "I had hoped," Paul said, "that Alan would bring you here one day. It is not true that the McCurdys eat their young."

"Only occasionally," Alan said. There were undertones of tension in his father's manner, he thought; and decided that with the trial, his mother's absence, the general state of the financial world, and now Wally Trent's death, it would have been remarkable if there had been no signs of strain. When one accepted responsibility, one paid the price. Long ago he had learned that. He hoped that the price his father was paying was not too high.

Nancy said in her calm easy way, "Alan told me about your talk. We are both grateful." Her sudden smile transformed her face and seemed to bring light into her eyes. "All day," she said, "we prescribe for others. But when it comes to prescribing for ourselves, 'Physician, heal thyself' is a tall order."

Paul thought of himself and Marty, himself and Susan, himself and Wally Trent. "It always is," he said. "For anyone." He sipped his drink, set it down. They had come for a reason, he thought; it was up to him to understand that. "Do you want to tell me about you two?" he said gently. "I don't want to pry, but—"

Again that sudden, brilliant smile. "You understand, don't you?" Nancy said. She looked at Alan and waited.

Alan said slowly, "We've got a long row to hoe, both of us." He hesitated. "And it may sound funny, but we can't see—complicating the whole process of learning, developing—unnecessarily." It was a lame finish, and he was aware of it.

"Unnecessarily with marriage?" Paul said. "Is that what you mean?"

There was silence. Nancy was smiling again. Alan felt himself relax. "She's right," he said, "you do dig, don't you?" There was a measure of pride in his voice. He paused again. "We were afraid you'd go formal and conventional on us. I think Mother would."

Paul took his time. "Maybe I ought to," he said at last, and smiled faintly. "I don't know." Recently, he thought, matters that were once black and white had started turning up in shades of tattletale gray; and definitive answers seemed to have become part of the past. "It has been a long time since I have heard or even thought of the phrase 'living in sin.' And even when the phrase and the thinking behind it were in vogue, I think there were many, too many, formalized relations that were far worse, dishonest, a sham"

They were both silent, watching him carefully.

They want my judgment, he thought; in a way, they need it for their own peace of mind. Sudie would not; nor Jim; there was the basic difference among the children. Would Bruce? Maybe yes, maybe no; in this matter too Paul was no longer sure. But these two were asking for help. And this time, he thought, I will not turn my back. "Do what you think is best," he said. He smiled. "And whatever it is, you will have what used to be called parental blessing. Without reservation. We will be more than delighted to have Nancy either officially or unofficially as part of the family."

It was late that evening when he saw Nancy and Alan to the door, came back into his study and tried to place a call to Susan in Boston. But his dialing produced only the intermittent buzz of a busy signal—whether from all circuits being in use, which seemed unlikely, or from unidentified line trouble, he had no idea.

Nor was he sure what Susan's reaction would be had he been able to reach her; propriety played a large part in Susan's life. But it would have been good to share Nancy and Alan's pleasure with her, and in the end it was with reluctance that he gave up and went upstairs.

The important thing was that he had made his judgment, and even now found it without flaw; and the relieved reaction both Alan and Nancy had showed was a warm thing to remember.

For the first time since Susan had left, he slept well, and awakened refreshed to face the new day in court.

The members of the jury had been admonished by the judge, of course, not to discuss the case with one another or with anyone else, but habit clings relentlessly.

Over his first can of pre-dinner beer, "I seen right from the start what he wants," Harry Smith the truck driver told his wife. "The crum-bum wants to get his hooks on all the moola, that's all it is." He shook his head wonderingly. "An' you tell me why. He's never done any work. He's already got all the loot he can spend and then some. Why, I read in the paper that just for doin' nothin' he gets more in a week than I earn in a year. Why, he gets more than Catfish Hunter. How about that?"

The television set was on, a domestic drama in progress. Harry's wife watched it, apparently able to listen to two conversations at once. "Maybe he's got reasons," she said. "And he's kind of cute."

"And what does that have to do with it?" Harry had a long swallow of his beer. "What kind of reasons?"

"Maybe he wants to, you know, travel. Like Europe an' Paris an' like that." She paused reflectively. "Places I always wanted to see."

Harry finished his beer, stood up, crushed the beer can in his big hands, and marched to the refrigerator for another. Over his shoulder, "With the dough he's already got," he said, "he could buy Paris, or at least the whatchamacallit Tower." He opened the fresh can relentlessly. "He's like some guys I know. They want it all. There's a word for that, but I can't remember it. Anyway, he's just a jerk." He walked back to his chair.

The wife's eyes were on the television screen. "Harry! Harry! Look! Just what I told you, remember? I said she was going to have a baby, didn't I? Well, didn't I?"

Harry sat down. "Who cares?"

"I do." Harry's wife blinked rapidly, never taking her eyes from the screen. "Suppose she dies in childbirth?"

"Oh, for Chrissake," Harry said, and attacked the fresh can of beer.

James Wang, the jury foreman, said, "I believe that a man's property is his to do with as he likes. His wishes should be respected."

His wife, Mary, also University of California trained, smiled and nodded and said nothing.

"On the other hand," James Wang said, "if it is shown beyond question that old Mr. McCurdy was not really of sound mind after his stroke, or that his son, Paul McCurdy, did indeed exert undue influence— We shall have to see."

"More tea?" his wife said.

"Thank you." James Wang was silent, thoughtful. "It is interesting," he said. "And it will be even more interesting when the case is given to us and we go into the jury room." He smiled. "We are a mixed bag, we jurors."

"You will handle it," his wife said.

Mrs. Beatty at dinner said, "I can't talk about it. The judge told us not to."

Luther Beatty, husband, said, "Now, Mother."

Martha Beatty, sixteen, said, "Oh, Mom!"

"Well," Mrs. Beatty said, "nothing much has happened yet. Old Mr. McCurdy had breakfast every morning at seven o'clock and never went to church and then he had a stroke. That's all I know so far."

"But what about the young one, you know, the nephew, the one they call Marty?" This was Martha. "I saw his picture in the paper. He's real neat-looking, sort of like Paul Newman, only younger. What about him?"

"He hasn't said a word," Mrs. Beatty said. "He lets the other one do all his talking while he just sits there."

"Lawyers," Luther Beatty said, and shook his head sadly. "I'll bet they're costing a bundle." He paused. "That's what I should of been, a lawyer."

"Anyway," Mrs. Beatty said, "that's all I know so far." Her disappointment was plain. "It isn't at all like Perry Mason."

"Maybe it'll pick up," Luther said.

"I'd like to meet him," Martha said. "The one they call Marty, I mean. Maybe he'd take me out on his yacht."

"You stay away from yachts, young lady," Mrs. Beatty said. "Things happen to girls when they go on yachts."

"Oh, Mom! You're so—old-fashioned!"

Walter Jensen, the black postal clerk, said, "I feel kind of sorry for old Mr. McCurdy. We're getting to know him." He smiled suddenly. "He liked tomato juice every morning for breakfast, with lemon juice and Worcestershire sauce in it. How about that?"

"Lots of vitamin C and low carbohydrates," his wife said. She was a dietitian's assistant at the hospital. "I'll bet the doctor had him watching his lipids. More people should."

"Well, anyway," Walter Jensen said, "that young fellow Gibbs is giving us a picture of how the old man was before his stroke." He shook his head. "I don't think I'm going to like what comes out about him after the stroke." He paused. "You know, like in a movie when you know somebody's going to be put down, and you wish it wouldn't happen."

"With all the money that old man had," his wife said, "I can't work up much sympathy for him. Especially him being a banker. You know what they do to poor folks."

30

Millicent Potter was back on the stand, her no-nonsense hat anchored onto her tightly drawn gray hair, her hands folded in her lap, knees close, and feet planted together pointing straight ahead.

"You have given us a very clear picture of the McCurdy household routine, Miss Potter," Billy said. "Before Mr. McCurdy's—seizure, this is. I believe you referred to it as his affliction?"

"He was a fine man," Miss Potter said, "but those who don't turn to the Lord—" She left the sentence unfinished, her disapproval plain.

Get off that subject as fast as you can, Billy told himself. It was a damn-fool question to ask anyway. "Do you recall the day of Mr. McCurdy's stroke?" he said.

Miss Potter's expression softened. "I remember it very well. Everything changed."

John McKenzie started to rise.

The judge said, "I assume that you will see that that answer is amplified, made specific, Mr. Gibbs?"

"Yes, your honor."

The judge nodded. "Proceed."

Billy turned back to the witness stand. "Will you tell us, please, from your own knowledge, Miss Potter, just what happened? Only to your own knowledge, Miss Potter, what you saw and heard."

Miss Potter nodded shortly. "The old gentleman had his breakfast as always. It was a Thursday, and it was a nice morning, so he was going to walk down to the bank. He went out the front door the way he always did, at seven-thirty sharp. Just like any other day." She was silent.

"And?"

Miss Potter shook her head. "That's all there was. He was just like always when he walked out. The next time I saw him, it wasn't the same man at all."

Billy said quickly, "We will be more specific, your honor."

"I hope so, Mr. Gibbs. The jury must have facts."

Billy turned back to the witness. He was conscious that the jury watched him with new attention. The courtroom was still. "When and how did you first hear of Mr. McCurdy's—seizure?" he said.

"About eleven o'clock that morning," Miss Potter said. "Near enough. That was when his secretary, Miss Wood, that was, usually called if Mr. McCurdy was bringing guests for lunch."

"Miss Wood called you?"

"That's what I said." Miss Potter paused. "She sounded upset, as well she might. She said that Mr. McCurdy had been taken ill at the bank and they had taken him to the hospital."

"That was all she said?"

"That was enough. Him, who'd never been ill a day in his life. Like a tall redwood he was, big and strong. I knew then that it was something—bad." She glared at Billy as if expecting challenge.

Billy half expected interruption from John McKenzie. There was none. "And what did you do then, Miss Potter?"

"I went to the kitchen and called Frances the maid and Tim Allen and Cook together and told them." Miss Potter sniffed. "Cook began to cry. Like a big baby, she was. She wanted to know what was going to happen to all of us, and I told her that until we heard otherwise, the house would run as it always had, and that was that."

In the jury box, the judge noticed, little Ms. Carstairs nodded with decisive approval. Exactly right, her expression seemed to say, carry on! In character, the judge thought, and stifled a smile.

Billy said, "And did the house run as it had, Miss Potter?"

"It did." Miss Potter pointed with her chin at the table where Paul sat. "He, young Mr. McCurdy, came over the next day and told me what had happened. He said he didn't know when the old gentleman would be coming home, but that we were to be ready for him when he did. And we were. Two weeks, it was."

"During those two weeks, Miss Potter," Billy said, "did you visit Mr. McCurdy in the hospital?"

"No." Miss Potter paused for emphasis. "It wasn't my place. I was paid to run his house, and that is what I did."

Again Ms. Carstairs showed approval, the judge noticed. For her at least Miss Potter was emerging as a wholly respectable and dependable witness, one whose word could be taken without question.

And, the judge thought, since Millicent Potter was probably one of young Mr. Gibbs's most important witnesses, if not *the* most important, establishing Miss Potter's credence had been imperative, and young Gibbs had done it well.

Walter Jensen, the postal clerk, listened carefully. It was obvious, he thought, that beneath her snappish front, Miss Potter had a large soft spot for old Joe McCurdy, and Walter Jensen wondered how she would feel when it came to telling about the old boy's decline, as she would certainly have to.

James Wang sat impassive, judgment suspended.

"So after two weeks," Billy said quietly, but loud enough for the jury to hear, "Mr. McCurdy came home, is that right, Miss Potter?"

For once Miss Potter did not reply. She merely inclined her head.

"Tell us about the homecoming," Billy said.

Miss Potter closed her eyes. It was a few moments before she spoke. Memory was both clear and painful:

They helped him out of the ambulance that gray morning and it took two men to get him up to the front porch, one shaky step at a time. He had suddenly become a weak, tired old man, merely a husk; that was Miss Potter's first thought. She could not remember when last she had shed tears, but they were close now as she held the front door wide.

Joe McCurdy smiled at her. It was a grimace, only one side of his mouth lifting naturally. When he spoke, the words were indistinct. "It is good to see you again, Miss Potter," he said. "I thank you for taking care of things in my absence."

Then slowly across the hall, and the long, laborious climb up the carpeted stairs, a white-coated attendant on either side. Halfway up they stopped.

"We could carry you, Mr. McCurdy," one of the attendants said.

"You will not." Indistinct, but unequivocal. "I am not totally helpless yet."

On they went, pausing only briefly at the head of the stairs, and then down the hall and into the master suite.

Miss Potter had not even noticed the nurse, but suddenly there she was, following the old man and the two attendants, and closing the door firmly after her.

Miss Potter went slowly back down the stairs. Cook, Frances, and

Tim Allen were watching surreptitiously from the dining-room doorway.

"Jesus," Tim said. "You wouldn't know him, would you?"

Her own thought exactly, but Miss Potter would have none of it. "That," she said, "will be enough blasphemy in this house."

It was quite a picture, Marty thought, and found in it no pleasure. He hoped the old boy had kept his head high, defiant even in shattering adversity. He had.

"After Nurse had him settled," Miss Potter said, "he sent for me. He hadn't gone to bed; he was in a big chair by the windows that looked out on the gardens. 'This is Nurse Carter, Miss Potter,' he said. 'She tells me what I can and cannot do.' "

" 'You should be in bed,' the nurse said, and the old gentleman gave her that crooked smile, and said, 'But there are still some things I decide for myself.' And he did, too. Nurse would grumble, but it didn't do her any good.

" 'I am not going to live the rest of my life as a cripple,' the old gentleman told me one day. He had two canes and he had almost worn a path in the carpet going back and forth across that big room. Nurse said he would tire himself out. He didn't pay any attention to her. The doctor said to take it slow and easy. I heard him. The old gentleman said there wasn't time for slow and easy, that one day soon he would have all the rest there was—in a box in the ground—but that in the meantime he wasn't about to throw in the sponge, whatever that meant."

Paul sat at his table, his hands in his lap, eyes staring straight ahead. Once he glanced at Marty, and could find no expression at all in Marty's face. We are letting the world pry into our lives, Paul thought, as we never have before. He was glad Susan was not here to watch. And this is just the beginning. Bitter thought. It was anger that he felt, directed at Marty, at Charles Goodwin, at Billy Gibbs for his patient, subtle questioning, at the jury for their eager interest, at the packed courtroom. Easy, he told himself, easy; you can't hate everybody. Or could he?

Billy walked to the table where Marty sat, picked up papers and pretended to study them. "Here we go," he said in an undertone that scarcely reached Marty's ears. "Now we get down to the meat." He turned, walked back to the witness stand, and positioned himself so that he spoke both to Miss Potter and to the jury.

"Obviously, Miss Potter," he said, "Mr. McCurdy during this period was in no condition to resume the household routine you have so ably described. Is that not true?"

Miss Potter opened her mouth. She closed it again carefully. Her eventual reply was unexpectedly gentle, even halting. "He couldn't do much of anything," she said, "except sit in that big chair by the windows resting between his walks back and forth across the room. They tired him terribly."

Marty glanced at Paul. Paul's face was set, even angry, and he looked, not at the woman in the witness chair, but at some indeterminate spot on the far courtroom wall as if trying to remove himself from the scene. I guess I can't blame him much, Marty thought. And then came the reverse side of the concept: but he asked for it, and he can stop it anytime.

"While he sat, resting himself," Billy said, "did he do anything, Miss Potter? Did he read? Listen to the radio? Watch television?"

"He stared out the windows." Miss Potter hesitated.

"Go on, Miss Potter."

"And he—talked," Miss Potter said.

A fresh rustle of interest in the courtroom, the judge thought; you could close your eyes and almost guess what audience and jury reaction might be. He glanced at the jury for verification.

Timothy La Grange—the judge fixed his name on the list—sat quiet with a controlled smile on his lips and his eyelids half lowered as he seemed to consider the lesser creatures around him. Occupation: hairdresser. Idly the judge wondered why John McKenzie had not used one of his peremptory challenges to dismiss Timothy La Grange, who might very well have a deep-seated antagonism against large, aggressive, robust males like old Joe McCurdy. On the other hand, he told himself, great inherited wealth would certainly not offend La Grange, as it might some others, so maybe the balance was even after all.

The courtroom waited in silence for Billy's next question. He was aware of the hush, and he let it endure. " 'Talked,' " he said at last in a quiet, wondering voice. "To whom, Miss Potter? To the nurse? To you?"

Very quietly, "No."

"Then?"

Miss Potter's mouth was set in a thin, straight line. She shook her head in angry refusal.

Billy looked questioningly at the judge.

"The witness will answer the question," the judge said quietly. A God-fearing woman, he thought, refusing to lie, and unwilling to tell the truth; a painful predicament. "Did you hear me, Miss Potter?"

"I heard." Miss Potter took a deep breath and tried evasion. "I wasn't in the room all that often," she said. "I came up only when he sent for me."

In a way, Billy thought, it was even better, more convincing like this, having to drag it out of the old girl; it gave her testimony greater weight. He went about it gently. "When he sent for you," he said, "it was merely to discuss something with you, and then you left immediately, is that it?"

"Not—always." Miss Potter considered her options and found no escape. Her voice expressed her unhappiness. "Sometimes he just wanted me to—sit in the room. He liked my company, he said." She could not resist a single scornful sniff. "I never tried to order him around like Nurse did."

"And," Billy said, his quiet voice carrying easily through the courtroom, "it was during these times that you heard him talking, Miss Potter?"

Miss Potter inclined her head in silence.

"The witness will answer," the judge said.

Miss Potter glared at Billy, her tormentor. "Yes," she said. It was almost a hiss.

"And he was not talking to you?"

"I told you, young man." Miss Potter paused, thought of the judge, and added, "No. He wasn't talking to me."

Billy took a few steps away from the witness-box railing, turned, and walked back, again positioning himself so that he spoke to the jury as well. "He talked to himself, perhaps?" He smiled. "People do. I do myself at times."

Miss Potter shook her head. "No."

Billy took his time. "I am afraid," he said, "that you have us all"—he made a swift, a small gesture of bafflement—"bursting with curiosity, Miss Potter. If he wasn't talking to you, or to himself, then—?" He left the question hang.

Miss Potter drew a deep breath. Silence grew and stretched. "He talked to the flowers," she said at last.

The silence was complete. After a slow take truck driver Harry Smith's eyes, the judge noticed, opened wide. He stared at Miss Potter. Slowly he began to shake his head in incredulity.

"Which flowers were those, Miss Potter?" Billy said gently. "Were there flowers in the room?"

"In the garden." Miss Potter's voice was impatient now, as if the subject once broached should be pursued briskly, gotten over, and then forgotten for all time. "He gave them names, people names, I told you he didn't know one from the other."

"I believe you also said," Billy said, "that Mr. McCurdy never paid any attention to the flowers in the garden."

"He could change his mind, couldn't he?"

"Of course he could." Billy's voice was soothing. He was thoughtful for a few moments. "And so he gave them names, people names, and he talked to them. What did he say to them, Miss Potter?"

There was no hesitation now. "He asked them how they were, and whether they liked it there in the garden, and if the gardener was doing things the way they liked? He told them they were lucky to have all the care they had, but he thought he could understand how maybe they would rather be free, out in fields and meadows, and like that." Miss Potter's voice was rising. "I tried not to listen, can't you understand that?"

"I think I can, Miss Potter," Billy said quietly. "I think I can. Was this an isolated instance, Miss Potter? Did you hear him talking to the flowers only once?"

Miss Potter's defiance was gone. Only sadness remained. "Every time I sat with him," she said. "And Nurse heard him too. She thought he was—dotty."

"Objection, your honor," John McKenzie said. "Hearsay—"

"Well," Miss Potter said, defiance rising briefly again, "I heard her saying it often enough. I told her once to be quiet."

The judge tapped his gavel. The situation was not really comical; nevertheless he found it hard not to smile. "Objection sustained," he said. "The jury will disregard those last remarks." As if they can, he told himself, or will; but there it is. "Proceed, Mr. Gibbs."

Billy nodded. He glanced at Marty, and then returned to Miss Potter. I don't much like what I'm doing, he thought, but I am doing it anyway. Why? Because if I am going to represent my client well, it has to be done. Was that an answer, he asked himself, or merely an excuse? No matter. "During these times when you sat with Mr. McCurdy," he said, "and, we quite understand, tried not to listen, did you despite yourself hear other things he said to the flowers?"

Miss Potter closed her eyes. When she opened them again, she tried not to look at Billy. "Sometimes," she said slowly, "he told them about the bank. I mean," she said, "he'd ask one of them questions, like: 'Geraldine,' that was one of the names, 'Geraldine, you have forty thousand dollars from your late husband's insurance policy. What are you going to do with it?' Like that."

"And did he seem to hear an answer, Miss Potter?"

"I don't know. I guess so." And then, almost violently, "Yes! Because I heard him say, 'That is very wise of you, Geraldine. In your situation, I think safety in investment ought to be your primary concern.' "

There was more. Marty tuned it out, as apparently Miss Potter had been unable to do. The poor old guy, Marty thought. When I get to that point, I hope they shoot me. He glanced across at Paul's stony face. Their eyes met briefly. It was Paul who looked away.

Maybe I'll have kids, Marty thought, and maybe I won't. But if I do, I won't try to run their lives after I'm gone by words I have put down on a piece of paper, even if when I have those words put down I'm still playing with a full deck. Or think I am. Same thing, really. Wasn't that what this trial was all about? Does anyone realize it when he's off his rocker? Where did that thought come from?

He looked again at Paul. Did you really, consciously set it up the way you wanted, knowing that the old man, sitting talking to the flowers, would go along with whatever you said? Did you—? Billy's words drew his attention back to the courtroom.

"Did Mr. McCurdy have frequent visitors, Miss Potter? During this convalescent period, I mean."

Miss Potter pointed her chin at Paul. "He came every day, young Mr. McCurdy. Sometimes alone. Sometimes with papers, lots of papers for the old gentleman to sign. And sometimes, half a dozen times, maybe, that other one, the lawyer, Mr. McKenzie, was with him too, and they would talk with the old gentleman with the door closed."

The judge said mildly, "I assume you are about to open a fresh line of questioning, Mr. Gibbs?" For "fresh line of questioning," he thought, read "fresh can of worms."

"I am, your honor."

"Then I think we might recess now for lunch. Court will resume at two o'clock." He tapped the gavel gently, and rose from his chair.

31

Outside in the bright San Francisco fall day Marty found himself breathing deep as if to dispel the lingering courtroom odor. Billy walked with him. "Talking to the flowers," Marty said. "I didn't know about that. Where did you dig it up? From the Potter woman herself?"

"From the nurse." Billy's voice was deliberately noncommittal. "She hates Potter's guts, and she wasn't all that happy with your grandfather either. I gathered that she didn't get very far in ordering him around, and she resented it."

"Nobody ordered him around," Marty said. Damn it, he thought, I am proud of the old son of a bitch. Or, I was. He and his father made a name that still means something in this part of the world. How many can say the same?

They walked in silence to the restaurant, where they sat at the same table they had occupied yesterday. Today it was set for two instead of three. "I'm going to have a drink," Marty said.

Billy nodded. "I'll join you."

They ordered, and while they waited, "How much more is there?" Marty said. "How far do you have to go?"

"There is quite a bit." Billy paused. "And I am going to use it all. Call it overkill. But with a jury there is no way of telling how much is enough."

Their drinks arrived. Marty sipped his and set it down. "Okay, what else is there? Give me a rundown."

"He forgot things. Potter and others will testify to that."

"Everybody forgets sometimes."

"Look," Billy said, "no one thing he did or didn't do is conclusive.

I took an abnormal psychology course once, and the professor warned us at the beginning that as we studied case histories we were going to find that almost every symptom of abnormality was in ourselves too. The difference was not of kind, but of degree. You had to look at the total picture and study the balance."

Marty thought about it. He nodded slowly. "Okay. Go on."

"He wrote letters to the newspapers. Lots of people do that too, but some that he wrote, and the papers printed, are real beauties."

"About what?"

Billy shook his head. "Everything. The AAU and the option clause in pro baseball, the Olympic Committee and high-rise buildings, increased payrolls in Washington and the kinds of cars Detroit built, girdled grapes and bad French wine. You name it." He looked at his watch. "We'd better order. We can talk while we eat. I can't be late."

Over coffee, "Have I got it all?" Marty said.

Billy shook his head. "The chauffeur, Tim Allen. He used to drive your grandfather over to Muir Woods. He'd get out and talk to the trees the way he did to the flowers, and he was forever telling Tim to stop the car to pick up some hitchhiker, usually a shaggy turned-off kid, take him in the back seat, and talk about everything under the sun."

Marty said nothing.

"Then," Billy said, "there's Robert Falcon, you know him? President of the University of California. Your grandfather wanted to endow a Chair for Revolutionary Study. Not the 1776 Revolution, but the one he thought was going on right now, here and other places." Billy paused. "Not a bad idea, maybe, but you can imagine what the Regents would have said."

Walking back to the courthouse, "After he could get around pretty well," Billy said, "he started going down to the bank again every day. He had a desk on the main floor, and he'd talk to everybody about everything and anything, and he started bringing strange types home for lunch. Tim Allen told me about those. Potter will have to talk about them too." He glanced at Marty's face. "Heard enough?"

"Yes."

Billy stopped at the foot of the courthouse steps. "Shall we quit?"

"If Paul will compromise."

"I don't think he will."

"Then we don't quit."

"Okay," Billy said. "I can talk to McKenzie and see if there's any chance of a settlement. Shall I?"

"Yes. This weekend. Work on it. I'm going down to LA. It's past time."

What was happening in Los Angeles had never really been out of Marty's mind. Twice he had called Jerry Hopkins at the plant, each time coming away from the phone with a feeling almost of relief that he could in conscience concentrate on what was happening here in San Francisco knowing that the plant was in good hands.

It was not all wine and roses, of course; and sooner or later he was going to have to involve himself even more deeply, or else, as Billy and Paul had suggested, walk away from the entire situation and let happen what might.

"Pretty much all quiet on the home front," Jerry Hopkins had said during that first telephone call. Jerry was young, breezy, and filled with confidence. "There are going to be some problems—some pretty big ones, but they're a little way down the road. For the present, we'll make out."

"Walter Jordan?" Marty said.

Was there a smile now in Jerry's voice? "You put something of the fear of the Lord in him. And the man, my man, that is, John Black, apparently decided it wouldn't hurt to give us a little backup, so he talked to Jordan too, and what he said, I don't know, but Jordan has been a very cooperative fellow ever since. John Black has a way of getting his point across."

Marty thought of the solid, stocky man in that big office at the heart of giant Coast Aircraft, and decided that John Black would indeed be able to make himself understood. And it was oddly comforting to know that Black had thought to intervene in even this minor way.

On the other hand, Marty told himself, what merely amounted to Black's sympathy for the plant's predicament was certainly no guarantee of any kind of success. Black had made it clear that whatever his personal inclinations, his duty was to Coast Aircraft and the Coast Aircraft stockholders, and what might happen to a minor vendor like McCurdy Aircraft was really a matter of relatively little importance.

"Okay," Marty said. "What's your first problem, and when does it turn critical?"

There was no hesitation. "Money. The first of the month we're going to need more cash than we have. And from what I understand, credit isn't readily available."

Understatement, Marty thought. "That's why I'm up here in the middle of a lawsuit," he said. "How much will you need?"

Jerry Hopkins was prepared. "We can squeak along for maybe another month on a hundred thou. That merely postpones the real day of reckoning, but as I understand it, that's how you want it."

"Exactly," Marty said. He was silent for a few moments. Then, "With a hundred thousand dollars, will you have to lay people off?"

"No." Jerry's voice altered subtly. "I can cut the figure if layoffs are the route you want to go."

"It is not," Marty said. "A hundred thousand it is, and I'll get back to you."

The rest of the conversation was generalities, important, but not urgent. Marty sat for a long time after he hung up. He was not used to money matters, he told himself, and it was quite possible that he was going about things in the wrong way and in the wrong direction. The hell with it. Sometimes you played your hunches, and not infrequently they paid off—if you went with them all the way, without hedging.

He stood up. Maybe he would be able to raise the money Jerry Hopkins needed. One thing was sure: he wasn't going to find money if he didn't try.

He called Jerry Hopkins three days later. "You'll have the money for the first of the month. I'll be down this weekend and give you a check."

There was a short silence. Then, "Just like that," Jerry said. "Okay. You got the money. I'll make it stretch. You found a line of credit we can use?"

"This," Marty said, "is a one-shot." A personal loan with *Westerly* as security. He hung up.

Now, sitting in the courtroom this late afternoon, thinking of Los Angeles, the plant, Jerry Hopkins, Walter Jordan, John Black at

Coast—and Liz, and whether he should ask her to go down with him—he heard only vaguely Billy's continuing questioning of Millicent Potter, and Miss Potter's sometimes acid replies.

The courtroom was quiet, even somnolent, the jurors trying to look interested without much success.

Billy said, "These times when Mr. Paul McCurdy and Mr. John McKenzie were with Mr. Joseph McCurdy, Miss Potter, behind closed doors as you have testified—do you know what they discussed?"

"Objection, your honor," John McKenzie said. "The question calls for conjecture on the part of the witness."

Marty's attention was caught now. He watched the judge.

"Sustained," the judge said. "Strike the question."

Marty watched Billy. It's the way he wanted it, he thought suddenly; objection is exactly what he planned on. He glanced at the jury. Billy had them alert now.

Billy took his time. "I will put it another way, Miss Potter," he said at last. "On one of these occasions, were you called into the room where Mr. Paul McCurdy, Mr. John McKenzie, and Mr. Joesph McCurdy had been with the doors closed?"

Miss Potter sniffed. "That I was."

"Tell the jury about that occasion, please."

Miss Potter faced the jury. "Him," she said, and pointed with her chin, "Mr. Paul McCurdy, came downstairs. Nurse, Cook, and I were in the kitchen having a cup of tea. He asked us if we would come upstairs."

"All three of you?"

"That is what I said, young man." Miss Potter paused and then went on. "So we did, and he led us into the master bedroom."

"Mr. McKenzie was there?"

"He was."

"And Mr. Joseph McCurdy?"

"Of course."

Billy took a turn away from the witness stand, slowly returned. "Where exactly was Mr. Joseph McCurdy, Miss Potter?"

"In his chair."

"By the windows?"

"Yes."

"Where he talked with the flowers?"

Miss Potter's mouth was a thin straight line. "Yes."

Good boy, Marty thought; you're doing fine.

"Did you know, Miss Potter," Billy said, "why Mr. Paul McCurdy had asked the three of you to come upstairs and into the bedroom?"

"No."

"But you found out?"

"Of course."

"Will you tell the jury why it was, please, Miss Potter?"

Miss Potter was quite aware of being center stage. She took her time in answering. "To witness the old gentleman's will." In the silence Miss Potter pointed, this time with her finger. "He had it, Mr. McKenzie, and he spread it out on his attaché case on the old gentleman's lap and gave him a pen and showed him where to sign. Then we all signed. All the old gentleman said was 'Thank you.' "

32

Marty sent the Mercedes scudding down Interstate 5, one eye on the road, one on the mirror in case a trooper should come into view. It was childish, he knew, to take his annoyance out in speed, but there were times when moderation simply would not do. The annoyance was because of Liz.

"It's a nice invitation, Marty," she said, "and I think a weekend in Los Angeles might be fun. But no, thanks anyway."

"Any special reason?"

"No."

Marty waited, but she added nothing, and this was a decisive side of Liz he had rarely if ever seen before. "Okay," he said.

"Have a safe trip," Liz said, and hung up.

Now, alone, with only the rushing sound of the wind and the faint hum of the tires for company, he told himself that she had every right to refuse. Why then should he take umbrage because she had? Face it, he was, in fact, acting like an adolescent fool. Perfectly true; but no help at all.

The trouble, of course, was that Liz was an enigma. You thought you knew her well, and it turned out you didn't know her at all. Even in intimacy, about as close as a man and a woman could get, or supposed to be, now that he looked back on it Marty decided that he had never really gotten *to* Liz, penetrated her defenses, reached her core. It was as if a part of her always stood off watching ("I spend quite a bit of my time Marty-watching") and appraising and coming to God only knew what secret conclusions. And that, he thought, puts me pretty much in the category of a bug impaled on a pin for examination. A humbling thought.

He turned his thoughts to the trial. I wish I had known the old boy better, warts and prickles and all. He was a man; and when you've said that, you've said just about everything.

He had made his own way as few ever did. He had had a place to start, the bank already in existence handed down to him by his father, but what he had done with that bank was the important thing; the billion-dollar-plus financial structure that was McCurdy National was *his* monument. That, and the fortune he had amassed and chosen to pass along with strings attached.

But was "chosen" the word? If you believed the implications of Billy's artful questioning of Millicent Potter, that the remnant of a man who talked with flowers was capable only of doing what Paul and John McKenzie told him to, then the will he signed in Millicent Potter's presence could very well represent no wishes of his own, but simply what Paul wanted, and got.

And what of the Harlows, mother and illegitimate son, whom Billy had unearthed? Funny that should have popped into his mind right now. It scarcely fitted with the picture of devotion Millicent Potter had sketched when she told about that scene in the study, the old boy surprised, his dead wife's picture in his hands.

Paul had to know about the Harlows, of course; it would come as no surprise to him if Billy managed to work them into testimony. Rick Harlow's relationship to Paul was what, half brother? Much younger, of course, only four years older than Marty himself, which meant that he had been born in 1943, but age difference did not alter the relationship.

The important thing was that for lack of a single piece of paper, a marriage certificate in his mother's name, Rick Harlow had to be satisfied with a mere bequest instead of sharing equally with Paul and Joe Jr., and now Marty, the fruits of old Joe's financial wizardry.

Unfair? Probably, but that was the way it was. And again the concept of sheer accident of breeding and birth that had put himself, Marty McCurdy, into his own comfortable situation came to mind. He was in a thoughtful mood as he came into Los Angeles and drove out Sunset Boulevard to Stone Canyon.

Molly Moto met him at the door. He thought he could see pleasure in her face, and he had the warm feeling that he was home if only temporarily. Odd, he had never really thought in terms of home before. He was, he thought, seeing many things in a new light.

Jerry Hopkins was waiting in the study. They shook hands and walked together out on the cantilevered porch, where Molly Moto brought them beer and chile-flavored taco chips.

"Here's your check," Marty said. "I've endorsed it to the plant." And now I've pushed *Westerly* into the pot, he thought, and said nothing.

"I'll squeeze it till it hurts," Jerry said, "but this only postpones the reckoning."

"Understood." Marty tasted his beer, set it down. "How do you like the plant?"

Jerry grinned. "My own boss. Fun. It could be—" He stopped and shook his head. "Dreaming," he said.

Right here on this porch the day of the funeral, Marty thought, Paul had spoken of dreams, hadn't he? The wine industry starting with a dream? The movies? Even giant Coast Aircraft? And how about the bank itself? Had old Joe McCurdy dreamed? What else could have driven him to take the chances Marty was only now beginning to understand? "Tell me what you think it could be," he said, and settled himself to listen.

It was obvious that Jerry Hopkins had given considerable thought to the matter. "Not just a run-of-the-mill vendor," he said. "That way you're competing with half of Southern California. It could be a specialized vendor, not only fabricating and assembling components for Coast and Lockheed and McDonnell-Douglas and the rest, but designing them too. That way you're tied right in with the big boys and they can't cut you off and take the work back into their own shops."

Marty thought about it. "Would John Black hold still for that?"

"That depends on what kinds of things we'd take." Jerry paused. "There are nasty little components, there always are, that cause more trouble than they're worth. Constant headaches. Coast would love to throw some of those lock, stock, and barrel to a vendor who could produce." He paused again. "But for the vendor that would take considerable financial backing." He grinned. "So it's not something to think about right now."

It all came right down to finances, Marty thought, in order to convert dreams into reality. He nodded. "If it did become possible," he said slowly, "would you care to give it a whirl?"

"I don't know," Jerry said, and then grinned suddenly and made a small quick gesture of negation. "The hell I don't. The answer is yes. I'd love to take a whirl at it. Maybe that isn't the prudent way to think, but—"

"You'd be leaving Coast," Marty said.

"That's right, walking out on what they call the security I've built up." Jerry shook his head. "That's crap." He grinned again. "It probably sounds cocky, but the way I see it, the only security is in yourself."

I've never thought about it, Marty told himself, because I've never had to; and he found the concept interesting. "Explain that."

Jerry nodded. "I have an uncle," he said. "He worked for Studebaker in South Bend. Doing fine, raising his kids, buying a house, money in the bank and seniority on the job. Security." He shook his head. "But Studebaker closed the South Bend operation and moved to Canada, and South Bend houses were suddenly a glut on the market, and my uncle didn't want to move to Canada anyway, and the money in the bank didn't last very long, and where was the security then?"

Marty was silent, listening; and learning, he thought.

"No," Jerry said. "The way I see it, if you're good enough at what you do, then sometimes, maybe not very often, a chance will come along, call it opportunity, and you'd better take a good hard look before you turn it down because it might be just what you've been waiting for without even knowing it, and it leads right in the direction you've really been wanting to go all along."

Thoughts of old Joe McCurdy again. Why was it, Marty asked himself, that he was forever trying these days to put himself into the old man's mind? What would Joe have thought of young Jerry Hopkins' ideas? The answer came loud and clear: he would have applauded. "I think we could get along, you and I," he said.

Jerry nodded. "If I didn't think so too, I wouldn't even consider it." He stood up and gestured with the check. "I'll see that this goes to work. If it turns out that you think you can manage the financing, and you want to talk about it—" He paused, grinning. "Why, you've got somebody who'll listen real hard."

Marty sat for a time in the sun after Jerry Hopkins had left. I'm getting in deeper and deeper, he thought, because if I did take him on to run the plant, I would be responsible for him, no? Yes. And for all the men who worked at the plant. And for their families. In a way I am responsible for them now, but only in a way, because I am not yet totally committed.

That, he decided, was hairsplitting, weaseling; and it angered him. I told Liz I was responsible, didn't I, and either I am, or I am not; there is no halfway.

With sudden decision he stood up, walked into the study, and sat down at the desk to search for a telephone number. Saturday or not, Howard Carter, Assistant DA, was in his office. "Marty McCurdy here," Marty said. "I've been in San Francisco. What's going on in my father's plane crash?"

"The investigation is proceeding, Mr. McCurdy."

Some of the annoyance, even anger, of the day remained. Marty said, "Don't pat me on the head and tell me everything is all right. I want some facts."

Carter's voice altered subtly. "There are certain routines, Mr. McCurdy, that have to be followed. We do not give out information at random. Our policy—"

"If I have to," Marty said, "I'll get John Carrington and go with him to see the DA himself. You're talking about my father, and I want to know what's doing. I want to know you haven't just been sitting on your pin-striped ass."

"I resent that, Mr. McCurdy."

"Go right ahead and resent it. But make up your mind. Are you going to fill me in, or do I go to your boss?"

There was a short silence. Then, with slow reluctance, "If you think you can find my office—" Carter began.

"I'll find it." Marty stood up, the phone still at his ear. "I'm on my way."

33

Susan had a skycap collect her bags from the carrousel, wheel them outside, and put them in a taxi. She tipped him well and settled back in the seat for what was going to be a ride she did not relish.

She had not examined too closely her motives for leaving Boston so suddenly because she was afraid that if she did she would find them at best flighty or humiliating, and at worst irresponsible even to the point of ignobility. And she was not, or never had been, an impulsive person.

She looked idly, distastefully from the cab window. The last time she had taken this trip, she remembered, had been after their return from young Joe McCurdy's funeral down in Los Angeles, and Paul had been preoccupied, she recalled, with, of course, some kind of bank business. Among other things, she seemed to remember, something to do with Wally Trent. Men, Paul in particular, could make so much out of what was really so little.

At the airport it had been bright; as they neared San Francisco the sunlight began to diminish as afternoon fog rolled in. Watching the gathering haze, Susan could imagine how it would be looking out to the Golden Gate and the great red bridge and watching the gray wall approach in its soundless, irresistible way. And the foghorns would start up, voices of danger, of doom, a cacophony of despair to her way of thinking, and how Paul could, as he said, actually enjoy their sound was more than she could imagine. She closed her eyes and shivered faintly. Why have I come back? It is—demeaning.

The cab driver, bearing the size of the skycap's tip in mind, carried her bags up to the front door of the house. Susan paid him and tipped him well. She rang the bell and Teresa appeared almost immediately, an instant broad smile showing her gold teeth. "Hello, Teresa."

"Ah, señora," Teresa said. It was only in moments of emotion that she lapsed into Spanish. "*Bienvenido.* Welcome." She picked up Susan's bags and started inside.

"Mrs. McCurdy." A pleasant female voice from the steps below.

Susan turned. She did not recognize the young woman, but she approved of what she saw. Obviously a person of breeding, of quiet confidence, carrying her stunning looks and her marvelous young figure with awareness and justifiable pride, but without arrogance. "I do not believe—" Susan began.

"No, Mrs. McCurdy, we have not met. I saw you at the McCurdy funeral in Los Angeles. My name is Elizabeth Palmer. I am a friend of Marty's."

"I see." Susan did not see; it was merely what one said under the circumstances. She waited.

"I came to see your husband," Liz said, "but he isn't here." She wore now a different, almost strange expression. "Another funeral," she said. "A coincidence?" She paused. "I wonder if you and I could talk instead?"

Susan hesitated. "About what, Miss Palmer?"

"About Marty. And your husband."

"And this wretched will-contest business?"

Liz nodded. "Exactly," she said.

Again the hesitation, the reluctance. "I am just home," Susan said. "I have had a long flight, and I am tired." The words suddenly seemed to scream at her, mock her; they were the words of a woman who sidestepped all responsibility. Was that what she had become? "Come in, anyway," she said suddenly, and held the door open.

They sat in the study facing the fireplace, where, in reaction to the fog outside, Teresa lighted the already set fire when she brought in the tea tray. Susan poured, the movements so automatic her mind was not conscious of them. "Did Marty send you?"

"Good heavens, no." Liz could even smile at the thought. "He's in Los Angeles and he wouldn't like it if he even knew I was here."

"Then I am afraid I don't understand."

"Two men," Liz said, "two strong men, your husband and Marty."

Susan set her teacup down. "Is that how you see them?" Marty perhaps; but Paul? Was that how he seemed to others, especially to other women?

"Don't you?"

"I—" Susan began, and there she stopped. This young woman was remarkably blunt, quietly forceful. Susan felt on the defensive. "Go on," she said.

"They're in a fight," Liz said. "Neither of them likes to lose—in anything." She smiled; it was the sudden brilliant smile she showed only rarely. "I know Marty doesn't. I've seen him. I don't think your husband is any different, maybe only a little quieter."

Susan picked up her teacup again. "I suppose you are right."

"In some fights," Liz said, "maybe in most fights, nobody wins." She paused. "I think women have known that for a long time. I'm not sure men will ever learn it."

I have never even thought about it, Susan told herself; and was annoyed that it was so, because the concept struck her now with impact.

"At first," Liz said, "I thought Marty had started this fight out of just plain stubbornness. I was wrong. Conviction, responsibility, pride—those are his reasons. I see that now. And I admit that I find his reasons admirable." She smiled faintly. "Maybe I'm prejudiced."

"You're in love with him."

"Maybe. That's the easy inference."

Susan set her teacup down again. "You seem to know him well."

Another smile. Was there in it a hint of pity, as if Liz felt sorry for an older woman who could not bring herself to speak frankly? "I know him very well," Liz said, "as well as a woman can know a man. Does that answer your question?"

It had been a long time since Susan had felt flustered. She took her time, gathering herself in silence. "What is it you want me to do?" she said. "Relay all this to my husband?"

"That's just it," Liz said. "I don't know. But it can't go on this way. It has to be stopped. Maybe you can help."

Susan sat quietly, staring into the fire. We are in agreement, she thought suddenly, and found both ease and comfort in the knowledge. Have I felt this way all along and only now realized it? It was as if a light had been turned on in what had been darkness. "I think," she said slowly, "that they are tearing themselves apart." A thought until now hidden; spoken aloud, it seemed to free restraint. There was luxury in the new sense of release. "I can't imagine that Marty likes what is being done to my father-in-law's—image. I know Paul doesn't." The words had been waiting to be spoken. "He—my father-in-law was not the ridiculous, confused old man they are making him out. Not for a moment. What he did, whatever he did, he did for a purpose. Always. And they are making him appear a—doddering old fool."

"You knew him well?"

How can I explain it? "He was always there. He and Martha. They were the ones who understood—oh, I know it sounds odd, but it was true—that here I was a stranger in a strange land. It was their land, and they loved it, and they tried to make me feel at home, secure. That was the word: secure." Her voice dropped. "And then all at once," she said, "Martha was gone. But Joe was still there, bigger than life. You could count on him. Always."

I think I can understand, Liz thought. I feel I am getting to see him, and that is the picture I have of him too. I wish I had known him. "But after his stroke?" she said.

"He—fought it. Alone upstairs in that corner room. 'I'll whip it, Susie,' he told me. And I knew he would." Susan smiled suddenly. "The only person in the world who ever called me Susie." The smile was gone. "And he did whip it, all of it, the walking, the use of his arm, the talking, all of it. And now—" She was silent.

All at once they were no longer strangers, but allies, Liz thought, brought together by an unlikely concatenation of circumstances, in effect representing opposing sides and yet holding identical views.

"I am used to letting Paul handle this kind of thing," Susan said. "But you are right, it can't go on." She was close to tears, and lest it show, she stood up quickly, walked to the windows, and stood for a while with her back to the room. "The gardens," she said. "Martha loved them. Joe—knew nothing at all about them."

Liz said gently, "He talked to the flowers, the radio says."

Susan turned to face the room. She had the strange feeling that her thoughts now were being guided by she knew not what force. She said slowly, wonderingly, "Of course he did. Just as he talked to me and the nurse and Millicent Potter and anybody else who was handy. Just as he drove himself to walk endlessly back and forth across that room until he was exhausted. And for the same reason." There was deep conviction in her voice. "Exercise. His speech muscles were affected, just as the muscles of his arm and leg were. And he drove himself to regain their use. All of them." She paused, watching Liz steadily. "Can you think of any other reason?"

Liz was smiling now. "Do you know," she said, "I can't."

Susan saw Liz to the door, and they shook hands. "I think," Susan said, "that you are in love with him. You don't mind my saying that?" And again this young woman surprised her.

"Not at all," Liz said, and smiled. "So I will be equally blunt. Are you in love with your husband?"

Susan opened her mouth and closed it again in silence.

Liz said, "I hope you don't find the question offensive, because I think it is important." She smiled again. "I think we all listen more closely to those we care for. And those who care for us." She turned away then without waiting for comment.

Hans was in the car, sitting erect in the passenger seat. He gave her hand a quick swipe with his tongue when she slid in beneath the wheel, and his expression seemed to ask: where now?

"Let's hope that Billy is in."

Billy was, in loafers, chino trousers, and a short-sleeved shirt, his hair rumpled and his expression preoccupied as he came to the door of the small apartment he had taken for the trial period. "Well," he said, "well, well. This is a pleasant surprise." He held the door wide.

It was a modest apartment, furnished in by-the-yard decorator taste, as characterless as an empty refrigerator. Papers were spread on the dinette table, and a cassette tape recorder lay among them. "Tools of the trade," Billy said. He was smiling. "Yours are probably much neater." He was talking too much, he thought, and found it impossible to stop. "I thought of calling you to see if you were free anytime during this weekend—" He shook his head. "It didn't seem like the thing to do. I don't know why." He waited until Liz was seated on the sofa, and then sank into a matching chair. He studied her face. "I take it this isn't exactly a social call?"

"Billy," Liz said. Her voice was soft. "Billy, slow down."

"Racing my motor?" His smile was rueful. "It's the effect you have on me." His smile disappeared. "Okay, what do we talk about? Marty?"

"His grandfather."

Billy settled back in his chair. "I'm getting to like the old guy. He was an original." His voice changed. "Maybe *the* original. In a lot of ways Marty fits the pattern. You've seen it?"

She had indeed seen it, and after her talk with Susan it was even clearer now. Liz said, "I keep thinking of Joe McCurdy up in that room driving himself to walk back and forth until he was exhausted, then sitting down to rest in that chair." Marty, she thought, would have done the same. There are some who do not give up.

"And," Billy said, "talking to the flowers?" He shook his head. "I didn't particularly like bringing that out, but there it was."

Liz's voice was quiet now. "You're wrong, you know. Susan McCurdy had it right." So simple, so obvious. "He had to talk to regain his speech. There was nothing wrong with his mind. You have all said it: he simply didn't care what people thought, so he went right ahead with the talking practice he had set himself whether Nurse was there in the room or Millicent Potter or anybody else.

Who else but the flowers would he have talked to about financial matters, things he had talked about all his life?"

Billy got slowly out of his chair and took a few paces toward the windows, turned, and came back as if he were still in the courtroom, taking time to set his thoughts in order. Still standing, looking down at Liz as at Millicent Potter, he said at last, "An interesting theory."

"But you don't believe it?"

"There are so many other—factors."

Liz watched him carefully in silence.

"I told Marty about them," Billy said. "Letters to the papers, talking to the redwood trees, picking up hitchhikers and talking to them, trying to endow a Chair for Revolutionary Study at UC." He paused. "And then that Mary Harlow affair and the illegitimate son." He shook his head. "I think he was off his rocker all right." He seemed to be reassuring himself.

"Are you implying that men who have illicit affairs are unbalanced?" Liz paused. "Because if you are, you have to include yourself, don't you?"

Billy sat down again. "You play rough," he said.

"I can't help that," Liz said. "I was taught to look at things as they are, not as I wish they were. I was taught to look for the truth, and if that sounds pompous it is still the way it is." Let's make it plain, she thought. "Because he had a stroke," she said, "and made a will your client doesn't like, you try to build the case that his eccentricities were actually insanities, or at the least evidence of total senility." She shook her head. "I don't believe it, and I am not sure you do."

"The question," Billy said, "is whether the jury will."

Liz was silent for a long time. "I see," she said at last, "that is it, isn't it? Not whether it is really true, but only whether that collection of people on the jury can be convinced that it is." She shook her head again. "We look at things differently, Billy."

The room was still. Billy closed his eyes. He opened them again and for a long time looked across the room at nothing. He said at last, "How did we get to this point anyway?" He looked at Liz.

"I'm afraid," Liz said slowly, "by a kind of inevitable process, a sort of chain reaction. Maybe sooner or later it had to be."

"That's nonsense."

"Maybe, Billy, but I don't think so."

Billy's smile was bitter. "You've really made my day, Liz."

"I'm sorry about that. I hoped I was giving you an interpretation you might have missed, explaining why Joe McCurdy talked to the flowers."

"An interpretation that leads right straight to defeat."

"Or the truth." Liz stood up. "Maybe one leads to the other. I'm sorry, Billy. I mean that."

He too had risen. He was taller than she, far stronger, but his was the position of weakness. "Are you going to take your theory to McKenzie?"

"I don't know yet." Liz paused. "Maybe you'll want to take it to him yourself." She held out her hand. It was cool and firm. "Goodbye, Billy." There was finality in the words. She let herself out and closed the door gently.

Outside, the fog was thicker now; its moisture glistened on the pavement. Liz got into her car, and Hans thrust his muzzle against her hand. His tail thumped the door panel. "Oh, God," Liz said, "why do I have to be like that? Can you tell me, Hans?" She fondled his ears. "Now we go home," she said. "At least you don't get mad at me."

34

The phone call was not, of course, from Pete Mankowski as Sudie had hoped. That, whether she liked it or not, was over, finished, and maybe one day the scars on her psyche would disappear.

"My name is Robert Story," the voice on the phone said quietly. "I'm calling because there has been an accident, and your brother is hurt."

Just like that. Alan? Bruce? Of course not. "Jim?" Sudie said. And then quickly, "Where? I'll come, of course."

Robert Story was waiting in the hospital lobby. "You're Sudie." He nodded and took her arm. His hand was surprisingly strong, and comforting; a take-charge guy. "He's in surgery. We'll wait upstairs." There was no more talk until they were seated on the straight bench in the empty waiting room. "You'll have questions," Robert Story said then. "I'll try, but I probably can't answer them."

It was unreal, Sudie thought. "Surgery? What are they doing to him? Why?" She was conscious that her voice was too loud, but it was beyond her control. "I mean—!"

"Easy. There was a hassle," Robert Story said. "If even the cops know what it was about, they aren't saying, anyway not to me. Probably one of those senselesss things."

Sudie shook her head. "Not—Jim. He'd—run! What happened?"

"Somebody put a knife in him."

"No," Sudie said. Automatically she brushed her hair back from her face with both hands. "No," she said again. Her voice rose. "I—don't believe you. I don't even know who you are! You're just a voice on the phone!"

"I'm your brother's lawyer. Your father hired me before. They found my card in Jim's pocket and called me." He paused. "They wanted a next-of-kin, somebody. Your father was out. I left a message. The best I could do. Then I called you."

"How did you even know there was a me?"

"I know you. Jim talked about you. His twin. Patient beyond the call of duty."

"Then he was stoned." And now? "Will he be—all right?"

"I hope so."

Paul walked home, in the exercise finding a lessening of the tension that had been building within him all week. Had this been the reason his father had also walked, rather than ridden, to and from the bank every day? Strange, he had never thought about that before; boys, he decided, merely accepted what their parents did without probing for reasons.

Wally Trent was gone. That fact had come clear to him now, and with its realization there had come too the sense of loss that had been missing before. And, concomitant, a sense of guilt, inescapable, justified or not.

Wally was a grown man, allegedly responsible for his actions. And what he had done by playing fast and loose with bank funds, whether out of greed or just plain bad judgment, was indefensible, inevitably setting in train unpleasant and just possibly chaotic results which even Wally ought to have foreseen.

Jordan had said about McCurdy Aircraft that there were always rumors, which was not necessarily true. But Paul knew now how Jordan had felt because there were rumors about McCurdy National, and some of them had found their way into print. "McCurdy National's Foreign Losses Reckoned in Millions . . ." Enough gossip to depress the price of McCurdy National stock; not enough to cause any kind of panic—yet. But, coupled with word of crop losses in the vineyards, the publicity this damnable trial was causing, *and* Charles Goodwin's reaction, Wally Trent's transgressions were not easily forgotten. Or forgiven.

But suppose instead of shutting him off that night when he phoned, Paul asked himself, I had been sympathetic, asked him over, listened to his maundering self-pity, in effect held his hand? Would he be alive now? The question was unanswerable, and therein lay the pain. Uncertainty was something you lived with. Forever.

The fog was heavier now. Paul breathed deep as he walked, savoring the faint salt flavor in the air. He loved fogs. And Susan hated them. Susan. She had been much in his thoughts all day. Maybe I don't know much about dealing with people, only with balance sheets.

He reached the house, went quickly up the steps, let himself in, and there he stopped, his hand still on the doorknob. Susan was standing in the study doorway.

They were strangers, that was Paul's first thought, and he wondered if it was in Susan's mind too, because for long moments neither spoke. It was Susan who broke the silence. "I should have given you warning," she said.

Paul closed the door gently. "I'm just glad that you are back. You—look great. In fact, you are quite the most beautiful thing I have ever seen. I've missed you, terribly."

Susan was afraid to speak; tears were very close. Somehow he understood, and came toward her, smiling, to take her in his arms and hold her close for a long time.

Home, Susan thought; this is home. I know that now. The enormity of the knowledge was stunning, and needed further examination, which could wait. Together they walked into the study and, still in silence, sat down on the sofa facing the fire.

"I'm all right now," Susan said. She could even smile brightly, too brightly, as she tried to make conversation. "Teresa said you had gone to a funeral."

Should he say it? How could it be avoided? "Wally Trent's."

The room was suddenly still. Susan withdrew from the protective arm to look carefully at Paul's face. "When?" she said. "And how?"

"A few days ago. After you left." Paul shook his head gently. "It doesn't matter. He's dead. Sleeping pills—"

"Suicide?" Susan's voice was incredulous. "Wally? Loving to live the way he did? No, not Wally."

He had not even considered suicide, Paul told himself; and yet it was the first thing you usually thought of when sleeping pills were involved, wasn't it? Had he unconsciously rejected the possibility because the implications were too painful? There were times, it seemed, when his mind played tricks on him. He kept his voice as emotionless as he could. "He had been drinking. Alan said there was a synergistic effect. There frequently is. Damn it—" Suddenly unable to sit still, he stood up, walked a few steps away from the sofa, turned, and came back. Standing, looking down at Susan. "He's dead. That's the only thing that matters."

"You're blaming yourself. Why?"

"Nonsense."

Susan sat quietly, watching him steadily.

"Damn it," Paul said, "you are just home. I shouldn't have told you about Wally. Let's forget it, him.'"

"Don't I have a right to know what's bothering you?"

It was then that Teresa appeared in the study doorway, a penciled note in her hand. Paul and Susan looked at her and waited. "A Mr. Robert Story telephoned while you were gone," Teresa said.

Jim again, Paul thought. "He wants me to call him?"

Teresa held out the note. "He didn't give a telephone number. This is the address where you can reach him."

Paul nodded. "Thank you, Teresa." He glanced at the note; the Berkeley address meant nothing. A police station, perhaps? Oh, God, what had Jim done now?

"What is it?" Susan said. "Is it important?"

She's just home, Paul thought, she's tired, and already the news of Wally Trent had upset her. Now this, whatever it was; too much. "Probably not," he said. "But I'll have to go see anyway."

They were strangers again, the moment of closeness past. Well, perhaps not total strangers at that, Susan thought; Elizabeth Palmer had made the point: he is a strong man, and others depend on him.

She could even find a measure of pride in the thought. "Of course," she said.

"I won't be long. Across the Bay and back." Tomorrow I will tell her about it, whatever it is. He smiled and walked quickly out of the room.

Across the Bay on the lighted bridge, windows up against the fog and dampness, windshield wipers going at their steady pace, the foghorns only faint sounds somewhere out in the darkness. Susan was home, that was the important thing, and tomorrow he and she could sort it all out.

He came into the hospital almost disbelieving. Teresa could have had the address wrong, of course, but he had a sinking feeling that she had not. At the information desk, "I am looking for a Mr. Robert Story," he said, "and possibly also my son, James McCurdy."

There was no hesitation. "Fourth floor. The elevator to your right."

Paul came into the formal, characterless waiting room, and Sudie jumped to her feet and ran to him. "Jim?" Paul said.

"Yes, sir. He's in surgery. A knife wound," Story said.

Sudie said, "We don't even know what happened!" Her voice was filled with protest. She explained about the card in Jim's pocket, the police call to Robert Story. "And that's all we know!"

"It's enough." Paul's voice was grave. A marijuana charge or something like it was one thing, he thought; this was quite another, and he should have brought Susan—he saw that now. "I'd better telephone your mother." He looked again at Story. "You have no—progress report?"

"No, sir. They already had him in surgery when I arrived." Bob glanced at his watch. "Almost two hours ago."

Sudie said, "Mother is—still in Boston?"

So the children all knew, Paul thought; and why should they not? Their ties to Susan were even closer than his, part of her flesh, her being. "She came home this evening."

Sudie's eyes were wide. "Why didn't you bring her? Oh, Daddy!"

"I'll try to get her now," Paul said. The words and the thought were inadequate. He started down the hall in search of a telephone; Robert Story's hurrying footsteps caught up with him.

"The doctor has come out. He's with Sudie now."

He was young, and his mask hung loose around his neck; he still wore his green operating cap. The waiting room seemed even smaller, colder than before. "I am sorry, Mr. McCurdy." His voice sounded sincere, and Paul was reminded of Nancy saying that they never got used to death. "We did all we could. It wasn't enough."

Sudie stood motionless, stunned. Paul put his arm around her shoulders and drew her close. "Thank you, Doctor. I am sure you did. Are there—formalities?"

"Let me take care of them," Robert Story said.

Paul nodded. "Thank you." He looked down at Sudie. Tears ran down the sides of her nose. "You?"

"I want to go home."

Paul nodded again. "Come with me."

"I can't! My car is on the street, and, and—everything!"

"I'll see that she gets to San Francisco, sir," Robert Story said. "You'll want to see Mrs. McCurdy first." A statement, no question.

My duty pointed out to me, Paul thought, and said, "Yes." He bent to kiss Sudie's wet cheek. "Nothing you could have done, honey. Nothing anyone could have done."

"Are you sure?" As that day in his office, the girl-child was suddenly if maybe only temporarily a woman grown.

"No," Paul said, "I'm not. I find I am not sure of many things these days." He gave her shoulders a final squeeze and walked out. He felt old and tired as he rode down in the elevator and walked out of the building into the fog.

35

Marty sat after dinner Saturday night stretched out in a chair on the cantilevered porch looking out at the lights of the city, nursing anger and a sense of frustration.

Assistant DA Howard Carter was an obnoxious little son of a bitch. That was just for starters. And the talk in Carter's crowded little cubbyhole that he called an office had been difficult from the beginning.

"I resent your attitude," Carter said.

"As I said on the phone, you go right ahead and resent it," Marty said, "as long as you tell me what I want to know." Maybe that was not the way to handle the little jerk, but Marty doubted if any other approach would have worked better. "I'm listening."

Carter seemed about to resist, thought better of it, closed his mouth with a snap, and opened the folder on his desk. He began to read the dry, routine facts: date and time of the crash; type and serial number of the aircraft; testimony of the tower operator; results of the findings at Coast Aircraft in sifting the wreckage; testimony that the aircraft had been parked at the McCurdy Aircraft plant field for two days following its overhaul in the Coast Aircraft shops, and that on one of those days, it had been flown without incident; the results of routine investigation into insurance coverage; the coroner's report on the remains of Joseph McCurdy.

He closed the folder. "This is what we have," he said. "Do you find in it anything of significance, *Mister* McCurdy?"

Marty held tight to his temper. "Dynamite," he said, "doesn't come as standard equipment on Coast aircraft as far as I know."

"I am aware of it." Carter paused. He seemed reluctant to add anything, but he could not resist saying, "But the evidence shows that the dynamite was not in the aircraft when it left the Coast shops after overhaul."

"Not so," Marty said.

Carter produced a tight little smile. "The aircraft was flown from Coast Aircraft to the McCurdy field, it wasn't towed clear across a good part of Los Angeles. And it was flown again without incident the day before the explosion and crash. It follows that the dynamite had not yet been introduced into that engine nacelle." There was a hint of triumph in his voice.

Marty shook his head. "Dynamite doesn't go off by itself. It takes a detonator to explode it, and it takes something to set off the detonator. Everything could have been inside that nacelle just waiting for whatever was going to activate it to be set."

Carter thought about it. If he was disappointed, it did not show. He said slowly, "What would activate it?"

"I don't know. I could design a dozen things that would work, and there are probably a hundred others I wouldn't even think of."

"You could design the—explosive package?"

"Of course I could," Marty said. There was disgust in his voice. "Any engineer could. The question is, who would want to? And why?"

"And," Carter said, "would have the opportunity."

Marty stared at the bristly little man. "You know," he said, "for the first time you and I are on the same wavelength."

Now, sitting looking out at the city lights: no, it was not a pleasant talk, Marty thought, and what I learned was exactly nothing.

Bullets sometimes showed distinct rifling marks and could be traced to particular guns. Even knives, as Marty understood it, sometimes made distinctive wounds. But when dynamite exploded, all that was left were some pieces out of which little could be made.

But damn it, Marty thought, the police are supposed to know their business. What was it the Seabees had had as their motto: The difficult we do immediately; the impossible takes a little longer? Why couldn't others operate on the same principle?

All right, he told himself, you're a smart fellow, and you have a motivation they don't: he was your father, and you are involved, and you are not going to get to the bottom of this whole mess until you know all the answers—so how would you go about it?

From the other end, he thought suddenly. Never mind the evidence; it told almost nothing. Who would want to set the explosive charge? And, as Carter had said, who would have had the opportunity?

He sat late thinking of possibilities, and thinking too of Liz, who would have been a good backboard against which to bounce ideas, merely by her presence providing too a satisfying warmth that closed off loneliness. When at last he went to bed, he felt a trifle easier in his mind, the frustration at least for the present reduced to bearable proportions.

He was up early Sunday morning, and went for a brisk twenty-length swim in the pool before breakfast again on the porch.

The day was bright and clear, smog not yet gathering, and the ocean lay sparkling all the way to infinity. Down at Newport by mid-morning the breeze would be up, and to be out on the water, putting *Westerly* through her paces, would have been ease and comfort, and could not now be merely whenever he chose, as before. Besides, *Westerly* was in hock.

Molly Moto came out to clear away the breakfast dishes. "More coffee?"

"Thanks, no."

"Your father—" Molly began, and stopped.

"He drank a lot of coffee?" Idle question.

"Always." Molly paused. "Even on that morning he would not leave until he had had his three cups."

That morning, Marty thought, when he had gone off to fly to his death? Sitting here over that third cup of coffee, had he had any premonition? Why should he? "Molly. Molly."

She was already at the doorway. She stopped and returned, the tray in her hands.

"Sit down, Molly," Marty said, and took his time setting his thoughts in order. "You said that *even on that morning* he would not leave until he had his third cup of coffee."

Molly nodded.

"What did you mean by that?"

Molly hesitated. "Why, I don't know. He stayed for his coffee like he always did."

Easy, he told himself; slow and easy. "But the way you said it, Molly," he said, "there must have been some reason why on that particular morning he might have skipped that third cup. Mustn't there?"

Molly thought about it. "He said he would probably be late, but he didn't care." She smiled faintly. "He was always late."

Yes. Marty remembered that well. Maybe it was in reaction that he himself was almost religiously punctual. Still. "What would he be late for that morning?"

Molly shook her head. "I don't know. There was a telephone call while he was at breakfast."

"From whom?"

Again, "I don't know. He answered it himself." She sait quietly, composed, inscrutable.

Think, Marty told himself, think! He said slowly, "When he left, did he tell you where he was going? Anything at all?"

"Only the factory. He said he would be there sometime."

Obviously, Marty thought, because he was going flying and the plant was where the aircraft was parked. Wait a minute. "*Only* the factory," he said. "What does that mean, Molly?"

Molly's voice was patient. "He went there a lot. Every day."

No; that Marty did not remember. "For how long?" he said.

"The last week, ten days."

"All at once, just like that he started going every day?"

"I think maybe."

"Did he tell you why?"

Molly shook her head. The movement was emphatic.

"Did he seem—different? Worried about anything?"

"I don't know."

Marty was silent for a long time while Molly waited patiently. He said at last, "Thanks, Molly," and sat on in the sun after she had gone, staring at the distant, shining ocean, and then at last he went inside to the study desk, and got out the telephone books.

Hopkins, Jerry. Well, at least his name was not Smith or Jones; that would have made the search impossible. But Hopkins was bad enough, and it took almost thirty minutes, a number of telephone calls and several voices filled with annoyance at being disturbed this early on Sunday morning. But finally the right Jerry Hopkins was on the line.

Marty said, "Do you know Tom Chambers, the project engineer on the Executive model?"

There was a smile in Jerry's voice. "I know him well."

"I want you and him at the plant tomorrow morning," Marty said. "Early."

"Oh?"

"And I want an Executive aircraft flown in there even earlier, and parked. There are tie-down anchors set in the pavement."

There was a long pause. Then, "Anything else? How about a fighter-bomber? Or maybe one of the big jet transports? Are you serious? Because I'll have to go to John Black to arrange it. And I'll have to tell him something. And this is Sunday."

"Tell him," Marty said slowly, "that I'm riding a hunch. All the way. I think he'll understand." He hung up.

It was going to be a long day, he thought. Maybe to pass the time he would drive down to the beach and see if the surf was running high at the Wedge, do a little surfing to tire himself out. And just possibly bang yourself up? Wouldn't that be great? Am I so involved that I can't even do that? And the answer, unmistakable, was: yes, you have accepted responsibilities, and that is that; your life is no longer solely your own.

He sat for a long time thinking about it, because the implications were vast. Then he roused himself at last, and dialed Liz's number in Berkeley. There was sleep in her voice when she answered.

"Slugabed," Marty said. "I've been up for hours." At least it seemed like it.

"The consensus here," Liz said, "is that all Southern Californians are barbarians." She yawned audibly. "What's on your mind?"

No hesitation. "I wish you were here."

"That sounds carnal."

Marty could smile faintly. "Maybe a little of that too, but mostly something else. I wish you were here to hold my hand, and just talk to me. What was it the poet said, that no man is an island? You can probably quote it entire."

Liz said slowly, "Is this Joseph Martin McCurdy III?"

"The same."

"You sound like an impostor."

"Maybe I am," Marty said. "Maybe I have been all along." He took a deep breath. "The word is 'need,' woman. I need someone, and I think it's you," he said, and hung up slowly.

One more call, to Billy's rented San Francisco apartment this time. Billy's voice too was sleepy. Had Billy and Liz been together? Never mind. "I'm not going to be in court tomorrow," Marty said. "Is that against the law, or something?"

Billy said at last, "In a civil suit, no. But I'd rather you were here for a number of reasons."

"What are they?"

"If you aren't going to be here," Billy said, "there's no point in spelling them out."

Marty said slowly, "Somebody been rubbing you the wrong way?"

"I'll survive. It's definite? You're not going to show tomorrow?"

"It's definite."

"Okay," Billy said then, "I'll argue your goddamn case." The line went dead.

Marty hung up, and sat quietly, staring at nothing. It was going to be a long day.

Paul too was up early this Sunday morning, the bad taste of last night's events still depressing his thoughts. Driving back across the bridge from Berkeley after leaving the hospital, he had tried not to think what Susan's reaction was going to be when he told her the sad news, but recriminations, of course, would inevitably be a part of it, and unconsciously he was prepared. There were no recriminations.

Susan had sat quietly on the sofa facing the fire, staring straight into the flames while, sitting beside her and holding one of her hands in his, Paul told her what had happened. "I thought it was—something else," he said, "and nothing to concern you with tonight."

She turned her head then and looked for long moments into his face. "Go on."

"He was arrested on a drug charge," Paul said. He watched her eyes close briefly, open again. "I arranged for an East Bay lawyer to handle it, Robert Story. He was the one who called this afternoon. I assumed it was more of the same." Patient and logical, and knowing all along that it was somehow wrong.

Susan merely nodded. "You couldn't have known that it was—the other thing." Her voice was entirely calm. "And you could not have known that Wally Trent would kill himself either." She turned to look at him. "Could you?"

"There is nothing to show that Wally did—" Paul stopped. "I could not have known," he said. And then, in a different voice, "Even if you had gone with me tonight, there would have been nothing to do. I didn't see Jim. Nobody saw him."

"But you were there. And Sudie. And I would have been there. For once, not—locked out." She nodded again and stood up. "You always have tried to—save me pain, worry, anguish, and you meant well. I think you always do." Her voice altered subtly. "A long time ago I read somewhere that the road to hell is paved with good intentions." She walked out of the room and up the stairs without haste. Paul heard her bedroom door close firmly.

He sat down again and stared at the flames. "Locked out" was her phrase, he thought; and found its impact staggering. When he was growing up, he remembered, he had listened with amusement to his father telling his mother what had happened at the bank each day, sometimes in profane language, frequently in detail Paul was sure his mother did not understand.

But the boy himself, Paul thought now, had badly missed the point. His mother had never been "locked out"; he saw that now. Such a simple thing, and so—devastating. Why had he not thought of it before?

"Mother isn't here, Daddy?" Sudie's voice from the study doorway.

Paul got up from the sofa and turned to face her. Robert Story, he saw, stood behind her waiting in the hall. "She's gone upstairs."

"You—told her?"

Paul nodded.

"I see." It was the woman, not the girl-child speaking now. "I'll go see her." Sudie turned to Story. "Thank you, Bob, for—everything."

He nodded gravely. "When you're ready to go back to Berkeley, I'll be happy to come for you. Anytime."

"I'll call you." She started to turn away and then turned back briefly. "Good night, Daddy." She was gone, running up the stairs.

Story said, "Good night, sir."

"Come in, young man. Sit down. Have a glass of brandy with me." Suddenly I don't want to be alone, he thought; not ever again.

Now, sitting at breakfast, he wondered that he and young Story had found so much to talk about. The subject of Jim was never mentioned. Instead, conversation like a soothing compress spread itself over the new wound. "Baseball was your game at college," Paul said. "I played some golf."

"Yes, sir. I know. You were Captain of Stanford's team, and you won the state amateur title four times."

"Only three," Paul said. "As you would say it, I blew the fourth. When you let your concentration lapse, I think in anything, you are asking for trouble."

"I'd never thought of it that way before," Story said, "but I think you're right."

The two women were together upstairs, Paul thought, and tried not to wonder what they might be saying, or thinking. And Jim was dead, as dead as Wally Trent. He put that aside too. "Have you been following our trial?" he said, and sipped his brandy.

"As best I could, sir. What's been in the papers." Story's voice was careful, guarded. He avoided Paul's eyes.

"I would like your opinion," Paul said.

Hesitation plain, "Well, sir, as a lawyer, I don't know a great deal about wills. I've studied some on the subject, but—"

"Not as a lawyer," Paul said. "As a spectator. Suppose you were sitting in the jury?"

"I—don't know what to say, sir."

"I think you do," Paul said, "but just don't want to say it. I can appreciate that. My father," he said, "living in this house after his stroke." It astonished him that he could speak so dispassionately. "The question of course is whether he was of sound mind when he drew up his will and signed it. What's your opinion?"

Story took his time. He said at last, clearly uncomfortable, "Well, sir, as I said, it's only through the papers that I know anything at all, and that isn't very much. I mean—"

"I understand," Paul said. It is as I thought, he told himself, even the relatively scanty newspaper reports inevitably give the impression that Father's mind was badly affected. Talking to those damned flowers. "I won't embarrass you further," he said.

Story hesitated. "I'm sorry," he said.

One more bit of the conversation repeated itself now in Paul's mind as he sat at the breakfast table. It had been after they had finished their brandy and just as the young man was leaving.

Story hesitated, his hand on the doorknob. "Uh, I don't quite know how to say this, sir," he said. "I know that she, Sudie, is only nineteen. And I'm—older of course. But—I just met her today, tonight, but we were together for quite a while, and, well, I'd like to see more of her." A third pause. "If that's all right?"

Imagine finding this kind of deference today, Paul thought. He nodded gravely. And what of the football player? he wondered. "I think," he said, "that is a matter for you and Sudie to settle between you. It's fine with me."

Relief was plain to see. "Thank you, sir. Thank you very much."

36

A gentle, salt-laden breeze swept in from the ocean, and the early-morning air was cool and fresh. The Executive model aircraft tied down on the plant runway was identical to the plane in which Joe McCurdy had crashed, even to the beige-and-white paint job.

Jerry Hopkins said, "John Black says he hopes you know what you're doing, and he doesn't really know why he's going along."

Tom Chambers said, "Let's get on with it, whatever it is. I've got a morning full of nit-picking conferences."

Fifty yards away toward the main plant building a guard came out of his little shack, stared curiously at the three men for a few moments, and then walked back inside. Marty took note.

Then, to Jerry and Tom: "My father's plane was parked here, right out in the open, and in this position." The tie-down anchors set into the pavement firmly established location. "The starboard side is toward the plant and that guard shack."

Both men looked from plane to shack, and nodded. Tom Chambers said, "And the explosion was in the port nacelle, the one that's hidden."

"Exactly." Marty nodded. "And the plane had been flown the day before, without incident. Does that suggest anything?"

Tom Chambers said slowly, "Either the explosive wasn't in the plane then, or— That's what we're trying to do, is it? Just stand here and figure out exactly what happened?" Again the negative headshake. "That's a little far out."

Jerry Hopkins was watching Marty carefully.

"It would be," Marty said, "but what we're trying to do is the reverse—figure out some things that couldn't have happened, narrow down the field of possibilities." He was sure of himself, but still he wanted corroboration.

"Such as?" Tom Chambers again, but there was some interest in his voice now.

"Okay," Marty said. "You started to say it, either the dynamite wasn't in the plane the day before—let's just take that. Suppose it wasn't? Could it have been put in after that safe flight and before the flight that crashed?" He looked from one to the other.

Tom Chambers said, "Go on. You've got something in mind. Maybe I'm beginning to see it, but spell it out anyway."

Marty said slowly, "The plane was clear out over the valley before it exploded. It had been in the air, say, fifteen, twenty minutes. Does that suggest anything? Damn it, I want your answers. I know what mine are. I want to see if yours are the same."

"Well." This was Jerry. "It had to be a delayed-action explosive package. If it was hooked, say, to ignition, it would have gone off right here on the ground."

Marty nodded. "Right."

Tom Chambers said, "You're thinking in pretty sophisticated terms? A timing device, say, or something hooked to throttle linkage, or maybe a pressure switch, that kind of thing?" He nodded in answer to his own question. "It had to be something that took some planning, right?"

Marty nodded again. "Okay, now back to my question: Could it have been put into the plane after the safe flight and before the flight that crashed?" He looked from one to the other in silence.

Jerry shook his head slowly. "While the aircraft was parked right here in front of God and everybody? No way, without somebody seeing it. Whatever it was, if it had to be installed and hooked up, it would take time and it couldn't be hidden. You'd have to unbutton the cowl panels and take them off—" He shook his head again. "You'd have that guard over here asking what the hell you were doing, and did you have a work order."

Tom Chambers said, "How about during the night?"

Jerry smiled. "You goddamn engineers, you wave your hands over a drawing and figure that's all there is to it. I used to be a pretty fair country mechanic on final assembly and out on the flight line, but I sure as hell wouldn't even try to make any kind of installation in the dark, and I don't know anybody who would. Night is out."

Marty said, "And day is out too. That leaves what?"

Tom Chambers said slowly, "You tell us. Because I don't like what you're thinking."

"I don't like it either," Marty said, "but give me another answer." He paused. "If the explosive package couldn't have been installed here, then it had to have been installed at Coast during overhaul, isn't that right?"

There was silence. Again the guard came out of his shack for a long look, and then slowly walked toward the three men. Marty watched him approach. "Hi, Pete," he said.

The guard smiled. "I thought I recognized you, but I wasn't sure, that's why I come over." He hesitated. "Everything okay?"

"Everything's fine." This was Jerry Hopkins. "You check on things."

"That's what they pay me for." The guard hesitated again. "This plane is a dead ringer for the one your daddy flew. I did a double take when it landed here this morning." His question was implicit, directed at Marty.

"It's okay, Pete," Marty said. "We're just trying something."

The guard nodded, and walked slowly back to his shack.

Tom Chambers said, "You're saying that the package was installed at Coast, and that the aircraft flew here from there, and then flew again the day before the crash, with the explosive riding right along?" He nodded. "We wondered why dynamite."

"It's easy to get," Marty said, "and it's safe to handle."

Jerry Hopkins said softly, "Jesus!" And then, "You're not saying the thing was set to go off that far ahead? While the plane was still in the Coast shops?"

Tom Chambers said, "No. It wouldn't have to be. A simple switch to activate, say, a timing device. That's all it would take."

"And that," Marty said, "could have been done right here on the ground in plain sight of the guard."

He walked around the aircraft. The two men followed him. Marty pointed at the smooth contour of the port-engine nacelle. "That inspection door. Flip it open. Like this."

He opened the small door, put his hand inside, withdrew his hand, and snapped the door shut again. The entire operation had taken less than five seconds. "All done," he said. "The switch is thrown. The timer is activated. In, say, thirty minutes you have an explosion." He looked at them both. "How about it?"

Jerry Hopkins said slowly, "John Black is going to blow a gasket, and fat-ass Granger in Sales and Service is going to shit in his pants."

Tom Chambers was silent, thoughtful. "You've got to have at least two people, is that what you're thinking? One at Coast. And one here to activate the timer, if that's what it was. Right?"

Jerry Hopkins said again softly, "Jesus! It gets more complicated by the minute." He looked at Marty. "So maybe we know how," he said, "but do we know why?"

"Maybe we can guess. That," Marty said, "is where you and I get together and start checking."

Tom Chambers nodded. "That's all you wanted from me? That, and now to plug John Black in?"

"It was quite a bit," Marty said. "Thanks."

"I hope," Chambers said, "that you catch the bastards and hang them up by their balls."

Marty and Jerry Hopkins sat in Jerry's office, Jerry behind the desk. "By rights, this chair is yours," Jerry said.

Marty shook his head. "You're the man who knows how to keep everything moving." He smiled without shame. "Only a little while ago I thought there was nothing I couldn't do." He was thinking of Liz, of Billy's competence in court, of Paul and McKenzie holding firm; seeing all this and other matters now with different eyes "I know better now. Maybe with a few years' experience I could do the job as well as you can, and maybe not, but we aren't even going to try to find out. For the time being you're it, and we're going to try to make it permanent."

Jerry hesitated. "The time being is maybe a month on that money you raised."

"I've been thinking about that," Marty said. "I'll have another hundred thousand for you before that runs out." There was nothing in his voice. No other way, he thought: sell *Westerly*, that was the only answer. But not quite yet. There was maybe one more thing *Westerly* could do for him before he let her go. "Now let's do some guessing," he said, and settled back in his visitor's chair.

"You take a plant like this," he began, "and the way it was run, it didn't amount to much. It was what it was, a rich man's toy. You've seen the books, production figures, plant investment, and all."

"Gold-plated," Jerry said. "Somebody didn't care much about profits."

Marty nodded. "They weren't important. Then what happened all of a sudden? The plant began running at full speed instead of half throttle. And in some wrong directions." It seemed now as if he had never stopped thinking about it, wondering about it, searching for the handle. "Why?" he said.

Jerry's eyebrows rose. "You're asking me? I wasn't even here."

"Neither was I, and that's good. Isn't that why they bring in outside consultants, to take a fresh look?"

Jerry thought about it. "All I can say," he said at last, "is if somebody wanted to run this operation right into the ground, he couldn't have figured out a better way." He watched Marty's face, and slowly shook his head. "Now what the hell did I say that made you so happy?"

"Not happy." Marty was unsmiling. "But satisfied that we're thinking the same way." He raised his hand to forestall protest. "I told you we were going to be doing some guessing. Let's assume that was the idea—to run the plant right into the ground. Why would somebody want to do that?"

"You ask the damnedest questions." Jerry's smile disappeared. "Usually when that's done," he said, "it's to milk the operation of all of its profits, and then get rid of it for a tax loss. At least that's how I understand it."

"I think you're close," Marty said, "but not quite right. My father wouldn't have thought in terms of tax loss. He enjoyed having a plant that was part of the aircraft industry. I think he felt it gave him prestige without much work."

Jerry picked up a pencil, looked at it, and set it down. "Maybe," he said, "I'm beginning to dig you. Shall I try it for size?" Marty nodded. "Okay," Jerry said, "what if somebody wanted the plant run into the ground so it would be sold? Cheap. So that somebody could maybe buy it at a bargain. How about that?"

Marty said slowly, "With what you know, your experience in manufacturing, and what you've seen since you've been here—does it fit?"

Jerry nodded soberly. "It fits."

"And," Marty said, "if my father, who didn't pay too much attention to what was going on most of the time, maybe tuned in on some of the rumors that were going around and decided to have a look for himself?" He let the question hang.

"He'd be in the way." Jerry's voice was solemn. "Is that what you're saying?"

"Guessing."

For the third time that morning Jerry said softly, "Jesus!" And then, "What a can of worms you're opening."

"Yes."

Marty stood up suddenly. "Have you ever done any sailing?"

"What in the world does that have—?" Jerry stopped. The man wasn't just making idle conversation. He had a reason, whatever it was. "Some," Jerry said, "but not in your class. Weekends I used to crew on a friend's thirty-footer down at Balboa."

"That's good enough. I'll give you a call. We'll take my boat out one day." While she is still mine, he thought sadly. But there is no other way. "I'll be in touch."

37

Susan was up early too on this Monday morning, down to join Paul at breakfast. She was, as always, immaculately groomed; and she wore a tailored housecoat of Thai silk in blues and greens that went well with her dark coloring. She showed no signs of her grief.

"I will make arrangements this morning for—Jim," she said. "I think only family. You agree?"

"Whatever you think best." Tomato juice with Worcestershire sauce and lemon every morning, Paul thought; and why should that have come to his mind now? Probably because these days his father was never far from his thoughts.

Susan said, "Yes? Whatever you are thinking."

It was their first time alone since that painful scene when Paul had returned from the Berkeley hospital; and the tension between them was almost palpable. "I'm sorry about Saturday night," he said. "I was wrong. I see that now."

"It can't be helped." She was not making it any easier for him, Susan thought, and wished that it were in her to behave otherwise. "Are you going to court today?"

"First the bank, then court, yes." Paul paused. "Unless—" he began.

Susan shook her head. "I'll manage. Sudie will help."

Again he was at fault, Paul told himself, because he had not even given thought to what was proper at a time like this. "Maybe—"

"No," Susan said with finality. "There is nothing to be gained." And then because the question had to be asked, "Do we know anything at all about—what happened to Jim?"

Bob Story had spent a good share of yesterday with the authorities, the DA's people and the police. His report was scanty. "Very little," Paul said. "There was a disturbance near Sather Gate. Precisely what it was all about, no one seems to know, or is willing to tell. Jim appears to have been—involved—" He paused again. "Jim's—friends, as Sudie knows—" He shook his head. "Maybe it was my fault."

Susan said unexpectedly, "Or mine." She was silent for a few moments. That Elizabeth Palmer was very much in her thoughts this morning, and she could not have said why, except perhaps that all of them, Jim, Marty, Elizabeth Palmer, could be lumped together into the generation on the far side of the gap everyone talked about. And she and Paul had not been able to reach Jim; but maybe the others were not entirely beyond communication. If they tried. "I know very little about finances," she began, and there stopped to choose her words. "But maybe," she said, "there comes a time when purely financial thinking ought to be put aside?" She hesitated, expecting a "now now leave these matters to me" reply. Paul surprised her.

"Maybe," he said. "I haven't thought so, but perhaps as in other directions, I have been wrong. You are talking of course of the trial?"

Susan took a deep breath. "Would it—hurt you to give in to Marty?"

A strange way to put it, Paul thought. "Hurt me how?"

"Your pride."

Good God, was that how it looked? But John McKenzie had hinted as much; and Marty had come right out and said it; and maybe if Charles Goodwin and his self-appointed-watchdog attitude hadn't been part of the whole equation, pride would have been the easy answer. The clock in the hall struck the half hour. Paul automatically checked his own watch. "Time to go." He stood up. "Bruce wanted particularly to see me."

"Bruce," Susan said, and left it there.

"Bank business." Paul walked around the table and bent to kiss Susan's cheek. "If there is anything you want, call."

Bruce was waiting in Helen Soong's outer office. He followed his father into the corner office and closed the door. Both he and Alan had been to the big house yesterday for a stiff, almost silent luncheon, and there was no need now to express further platitudes about a death in the family. "I wanted to give you this," he said, and held out a white envelope. His face showed nothing.

Paul took it. "Sit down." He lowered himself into his own chair, opened the envelope, took out the letter, and read it through. He looked up slowly. "You're resigning?" he said. "Why?"

"I shouldn't think you would need to ask."

There was strength in the boy, Paul thought, where before there had been uncertainty. Everyone seemed to be changing before his eyes. "There have been too many misunderstandings," he said, "because each side assumed that the other knew what it meant. Speak up."

"All right." Bruce's voice was not belligerent, but neither was it apologetic. "Polly. I've found her. She is back in Modesto, and she won't come here, so I am going there."

"That's a pretty big decision."

"What you mean," Bruce said, "is, is she worth it? To me, yes. You probably know a lot more about this, about her and her family, than you let on. You usually do know a lot of things you don't talk about. If it's her background—"

"My mother," Paul said, "your grandmother, came from a very humble background. And her mother had walked halfway across this continent beside a covered wagon. Barefoot. Are you accusing me of that kind of snobbery?"

"Maybe I am," Bruce said. His voice was quiet. "You don't think she's right for me. You made that clear."

"I don't recall saying anything to that effect."

"Some things don't have to be said." Bruce stood up. He was an impressive man, tall, broad, muscular; and, more to the point, under control. "I think she is right for me. I'd rather have it that you and Mother thought so too, but if I can't have that, I can still have Polly." He nodded at the letter on Paul's desk. "I ought to give at least two weeks' notice. Will you accept a week?"

Paul nodded in silence. He watched the boy let himself out, and when the door was closed, he shut his eyes. Mistakes, mistakes, mistakes. Susan, Wally Trent, Jim, now this one. Marty too? The question echoed in his mind. When the intercom buzzed he sat up and flipped the switch. "Yes?"

"Mr. Goodwin is on the line," Helen Soong said. "And it is almost time to go to court. Unless you want me to call Mr. McKenzie and say that because of the death of your son—"

"No," Paul said. At least Helen Soong had spared him painful, effusive expressions of sympathy. Later in her quiet way she would drop a word. Paul wished more would behave in the same way. "I'll take the call." He reached for the phone.

Charles Goodwin said, "I am afraid that matters are getting out of hand, Paul. I'm sorry, but there it is. Wally Trent is dead. Your son—have you seen the morning papers? And this trial of yours is making headlines. Those things aside from all else, the foreign transactions, the vineyard losses. I don't need to tell you that none of this is good for the bank. Publicity of this kind, scandal is precisely what we do not want at this time. I hope you can appreciate that."

Paul was staring at the far wall. Others make mistakes too, he thought suddenly; sometimes they push too hard, just as I did with

Bruce. I understand the boy's attitude now, and I sympathize with it.

"Did you hear me, Paul?"

Paul took a deep breath. "I heard you, Charles." His voice was quiet, almost uninflected. "Now let me say what I think. First, my personal life is my own, no concern of yours. Second, I am chief executive officer of this bank, and while I will be glad to listen to your suggestions, as long as I retain my position I will take no orders. If you wish to force this confrontation you mentioned, go right ahead, Charles, take your complaints to the board and we will fight it out there. I hope I make myself clear."

There was a short silence. "That is your final word?"

"That is my final word. And now I am due in court." He hung up. It was far from finished, he thought.

Billy Gibbs was alone at his table in the courtroom when they all stood for Judge Geary's entrance. Paul, with Charles Goodwin still in mind, noticed Marty's absence, glanced at John McKenzie, and saw that he was aware of it too. So was the judge. "Are you prepared to continue, Mr. Gibbs?" the judge said.

"Yes, your honor." Billy was still standing. "My client is unavoidably detained in Los Angeles. With the court's permission, we shall proceed without him." Bad tactics, he thought; the jury could very well get the idea that Marty did not care, and that could really upset the applecart. But there it was. "I call Millicent Potter to return to the stand."

The same no-nonsense hat; as far as Billy could remember, the same dress; certainly the same feet-and-knees-together-facing-straight-forward posture. And the weekend had done nothing to soften either Miss Potter's expression or her attitude.

"Now, Miss Potter," Billy began, "when court adjourned for the weekend, you had told us how you, Cook, and Nurse witnessed Mr. Joseph McCurdy's will in the upstairs bedroom, in the presence also of Mr. Paul McCurdy and Mr. John McKenzie, both of whom are sitting here in the courtroom."

"That's the way it was."

Billy walked to his table and came back with papers. "I have here a certified copy of Mr. Joseph McCurdy's last will and testament,

Miss Potter." He folded back the pages and held the document out. "Is that your signature?"

Miss Potter took one quick look. "It is."

Billy refolded the will copy and carried it back to the table. He returned slowly to the witness stand. "Did you at any time witness another will for Mr. McCurdy, Miss Potter?"

"Only the one."

"Then we have established that the last will and testament of Mr. McCurdy, that which is challenged here in this court, was witnessed under the circumstances you describe." He glanced at John McKenzie.

McKenzie rose. "We will so stipulate, your honor."

The jury stirred quietly. Ms. Carstairs, the judge noticed, wore an I-told-you-so expression which clearly indicated that wherever men were concerned, there would inevitably be shenanigans.

Paul watched, listened, and thought of Susan and Sudie at their dismal task of making funeral arrangements. And of course of Charles Goodwin. How would he react? Would he indeed force that confrontation—as he very well could?

Billy was uncomfortable. That scene with Liz had been very much on his mind ever since Saturday evening; it was the kind of thing that gnawed at your confidence and made you begin to wonder about your basic tenets.

Had Liz indeed gone to McKenzie with that devastatingly simple theory of hers about why old Joe carried on his conversations with the flowers? Because it did have a ring of authenticity, and in cross-examination of Millicent Potter, Billy had no doubt that John McKenzie would make the most of it.

It behooved him, Billy thought, to move along to other areas in which Miss Potter's testimony could be made to support the idea that old Joe McCurdy was no longer in control of himself, and that Paul McCurdy and John McKenzie took full advantage of it.

He approached the witness stand again. As he turned so that his voice would carry well to the jury, he saw Liz sitting in the back of the room. She was watching him closely. He forced himself to concentrate. "Now, Miss Potter," Billy said, and even smiled, hoping to show his confidence, "after the signing of the will and the witnessing, did the visits of Mr. Paul McCurdy and Mr. John McKenzie to

Mr. McCurdy cease?" He made himself concentrate on the witness and the jury and ignore Liz.

"They did not. Almost every day like," Miss Potter paused. "Well, not quite every day. Maybe three, four times a week they came."

"And spent time alone with Mr. McCurdy?"

"Always. With the door closed."

"And so you of course had no idea what they discussed."

"All I know was that those—discussions tired him something terrible."

McKenzie was on his feet. "I think we must make an objection here, your honor. The conclusion of the witness—"

"Well," Miss Potter said sharply, "he told me so himself. Time was, he said, when making decisions was easy, and once they were made they could be forgotten. Now, he said, he tired himself out just looking at them."

Judge Geary said slowly, "Mr. McKenzie?"

"I withdraw the objection, your honor." McKenzie sat down slowly.

Billy said, "Did he tell you what kinds of decisions he was asked to examine?"

"No. I certainly didn't ask."

Liz was back there watching, listening, and Billy could not put that from his mind. Once he would have welcomed her presence in order that she might see on the ground of his choosing, the courtroom, his skill and competence at work. Now, after Saturday evening, he was afraid that she was predisposed to find subterfuge and downright dishonesty in his every question, and how could a man make any headway against that? He wished Marty were here, and then Liz would see that he, Billy, was not the only one who thought as he did, and that if any blame was justified, it had to be shared. Damn it, Marty ought to be here!

Billy had taken his few steps away from the witness stand. He turned now and walked back slowly, putting his thoughts in sequence. First he would question Miss Potter about the old man's letters to the newspapers; next about the memory lapses; and then about his later daily visits to the bank and the odd guests he brought home for lunch. Finally, he thought, he would ask Millicent Potter if Mary and Rick Harlow, one or both, ever came to the house, and if she was aware of their relationship to Joe McCurdy. As far as Billy knew, neither mother nor illegitimate son had ever visited the old man, but the mere asking of the question would plant the idea in the jury's mind.

"Now about those letters Mr. McCurdy wrote to the newspapers, Miss Potter . . ."

Marty was sitting again in Howard Carter's small office. "No proof," he said, "but I think the guesswork will stand up." He told of his meeting with Tom Chambers and Jerry Hopkins at the aircraft parked on the plant runway, and their deductions concerning it.

Carter said at last, "How do you know your father's airplane was parked in the same spot, facing in the same direction?"

"There are tie-down anchors set into the pavement, one for each wing and one for the tail. There's only one way the aircraft could be parked and tied down."

Carter leaned back in his chair, and rocked slowly back and forth. "As you said," he said, "guesswork. But I'll admit it sounds good." The admission seemed painful.

"It means connivance, of course," Marty said. "Someone at Coast has to be involved. I have an idea that John Black will take steps to flush him out." It was more than an idea; it was a certainty. And John Black would not deal gently in a matter like this which could ruin Coast's reputation.

Carter rocked on and the chair squeaked monotonously. He said at last, "Assuming *arguendo* that you are right. Where is the motive?"

"That," Marty said, "is a little complicated. It goes clear back to the financial condition of the plant. . . ." He told of his session with Jerry Hopkins in Jerry's office, and when he had finished, Carter said slowly, "Interesting. Can you prove it?"

"Maybe. What kind of proof do you want?"

Carter's voice was condescending, a parent explaining to a child. "Something I might be able to build a case around, Mr. McCurdy, something I could take to a grand jury and to court." His voice sharpened. "Theories are fine. Theories are lovely. They are also a dime a dozen and usually not worth even that."

Marty stood up. "I didn't really expect cooperation, so I'm not disappointed." Annoyed, yes; but that he had expected. "But if I bring you proof, what assurance do I have that you'll get your ass out of that chair and do something with it?"

The muscles in Carter's cheeks worked. "You bring me proof—" He shook his head, refusing to give Marty the satisfaction of a completed statement. "How do you intend to get it?"

"By watching the weather," Marty said, and walked out.

Driving back out to Stone Canyon he switched on the car radio to the news and weather station. News bulletins and commercials flowed endlessly. Mentally he tuned them out.

He would like to know how Billy was doing in the San Francisco courtroom, how the jury was reacting, but that could wait. You concentrated on one thing at a time, and right now what was happening, or was about to happen, here in the Los Angeles area was the important thing.

A weather report came on at last. He listened to it with growing disgust—light smog in the basin; light, variable westerly winds; scattered clouds; the chance for precipitation near zero.

At the Stone Canyon house there were no messages, Molly Moto said. And that too was not surprising. Marty walked out on the porch and stared at the ocean.

There was a freighter northbound on the horizon, trailing black smoke in a thin horizontal line that disappeared quickly. Marty studied it thoughtfully. And then he went back into the study, sat down at the desk, and reached for the telephone. There was no need to look up the number. It was, he told himself, something he might have thought of sooner.

The phone rang four times, five, and Marty could picture the scene. Rollie would be behind the café counter, probably a can of beer wrapped in one huge paw, deep in conversation with any of the wet-suited surfers who happened to be in the joint for chili or coffee or just plain talk; and Rollie would look at the wall phone and snarl an obscenity, and only if it rang long enough to bother him would he put down his beer and go to answer.

The phone came alive. "Yeah?" Rollie's voice.

"Marty McCurdy here."

There was no hesitation. "Hey, baby, how they hanging?"

"Loose." Not true; I'm uptight, Marty thought. No matter. Maybe it was better that way. "How's the surf?"

"Baby, it's coming! Down at Onofre it's beginning to separate the men from the boys. The word's out. Where're you?"

Well, well, Marty thought, and began to smile. "Too far," he said, "and in store clothes."

"Better climb into trunks and get your ass down here, baby. I got this feeling that we're going to have us a king surf before we're through."

"Thanks, Rollie." Marty hung up. Then he made himself sit and think quietly when the temptation was to jump into immediate action.

A rising surf might mean something, and then again it might not. A big storm a thousand miles, two thousand miles offshore could have built normal swells into mountainous seas and sent them hurtling eastward unhindered to land only now on the California coast. And mere swells at sea were not what he wanted. As on that late afternoon and evening so long ago, what he wanted now was wind, lots of it, and maybe, just maybe, wind was what the rising surf was foretelling. A hunch, no more, but you played your hunches, or sat and did nothing.

He picked up the phone again, and, remembering the number, dialed. To the Coast Aircraft operator: "John Black, please." And to one of those two efficient, brushed-up secretaries in Black's outer office: "Martin McCurdy here. Is he in?"

"One moment, please." And then, almost immediately, John Black's voice saying hello, and adding, "I don't like what you've turned up, young man, but I don't suppose you do either. From what Tom Chambers tells me, there has to be somebody in our shop."

"Yes, sir. There has to be."

"We'll find him."

No ifs, ands, or buts, Marty thought; merely the flat statement, convincing, and reassuring. With some men, yes, and women too, like Liz, when they said they would do something, you could relax and know that it would be done. It was good to deal with someone like that. "All I want," he said, "is a name. Soon."

Black's voice altered subtly. "I can't promise when," he said.

"No, sir, I understand that." Marty paused. "But if it does work out that way, even if you're only reasonably sure he's the one, will you get the name to me?"

"You're up to something?"

"Yes, sir." And then in honesty, "Maybe a long shot, but I'm going to play it. Anytime within the next, say, two hours and a half, you can get a message to me at the Balboa Bay Club."

"And after that?"

Marty shook his head. "I'll be out of touch, and probably pretty busy. I'll have to play it alone."

"Luck." Was there a smile in John Black's voice?

Marty disconnected and dialed the number of the plant. To Jerry Hopkins, "I think a little sail this afternoon," he said. "You, Walter Jordan, and I. If you want, I'll talk to him."

"No need. I'll tell him you want us both."

Another who could be counted on, Marty thought; and found comfort in the knowledge. "The Bay Club," he said. "Do you know *Westerly?*"

"Brother! I've admired her for years."

"I'll be on board."

38

From the rear of the courtroom Liz had watched and listened throughout the morning as Billy led Millicent Potter through her sometimes reluctant and at times almost belligerent testimony.

Letters old Joe McCurdy had written to the newspapers; his lapses of memory; the odd guests he had brought home to lunch after he had been able to go down to the bank again, among them the man who had shined his shoes for twenty years—all of these matters explored by questions carefully aimed at showing a personality altered beyond the bounds of eccentricity well into the realm of incapacity. Well, to Liz's mind, they showed nothing of the sort.

She was probably biased in Joe McCurdy's favor, she told herself, but to her the picture the testimony drew was that of a tired, lonely old man fighting a gallant if sometimes pitiful battle against boredom, lassitude, and almost total loss of the strength and vigor that had been his essence; a giant, crippled, but still defiant, Samson Agonistes.

Billy was good; and what his effect was on the jury she would not even try to guess. He was like an actor on the stage, but with a difference: he was speaking lines of his own invention, and so he was responsible for their content. He was, as he had said, an advocate, doing everything he could to advance his client's case. It was logical, even reasonable, she was sure; and she didn't like it.

She was not pronouncing moral judgment, she told herself; she was merely expressing personal opinion, prejudice, call it what you would. And she was quite aware that in an imperfect world advocates were necessary and were obligated to do the best they could for their clients, precisely as Billy was doing now. Still.

At their table, Paul and John McKenzie sat quiet, impassive. What Paul's feelings were, Liz could only guess. Certainly he was not happy at having private family matters dragged out into the open, but he gave no outward sign. From time to time he glanced at the table where Marty ought to have been sitting, but there again, it was impossible to tell what he was thinking. And the questions and answers went on.

It was Judge Geary who put a temporary stop to them. "It is a little past noon, Mr. Gibbs," the judge said. "Would this be a convenient point in your questioning for a luncheon adjournment?"

"Perfectly convenient, your honor." Billy was smiling. More than convenient, he thought: welcome. He would begin the afternoon with queries concerning Mary and Rick Harlow. Coming immediately after adjournment, he thought the subject would have greater impact.

Marty had the hatches open and the sail covers off and stowed. He had changed to shorts, topsiders, and a tee shirt that clung to his broad shoulders. Here in the harbor there was a little wind, but out beyond the jetties there would be breeze enough to put *Westerly* through her paces even without the good wind Marty still hoped for. He had thought about breaking out the big overlapping jib, and decided against it. He had no idea how competent a sailor Jerry Hopkins was, and in any kind of blow, that big jib was nothing for inexperience to cope with. Working sails would have to do.

He made himself relax now in *Westerly*'s cockpit, tried not to hope for a call from John Black, and let his thoughts run free while he waited.

Only short weeks ago he had sat here with Liz, with nothing more on his mind, as he remembered saying, than a drink or two, dinner, and bed. What was happening at the plant or in San Francisco at the time was of no interest to him. Looking back now, it seemed impossible that it had been so.

He had known Walter Jordan only casually as his father's plant manager, a man who had expressed his mild contempt for sailboats and those who enjoyed them. Now he thought he knew Walter Jordan very well indeed.

He had never even heard the names George Granger, Tom Chambers, John Black, and Jerry Hopkins. He was now, it appeared, inextricably entangled with all of them.

His uncle Paul had been a distant, almost shadowy figure behind a prominent name; and there had been no such person as John McKenzie. Old Joe McCurdy had already disappeared into the void of passing time.

Marty had seen Billy only occasionally, and their meetings had been "Hi, how are things going?" Of Billy's obvious yearning for Liz, he had had no idea, and probably would not have cared a bit if he had.

And Liz herself? He knew her no better now than he had that day when the club waiter walked out on the slip with word of the telephone call which began it all. Even now he was not at all sure what his feelings toward her were. When he thought about her, he seemed to blow hot and cold.

It was trite, of course, to say that it was difficult if not impossible to see yourself as others saw you, but the fact of the matter was that he had never even bothered to think about it before. Now, with Liz in mind, the outside view of Marty McCurdy suddenly took on some importance.

He saw Jerry Hopkins and Walter Jordan walk out of the club building and start down to the float.

No phone call yet from John Black; no name. Damn. Then he would have to play it by ear. And there was no point in trying to stall. By the time Jerry and Walter Jordan reached *Westerly*'s side,

Marty had the engine blowers already whining softly as they cleared away any possible explosive fumes.

Jerry stepped over the gunwale and dropped down into the cockpit first. He gestured with both hands toward himself. "Store clothes," he said.

"You can find something in the hanging locker below." Marty turned then to Walter Jordan. "Welcome aboard."

Jordan stepped down gingerly. "I must say, I do not understand this. I think you know how I feel about boats."

"Just a conference," Marty said.

"Conferences are usually held in offices."

Marty was smiling. "We'll try fresh air and sunshine for a change." He started the engine. It caught at once, and he listened to the bubbling exhaust as he throttled down to near idle. "Just sit down and relax," he said to Jordan. "You're the passenger."

Jerry came up into the cockpit in shorts, topsiders, and a sweat shirt. He was smiling. "Cast off?" he said.

He could wait indefinitely for a phone call that might never come, Marty told himself. "Yes," he said. And then, quickly, "No. Hold it." A waiter was coming down the slip.

"A phone call for you, Marty."

Marty nodded. "Okay." He hoped his voice was unconcerned. "Back in a minute." He stepped down to the slip and walked quickly to the club building.

It was one of the efficient, brushed-up secretaries on the line. "Mr. Black is calling. Just a moment, please."

John Black's voice was solemn. "I think that the name you want is Willard Bates. He's a mechanic. Our plant protection people are taking him into custody now. They will be in touch with the authorities. But I am afraid it does not stop there. It would appear that a vice-president is also involved."

Of course, of course, Marty thought. There would have to be someone other than a mere mechanic; someone to direct the operation. "Would that be Granger?" he said.

There was a pause. Then, "You make shrewd guesses," John Black said. His voice changed. "That's all I can tell you at present."

"I think it's enough," Marty said. I hope it is, he thought as he walked back down to *Westerly*. Damn it, I know it is. His thoughts were a high, fierce chant. "Okay," he said as he dropped down into the cockpit, "let's cast off."

They backed out of the slip into open water, swung, and headed down the bay. The water gurgled along *Westerly*'s sleek sides and trailed a flat wake astern. Walter Jordan sat expressionless, his eyes on Marty at the wheel. Jerry Hopkins was standing, leaning against the cabin trunk, his arms folded on the overhead. He was smiling at the water, the sky, the fresh feel of the wind of their passage against his face.

Down the channel between the stone jetties, out toward the bell buoy that rolled to the incoming swells and tolled their number. There, in the beginning of deep water, *Westerly*'s motion changed abruptly, and what had been effortless domination of the mild chop in the bay now became obedient gentle rolling to the long Pacific swells.

Rollie had been right, Marty thought. Down at San Onofre, curved inward by the drag of the submarine ridge, these swells would already be building to a big surf and the word would have spread. To Jerry he said, "Take the wheel. Hold her on the wind. I'll hoist sail." As he went forward and uncleated the jib halyard he studied the western horizon and saw the first trace of the clouds he was hoping for. So far, so good. Willard Bates and George Granger; the names repeated themselves in his mind. He had no idea if what he had in mind would work, but all a man could do was try.

Sails up and halyards sweated taut, Marty dropped back into the cockpit, breathing deeply but not hard. He took the wheel, fell off the wind, bent to switch off the engine, and *Westerly* came alive.

Suddenly she was no longer slave to the motion of the swells, but their mistress. With wind filling her sails she heeled against the deep weight of her keel, buried her lee side almost to the rail, and drove almost contemptuously through the swells, throwing spray into the air, and sending white water hissing along her sides to spread astern in a now turbulent wake.

Jerry, sitting on the weather seat, legs braced, was grinning broadly. "She really makes it happen, doesn't she?"

Walter Jordan was crowded against the lee coaming. He swallowed hard. His glasses were already beaded with spray, and his expression unhappy. He squinted through the mist at Marty. "I don't know what you think you are doing," he said, "but I don't like this, you know."

Marty's eyes were again on those gathering clouds ahead. "It will get better," he said, "as it goes along."

Jordan was frowning now. "That means what?"

Marty said, "We may get some real sailing wind if we're lucky. This is just a little breeze." He was keeping himself under tight control, when the temptation was to bear down. Willard Bates and George Granger, he thought; and the anger that had lain dormant in his mind was beginning to build.

There was no reason why she should have gone back for the afternoon session of the trial, Liz told herself; but she simply could not stay away. Morbid fascination, she supposed was the phrase.

She had encountered Billy on the courthouse steps after a solitary lunch. The meeting had been somewhat strained.

"Enjoying the spectacle?" Billy said, which was unlike him.

Liz ignored the question. "Marty is still in Los Angeles?"

"He is. Doing what, I haven't the faintest idea. He ought to be here."

She had been thinking about that. "For his effect on the jury?" Liz said.

Billy hesitated. Then he nodded shortly. "For his effect on the jury," he said. "That is the name of the game." He turned away and walked quickly up the steps and into the building.

Now, sitting quietly in the rear of the courtroom again, Liz watched and listened while the play went on. Billy was taking a new direction with Millicent Potter that seemed almost to be backtracking, and Liz did not understand where he was going.

"You testified that before his seizure Mr. McCurdy was a sociable man, is that not so, Miss Potter?" Billy said. He paused. "He entertained quite a bit at home?"

"That is what I said."

"Frequent visitors?"

"I suppose you would say that."

"Banking friends, other business acquaintances?"

At their table, Paul leaned closer to John McKenzie. "Where is he going?"

McKenzie shook his head gently. "I have an idea we'll find out shortly. I don't think this is just a fishing expedition."

Miss Potter assumed that many of the visitors were from the bank or from outside business, but she could not say definitely.

On the bench Judge Geary listened carefully, wearing now a faint frown. He too wondered where Billy was going, and decided that he would allow him a few more apparently pointless questions before he interfered.

"Did you know many of these visitors by name, Miss Potter?"

"Some of them."

Billy consulted his notes. "Mr. Gilmore?"

"He was from the bank."

"Mr. Markham?"

"So was he."

"Mr. Carson?"

"He's the mayor."

Billy took a few steps away from the witness stand, turned, and walked slowly back. "Mary Harlow?" he said. "Her son, Richard?"

Paul came out of his thoughts and said almost inaudibly, "Oh, my god!"

McKenzie turned quickly. "That means what?"

"You've got to stop that," Paul said. "It has nothing to do with this. Nothing." His whisper was urgent.

"I can't work blind. I warned you about that."

"Never mind. Just stop it!" It was a command.

Miss Potter was saying, "I don't remember those names. But there were sometimes so many."

McKenzie rose slowly. "Your honor, may we request a short recess? I must confer with my client on a matter of considerable urgency."

"It can't wait, Mr. McKenzie?"

"I am afraid not, your honor."

Judge Geary looked at Billy. "Have you objections, Mr. Gibbs?"

"None, your honor." Billy was smiling. It couldn't be better, he thought; they were touching a sensitive spot and they had the jury's full attention now. The name Harlow would stick in their minds.

Judge Geary nodded. "Very well." He was looking again at McKenzie. "Fifteen minutes, counselor?"

"That should be ample. Thank you, your honor." McKenzie waited until the judge had left the courtroom, and then sat down again. "Now," he said, "what's this all about? Who are Mary and Richard Harlow? They are in the will, but that's all I know."

This along with everything else. "I wish it was all I knew too," Paul said. "She was a little hot pants, and Richard, Rick, was the result."

"A McCurdy?"

"In a manner of speaking." Paul's face was expressionless. "No wedding bells. No marriage certificate. It was wartime."

"Your child?"

"Good God, no."

"Then how do you know about it?"

"Father told me when he wanted them in the will." Paul paused. "It's a long story."

"You have about fourteen minutes left to tell it."

The wind was rising, and the driven swells were beginning to build. Here and there the top of a swell would crest into white water quickly windblown into spray. The sky had lost its clarity and dark clouds scudded across the gray background. Close-hauled, *Westerly* had her rail almost under; and with a bone in her teeth she thrashed into and through the rising swells as if bursting through moving barriers in her eagerness to be free.

Marty, braced in the lee corner of the stern seat, one hand on the wheel, kept his eyes on the luff of the jib, holding the boat as high as she would point and still keep driving. From time to time he glanced at Walter Jordan.

Jerry Hopkins was still on the weather seat, firmly braced. He watched the seas, the towering mainsail, and Marty, seeing plainly now the side of the man he had merely glimpsed before. There was, Jerry thought, no give in him. None. And no pity. Because what he was doing to Walter Jordan was almost inhuman.

Jordan was huddled on the lee seat in the partial shelter of the cabin trunk. He had taken off his glasses and tucked them into the breast pocket of his now sodden jacket, and his eyes without their comforting lenses seemed to peer fearfully at the world—and particularly at Marty. Jordan's face was wet with spray, and his hair plastered against his skull, but it was the color of the face that held Jerry's attention. The skin was almost gray, and lifeless, the skin of a man in collapse—or in death. He had not said a word.

Jerry looked again at the face of the man at the wheel. It was set, expressionless, all feeling either wiped away or held under tight control. There existed only the man, the boat, and the wind and sea. He held the wheel with one hand, but his control was absolute; each minute movement brought into play the heavy muscles beneath his wet tee shirt, and *Westerly* obeyed without hesitation.

The man was a superb seaman, Jerry thought, even as good as his reputation. It was no wonder that with his skill and the set determination he now displayed those Honolulu races had come out as they had. And a man who could safely take this same boat those thousands of miles in sometimes violent weather was not about to make dangerous mistakes of judgment on a mere day sail like this, was he? *Was he?*

Jerry glanced aloft again. He could see no sign of excessive strain in that towering mainmast, nor had he expected to. But strain was there. All that held that or any mast in place and intact were the shrouds, and the swaged fitting of only a single shroud *could* fail, and in this rising sea that could be the ball game. It was not exactly fear he felt, but almost. But what had to be holding Jordan in a state of near catalepsy was sheer terror. And Marty was well aware of it.

And that is precisely why we're here, Jerry suddenly realized.

The rail was under now, and the lee deck was awash to the cockpit coaming. Mainsail and jib were as taut as stretched fabric could be, and the sounds of *Westerly*'s hull crashing into and through the seas blended with a high-pitched keening of wind through rigging as their broadening wake churned astern in a tossing vee.

Ahead there was only more darkness in the sky ominously spreading. The rhythm of the swells was broken now into confused seas of tossing gray water. Spindrift filled the air.

We're heading right into it, Jerry thought, and glanced once more at Walter Jordan. His mouth was open and he was breathing in short gasps as he clung to his seat and tried to look in all directions at once.

Marty's face was still set; water streamed down his face and his eyes were squinted against wind and spray. Jerry had to shout against the sounds of wind and waves. "Driving her pretty hard, aren't we?"

Marty's expression did not change. "We'll see what she can do!" His voice, raised above its normal pitch, carried clearly.

Jerry wiped water from his eyes. "Don't you think we might ease her off, maybe come about and run for it?"

"No!" Unequivocal, unyielding.

Jerry thought, he is going to take us right under and never ease up a bit. That fellow with the white whale came to mind, driven by his obsession, completely off his rocker. But why me? The question asked itself. "Look—" Jerry shouted, and started to rise.

Marty's voice cut like a lash, and its threat was plain. "Stay where you are! I'm sailing this boat!" Under, if I have to, he thought; and glanced again at Jordan. And maybe I will have to. He raised his voice in a great shout. "Jordan!"

For a moment the man seemed not to hear. Then, slowly, his head turned and his eyes, filled with terror, focused on Marty's face.

"The phone call I had was from John Black!" Marty shouted. "He gave me two names!"

Westerly rose to a heavy sea, crashed through its crest, and slammed down into the following trough with a jar that went clear down to her keel. She seemed to shake herself as she rose again. Cold gray water slopped over the cockpit coaming, soaking Jordan to the skin. He trembled, but other than that made no move. His eyes had not left Marty's face.

"Willard Bates, the mechanic!" Marty shouted. "They've taken him off to jail!" Was he getting through, or had he gone too far already and reduced the man to total helplessness, beyond feeling and the power to respond? "The charge will be murder!"

Jordan closed his eyes and brushed ineffectually at his face with the back of his hand. He shook his head as if to clear it, and his eyes opened again to stare once more at Marty's face.

Unreal, Jerry thought; totally, absolutely unreal. One man does not do this to another except in movies or on TV. But the crashing seas were real, and the feel of the boat laboring now as she fought her way up each steep slope to crash again into the trough, burying her sharp bow, streaming water along her deck, over the coaming to slosh in the cockpit around their feet before it drained away. It was real enough, he told himself, but how long could it last? And the temptation to claw his way across the cockpit and try to interfere was almost overpowering. But what was in Marty's face held him motionless and only silently protesting.

"The other name is George Granger!" Marty shouted. "He—!"

Jordan came off his seat in a lurching rush, arms extended, fingers hooked in a clawing spasm. He almost fell on Marty's half-bent arm, tried to force his way past it, and failed.

Marty straightened the arm with the full strength of his shoulder, and Jordan stumbled backward, crashed into the cabin trunk, and slid to the deck to lie in a huddle, his eyes still fixed, staring up at his tormentor.

"Bates and Granger!" Marty shouted amidst the crashing of *Westerly*'s struggles and the keening howl of the wind. "They'll talk! So will you—if you're still alive!"

Westerly dropped sickeningly, and slammed against the bottom of the trough. Water poured over everything. Jordan grabbed wildly at the seat for support. "Stop!" His voice was a scream. "Make it stop!"

Marty watched him coldly. He seemed unaware of the tumult around them. "And?"

"Anything!" Jordan's voice was even higher than before. "Bates, Granger—yes!" He took a deep, shuddering breath. "I'll tell you anything!"

They came between the jetties into the calmer water of the harbor under power, mainsail down and loosely furled, jib and jigger still set as steadying sails.

From the clubhouse the waiter saw *Westerly* and hurried down to meet her.

Jordan sat slumped on the same cockpit seat. He had not bothered to put his glasses back on, and he looked up at Marty with a show of defiance that was transparently impotent. "I'll deny everything. You understand that? Everything!"

Marty guided *Westerly* into her slip, and brought her to a halt with only a touch of reverse engine. Jerry stepped ashore and began to make fast her lines. The waiter was coming down to the slip.

"Everything!" Jordan was saying, louder now. "You'll see!"

Marty switched off the engine.

The waiter said, "This came." He held out a slip of paper. "Billy Gibbs. There's his number, but he said you don't need to call because he might not be there. He wants you back in San Francisco as fast as you can get there."

Marty took the paper slowly. "What's up?"

"He didn't say, except that you'd better get the hell up there because the whole picture has changed."

"Okay," Marty said wearily, "if he calls again, I'm on my way."

"Everything!" Jordan said. "Do you hear me? Everything!" And then, "You aren't even listening!"

Jerry Hopkins had dropped down into the cockpit. He did not look at Jordan. Marty said at last, "No, I'm not listening. There's no need. We've already heard it all. Both of us."

39

They sat, as before, in Judge Geary's chambers—Paul and John McKenzie facing Marty and Billy Gibbs. The judge was in shirt sleeves, his black robe still on its hanger. He looked at all four. "Well, gentlemen?"

John McKenzie said slowly, "We asked for this conference, Steven, because certain events have taken place, and because the courtroom testimony is taking a new, and I might say vicious, direction." If he was aware he was addressing the judge informally, he gave no sign.

"What you mean," Billy said, "is that we're touching a very sore point."

"Which is not relevant or in any way material to this case," McKenzie said.

Billy shook his head. "I think his honor should make that determination."

Marty said, "Okay, somebody fill me in."

Paul said, "If you had been here, you would know what is being discussed."

Marty's smile was crooked. "I've been sailing."

In the silence, "What we're talking about at the moment," Billy said, "is Mary Harlow and her son, Richard. As soon as I mentioned them yesterday things got exciting." The urgent request for a recess; the whispered conference; the request for adjournment, grudgingly granted; the call for this conference.

Judge Geary said to Marty, "I am in the dark too, Mr. McCurdy. I have as yet no idea who Mary and Richard Harlow are." He looked from Billy Gibbs to John McKenzie. "Perhaps someone will enlighten me?"

"To put it bluntly, your honor," Billy said, "Richard Harlow is a McCurdy bastard."

"I see," the judge said at last. He looked at Paul. "A sensitive subject, I agree." He looked then at Billy. "And you believe you can show the relevance of the relationship to this case, Mr. Gibbs?"

Paul said wearily, "It doesn't matter. The time comes," he said, "to cry 'stop.'" He was looking straight at Marty. "You don't care," he said. His voice was sharper now, and tinged with bitterness. "While your counsel does his considerable best to show that the finest man I have ever known ended his life as a doddering old fool" —he paused—"you go sailing. I hope you enjoyed it."

"Not particularly." Marty's voice held nothing. "Since you raise the point." He was damned if he would say more.

Billy Gibbs said, "May I ask what you have in mind, Mr. McCurdy?"

Paul said slowly, "Perhaps much of—all that has happened is my fault. I don't know. I am no longer sure of a number of things." Again he looked at Marty. "I envy you your serene conviction that whatever you do is right, or justified. I no longer think that way."

Marty opened his mouth and closed it again in silence. Serene conviction? Hardly. It would be a long time, if ever, before he forgot that scene with Jordan, beating a man into submission, destroying at least a part of him. Justified? That question could never be fully answered. And his relationships with Liz, with Billy, with Paul himself, were they totally right, or justified? "Go on," he said. "You're making the speech."

There was a faint tightening of the muscles around Paul's mouth, but he merely nodded. "Yes. In the past few days I have lost a very good friend. I have one son dead, and another son about to leave the family." Plus the strain between himself and Susan. And of course

Goodwin. He shook his head. "Now this matter of Mary and Richard Harlow almost certain to come out into the open to—discredit the dead. I no longer have the stomach for this kind of warfare."

The room was still. There was more to come, the judge thought.

"While we are here in private," Paul said slowly, "I want to tell you something about the man you have been—maligning."

Billy stirred in his chair and started to speak.

Paul forestalled him quickly. "You may have your say when I am through." There was command in his voice. "It was wartime," he said then. "Mary Harlow was an attractive female of—easy virtue. I think, as my father did, that from the beginning she had drawn a bead on the McCurdy wealth. When she was pregnant she came to see my father. They came to an arrangement. A check went to her every month through—circuitous channels about which not even I knew until Father drew up his will. True to his bargain, he included a sizable bequest to Mary and her son and explained to me the reason. You question his lucidity or his judgment?" Paul shook his head. "He knew precisely what he was doing and would hear no argument against it. It was, he told me, a matter of personal honor. He had given his word."

Marty was frowning. There were undertones and harmonics which puzzled him.

Paul smiled at him. "You are wondering what there was out of the ordinary in a man's paying for his own—indiscretion?" The smile disappeared. "I will tell you what there was. Rick Harlow was not my father's indiscretion. He was Joe's—your father's. Joe sired Rick and then went off to war to fly airplanes. He never knew about the boy. Father never told him, and made me promise not to tell him either. There was no point in it, he said. He was perfectly willing to bear the responsibility. That was the kind of man he was." He stood up. "Come to the bank tomorrow," he said to Marty. "We will discuss your invasion of the trust. Anything to—stop this dirty business." He started for the door.

"Hold it," Marty said. "I had my last sail in *Westerly* yesterday. I have already mortgaged her and now I am selling her to raise money for the plant. Somehow, we'll make out. But just for the record, yesterday's sail was not for pleasure. I had—other things in mind. I'm not very proud of what I did, but I did it, and I would probably do it again. It—seemed the only way."

They listened in silence while he told about the demonstration at the airplane on the plant runway, of his talk with Jerry Hopkins, finally of the telephone call from John Black and that wild sail with Jordan aboard. "It's done now," he finished, and he too stood up. "I'm not very happy either with what we've been doing," he said. "Do whatever it takes to end it, Billy." He looked again at Paul. "Okay?"

Paul hesitated. "Jim's funeral is this afternoon," he said slowly. "Susan and I would be—pleased if you would come."

In a sense, Marty thought, it was ending as it had begun, he, Susan, and Paul sitting together during the service, and driving together to the graveside. Alan, Sudie, and Bruce followed in another car.

When it was over, they shook hands solemnly. "The bank tomorrow," Paul said. "We will work something out."

Susan said, "But first, now, let us repay that drink you gave us." Her smile was gentle, and at the moment she had no tears. They would come later. "A family affair," she said.

Marty was looking beyond her. Liz stood there watching; Marty-watching, he thought, and what was in her face, in her eyes made it all worthwhile. "I'll bring a guest," he said, "if I may."

Paul walked over to Bruce. "Tomorrow too," he said, "I want to take a little ride with you, to Modesto. To meet your Polly and persuade her to come back here. I have torn up your resignation."

He turned away then and started back to Susan's side feeling better, easier in his mind than in a long time. A funeral was an end, but it could also be a beginning. Many things were changed; some, of course, were not. There was still Charles Goodwin beyond his term trying to retain command—*as Father did through his will,* Paul thought; and matters suddenly appeared in a new light.

Decisions belong to us now, he told himself, the responsibilities are ours. And the logical conclusion followed quickly; so I will handle Charles because I have to; I will do what *I* think is right.

He saw Susan waiting for him, watching him: but I will not be alone, he told himself, never again alone. There was warmth in the concept.

He reached Susan's side and she tucked her arm through his. Together they turned away. Her voice was quiet, comforting, meant only for his ears. "Let's go home," she said.